LITTLE BONES

PATRICIA GIBNEY

SPHERE

SPHERE

First published in 2021 by Bookouture, an imprint of Storyfire Ltd.
This paperback edition published in 2024 by Sphere

1 3 5 7 9 10 8 6 4 2

A CIP catalogue record for this book
is available from the British Library.

ISBN 978-1-4087-2854-3

Printed and bound in Great Britain by
Clays Ltd, Elcograf S.p.A.

Papers used by Sphere are from well-managed forests
and other responsible sources.

Sphere
An imprint of
Little, Brown Book Group
Carmelite House
50 Victoria Embankment
London EC4Y 0DZ

An Hachette UK Company

www.hachette.co.uk
www.littlebrown.co.uk

For Liam Gibney

PROLOGUE

She had to save her children. That was what mothers did. They saved their children.

When he was smashing his fist into her stomach, her only thought was her babies upstairs. And if she had to save them, she must extricate herself from the murderous relationship. But how? And was it already too late?

'Please, that's enough,' she whimpered, struggling up onto her knees. 'Please, stop.'

Something caused him to pause. Her helplessness? No. Weakness in others spurred him on.

Up until now, she had taken the beating in silence. She stared up into his flint-like grey eyes and frowned at the blood dripping from the small cut high in his hairline where she had struck him with the tip of the knife. The cut wasn't deep. Pity, but it had been enough to cause his explosion of rage. She had no idea where the knife had landed when he'd squeezed her wrist and unfurled her fingers, forcing her to release it.

He wiped the trickle of blood away before drawing back his arm to land another slap on her face. She cowered, desperately trying to defend herself. Any one of these thumps could be the blow to leave her debilitated, or the one to kill her. Who would protect her children then?

'Please …' She sheltered her head in cupped hands, hoping her fingers, rather than her head, would take the pressure from his fist.

'And who is going to make me? You? Not a chance in hell. You think I don't know what you were doing behind my back? I know! I bloody well know every fucking thing about you, and I told you before, you talk to no one. No one. You are mine!'

He grabbed her by the collar of her white blouse – stained black from the grime on his fists – and hauled her to her feet. She found herself staring at a chest full of curled hair, and unwillingly inhaled his disturbing scent of rage.

'I'm sorry. Truly sorry. Let's sit and talk it out,' she whispered, terrified by his insane lies.

'*Let's sit and talk it out*,' he mimicked, pushing her away, squeezing his hands into tightly scrunched-up balls, hiding the long fingers she thought she had loved. That had been her first mistake.

There never had been any love. Only torture and pain. She'd deluded herself with romantic notions to conceal the torturous hell in which she lived. She now recognised that he was consumed by psychopathic jealousy and a yearning for power, and she was nothing in his presence. A mouse in a trap. Clamped for ever. No escape. She sobbed, but quickly covered up her cries, fully aware that any display of weakness only provoked further violence.

Leaning against the cupboard for support, she scrabbled around for something, anything, to use as a weapon. But her hands fell to her sides when he stepped into her space and headbutted her.

She didn't fall over. She didn't cry out. She couldn't wake the children. Then she wondered how they were sleeping through the noise.

'You think I'm stupid?' he sneered. 'Skiving off to the shops without my say-so. Talking to all and sundry. I'm not bloody stupid. I know you must have slept with some dirty bollix. I have eyes everywhere. Everywhere, do you hear me? I know that bastard child is not mine. She doesn't even look like me. You betrayed me.' Sweat trickled from his temples. 'Never wanted a daughter anyhow.'

He turned and landed a punch to her stomach. She sank to her knees. As she fell, he thumped her ribs. 'I won't have to listen to her screeching any longer. Job done.'

She bit her lip so hard, blood trickled down her chin.

'What? What … what have you done to my baby?'

He laughed, loud and mocking. She realised in that instant that she would never escape him. No matter how long it took, he would eventually kill her.

He stopped laughing and sneered. 'She's gone to fluffy cloud land in the sky, where I won't have to listen to her squawking and squealing ever again. She wasn't even mine. Bitch.'

She dragged herself upright, knees wobbling and hips shuddering with pins and needles. A pit of fear opened up in her chest and she had nothing to douse the flames as they ignited with anger and rage and something else she couldn't quite put her finger on. A streak of madness had invaded her brain. Had she truly lost her mind?

She shoved him then, with the full force of her shoulder, dodging his flailing arm, and flew out the door and up the stairs. Into her three-year-old daughter's room. Rushed to the cot where the child still slept. The pillow from her own bed was in there. On top of her little girl. Whipping it off, she stared into the milky-white face, eyes closed, the tiny butterfly lips stretched in an unnatural grimace. She reached out and touched her daughter's forehead.

Cold. Oh God, so cold. Her hand flew backwards as if it had been plunged into ice.

'No, no, no, no …'

Then she saw the blood. So much blood for one so small.

She ran to her fifteen-month-old son's room. She found him lying on top of his Spider-Man duvet, one foot and one arm hanging through the bars of his cot, the way he always slept, starfish-like. She gulped, then held her breath. Pain coursed through every bone and sinew, and her muscles cramped in terror. She waited. She counted.

In. Out. In. Out. In. Out.

Relief flooded her veins and she sank to her knees. Her son was breathing. She ran her hand over his forehead and felt the warmth of his skin. She nudged his limbs back into the cot and draped the light duvet around him. He turned over, his breathing steady, dreamless.

What was she to do?

He was still downstairs, pacing the kitchen. She heard the soft thump of his feet on the floor, where a few moments earlier she had thought he was about to kill her. He was still going to kill her.

Her baby girl was dead.

'Oh my God!' She clamped a hand to her mouth, ran to the bathroom and vomited into the toilet. Blood and water spewed, swirling in the bowl. She returned to her son's room, her mind a riot of confusion.

She had to stop him. But how? He had taken her phone. She had no friends. She didn't know any neighbours. She'd never had a real family. She was alone. With her children. No, that was wrong. With her son, now that her little girl was dead. Her little girl was dead! Maybe she was safer in the arms of the angels, she thought, before vomiting bile on the carpeted floor by her son's cot.

Sobbing, she wiped her mouth, fought the rising trauma and grief and flew back to the bathroom. There, she searched the cupboard under the washbasin. Bleach? Could she throw it in his eyes? Would it kill him? She had no idea, but she took the bottle anyway. Opening the mirrored door above the sink, she eyed the toothpaste and brushes. No make-up or pills. He never allowed them. Then her eye fell on his razor. The old-style cut-throat he preferred to use. Dancing with danger, she thought, as she took the blade in her hand. It would have to do.

Beating down her nausea, and with every creaking muscle and bone in her body screaming in pain, she slowly descended the stairs.

He was in the kitchen, on his knees, his face a mask of serenity. The red mist of anger, of insanity, had lifted, like it always did after his rages. She had to use this lucid time to convince him to let her go. She paused in the hallway and prayed she could at least save her son.

She would hold the death of their daughter over him with the cut-throat in her hand. It was the only way to escape.

*

He could not believe what he was hearing. He'd come to the Mireann Stone to cleanse his spirit, here on the side of the sacred hill. Mother Earth. The centre of the country. He held his finger to his lips to silence any sound that might come out.

The tramp of footsteps. Coming towards him.

He squinted through the darkness to see two people walking up the hillside, a light like a sabre guiding them. One of them carried something wrapped in a blanket.

A pink hue skirted the horizon as the morning struggled to overcome the night. He'd spent hours on the hill, part of the ritual he'd hoped would fill him with renewal. He had too much trauma in his soul, too many secrets to hide. He needed release from the anguish that clouded like a shadow all around him.

He leaned back against the stone, making himself as small as possible while still being able to see them.

'We have to bury her.' A woman's voice. High-pitched. Like loud shrieking whispers.

'What are you talking about?'

'We can't leave her exposed to the elements. We have to put her somewhere. A bit deeper. So the animals won't … Oh God, I can't do this.'

'This was your idea, not mine. Do you think I can dig this dry earth with my bare hands?'

'She's so tiny, and the ground isn't that hard. We can dig a little. There's a load of rocks around. We can cover her with them too.'

It took them over an hour, and the cold light of morning was casting its rays on the mound under the tree when at last they made their way back down the hill.

He couldn't believe what he had witnessed, or the voices he'd heard. Voices he knew all too well. He did not want to believe any of it. But he would never forget it.

Abandoning his ritual and all thoughts of cleansing his spirit, he made his way home, consumed with more darkness than when he'd arrived.

It was the second day of November, and the souls of the dead were all around him.

TWO AND A HALF YEARS LATER

MONDAY

CHAPTER ONE

When Anita Boland's daughter, Isabel, rang her shortly after the nine o'clock TV news, whispering down the phone, asking her mother to mind the baby at nine the following morning, Anita was annoyed. It was just like Isabel to ask at the last minute. No thought that her mother might have a life, might have something else to be doing – not that she did have anything to be doing, but all the same, it rankled.

It was 8.57 the next morning when Anita reached the bungalow at Cloughton, eight kilometres from Ragmullin.

Without locking the car – no one locked anything out here in the countryside – she made her way to the back door, relishing the silence all around. She breathed in the air to fill herself with the freshness of nature, but the stench of slurry rose from the fields and caught in her throat. So much for country living; she preferred town life.

Opening the door, she immediately felt unnerved, for no good reason.

She stepped inside.

The air splintered with the high-pitched cry of a child. The wail was ancillary to the sound of silence. Anita knew her daughter was a terrible fusser and rarely let the child cry. Usually Isabel was all a-flutter through the house – television blaring, washing machine humming or hoover knocking against skirting boards – when she had an appointment in Ragmullin.

'Isabel?' Anita walked through the utility room.

No answer, save for the baby's hysterical cries.

An icicle of fear skated down Anita's spine. Her heart beat so wildly she thought it might break free from her chest. With her hand instinctively clutching her throat, she entered the kitchen, and froze.

Drawers hung from their moorings. The cupboard doors were open, a few pieces of crockery smashed here and there on the floor. The clothes horse lay askew against the wall and one chair was on its side.

'Isabel?' She called her daughter's name again, her voice a fearful whisper.

Was there an intruder in the house? She had to get to her grand-daughter. Where the hell was Isabel? Anita tiptoed through the kitchen towards the bedroom from where she'd heard the baby's cries.

She had stepped into the room before her eyes registered someone lying on the floor. The overriding smell was metallic, mixed with the foul odour of the baby's unchanged nappy.

'Isabel, sweetheart.' Her lips trembled as she took a tentative step towards the figure lying face down.

Isabel's short hair was matted with blood. Her pyjamas were torn, the cotton sliced and bloody. Anita raised her eyes to see baby Holly lying on her back in the cot, feet kicking frantically, her empty bottle on the floor. The child turned her head and her screams ceased, as if she'd recognised her grandmother through the wooden bars.

As she knelt beside her daughter's body, Anita's nursing training kicked in. She knew Isabel was dead. Still she laid a finger on her daughter's cold neck and checked for a pulse. There was nothing.

'Dear God in heaven,' she cried. Someone had brutally assaulted her Isabel. What if the assailant was still in the house?

The baby! She had to get little Holly out of here.

She traipsed through the blood – there was no other way to get to the cot – and lifted the baby girl, feeling the weight of the soiled nappy and the dampness on the Babygro. She clutched the child to her chest, and with a final heartbreaking glance at her beautiful daughter lying slaughtered on the floor, she ran from the room.

Only when she was out front, by the car, did she let a howl escape her lips, frightening the baby, who joined in her screams.

A flock of birds startled in the trees rose as one and swept across the sky in a black line of doom.

CHAPTER TWO

It was a mistake. A huge bloody mistake. Lottie spooned granola soaked in goat's milk – Katie's latest fad – down her throat. It stuck there, a big gluey lump.

Mark Boyd sat across from her, the wide wooden table between them. His cheeks were beginning to fill out, but his illness still shadowed him. The thing that concerned her most was the shroud of melancholy that hung like chain mail on his bony shoulders. The death of his mother hadn't helped, and he was worried about his sister, Grace, living alone in the west of Ireland, almost two hours' drive from Ragmullin. Lottie doubted Grace was worried about Boyd and knew for a fact the young woman was doing just fine.

No, it was the ever-present spectre of cancer that veiled his good humour. The fear that it might return, the damage it might do if it did. All that gave him a haunted look and tormented him even during his sleep. She'd felt his twists and turns and shouts in the dark when he stayed over, which was quite often now, and she didn't mind that.

Pushing the half-eaten bowl away, she recognised that what she was feeling had nothing to do with Boyd's illness – she had plenty of experience coping with sickness. It wasn't even their disastrous wedding, scuppered by their last case. No. It ran deeper than that. It was this cold, creepy house consumed with the horrors of her past. And she didn't know how to tell him that the move to Farranstown House had been one big messy mistake.

Boxes and bags littered every available space, and Lottie wanted to run out the door, across the field and down the hill, to stand on the shore of Lough Cullion and scream her heart out. Why had she moved out here? Leo Belfield, her half-brother in New York, was still wheeling and dealing their affairs, changing his mind and plans as quickly as the Irish weather. She had agreed to move as caretaker into Farranstown House until he decided how he wanted to proceed. He was taking his bloody time. Nothing ever went to plan where Lottie was concerned.

The turmoil crashing around her brain manifested itself physically and her hands shook. Boyd noticed.

'Penny for them,' he said.

'Feck's sake, Boyd, you sound like my mother.'

She picked up the breakfast dishes and, turning her back to him, brought them to the cracked ceramic sink.

'You should invite Rose over for dinner,' he said. 'She'd love to see the progress we've made on the house.'

Whirling around on the ball of her bare foot, Lottie let fly.

'Progress? Jesus, Boyd, look around you. It's a bloody mess. Everything is everywhere. I can't think straight, can't even walk from here to the front door without falling over bags of unpacked clothes, and ladders and paint tins and—'

'You should have hired professionals.'

'With what?'

'Look, Lottie, I didn't mean to upset you.'

He rolled down the sleeves of his white shirt and began fastening the cuffs at the wrist, until he realised one button was hanging by a single thread and the other had disappeared altogether.

A feeling of hopelessness engulfed Lottie. She turned away and wiped down the counter beside the sink with a tea towel, her nails breaking through the thin fabric and scratching against the wood. Crumbs fell to the floor and she heard him fetch the sweeping brush.

'Leave it,' she said through gritted teeth. 'I'll do it later.'

'Lighten up.' He came up behind her and kissed her cheek. It had the desired effect. She relaxed into his body and welcomed his arms around her.

'That's gross.' Sean waltzed into the kitchen. 'Are you not going to work today?'

'Are you not going to school?' Lottie said.

'Mam! It's the Easter holidays. What planet are you on?'

'Really?' Lottie stared at her six-foot-plus son buttering bread and mooching through the refrigerator. Her heart leapt in her ribcage as he closed the door and turned.

'What?' Sean said.

'Nothing.' In that split second of movement, her son had transformed into Adam, her dead husband. It was like a spear had split open the core of her heart. Adam hadn't seen his son grow up. Or his two daughters and little grandson.

Sean slapped three slices of cheese onto the bread and took a bite. With his mouth full, he said, 'I'm painting my room today. Want to help out, Mark?'

'Sure,' Boyd said, 'but it will have to be this evening. Your mother and I have to work. No Easter holidays for us.'

'Okay, I'll just spend a few hours on my game and we can paint when you get home.'

'You might be on holidays,' Lottie said, 'but you have to study.'

Sean rolled his eyes and sauntered out, letting the door swing shut behind him.

She quickly gathered her thoughts. 'Thanks for saying you'd help him with the painting. He really likes you.'

A commotion sounded outside the kitchen door before Katie burst in. 'I swear to God, I'm going to kill Sean Parker one of these days.'

'What's he done now?' Lottie said.

'He's here, isn't he? In my way everywhere I turn, and I've so much to do.'

'Like what?'

Katie quickly buttered two slices of bread while pouring the remainder of the goat's milk on a small bowl of cornflakes. 'I've to feed and dress Louis and get him to day care before I head to work. And I've hardly time to feed or dress myself. God!' She folded the bread and with both hands full elbowed the door open. 'Some of us have to work, you know.'

'Grand Central Station comes to mind,' Boyd said as the door shut behind Katie.

'Some days I feel like I'm in a scene from *One Flew Over the Cuckoo's Nest*.'

'I better get my stuff, or someone might think I live here.'

His chair scraped on the concrete floor as he shoved it to the table, and the soft thud of the door was more telling than if he had banged it.

She was aware he wanted to move in permanently. The sensible thing, she knew. They'd been on the brink of marriage, for God's sake. But still she stalled. Why?

Her dilemma was forgotten about when she received the call from the station.

*

Boyd let himself into his apartment, picked up the post from the floor and made his way into the living room. He rolled up the blinds. Light flooded the room. The air smelled stale, but he couldn't leave the windows open as he'd be out at work all day. A change of shirt was needed. No way could he spend the day with a button hanging off his cuff. He rooted in the wardrobe and took out a blue cotton slim-fit with a matching navy tie around the hanger.

After a quick shower, he dressed and glanced in the mirror, noting more grey flecked through his hair. He quickly turned away, ignoring the rest of his scrawny visage.

The night spent at Lottie's had been enjoyable. He loved being around her kids and little Louis, but he couldn't deny that Sean was his favourite. They could talk about hurling and cycling and play a few games of FIFA on Sean's PlayStation. For the first time in ages, Boyd felt he was part of a real family. That made him think of Grace. He needed to give his sister a call. Later. Tonight. Maybe tomorrow. He loved her dearly, but she was hard work at times. Most of the time.

He whistled as he returned to the living room. Picking up his keys, he cast an eye at the post. He flicked through the envelopes, bemoaning the fact that he had never set up online billing. He paused at the sight of familiar handwriting. Shit. His ex-wife. What could Jackie want from him now? Who wrote letters any more? Email, texts and phone calls had taken over, so it must be something she didn't want electronically monitored. Knowing her involvement with the criminal world, it could be nothing good.

He thought of how Jackie had left him to take up with a party-going criminal who could wine and dine her with his illegal income. They had fled to the Costa del Sol. Then a couple of years ago, Jackie had appeared back in Ragmullin when she'd followed her boyfriend after discovering his involvement in sex trafficking. She'd been instrumental in having him arrested but had skipped the country before any charges could be brought against her. Boyd wasn't even sure charges would have stood, but Jackie had been clever enough to flee.

Turning the envelope, his fingers hovered over the flap. Open it now and risk a bad mood for the day, or leave it until tonight and suffer it then? He even toyed with the idea of tearing it up and putting it in the trash. Instead, he slipped it into his inside jacket pocket. Later, then.

As he left his apartment, a little of the zing had left his step.

CHAPTER THREE

The envelope plopped loudly onto the hall floor.

Curled up in bed, twenty-seven-year-old Joyce Breslin tugged the sheet to her chin, smoothing down her long hair. Another restless night.

It was too early for the post. That usually arrived later in the day. But someone had walked up the narrow path and pushed something through her letter box. Even though her thoughts were totally irrational, she felt the follicles on her scalp itch and the hairs on her arms pulse with electricity.

She flung back the sheets and sat on the edge of the bed. This was madness. Of course it was just the postman.

But her antenna for danger was on high alert.

He'd come for her. She just knew it. Flying on shredded wings, torn by her past, she'd fled because she'd been left with no choice but to run. And now she was flightless. Stagnating in this three-bed semi with Nathan, a man she barely loved. The price of freedom had turned into another form of incarceration.

A shiver coursed through her body like an overflowing river, but the dam had yet to break. She could crest this wave and hopefully make it to the other side. *That's it, be positive.* Easy to say, but doing it was a whole other ball game.

Inhaling deeply, she floundered around on the floor for her fleece and pulled it over her head. On tiptoes she left the bedroom and stood on the landing.

Not a sound. Her child was still asleep.

Down the stairs carefully, so as not to put pressure on the creaking fourth-last step, she stepped onto the wooden floor. A soft hint of light bled in through the coloured glass at the top of the door. The heating had yet to kick in and she was suddenly cold. Very cold.

Another step forward, her eyes open wide, all sleep banished to the night-time horrors that stalked her.

There it lay. A white envelope. Like a blemish on the polished wood.

She wondered if she had the strength to even pick it up. To open it. To glance inside. She knew it was bad. Nothing came through the letter box this early in the morning. Nothing good, anyhow. Not for her.

Bending down, the legs of her satin pyjamas swimming around her bare feet, she reached out, her fingers floating over the envelope as if they might be burned by whatever lay sealed inside.

She studied it as it lay there. The front was blank. No name. No nothing. Maybe she was imagining it. Was it a mistake? Something for her neighbour, maybe? Something for Nathan? *That's it!* She sighed in relief, before deflating again.

No. She'd felt something ominous was on the way. And she had only herself to blame, having put in motion the actions that had surely led to this.

With her heart palpitating outrageously, she scooped up the envelope before she changed her mind.

Tore at the seal. Peered inside.

Her heart stopped beating for a few seconds and she lost her breath. Then the pace ratcheted up in her chest.

She upended the envelope.

A rusted razor blade clinked onto the floor, coming to rest under the radiator, followed by another. Two blades.

Her hand flew to her throat.

'No,' she whispered.

It was a warning. A warning that she had to flee. Take her child and run. Then she saw something else inside. A scrap of paper with a typed address and nothing else on it.

No! A small scream escaped from her throat.

They were coming for her. No longer floating out there in the ether of bad memories and haunted nightmares. They were here. And she had brought them back into her life.

'Dear God, help me,' she whispered to the ceiling.

Her hands trembled as she picked up one of the blades. She couldn't find the other and didn't care either. She stuffed it into the envelope, which she crumpled into her pocket, and took a deep breath.

Joyce was certain this would be the last day of her life.

By the end of the day, she would be wishing that was true.

CHAPTER FOUR

Lottie stood on the threshold of the open door, transfixed in horror. She tried to absorb the scene by sweeping her eyes over the room in front of her. Battling her anger, she straightened her spine and threw back her shoulders, physically and mentally transforming into work mode; becoming Detective Inspector Lottie Parker, not the mother, widow, lover, combatant, but the professional detective.

The victim's mother, Anita Boland, stood outside, her tears mingling with raindrops, clutching her granddaughter tightly to her chest. Lottie would do her best for Mrs Boland and the baby girl.

She was glad that SOCOs had placed steel plates on the floor to preserve the bloody shoe prints leading from the bedroom. Similar prints led from where the body lay to the baby's cot. They more than likely belonged to Mrs Boland, but they had to be preserved and analysed because some of them might be the killer's.

Before she moved fully into the bedroom, Lottie stared at a large wedding photo hanging on the wall in the hallway. The husband, Jack Gallagher, was tall and broad-shouldered. His bride, Isabel, only reached his shoulder. Her demeanour was mouse-like, but the hint of a smile added light to her face, and her fair hair glistened in the sunshine glowing behind them.

Lottie steeled herself before looking at the body.

Twenty-nine-year-old Isabel Gallagher lay face down on the wooden floor, her white cotton pyjamas now reddish brown in colour, torn and slit with a multitude of cuts. Short fair hair sticky with matted blood, her face invisible for the moment. That was good, wasn't it? That she didn't have to look at the woman's last expression. Enough to know Isabel was dead.

But what got to her were the pink fluffy bed socks on the woman's feet. The simple things, the mundane little things, found in a room of horror were what penetrated her professional veneer and broke Lottie's heart. She imagined Isabel slipping out of bed with her fluffy socks on to keep her feet warm on the cold floor, and now here she was, cold and dead, lying in her own blood.

Lottie made her way over to Jim McGlynn, SOCO team leader.

'It's not pretty,' he said redundantly.

She nodded, not trusting herself to speak.

A white, wooden-barred cot stood in the corner of the bedroom. The baby had been taken outside by the victim's mother, but how long had she been left here screaming and crying? Apparently untouched physically, but what damage had been caused psychologically to the little mite? Lottie shook her head to dispel the image.

'I take it Isabel didn't die quickly,' she said. There was too much blood pooled on the floor, spread out in an arc away from the body. The pastel wallpaper above and around the bed was spattered with red pearl drops.

'I've counted five wounds on her back. I'm not turning her over until the state pathologist gets here.'

'Might be a robbery gone wrong,' Lottie said. 'The kitchen is ransacked. Maybe someone thought the house was empty.'

'That's your job, Inspector.'

'Can you find any evidence of who … did it?' She clenched her hands, desperately struggling not to choke from the smell of death suspended above the body. It was so intense, she could taste it glued to the back of her throat through her mask. It made her think of her granola breakfast, and she gagged.

'God almighty, give me a chance, woman,' McGlynn said.

'Any sign of the murder weapon?' Lottie persisted.

McGlynn glared. She held his stare. The house hadn't been fully searched yet. The body was his priority for now. She knew all that, but still …

'The baby,' she said quietly, 'was here when … Christ, Jim, this is too horrific even for my strong stomach.'

The older man glanced towards the empty cot, shaking his head wearily before returning to concentrate on his work. He tried to remain detached from the human side of the crimes he dealt with, assessing things forensically, but sometimes she saw the glimmer of sorrow deep in his green eyes. He had to work up close and personal with the horror.

Leaving him to his grim task, she sidestepped Gerry, the photographer, and made her way through the bungalow. A wine-coloured faux-leather handbag lay sideways on the kitchen table among the detritus of breakfast dishes and open drawers. She bent over it and peered inside, leafing the flaps open with her gloved fingers. A set of keys, including a car key; a black wallet with a few till receipts sticking out of it. If it was a robbery, wouldn't the bag have been taken?

'Did you photograph this, Gerry?'

'I did. I'm videoing the house room by room. The kitchen is the only place I can find evidence of disturbance.' He paused before adding, 'And the bedroom, of course.'

'Of course. Thanks,' she added, taking out the wallet.

No cash or bank cards. Maybe they'd been taken then. A photo of the baby but none of the husband. Everything would be bagged, tagged and analysed later. Like the body. Taking a closer look inside the bag, she spotted the creased spine of a thin paperback peeking out. Mills & Boon. Something about a duke and a commoner. Was Isabel craving romance in her life, finding it only between the covers of a paperback?

A Credit Union book showed an account in her husband's name. Not a joint account, then. Two thousand euros in shares and five thousand outstanding on a loan.

In a zipped pocket she found a single lipstick, the only cosmetic in the bag. Ruby Passion. This, above everything else, filled her with an intense sense of sadness for the young woman. It would never again be hurriedly swiped across pale lips to add a spring of colour.

Calling over a SOCO, she asked for all the contents to be bagged as soon as possible, then she scanned the kitchen, taking note of the landline phone on the wall beside the refrigerator. She made a mental note to check the call data with the provider. It was then that she realised she'd seen no sign of Isabel's phone in her bag, her bedroom or anywhere else. No laptop or computer had been found yet either.

Outside, she pulled down her hood and shook out her hair. She whipped off the mask and gulped air, unsure how long it would take to rid her lungs of the putrid scent of death.

Boyd was comforting Anita, the victim's mother, who was now sitting in the passenger seat of his car, door open, still refusing to leave the scene. Her bare feet were clad in paper booties, her shoes taken away for inspection. Her stylish black leather jacket was unzipped, and the cool breeze fluttered her white cotton blouse. She wore deep blue denim jeans. Late fifties, Lottie thought, and admired the woman's style. Her own mother wore polyester trousers and knitted jumpers. But at the same time she had to acknowledge that Rose, in her seventies, with short silver hair, carried off her own look.

As an ambulance with paramedics stood idle, Lottie noticed that the baby was wrapped in a multitude of coats Boyd had gathered from the assembled squad cars. Beneath those, she was clothed in a white forensic suit, the legs dangling downwards. Her clothes had been taken for analysis. Jesus, Lottie thought, I hope the killer didn't touch her. She was sleeping soundly in her grandmother's arms. Anita's clothes would have to be analysed for transference too.

'Take them to the station, Boyd. Get Anita a cup of tea and I'll appoint a family liaison officer.'

Anita's eyes widened like saucers and she climbed out of the car.

'No! I can't leave my Isabel all alone in that awful house.' She buried her face in the child's curls. 'Have you contacted Jack, her husband? He was at work. Quality Electrical, just outside Ragmullin. He's an electrician. Oh God, I should have called him. I wasn't thinking straight,' she sobbed.

'Don't worry. We've sent for him. He should be here soon.' She'd sent Detectives Kirby and McKeown to the Quality Electrical premises to bring Jack Gallagher home.

Anita held the baby tighter. 'Holly comes with me. God knows what state Jack will be in. I can keep her calm and let him deal with his grief. Please.'

A wood pigeon cooed in the uppermost branches of the trees that edged the garden, adding an eerie tone to the small gathering.

Lottie said, 'It's okay, Anita, I'll be here with Isabel. You go with Detective Sergeant Boyd.' She turned to him. 'Find someone who can make up a bottle for the baby. And get a paediatrician to look her over.'

'Thank you.' Anita's voice trembled, and more tears dragged mascara down her ashen cheeks. She leaned against the car door.

Lottie put out a hand to support the distraught woman. 'You need to be strong, for yourself and your granddaughter. Holly, did you say?'

'Yes. Image of my Isabel. She was born on Christmas Day. Isabel wanted to call her Noelle, but Jack insisted on Holly. Truth is, she was so happy the child was healthy, she'd have agreed to any name. She'd had a difficult nine months. Constantly ill. She lost a stone in weight. Poor pet. And now she's … gone.'

Anita Boland swayed, and Boyd held her securely, his arm around her shoulders. Lottie's heart bled for her, thinking of the days and weeks ahead she'd have to endure. Finding her daughter's body was just the beginning of the trauma.

As Boyd eased the devastated woman to the car, he looked over his shoulder at Lottie, his eyes telling her he'd got this.

Once they'd driven off, she walked around the bungalow. It was situated on an isolated piece of land around eight kilometres from Ragmullin, the nearest neighbour over half a kilometre away. It seemed to be an older house in the process of being renovated. The outline of an extension was marked out on the ground to the rear. A cement mixer, unopened bags of cement and a dome of sand stood to one side, and the path around the house was unfinished. Had they run out of money, or changed their plans? A ten-year-old black Volkswagen Golf was parked further down. The drone of a tractor spreading slurry hugged the sky in the distance. She could smell it hanging in the air.

From the back door she watched the SOCOs working. There was no sign of forced entry and she had no idea if anything was missing from the house, but Isabel's husband would know more.

She checked her notes and saw that Jack Gallagher's boss had confirmed he had arrived at Quality Electrical, on the outskirts of town, at 7.10 a.m. It was now 10.10. Anita Boland had found her daughter's body and the crying baby just before nine o'clock, when she'd called round to care for baby Holly. Isabel had a 10.15 doctor's appointment in Ragmullin and Anita said she'd arrived early to allow her daughter time to get ready. Isabel had phoned her last night and again at around seven that morning to remind her. Lottie realised she should have asked Anita if her daughter possessed a mobile phone. She'd ask the husband when he arrived.

With no obvious sign of a break-in, she thought the door was most likely left unlocked as Isabel was expecting her mother's arrival. Multiple stab wounds. The baby, unharmed. Someone she knew?

Lottie made to return inside, but looked up quickly when she heard the screech of brakes on the road and the shift of gravel as a car drew up out front. She hurried around the side of the house, bracing herself to meet the grieving husband.

CHAPTER FIVE

Joyce had just sent a quick text and turned so quickly when she heard the sound at the top of the stairs that she tripped over her pyjama leg and fell backwards, hitting the side of her head against the corner of the radiator.

'Mummy. Are you okay?'

The little boy rushed down the stairs, his pyjamas half on, half off. He insisted on dressing himself each morning and he was getting better at it, but being only four, he never quite managed.

'Oh Evan, silly Mummy slipped on the floor.' She hauled herself upright and picked up her son, bear-hugging him. 'Breakfast first, then I'll find your clothes for today.'

'Blood, yuck.'

She noticed the blood on his fingers as he drew away from her. Shit, she'd cut her forehead. There was a red streak on the corner of the hall radiator.

In the kitchen, she fetched the cereal box and let him tip it into his bowl. She poured the milk herself. Enough mess to cope with for one morning.

She chewed on the edge of a piece of toast she'd popped out of the toaster before it was hardly warm. Decisions. She swallowed without tasting and searched the laundry basket for a clean work apron. No. Not today. She threw it back into the pile and walked around the table.

Her son was spooning milky Coco Pops into his mouth while humming to himself, oblivious to her turmoil. The envelope with the blade burned a hole in her fleece pocket. The warning terrified her. But it also strengthened her resolve. She'd have to leave.

'Honey, eat up. I'm dropping you early to day care. I don't want to be late for work. Okay?' It was a few hours before she was due at the café, but she needed time to think.

'Okay.'

Rushing him caused him to upend the bowl. Chocolatey milk swam down his chin and onto his white vest.

'Sorry, Mummy.'

'Don't worry, I'll get your T-shirt.' She found a clean but creased top. Only the collar would be seen under his sweatshirt. It would do.

'Is Daddy coming home soon?'

'Sure he is, sweetie.' She pulled off his soiled vest and tugged the clean T-shirt over his head, then rooted around in the basket for his sweatshirt. Dirty.

'Mum, it's yucky.'

'It's fine for today. Trust me.'

'Okay.'

She feathered his hair with a kiss and hugged him tightly. 'Go watch telly while I get dressed.'

'Sure.' He sounded a whole lot older than his years.

Upstairs, she pulled a suitcase out of the closet. Throwing it on the bed, she unzipped it. What could she take? Where would she go? No, this was ridiculous. She needed to think clearly. First she had to drop Evan off.

She ran a hand through her hair and it came away with a smear of blood. Her damn forehead. In the bathroom, she washed the cut, found a plaster and stuck it on. After brushing her teeth she ran a comb through her long black hair and wondered if she should dye it.

And what would she tell Nathan? Could she leave without telling him what was going on? He wasn't due home until later that evening from his driving job on the continent. Why was she so worried? Did she even trust him? After the envelope with the blades this morning, she knew the answer to that question. Joyce trusted no one.

She pulled on jeans and a black shirt, glancing out the window. What was she looking for? She hardly knew her neighbours on the small estate. Wouldn't recognise an unusual car. Wouldn't know if someone was out of place. Someone who might be watching her. Shivering, she picked up her fleece and zipped it on. The envelope in the pocket made her skin crawl. Still, she had to keep it close, a reminder of the danger she and Evan were in.

What next? First she had to drop off her son. He'd be safe at day care. Lots of little boys and girls to keep him occupied there while she decided what to do.

Downstairs, she went into the sitting room.

'Ready, sweetheart?' She waved his jacket.

Evan wasn't watching cartoons. He was making a jigsaw puzzle in the corner by the bookcase. *Good Morning Ireland* was showing the news behind him, the sound low. Crime-scene tape fluttered at the end of a narrow road. Joyce couldn't hear what the blonde presenter was saying. As she moved towards her son, a road sign flashed up on the screen: *Cloughton 1 km.*

She looked around for the remote to turn up the sound.

The reporter was standing by the crime-scene tape surrounded by shrubs and bushes. 'Gardaí have yet to confirm the exact nature of their investigation, but a spokesperson told me that a female has been the victim of a serious assault. Locals say that a married couple, Isabel and Jack Gallagher, reside at the property, which is situated up along this road behind me. The house is subject to intense garda activity. More once we have it. Back to you in the studio.'

Joyce was rooted to the spot.

She knew why she'd received the envelope with the razor blade.

She knew who lived in Cloughton.

And she knew she was next.

CHAPTER SIX

Kirby and McKeown exited the car.

'Where is he? Jack Gallagher?' Lottie said.

'He was on a job, fifteen kilometres from here,' Kirby said. 'We got his phone number from his boss, Michael Costello. I told him to head home. He's on his way.'

'Does he know? About his wife?'

Kirby shrugged. 'I informed him it was in connection with a break-in, but I'm afraid the media scrum at the end of the road will have broadcast the news by now. He might hear it on his van radio.'

'Shit,' Lottie said.

'He should be here any minute,' McKeown said. 'Uniforms have his licence plate number and they'll wave him straight through without interference from the media.'

'Wait here for him. Inform me the instant he arrives. And don't let him into the house.' She looked over Kirby's shoulder as another car arrived.

Out stepped Jane Dore, the state pathologist, dressed in a navy trouser suit, a teal blouse adding a splash of colour. She joined Lottie and suited up in the tent that had been erected at the back door. Another tent was being assembled at the front door, and crime-scene tape delineated inner and outer cordons around the property.

'Isabel Gallagher, aged twenty-nine,' Lottie informed the diminutive pathologist. 'Multiple stab wounds to her back. McGlynn's waiting for you before he turns the body over.'

'I heard her baby was in the room with her,' Jane said as she fastened her mask and covered her hair with her hood.

'She was found in her cot by her grandmother, who was first on the scene. Baby appears to be unharmed. That's what we know so far.'

'Let's get on with it then,' Jane said.

Lottie led her inside.

In the bedroom, Jane greeted the SOCO team leader and assessed the scene. 'Have you moved her at all, Jim?'

'Just to confirm death.'

'Has a doctor been in attendance?'

'Paramedics were first to arrive,' Lottie said. 'They knew straight away that the woman was dead, and the victim's mother, a nurse, had checked for a pulse.'

As Jane moved across the steel plates on the parquet floor, the room fell silent. No cameras whirring. Not a breath. Only the swish of the pathologist's forensic suit.

Lottie watched as Jane hunkered down and laid a hand softly on the neck of the dead woman.

'I can't give an accurate indication of time of death yet, but I'd say she's been dead no longer than four hours, possibly only three. I'll know more when I examine the body.'

It was now eleven o'clock. Lottie said, 'I've yet to interview the husband, Jack Gallagher, but it's been confirmed that he arrived at work at ten past seven this morning. Isabel must have been killed shortly after he left home.' Anita had found her around nine, which meant she'd died between seven and nine. Hopefully Jane could pin down the time of death more accurately later on.

Jane said, 'You can turn her over, Jim.'

Gently McGlynn eased Isabel's body onto her side and then onto her back.

31

Seeing the woman's face for the first time, Lottie gasped. 'Jesus.'

'Haematoma, centre of the forehead,' Jane said.

'Attacked straight on.' Lottie shook her head. 'She saw her attacker.'

Isabel Gallagher was thin-framed. Her arms, which had been beneath her body, were bony, with what looked like recent bruising. She was a small woman, maybe five two or three. Definitely no match for any sort of assailant, especially one wielding a knife and a heavy object.

'A deep indentation to the throat,' Jane continued. 'Possibly the source of the majority of the blood loss. I'd estimate this quickly followed the head injury. The wounds on her back may have occurred post mortem.' She lifted the pyjama top, and Lottie saw two more wounds sliced into the woman's torso, along with considerable bruising.

'Those bruises could have been from a struggle,' she said.

'Or the result of lividity. She died where she fell.'

'What do you think happened?' Lottie asked.

'Off the record I'd say she was attacked front on, fell, throat cut, flesh sliced, and then flipped over onto her front and stabbed in the back. I need to open her up to tell you anything further.' Jane glanced at McGlynn. 'It's okay to move her to the mortuary once you finish gathering what you can from on or around the body.' She stood and inclined her head. 'This is sick.'

'I know,' Lottie replied.

'Just a minute.' Jane crouched down again. 'Tweezers, Jim.'

Lottie watched as the pathologist peeled back two of the dead woman's fingers and extracted an object with the steel tweezers. 'What is it?'

'An old-fashioned razor blade,' Jane said.

Jim held out an evidence bag and the pathologist dropped the blade inside.

'Why had she got that in her hand?' Lottie said, bewildered.

Jane shrugged. 'I'll schedule the post-mortem immediately. We have to find the bastard who did this.'

Lottie was shocked at the vehemence in her tone. The pathologist was usually professional, distant even, but something about a mother being killed in front of her baby had rattled her.

Outside, a guttural scream broke through the stillness of the house.

Jack Gallagher was home.

CHAPTER SEVEN

The navy blue van was parked haphazardly just inside the gate, driver's door open. Restrained by Kirby and McKeown, Jack Gallagher twisted and turned, his face distorted, eyes wide, mouth gaping. His dark hair flopped about his ears and stuck to his forehead with the perspiration from his exertions.

He was taller and broader than his wedding photograph suggested. Muscles strained under the cotton of his navy work shirt.

'Let me through,' he yelled, high-pitched, maniacal. 'This is my house. My wife and daughter, are they still in there? Someone tell me the truth before I punch my way through.'

Lottie faced him, shivering from the palpable energy of his anxiety. She hated this part of the job, but she was also angry. It was obvious Gallagher had heard something about his wife's death. She'd wanted to keep it from him until the last minute in order to gauge his reaction. Too late now. She'd have to change direction.

'Mr Gallagher. Jack. I'm Detective Inspector Lottie Parker. I'm the senior investigating officer. Please try to be calm.'

'What happened?' His body slumped and the two detectives relaxed their hold on his arms but stayed close to him.

Lottie straightened her shoulders, on high alert in case he broke free and made a dash into the house. The old adage that it was usually the husband who did it flashed across her mind. She did not want him compromising any evidence they might later find.

'Take a few seconds to catch your breath, and I'll fill you in,' she said.

'Is Holly okay? They said Isabel's dead.'

'Who said that?'

'The vultures down the road. Tell me they're lying.'

'There's no easy way to say this, Mr Gallagher, but I'm sorry to tell you your wife is dead.'

Instead of breaking down in a blubbering heap, he bit his lip and nodded slowly.

'It's true, so. I worried it might come to this.' Then, with dark-ringed eyes filled with tears, 'Please tell me she didn't take Holly with her. I could never handle that.'

Confusion thwarted Lottie's prepared question. 'What do you mean?'

'Isabel … well … you know. She was depressed. In an awful way since Holly was born. Before that, too. During the pregnancy.' He swept his fingers through his unruly fringe, swiping it back to reveal a smooth forehead. 'Tell me the truth. I need to know what went on in my house. Where is my daughter?'

'Your mother-in-law is caring for her. Holly was unharmed.'

'Thank God for that.' His body deflated as he sank to his knees. 'And Isabel? What did she do? I mean, how did she die?'

Lottie hunkered down in front of him. 'Mr Gallagher, have you any idea what might have occurred in your house this morning?'

His head shot up. Eyes sharp. 'What do you mean?'

Uneasiness crept into Lottie's chest. She shouldn't be having this conversation here; not while he was in this state. She needed to get him to the station. His clothes should be taken and analysed. Fingerprints and DNA. Not that it meant anything. He'd had ample time to wash, and burn his clothing, if he was guilty.

She stood and offered her hand. He took it and stood.

'Your wife was murdered, Jack. You need to accompany my detectives to Ragmullin garda station.'

'I'm going nowhere until I see Isabel.' Each word was hammered out with determination, as if he hadn't heard what she'd said.

'I'm afraid that's impossible. Your house is a crime scene.'

'Really?' His lip curled angrily. 'My wife was ill. Whatever she did, she can't be accused of a crime. That's a throwback to the Dark Ages.'

'Mr Gallagher, Isabel was murdered,' Lottie repeated.

'No. I don't believe you.' The angry red of moments ago paled, revealing thin blue veins on his skin. 'No. No way. How? My baby …' He doubled over, clutching his chest.

Shit, Lottie hoped he wasn't having a heart attack. She'd had enough drama for one morning.

Then he straightened, waxen-faced, hands trembling. 'I need to see Holly. Tell me, please. What happened?'

'Holly is fine. Unhurt. Your mother-in-law identified Isabel's body. There is nothing you can do here. I'd like you to accompany me to the station. It's just procedure. You won't be able to return home until my team and SOCOs complete their work. That could take a few days, unfortunately.'

'You're not serious.'

'I'm afraid I am.'

'I'll go with you.' He picked up his jacket from the ground, where it had fallen during his scuffle with Kirby and McKeown.

'Have you someone to stay with? Your parents? Sisters or brothers?'

'My parents are dead. There's only me.'

'Your mother-in-law?'

'I'll see what Anita says.'

She watched as he straightened himself, his eyes glued to the house, where SOCOs were scurrying around. With a resigned sigh, he followed McKeown to the car.

Lottie took a deep breath, trying to form an impression of Jack Gallagher. He seemed genuinely upset and distraught, but she'd met good actors and liars before. She'd have to be alert during the interview. But this morning, she felt anything but alert. She felt only anger.

Pointing to Gallagher's van, she instructed a SOCO to give it the once-over. 'And see if there's anything there that could be our murder weapon.'

CHAPTER EIGHT

Bubbles Day Care was located in a much more upmarket area than where Joyce lived. But that didn't worry her. Four walls didn't make a home. She'd lived in too many loveless abodes to be won over by appearances. But she admired the way the Foleys had converted their large garden into a safe environment for the children they looked after. The day care unit was built onto the house, and the first time she'd checked it out, she'd felt Evan would be safe with Sinéad Foley.

She glanced at her watch. Her shift at the café didn't start until twelve, but she knew Sinéad wouldn't mind taking Evan now.

'Hello, Joyce, you're early. Hi, Evan, in you go. Hang up your jacket. Your friends are inside.' Sinéad was motherly and joyful. At thirty-seven years old, she was about ten years older than Joyce.

'You've a full house today,' Joyce said.

'Easter holidays from school, so some of the juniors are here for the next two weeks.'

'Oh, I'm sorry for arriving early then.'

'Not at all. The more the merrier, as they say.' Sinéad picked Evan's jacket up from the floor, where he'd dropped it. 'What time will you be collecting him?'

Rocking from one foot to the other, Joyce contemplated the decisions she must make. Hard decisions. For now, she wanted everything to appear normal. 'Possibly a little earlier than usual. Is that okay?'

'Perfect. See you then.'

'Can I give him a hug before I go?'

'Evan, give your mum a hug.'

Joyce thought she might cry as her son dropped the toy he was playing with and ran into her arms.

'Love you,' he whispered into her ear.

She kissed him and held him tight before releasing him. 'Love you too, squirt.'

He ran back to the melee of children and picked up the dropped toy. An action hero figure. She wished that she had a superpower. Then she could hold on to her son for ever and fly away, far away from all the trouble that had hounded her life.

She walked back to her car, and sat in, her head thumping. She should call Nathan, but he'd be still driving and probably wouldn't answer the phone. Anyhow, she couldn't tell him the truth. She couldn't tell him anything, full stop. She bit her thumbnail down to the quick until it bled. What could she do?

She had to run. She knew that.

Otherwise she would be killed.

And maybe Evan would be killed too.

CHAPTER NINE

After watching McKeown drive off with Gallagher, Lottie turned to Kirby.

'What do you make of him?'

'Not sure, to be honest.' Kirby took a cigar from his pocket and scratched his head through his unruly curls. 'Do you suspect him?'

'I'm reserving my opinion until I interview him.'

Kirby walked with her to the boundary wall and lit the cigar. After taking a drag, he topped it and returned it to his pocket. 'He seemed genuinely upset. He's a big strong bloke. Took two of us to hold him back. He could have killed his wife, but he was at work.'

'Check that out. We don't have time of death yet, but just make sure he was where he said he was. We also need to know if anything has been stolen. Gallagher will have to give us an inventory, and I need to know if they kept cash or valuables inside. But looking around here, it doesn't seem like they had much.'

'Something's bothering you, isn't it?' Kirby could read her almost as well as Boyd could.

'I don't think it's a burglary gone wrong. Her handbag is still on the table. And if it was some random psycho or drug-fuelled murderer, why leave the baby alive? There was so much violence inflicted on Isabel; why not kill the baby too, unless Isabel was the sole target?'

'We need to discover all we can about Isabel Gallagher.'

'Yeah. I wonder did Jack know Anita was due to arrive to babysit?'

'What difference would that make?'

'Just thinking out loud. I'm heading back to the station to get what I can from him.'

'You think it was him, don't you?'

Lottie shrugged and tugged her sleeves down over her hands. 'All I know is that the excessive violence points to someone who lost control. That person could still be out there. God knows where they'll strike next. That's what scares me the most, Kirby. If it's not a domestic act of violence, then someone else could be in danger.'

Lottie flung her coat and bag on her desk and picked up the report McKeown had hastily compiled on the morning's events. Then she updated Superintendent Deborah Farrell, who officially appointed her as senior investigating officer. After briefing the super, she went to interview the victim's husband.

Walking along the corridor, her head down, thinking of all she had to organise, she bumped into Boyd.

'Anita Boland, Isabel's mother, is feeding the baby in Interview Room 1,' he said.

She gawped at him. 'Jesus, Boyd, could you not find somewhere more comfortable for them?'

'It was the best I could do at short notice. Mrs Boland wanted to return to her own house with the child, but forensics needed samples from her and the baby and I had to wait for the doctor to examine the little one before I could bring them home.' He tucked his jacket under his arm and rolled up the sleeves of his shirt.

'Was everything okay with the baby?'

'Yeah. Doc said she'd be fine once she got a bottle into her. No physical injuries.'

'In the greater scheme of things, that's a godsend.' Glancing through the scant paperwork in her hand, she added, 'Do you want to sit in on Jack Gallagher's interview?'

'I wouldn't mind giving him the once-over to see what he's made of.'

She eyed Boyd from under her lashes, noticing the tense line of his jaw and the irritating tap of his shoe on the floor. She'd have to keep a tight rein on him in the interview. 'Jack Gallagher was at work when his wife was killed.'

'Is that confirmed?' he said.

'Not officially, but Kirby's checking. Jane is prioritising the post-mortem and will inform me when she's ready to start. Once that's done, we should have a better idea of time of death. According to Jane, it could be within the two-hour period before Isabel's body was discovered.'

'Doesn't let the grieving husband off the hook, does it? Let's see what he has to say for himself.' Boyd pushed away from the wall and went to head down the corridor.

She put out a hand. Drew him back. Looked into his angry brown eyes. 'Boyd, relax. This man has just found out his wife was killed in front of their baby. We need to go easy on him.'

'But what if *he* was the one who killed her?' He walked on ahead of her down the stairs.

They were both letting their emotions run riot. Not a good combination for interrogating a grieving man who, for the moment, they had to treat as a suspect. She considered calling McKeown to replace Boyd at the table, but she decided Boyd was professional enough to park his preconceptions outside the door. He could control his feelings possibly better than she could.

*

The interview room was tiny, and the refurbishment budget had not extended to new furniture. Lottie eased in behind the old wooden desk and pushed her chair up against the wall, making room for Boyd to sit beside her. The old chair squeaked and rattled as she moved it. Hopefully it wouldn't collapse.

Once Boyd had set the recording to begin, with Gallagher's approval – it was a fact-gathering chat after all – and finished the introductions, she lifted her head. Before she could say a word, Gallagher spoke.

'What are you doing to find the bastard who killed my wife?' He ran calloused knuckles across reddened eyes. 'Tell me, please.'

Lottie felt her heart lurch in sympathy with the broken man sitting across from her.

'We have our technical personnel at your home, going over everything meticulously. No stone will be left unturned until we find out who did this.' She cringed as the clichés dripped from her lips, but what else could she tell him?

'I can guarantee you, if you leave anything unturned, I'll turn it myself.' He paused, then his lip drooped. 'I heard she was stabbed. My lovely quiet Isabel who wouldn't hurt a fly, stabbed! Why? Why do that to a poor defenceless woman?'

'We will find out, I assure you.'

'And what about my baby? She definitely wasn't hurt, was she?'

'A doctor has examined her. She's fine. You can see her soon. But we need information from you now, to help us advance our investigation.'

He stared at her, tears lingering in his eyes, trapped on his long lashes. She had to admit he cut a very sad figure. Gone was the aggressive manner with which he had appeared at the house earlier; gone was the fight from his hands as they lay limp on the table.

'I don't know why I have to be here. I want to see Holly.'

'In due course,' Lottie said. 'I have to build up a picture in order to discover what happened to your wife.'

'I heard she was mutilated.' The ease of his tone belied the harshness of his words. He gritted his teeth, spouting spittle as he spoke. 'Stabbed over and over. You're wasting my time and yours by having me in here when you should be out there searching for her killer.'

Lottie nudged Boyd's elbow. 'Would you mind getting Mr Gallagher a cup of tea?'

'Sugar? Milk?' Boyd stood.

'Whatever,' Gallagher said, and sank into the uncomfortable chair.

Boyd left the room. Lottie leaned towards Gallagher. 'I have the best team working on this investigation, but you have to talk to us. Please, Jack. There might be something you can tell us that will help us find Isabel's killer. Even something seemingly insignificant might provide us with a clue. We'll start when Detective Sergeant Boyd returns with your tea.'

'I don't want bloody tea. I want my daughter.'

Boyd arrived with a paper cup of milky tea from the vending machine. Gallagher slurped the tepid liquid, swallowed noisily and set down the cup.

'Tell me about Isabel,' Lottie began.

'What?' He looked up with watery eyes, his eyebrows clenched in a frown.

'How did you meet?'

'She worked in the office.'

'What office?'

'Quality Electrical. I'm an electrician. She used to work in the office.'

'What was her role there?'

'General dogsbody, if you ask me. That twat Michael Costello made her do everything from fetching his coffee to taking notes while he looked at her legs. She was really sad in that job.'

Lottie noted his choice of words. Wouldn't one say unhappy rather than sad? She let it pass.

'Why did she leave?'

'It was awkward, what with me on the books and her in the office. Do you understand?'

She didn't, but she supposed in a warped sort of way it had made sense to Isabel and Jack.

'She left the job after you got married?'

'No, a year before that. When we started going out.'

'Did she find another job after that?'

'A few hours a week at Bubbles Day Care.'

'The Foley place?' That was where Katie sent Louis, Lottie thought.

'Yeah. Passed the time for her, but then she started to get really ill with the pregnancy. About three or four months before Holly was born.'

'Was she working anywhere outside the home at the time of her death?'

Gallagher grimaced. 'No. She'd just had a baby, for fuck's sake.'

'What was she like as a wife and mother?'

'She was a good mother.'

'And as a wife?'

He scrunched up his lips and gave a slight shake of his head. 'She was my angel. But she had her ups and downs. Isabel was a little complicated.'

'How?'

He sighed before answering. 'I don't see what this has to do with you catching her killer.'

'Anything, no matter how inconsequential it might seem, could turn out to be crucial.' Lottie clasped her hands on the table and listened to Boyd scribble in his notebook, keeping her gaze firmly on Jack

Gallagher, who closed his eyes and rubbed them with rough fingers. When he took his hands away, red creases circled his eye sockets.

'What can I say that will help you?' He shrugged. 'I wasn't even at home when she …'

Lottie found it difficult to handle emotional men, and Jack Gallagher was fighting a battle to keep his emotions in check.

'This morning, what time did you leave for work?'

'The usual. Ten to seven.'

'Did you lock the door when you left the house?'

'No need to lock it when Isabel is there.'

'How was she when you were leaving?'

'Same as usual. A little grumpy. You know what women are like.' He threw an eye to Boyd for support, but found none there.

'Why was she grumpy?' Lottie asked.

'You know. Woman things. Things she wouldn't tell me about. It was a tough labour and birth. Twenty-two hours, and Holly was eventually born just as they were prepping Isabel for a C-section. I know it's been over three months, but she's been like a witch since Holly arrived. This morning she wanted me to feed Holly. Said she was exhausted. But I had to get to work.'

'She had an appointment at ten fifteen, didn't she?'

'Did she? She never told me that. Who was the appointment with?'

'Her doctor, according to Anita.' Lottie flicked the few miserable pages in the file, then closed it again.

As if registering the fact for the first time, Gallagher asked, 'Why was Anita at our house this morning?'

'To babysit Holly. How do you get on with your mother-in-law?'

'She's good for Isabel. Helps her out around the house and with Holly now and again. But I don't think she likes me.' He ran his hand across his sweaty brow and sniffed. 'I'm not good enough for her precious daughter. She gives out that I'm not doing as much as I should.

With the house, the baby. Every blasted thing. Jesus Christ, I work every hour God gives to save for the extension. Nothing I do will ever be good enough for Anita Boland.'

'You're finding it hard to finance the extension, are you?'

'I'm doing it bit by bit. I refurbished the kitchen. Just need to hire a JCB to dig the foundations to add another room.'

'Okay.' Lottie wondered if the Gallaghers were in debt. Money was a murder motivator. 'Do you have a bank loan?'

'No. I need to save first and then they might lend me something.'

'Credit Union loan?' She remembered the book in Isabel's handbag.

'Yeah. A few thousand. For the kitchen. Repayments are all up to date.'

'And you plan to do the work yourself?'

'There's a man who helps me out. Kevin Doran.'

Lottie made a note of the name. 'Is he a builder?'

'More like a handyman.'

'Has he been at your house recently?'

'Not for a few weeks, I think.'

'I'll need his contact details.' Lottie took down the number Gallagher recited from his phone. 'Is he local? Do you have his address?'

'I don't know. He just turns up when I need him.' Jack pocketed his phone then stared at Lottie. 'You don't think he could have done this, do you?'

'Do *you*?'

'If he touched her, I'll kill him myself.'

'I'll talk to him.' She could do without a grieving husband getting involved. 'Now, tell me, how were you and Isabel getting on?'

'What do you mean by that?'

'I'm trying to get a full picture of your relationship, to see what might have motivated someone to kill your wife.' Lottie blew out a soft breath. 'How was your marriage?'

'My marriage has nothing to do with this … this monster that killed my wife.'

'Everything has to do with her death, until we can eliminate whatever it is that has nothing to do with it.'

He leaned into the wooden chair with the stuffing coming out of the seat and stared at the ceiling. When he lowered his head, he was crying softly.

'Me and Isabel, we loved each other straight away. We clicked. Oh, we had our rows, but doesn't everybody? We married after a year of dating, and I set about renovating the house for her. She couldn't wait until I refurbished the kitchen. She wanted everything modern and streamlined. She loved cooking, though that changed a bit after having Holly. I've a well-paid job, but I'm not making enough to do all she wanted. It led to a couple of rows when I pared back her plans. But she seemed to lose interest in it once she was pregnant, and even more so after Holly arrived.'

'Was she diagnosed with post-partum depression?'

'She wasn't diagnosed with anything, as far as I know.'

'Was she on any medication?'

'She's not into pills for this and that. Didn't even want an epidural, though in the end she took it.'

'And she saw her doctor regularly after Holly's birth?'

'Only for the baby's vaccines and check-up. I'm sure there was nothing medically wrong with Isabel, Inspector. Holly wasn't sleeping through the night and Isabel was tired all the time, which was understandable. Nothing a good feed wouldn't fix. When she had a mind to cook, that is.'

Between the lines, Lottie was getting the impression that all had not been well in the Gallagher household.

'I see the way you're looking at me,' he said, 'and I don't like it. I did not kill my wife. I love … loved her. I don't know what the hell I'm going to do without her. Can I see my baby now?'

'In a few minutes. We need to have a word with Anita. In the meantime, can you provide me with a list of Isabel's friends?'

He twisted his large hands into each other. 'She hadn't any … many friends. Kept to herself. Too busy with Holly to be going out anywhere.'

'I couldn't find her mobile phone. Do you know where it might be?'

'She didn't have one. Too expensive. Used the landline when she needed to make a call.'

Where you could monitor her calls on the house phone bill, Lottie thought. Stop, she warned herself. She had nothing to point to him being controlling, but something itched under her skin where she couldn't reach to scratch.

'Did Isabel have a car?'

'An old Golf. It's at the back of the house. I drive the company van.'

'Did you keep cash in the house?'

'No … Wait. Do you think someone came to the house looking to rob us?'

'I'm still establishing facts. I didn't see cash or cards in her handbag.'

'She didn't have a bank card.'

'Cash?'

'A weekly allowance for groceries and baby stuff.'

He blushed, and Lottie gathered he realised this appeared suspicious.

'So she could have had cash in her wallet?'

'If so, there wouldn't have been much. We bought the groceries at the weekend. If anyone wanted to steal from us, good luck to them. We had nothing worth taking.'

'Did either of you have any enemies?'

'I don't know of anyone who could bear enough of a grudge to do something like that to my Isabel. And I don't know who could hate us enough to do it either.'

Boyd leaned across the table, his face close to Gallagher's. 'We need your permission to access your phone and financial records.'

Gallagher drew back, almost toppling his chair. 'You've got some cheek. My wife is lying dead in our house and you want to know if I have money in the bank? You know what you can do? You can stop looking at me for this, and find the monster who killed her.' He folded his arms and bit his lip.

Lottie watched him, more determined than ever to scrutinise the Gallaghers' bank statements. First, though, she'd have a chat with Anita.

CHAPTER TEN

Watching Anita Boland hold a bottle to her granddaughter's mouth, Lottie felt an ache clench her heart. As good as her own mother, Rose, had been when Katie, Chloe and Sean were babies, she had never seen her look on them with the same affection as Anita did with Holly. In later years, after Adam died, Rose had softened, helping out when she could, but they were young teenagers by then, and it hadn't been easy. Lottie hoped little Holly grew to appreciate her grandmother's love in the absence of her murdered mother's. At least the baby still had her dad. That was good, wasn't it?

'I need to go home,' Anita said. 'I have to get clothes for Holly.'

'You live here in Ragmullin, don't you?' Lottie said.

'Yes, Wisteria Villas. Sounds like an address out of a *Hollywood Wives* episode, but it's plain and simple, with a garden I can manage on my own.' Anita smiled sadly. 'I'd have preferred it if Isabel lived closer to me, but she was still only a ten-minute drive away. Too far, as it turns out.'

'You were first at the scene, so I'd like a quick word. Is that okay?'

'I want to take my grandchild out of here. I've had my fingerprints taken and supplied a DNA sample. What more do you want?' She kept her head bowed, a grey streak breaking the crown of dyed blonde hair in half. Lottie put out a hand to comfort her. The woman retreated into the chair, clutching the baby tighter.

'Just five minutes,' Lottie said. 'I want to find the person who killed your daughter. We can talk at the same time as you're feeding Holly. Is that okay?'

'I suppose so.' Anita raised her head, the lids of her eyes red from crying. 'What do you want to know?'

'Tell me about Isabel. What was she like? Was anything worrying her? Anyone causing her anxiety? That kind of thing.'

'I don't know what I can tell you that will help. Isabel was my everything. My husband, Fred, died when she was seven. Heart attack. So for more than twenty years it was just Isabel and me. Until she met Jack. Then I was out in the cold.'

'How was that?'

'Nothing major. But I was no longer her confidante. No longer her friend. Just her mother.' Anita sighed and shifted her weight as the baby continued to guzzle the bottle. 'Isabel was a bit of a loner growing up. Not many friends to speak of, and then Jack appears and whisks her off her feet, so to speak. She gave up that good office job at Quality Electrical because of him, and ended up working a few hours a day in Foley's. That's a crèche.'

'I know it.'

'Jack took her to that house in the arsehole of nowhere, an awful wreck of a place. She got pregnant not long after they were married, when I knew she didn't really want a baby. I think she was afraid any child she might have would endure a lonely childhood without friends like she did.'

'Why didn't Isabel have many friends growing up?'

'She was a loner. Her father was dead, as I said, and I had to work to keep up with the mortgage payments. School was daunting for her. She struggled. She lacked self-confidence and was the butt of bullies' jokes. I protected her as much as I could. Maybe that was a mistake …' Anita's voice drifted off as tears gathered in the corners of her eyes.

Lottie got the impression the woman had tried to cocoon Isabel from the world, and had failed. 'I'm sure Isabel was delighted to have you in her corner.'

'It was hard to know with her. She was a bit naïve, if I'm honest. She worked in AJ Lennon's Hardware a few years ago. There are branches throughout Ireland.'

Lottie nodded. She could see how painful this must be for Anita.

'She found it hard to deal with the irregular shifts there, and then she got the office job at Quality Electrical. Nine to five. That suited her, though I worried how she was coping. Her moods were quite dark at times, until she met Jack. He was the first guy to take any real interest in her, and she was besotted with him.' Bowing her head, Anita looked at the baby sucking contentedly on the bottle. 'In a way, I didn't blame her. He was really good to her. They seemed to be so in love. He's a bit older than her, so maybe she saw him as a father figure. Oh God, I don't know.'

'He's thirty-eight and Isabel was twenty-nine, is that right?'

Anita nodded. 'But he's older in other ways too … oh, all sorts of things.'

'Care to elaborate?' Lottie watched as Anita placed the baby on her shoulder and rubbed her back. Holly burped immediately.

'It has no bearing on what happened.'

'You can't know that. Tell me what you mean.'

'I don't believe Jack killed my daughter. He loved her and she loved him. Anyhow, he was working miles away, wasn't he?'

'That may be so, but—'

'Inspector.' Anita swallowed a sob, caressing the baby's hair. 'Whoever did this to Isabel is a monster. Jack's not a monster. He's clever with money, that's all I meant. He kept control of the budget. He had all his financial records locked in the garage. I know they were saving, but all the same, I think it hurt Isabel that he didn't trust her. '

Lottie considered this, and made a note to check out the garage. 'Is there anything else you want to say?'

'Will Holly be psychologically scarred for life now?'

'I'm sure she won't. She's young enough not to remember what happened.'

'But you saw the blood on her little face. Deep down, subconsciously, she'll always know something horrible happened in front of her eyes.' Anita gazed down at the baby. 'I suppose I should be grateful that she wasn't physically harmed.'

'That's one positive to take from this awful situation,' Lottie said, trying to keep the worry from her voice. The gruesome attack had left a sour taste in her mouth.

She looked closely at Anita. 'Jack told me Isabel didn't own a mobile phone. Do you find that odd?'

'They had a house phone. She told me they couldn't afford to pay for two mobiles plus a landline. She was at home most of the time, so she cancelled hers.'

'But she was a young woman and I'm sure she needed a mobile for social media. We didn't find any laptop or computer either.'

'Isabel despised social media. Said it was an intrusion into her privacy. She just wanted to build a life with Jack and Holly.'

'Right. You said she had a doctor's appointment this morning? Do you know what for?'

'I assume it was a check-up.'

'She wasn't taking Holly with her. Why?'

'I don't know. Maybe she wanted a few hours on her own.'

'Isabel was isolated out in Cloughton,' Lottie said, 'and Jack seems to think she might have been capable of harming herself. Was she depressed?'

'That's preposterous. Why would he even think that, let alone say it?'

'That's the impression he gave me.'

Anita thought for a moment. 'She'd become very withdrawn, but I didn't think she was depressed, just tired. Maybe that's why she had the doctor's appointment. Can you find out?'

'I'll do my best, but … patient confidentiality …'

'Maybe Jack could give permission for you to see Isabel's records?'

'Who was her GP? I'll see what I can find out.'

Anita sighed and gave her the name of a Ragmullin doctor.

Lottie said, 'Do you know if she intended to return to work at some stage?'

'She never said. After she met Jack, she didn't confide in me as much as she used to.'

Lottie was beginning to get the impression that Anita didn't know a whole lot about Isabel's recent life. Was that because either Jack or her daughter didn't want her to know?

'What friends did Isabel have?'

'Not many, I guess.'

'Other new mothers, maybe?'

Anita shrugged.

Lottie pressed on. 'Was she in any clubs where she'd have made friends?'

'What type of clubs?'

'Maybe tennis, or walking? A gym? That kind of thing.'

'She wasn't sporty, and like I said, she had moved on from me once she got with Jack. And then this little munchkin came along.'

'Did you see your daughter often?'

'Not as often as I'd have liked. They didn't invite me round much. Didn't stop me turning up now and again. She called me to sit with Holly from time to time, like she asked me to do this morning.'

'If you think of anyone else we can talk to who knew Isabel, let me know.'

'I will.'

'Did you ever meet Kevin Doran?'

Anita scrunched her eyes and leaned her head to one side. 'Don't think so. Who is he?'

'Jack mentioned that he helped him renovate the kitchen. Did odd jobs for him. Did you see him at the house this morning?'

Anita shook her head and settled Holly back on her lap. 'I didn't notice anyone around this morning. Only my lovely daughter and Holly. And all that blood. Dear God.'

'Don't worry. I'll contact this Kevin and see if he's been at the house recently, or noticed anything unusual.'

'Inspector, do you think Jack is okay to take Holly, or does he want me to mind her for a bit? He has no other family.'

'It would be good for you to be involved in Holly's care. They'll both need somewhere to live for a few days.'

Anita's eyes watered again, and tears fell on the baby's head. She wiped them away with whispered kisses. 'I'll do all I can to help. I love this little one as much as I loved my daughter, but Jack is her father. Holly will give him something to focus on, something to keep him sane through all this insanity.'

'Jack is in shock at the moment, like you are. You'll need support. I'm assigning a family liaison officer to help you both.'

'Thanks, but no,' Anita said, her cadence adamant. 'I need space to grieve. We won't be wanting outside help.'

Lottie laid a hand on her trembling fingers. 'Your daughter has been murdered. You saw the results of the attack first hand. The FLO will be there for comfort and support.' She didn't mention that she wanted eyes on Jack while he was still a viable suspect. He seemed too broken to be involved, but she'd seen it all, and anything was possible.

Anita took up the bottle and, seeing some formula remaining, put it back to the baby's mouth. She stared at Lottie with penetrating eyes. 'I know what you're thinking, Inspector. Jack would never hurt my Isabel.'

As she stood to leave, Lottie wondered if the woman was overdoing the platitudes.

CHAPTER ELEVEN

The office of Quality Electrical was located on the outskirts of Ragmullin. A large warehouse with a rolling door faced a two-storey office block. A wide yard separated the two buildings, stacked with wooden reels of cable and a couple of company vans parked up. It was only a kilometre outside town, but Kirby felt he was in the countryside.

A sixty-something man in overalls met Kirby and Garda Martina Brennan on the forecourt and told them that Michael Costello, the boss, was upstairs in the office. Leaving Martina to talk to the foreman, Kirby headed inside.

Costello looked to be in his forties, about five ten, wide-shouldered, sporting a thick beard and a head of ginger hair that fell in an unruly fashion over his freckled forehead. Behind horn-rimmed spectacles that Kirby imagined sported a designer label were eyes of an indiscriminate colour. He wore navy trousers, a white shirt and a green tie. His navy jacket had *QE* embroidered in gold thread on the pocket.

He offered his hand when Kirby entered the small office.

'Thanks for seeing me,' Kirby said.

'Will this take long? I've a meeting shortly.'

Sitting on a swivel chair, Kirby went to fold his arms, but his belly got in the way so he laid them on the table that separated the two men.

'So, what goes on around here?'

Flashing a mouthful of pristine white teeth, Costello removed his expensive-looking spectacles. 'I'm an electrical contractor. The building trade is booming once again and we're in demand. My crews can wire anything from a chicken coop to a high-rise office block.'

'Good, good,' Kirby said. 'You know why I'm here?'

'Awful business. Poor Isabel.' Costello buttoned his jacket. 'What is this world coming to at all?' His voice was soft and placating. A man used to smoothing over problems.

'How long has Jack Gallagher been employed by you?'

'Just shy of five years.'

'A good employee?'

'Exemplary.'

'No trouble in that time?'

'Jack is one of our best electricians. Eager to please. No job too big or too small for him. Punctual, courteous and hard-working.'

Costello's words sounded like a job reference. Blowing out his breath in frustration, Kirby said, 'Surely he must have some bad habits?'

'None that I know of.'

'What time did he arrive for work this morning?'

'I already gave that information to one of your colleagues over the phone, but I have it all here, anyhow.' Costello clicked the computer mouse and twisted the screen towards Kirby. It looked like a spreadsheet, with coloured columns containing lots of names and numbers.

'Can you explain it, please?'

'I'll give you a printout.' A button was pressed and the soft whirr of a printer sounded from behind Costello.

'That's great, thanks,' Kirby said, 'but if you don't mind, I'd like you to tell me yourself.'

'Sure, no problem. Jack clocked in at seven ten. His first job of the day was out in Bardstown. A wiring job on a new-build. His van was already loaded from the evening before, so he left the yard at once. You can check our CCTV if you want. I'm eager to help in whatever way I can. Oh, and there's a key-fob log from the gate here, when the workers come in and out. I assure you there's no need to suspect Jack of any wrongdoing.'

'And how do you come to that conclusion, seeing as you have no idea what we're dealing with?'

'Well, regardless, when he reached the house at Bardstown, he called me. The builders had been redeployed to another job and he had no way to gain access. The site was boarded up and locked. That call was around seven thirty.'

'Did he return here, then?'

'No. I contacted the house owner and they said they had a medical emergency and were at a Dublin hospital. So I told Jack to head to a house at Plodmore that had been on our books for a while. Simple job, to install a new fuse box.'

'Does it take long to get from Bardstown to Plodmore?'

'You have to travel along country roads, so maybe you should drive it yourself to see.' Costello placed his spectacles back on his nose and pushed them up.

Kirby bristled at the rebuke. 'Are you sure that's where he was when you told him to head home after our call?'

'As far as I know, that's where he was.'

'No way of checking?'

'I can call the occupier.'

'Just give me the contact details.'

'It's on the spreadsheet.' Costello smiled.

Taking the page without looking at it, Kirby said, 'What's Jack like? Besides being punctual, courteous and whatever else you told me?'

'He's a fine man. Always willing—'

'Yeah, yeah.' Kirby slapped the desk, losing patience. 'Had he any friends? Was he a loner? Did he drink? Join the lads in the pub after work? That kind of thing?'

'I have no idea what he did outside of work. Talk to his colleagues. They might be able to fill you in. I only concern myself with my employees on a professional basis. I'm not interested in the rest.'

'What do you mean by "the rest"?'

'Their relationships with each other. Friends or enemies, it doesn't matter to me as long as it doesn't interfere with their work. I'm a business-man, not a nanny.' He smiled again. It was starting to grate on Kirby.

'Do you know a Kevin Doran?' The boss had texted him, telling him to ask about Doran.

Costello shook his head. 'Not one of mine.'

Kirby glanced down at the spreadsheet, with its coloured columns. 'Where did Jack work before he started here?'

'I don't recall that.'

'Can you check your files?'

Shifting on his seat, Costello seemed to consider these questions for a lot longer than the previous interaction. 'Sorry. Data protection laws.'

'But you've just printed out Gallagher's work schedule for me; this is no different.'

'What you're asking for now is historic personal information, not relevant to his current employment. I'm sorry. I can't give it to you. Unless you get Jack's permission.'

'Okay. Thanks.' Kirby decided not to push it. 'Did you know Isabel?'

'She was lovely. Always ready to help out.'

'You knew her personally?'

'She worked here. Did you not know that?'

The boss had neglected to text that piece of information, and now Kirby felt foolish. 'When was that?'

'Must be over a year and a half ago. Jack convinced her to give up the job. She was so under his … She was in awe of him. I think she'd have jumped off a cliff if he'd asked her to.'

'Did she work in the office?'

'Yes. Isabel was limited in what she could do. She found it hard to work on her own initiative. Slow at the computer. Filed things in the wrong place. Bit of a scatterbrain.'

'But still you kept her on until she decided to leave. Why was that?'

'It helped to have a pretty face here to offset all those lads around the place.'

'If you say so.' Kirby was embarrassed by the man's words.

'Detective Kirby, Jack was insanely jealous if she even looked crooked at anyone. It was a bit awkward, to tell the truth, seeing that eighty per cent of my workers are male.'

'Thought you said he was everything bar a knight in shining armour.'

'A jealous knight. His work is exemplary.'

Kirby scratched his head. 'Was Isabel close to anyone else here, besides Jack?'

'Not that I know of.'

'Was there someone she didn't get on with?'

Costello stood and stretched out his shoulders. 'If you're asking if I know of anyone who would kill her, then I'm sorry, but I know of no such person. My reputation is my business, and I employ only the best people. Isabel was a lovely girl and it pains me to think she's dead.'

Kirby stood too. 'If you think of anything, contact me.'

'I will.' Costello picked up his keys and phone and moved around the desk. 'What's her name?'

Kirby turned at the door to see him looking through the window. 'Who?' he asked.

'That young garda you brought along with you. Nice tight trousers show off her assets quite well, don't you think? How does she carry all that equipment?'

Totally inappropriate talk, but Kirby couldn't think of a reply without 'arsehole' in it, so he just slammed the door on his way out. He thought of Martina Brennan, who was short and a tad overweight – though who was he to talk about weight. She was bright and breezy, always smiling. Maybe he'd chance asking her out, though he knew why he couldn't do that.

In the compound, he noticed a couple more vans to his right, parked in front of the unit, the rolling doors now open. Garda Brennan was chatting with two men, huddled together. They stopped and looked at him as he approached.

'Detective Kirby, ready to go?' she said.

'Are you lads not supposed to be out working?' Kirby said.

'We came back to base after hearing about Jack's wife. Garda Brennan wouldn't tell us much. What happened to her?'

'It's an ongoing investigation,' Kirby said, glad that Martina was clever enough not to divulge pertinent information, though he was sure the men knew full well what had happened to Isabel. 'Can I have a word for a few minutes?'

'We've talked to her.' The tall one broke away from his colleague. 'You coming, Ciaran?'

'Hold your horses, just a few more questions.'

The men turned and met Kirby's eyes with defiance.

'Lads, one minute,' Garda Brennan said, and smiled.

'What you want to know?'

'Your name is?' Kirby asked.

'She knows it,' the tall man said.

'This is Paulo Silva. From Brazil,' Garda Brennan said. 'Worked with Quality Electrical for three years but he's lived in Ireland for over fifteen. His colleague is Ciaran Grimes. He's worked here seven years.'

'Are you friends with Jack Gallagher?' Kirby said.

The smaller man, Ciaran, looked up at Paulo and shrugged. 'Jack doesn't say much.'

'Not drinking buddies, then?'

'I don't think Jack drinks.'

'What's he like around here?'

'Doesn't say much, as I said. Good morning. Goodbye. He never talks about his wife or baby. I talk about my Carla all the time. You want to see a photo?'

'No thanks. Did Jack ever show you photos of his family?'

'Are you for real?' Ciaran said. 'We couldn't even mention his wife's name or he'd blow a gasket.'

'Bit of a temper, then?'

'You could say that. We just kept our mouths shut,' Ciaran said, and Paulo nodded.

'Did either of you know Mrs Gallagher?'

The two men rocked on their feet like a comedy duo, one waiting for the other to speak. It was Ciaran who straightened his shoulders and replied.

'I haven't seen her since she left the office, before they got married. It's like Jack saw her as his princess to keep locked in his castle.'

'They had a baby three or four months ago. Did that make Jack happy?'

'We never even knew they'd had a baby,' Ciaran said, 'until my mother heard someone mention it in the post office.'

'Do either of you know Kevin Doran?'

Both men shook their heads.

'You sure?'

'Certain.'

'Know of any reason why someone would want to harm Mrs Gallagher?'

Both heads shaking in unison. 'Nope.'

'Thanks. I'll need your details in case we need to speak with you again.'

'I have them.' Garda Brennan tapped her notebook in her pocket.

At the car, Kirby leaned his elbows on the roof and surveyed the compound. 'Get anything useful out of them?'

'Don't think so, but I took notes. Sam … Detective McKeown says all information is important, even though it might not seem so at the time.'

'You and he are very cosy, aren't you?'

'What do you mean by that?'

Kirby grimaced when Garda Brennan blushed. 'Oh, nothing at all.'

'Not that it's any of your business or anything,' she said, opening the door, 'but I'm single.'

'Aye, but he's not.'

He leaped back from the car with the force of the bang she gave the door.

CHAPTER TWELVE

After Jack, Anita and Holly had left for Anita's house, Lottie set the team up in the incident room and doled out their tasks.

'McKeown, I want to know everything about this Kevin Doran, the handyman. All I have is his phone number, and it seems to be switched off or dead. Find out when he was last at the house. How often he works there. What else he does. His whole pedigree.'

'On it.'

'Lynch, search online to see what you can discover about the Gallaghers. Find someone to talk to who knew Isabel so that we can get to know her.'

'Sure.' Lynch gave her half of a crooked smile, glad to be back in the team after a period of icy isolation that had gradually thawed towards the end of their last major case.

Looking around, Lottie said, 'Where's Kirby?'

Lynch piped up. 'He went to Quality Electrical to confirm exactly where Jack Gallagher was until he arrived back home.'

'He's taking his time.' She glanced at the clock on the wall, which was set half an hour fast for some reason. 'Give him a call and see what he has so far.'

Lynch nodded.

'And phone the state pathologist for the time of Isabel Gallagher's post-mortem. Plus contact Isabel's doctor. See if you can wheedle out any information.'

The group dispersed and she grabbed Boyd to set out to the Gallagher house at Cloughton again. She phoned McGlynn and got his disgruntled permission to have a quick look in the garage. As Gallagher had not given them permission to access his financial or phone records, she hoped she might find something worthwhile.

They travelled in silence.

Once they arrived, they suited up. The sun was shining but a chilly breeze cut a sharp line around the side of the house. Standing in the garden with an increasingly belligerent Boyd by her side, she opened the garage door with the key she'd got from Gallagher.

'What's eating you, Boyd?'

'Nothing.'

'Listen, you need to lighten up a little.'

'It was him, I'm sure of it. It's usually the husband.'

'If it is, we need evidence to prove it, and if it isn't, we still need evidence to prove someone else did it. Either way, this is a fact-gathering exercise, so untwist your knickers and put on your logical hat.' She thought that would make him laugh. He just grunted.

They entered the garage. The only sound was the crinkle of their protective gear.

'Neat and tidy,' she said, sniffing the fusty air.

They moved further inside.

White fungus sprouted in a few corners, and the walls were stained brown with leaks from the roof. Everything seemed to have a space allocated in some kind of methodical order. One side of the garage was taken up with firewood, neatly piled as if the person who'd done it was a Jenga master. The other side was stacked high with empty paint cans in order of size. To her left was a bench with tools and electrical cables neatly rolled and held together with plastic ties. To her right, just inside the door, stood a four-drawer filing cabinet with its top drawer open and Boyd nosing through it.

She peered over his elbow. The file folders were scattered in a pile and did not seem to be in any sort of order. This was totally at odds with the neatness of everything else in the garage.

'It's a mess,' Boyd said, and opened the other drawers.

All were empty except for a forgotten roll of Sellotape. She couldn't tell if they had held files or documents at one time. As he moved off to rummage through the electrical equipment, she returned to the top drawer and extracted the bundle of paperwork. She brought it to the bench and began opening the files.

'There's no bank statements,' she said.

'Did you actually think he kept his bank statements out here?'

Concentrate on the job at hand, she warned herself, not rising to his bait.

The pages consisted mainly of invoices and receipts for electrical work, which made her think Jack worked freelance as well as for Quality Electrical. She shot off a quick text to Kirby to find out.

'Here's a phone bill printout,' she said. Placing the four pages to one side, she continued her search, praying for bank statements.

She was disappointed. There was nothing else of note. They might be lucky and find out something from the phone bill and invoices. And then again, maybe not.

She placed the invoices in a large evidence bag, which she titled, dated and signed.

'What about those?' Boyd pointed to the telephone bill printout.

'These are going in a separate bag. I want to examine them the minute we return to the office.'

He nodded and wandered round the cramped space lifting cables and tools.

'What do you hope to find?' she asked.

'The murder weapon.'

'I doubt the killer is that stupid. It's in the bottom of a lake by now.'

'No stone left unturned, to quote a certain detective inspector.' He glanced over his shoulder at her and she couldn't help but return his smile.

'Guilty as charged,' she said. 'Keep searching and I'll have a chat with McGlynn.'

The odour of fried food filtered through her mask as Lottie entered the kitchen for the second time that morning. She hadn't noticed it earlier, as the overriding smell had been death and blood. She walked around slowly, careful to take in anything she might have missed initially.

Breakfast seemed to have been cereal and toast. A teapot with a knitted cosy. Blue ceramic crockery, some smashed on the floor. Crumbs and congealed cereal. The sink was empty, the stainless steel gleaming. She opened the refrigerator and noted it was well stocked; there were also two bottles of formula, for when Anita was to mind little Holly, perhaps. Closing its door, she considered the kitchen again. Something was giving her an itch beneath her scalp. What was she missing? Was it the fact that there were no toys? No child's clothing on the back of chairs or on the toppled clothes rack.

She scanned her eyes over the countertops. The usual appliances and a tub of baby formula. In one corner a changing table with nappies, Sudocrem and cotton wool.

The walls were devoid of any paintings or photographs except for the wedding photo in the hall. The only nod to decor was functional.

A small wall calendar pinned above the phone caught her eye. Flicking the pages, she noticed the blank dates. She let it fall back to April, the current month. Today's date had a small x. Another x on

Friday. February had a note on the eighth. *Six-week check-up* written in cramped script. Nothing else anywhere. She supposed Isabel kept track of appointments this way, as she had no mobile phone. Lottie would die without her phone diary.

She moved on.

The sitting room was the largest of the rooms. The fireplace had been fitted with a black stove, the glass gleaming. A basket of kindling stood beside it. She ran her gloved finger over the mantelpiece; no dust or soot came away. The suite was white leather with orange cushions, all perfectly symmetrical. Again, no pictures or photographs on the walls. Plain magnolia paint, expertly applied. She had to hand it to the Gallaghers; they kept a clean house. It was bare and minimalist. No baby play mat or soft toys.

She glanced into the main bedroom, where McGlynn was working silently, the body now removed to the morgue. The blood-spattered cot seemed to mock her, and she took a step back. A quick glance from Jim warned her he didn't want to be disturbed.

Two other bedrooms had their doors open, and SOCO team members worked like ants. One room was completely empty, unfurnished and unpainted. The other had a single bed with plain white linen and a cream blind. No dust on anything.

The bathroom was similarly pristine. She opened the mirrored cabinet door without glancing at herself. She could do without seeing her haggard face with its confused expression. Two toothbrushes standing in a white ceramic holder. In her house everyone threw their brushes into a single grimy glass from the kitchen. Here, the toothpaste tube had its cap on securely. There was no congealed toothpaste lining the sink like in her bathroom.

A bottle of mouthwash, almost full. No pills for headaches or ointment for piles. In the cabinet, a straight razor and a box of blades. She thought of the blade they'd found on Isabel's body. Did it come from here or had it been brought by her killer? She asked for the blades to be examined.

Closing the cabinet door, she noticed an electric shaver secured to the wall with a clip. The bath was clean and the shower glass without scum or water drops. Had Isabel cleaned it after Jack had left for work?

As she moved back to the hall, her impression was of a woman under the control of someone else. There was no evidence of Isabel or Holly actually living a happy life here. No photographic montage of Holly on the walls. Nothing.

She moved back to the main bedroom.

'Jim, can I have a look through the wardrobe?'

'Not much to see, but fire ahead.'

She opened the nearest door. Her initial reaction was one of envy. If only she could keep her clothing as evenly folded. Not a hope in hell, she thought. Then she noticed that most of the clothes were Jack's. Shirts and jumpers. Behind the other door, two suits hung side by side, and four pairs of trousers and jeans. Ironed and pressed. Hanging on the opposite side were a couple of light summer dresses, a few hoodies and two pairs of jeans for Isabel. Three drawers beneath. Two held T-shirts and a selection of loungewear. All Primark. The other held underwear, practical, nothing fancy.

She felt pity for the young woman. Not that she herself had fancy underwear, but something about the well-worn cotton undergarments gave her a sense that Isabel hadn't spent much money on herself. Or hadn't been allowed to.

Shutting the drawer, she moved to the chest of drawers, and at last she discovered items belonging to the baby. Babygros, vests and socks. No frilly baby dresses. No Minnie Mouse tights. Holly seemed to be allowed only the most functional of clothing, like her mother. What had it been like to live like this? There was no evidence of poverty in the home, and Jack had a good job. Was he saving every cent for the building work outside? She really needed to see their bank statements and life insurance policies, if only to eliminate any wrongdoing on Jack's part in the death of his wife.

She rose to her feet. 'Jim, did any of your team come across toys or baby things?'

'There was a rag doll in the cot, which we've sent for analysis. A lot of blood spatter on it.'

'Grand. Thanks.' Lottie tried to offload the invisible weight that had settled on her shoulders.

'Why do you ask?'

'It's just that this house seems more like a bachelor pad.'

'I've seen many a bachelor pad in my time, and let me tell you, none of them were as tidy as this house.' McGlynn dipped his head back to his work. 'But I get what you mean. I'd be grilling that husband long and hard.'

'Thanks, Jim, I intend to.' At the door, she turned. 'Have you found anything to help me?'

'No evidence of the killer except for the possibility of picking up a boot print beneath that mess.' He indicated the blood on the floor.

'A boot print? That's good.'

'I know the mother-in-law walked through the house, but we're analysing everything. I'll let you know when I know more.'

'Wouldn't the killer have been covered in blood?'

'There'd be spray from the neck wound, but you and I know today's killers are clever. I blame television.'

'Thanks.'

Walking back down the hallway, Lottie looked around for the family's shoes. She found them in the utility room. A selection of coats and scarves hung above the shoe rack. She searched the pockets and found loose change and a pair of gloves. One of the scarves matched the gloves, a red knitted affair; the other was blue with a yellow trim. These were the only colourful items of clothing she'd come across in the house.

Jack Gallagher's shoes were size thirteen. A polished black leather pair and another in brown. Soles clean. Scrubbed? SOCOs would take possession of his work boots, which he must be wearing, but he might have more than one pair. For Isabel there was a pair of well-worn black Converse and a couple of unbranded light runners.

As she left through the back door, she noticed a holy water font hanging on the jamb. A silver crucifix perched over the font. And the font was full. Catholics, then. Not that it made the slightest bit of difference. Isabel was dead and Lottie hadn't a clue as to who had killed the young mother. She went out to look for Boyd, who was probably sneaking a smoke somewhere.

*

The detective was walking around the perimeter, his eyes scanning the distance. What was he looking for? They'd both been inside the garage, but Kevin knew there were no secrets to be found in there. He knew where all the secrets were buried.

He pulled up the collar of his heavy work jacket. The rough wool cut into his thin neck, and he inhaled the earthy scent of the boggy land where he was positioned. A bird cawed, and he glanced up through the branches with their sprouting leaves. He couldn't see the bird, but the sound had betrayed its hiding place. He himself could be found just as easily. He had to be careful. No one could know he was here. He was like everyone's shadow, following them around, sticking to their heels, but no one noticed him. That was what Isabel had told him. Suited him fine today.

He had been waiting there in the shade of an old tree, two fields behind the house to the right, for a good few hours. He had a great view. The house sat exposed on a hillock, visible from where he stood. He'd noticed earlier that the chimney wasn't sending smoke in a trail up to the clear April sky. Isabel always lit the stove once Jack left for work. It was the best way to heat the house, she'd told him. But Kevin knew that was because Jack was too much of a skinflint to fill the oil tank once winter was officially over. Didn't matter that the temperature in April was sometimes lower than January. No, Jack was too mean. Kevin spat on the ground whenever Jack's name entered his head. Today he spat with renewed venom.

What the hell were they all doing up there? Isabel's mother's car was parked in the yard. He'd seen her run out shortly after she'd entered the house, with the child in her arms. Then garda cars started to arrive, followed by the technical van. He'd sunk back into the shadows, not daring to leave his spot. They'd want to talk to him, no doubt, but Kevin did not want to talk to them. Not to anyone. Not now. Not ever.

It was still possible Isabel was okay, wasn't it? Maybe her mother had panicked over something, or they'd had an argument. But why hadn't she followed Anita out? No, this was serious. In his heart, Kevin knew Isabel was dead. Once he'd come to that conclusion, he was too stunned to move, so he'd been frozen in the same spot for the last few hours, his mind in turmoil.

Yes, the guards would want to talk to him, he reminded himself, but he wouldn't talk to them. He knew too much; he knew too little. Which was it? All those blackouts when he couldn't remember a thing. Did he really not know what had happened in the house? Had he been inside earlier? Had he seen Isabel and lost control? No, no, not that. He shook his head wildly. He couldn't think the unthinkable.

Sliding down the uneven bark, tendrils of wood sticking to his wool jacket, he sat on the grass, cradled his head in his hands and cried like a baby. For a long time.

When he stopped crying, he stood, pulled his black knitted beanie down over his ears and looked up at the house on the hillock. Before he moved on, he watched the two detectives get back into their car and drive away.

CHAPTER THIRTEEN

Boyd drove, and when he turned onto the main road, Lottie glanced at him.

'I got such an uneasy feeling in that house,' she said. 'Did you feel it?'

'It's a murder scene, so it should make you uneasy.'

'Find anything else in the garage?'

'Nope. I walked the perimeter of the yard. Work seems to have been started on the extension, but it appears to be a while since anything's been done.' He lowered the window to let fresh air permeate around them. 'Is that too cold for you?'

'For Christ's sake, Boyd. I'm boiling mad. I could explode.'

'Then tell me what's spooked you.'

'Everything was basic.' She explained about the clothing, the lack of toys for Holly and the cleanliness of every surface.

'Maybe Isabel was just house-proud or bored being at home all day.'

'She had a three-and-a-half-month-old child – there's no room for boredom. The house should show some evidence that they had a baby, that the baby had something besides one rag doll. It's like Isabel owned nothing.'

'We can ask Anita about it.'

'We can bloody well ask Jack Gallagher.'

'I agree,' he said.

They spent the rest of the short drive in absolute silence. As he turned the car up Bishop's Street towards the station, Lottie looked at him again.

'Boyd, she had no money or bank cards of her own.'

'Maybe she didn't trust herself with money.'

'Or Jack didn't trust her. How was she to pay for her doctor's appointment?'

'Another question for Mr Gallagher,' he said, and pulled in behind the station.

She could have given the phone bill to Lynch to go through – she was good at that type of thing – but the detective was already scrutinising social media to see if Jack or Isabel had any accounts.

Lottie needed to be doing something constructive while waiting to discover if any CCTV footage had been secured from neighbouring areas. The Gallagher bungalow sat on the top of a hill, with fields stretching for miles around. No more than three farmhouses lined the narrow road, with at least half a kilometre between each of them. So far the door-to-door reports had concluded that no one had seen anything and they knew little about the Gallaghers. More intensive interviews might elicit further information, but from initial reports it didn't look promising.

Laying photocopies of the landline phone bill on her desk – last month's bill – she looked for recurring numbers. She flicked through the interview notes and found Anita's mobile and landline numbers, plus Jack's mobile. She needed to get hold of his phone.

This was definitely a job for Maria Lynch.

'Favour to ask,' she said. 'Can you analyse this bill to identify the owners of the numbers?'

'Sure,' Lynch replied. 'Any I can't identify I'll ring the number and see who answers? Quickest way.'

'Do that. Let me know as soon as possible. How are you doing with the social media?'

Lynch sighed. 'Isabel doesn't appear to have any accounts, though Jack has a Facebook business page and a website for freelance electrical work. Very basic WordPress. I'll have to get Gary in technical to have a look at it.'

'Do that. And see what you can get from Jack's Facebook page.'

'It's password-protected. Another job for Gary.'

'Tell him it's urgent.' Lottie thought for a moment. 'Check with Revenue. See if his tax affairs are up to date.'

'Will do.'

'Anything about either of them in the local news archives?'

'Nope.'

'Talk to McKeown so that you don't duplicate work.'

Lynch grimaced.

'Is that a problem for you?' Lottie asked, knowing full well that it was. Lynch had blamed McKeown for ratting Lottie out on an earlier case. This had resulted in Lottie's suspension, after which she'd been reinstated without any wrongdoing having been proved.

'No problem. It's fine,' Lynch said, but her teeth were clenched.

'Great.' Lottie turned on her heel.

'Oh,' Lynch added, 'Isabel Gallagher's post-mortem is scheduled for three this afternoon.'

'Thanks.'

McKeown approached Lottie as she made for her own office and followed her inside.

'I've carried out a quick search on this Kevin Doran character. There's quite a few men with that name, but they all check out. So no sign of your handyman appearing on anything official. Nothing on PULSE. It might not even be his real name.'

'Dig deeper.'

As he trudged back to his desk, swearing under his breath, she doubled back from her office and went into the incident room. It was stifling hot. She turned down the radiators, pulled off her sweater and rolled up the frayed sleeves of her white T-shirt. Folding her arms, she leaned against a desk and studied the picture of the Gallaghers' wedding photo she'd taken at the house.

Anita had sent her a couple of photos from her phone, so she pinned those to the board as well. Isabel dressed in a hoodie zipped to the neck, aged about twenty-one or two. Eyes dark hollows with a sad gaze. Isabel holding newborn Holly in her arms. Drawing her gaze over all three photos, she noted marked differences in the young woman. Her eyes in the wedding photo were bright blue, reflecting the light, full of life, but in the others they seemed … dead.

'What happened to you, sweetheart?' she said to Isabel's image.

'Talking to yourself is the first sign—'

'Of madness. I know, Boyd. But look at these photos. Tell me what you see.'

He stood beside her, the heat from his body radiating against her own. She resisted the urge to clasp his hand, just to ground herself.

'Jesus,' he said. He lowered his voice to a whisper. 'I see it.'

'Tell me what you see?'

'Her eyes are so sad, troubled. She looks haunted.'

CHAPTER FOURTEEN

It was a lovely day for a climb. Dervla Byrne donned her hiking boots and, after locking her green Fiat Punto, set off up the side of Misneach Hill. She knew all about the mythology surrounding the hill, with its megalithic tomb and extraordinary Mireann Stone. The site of Mother Earth, a so-called friend had told her. The site of a lot of personal anguish, she recalled, but it was Easter week and that filled her with some hope for her own resurrection. She might yet be saved.

She knew the route up the hillside and held tight to her stick, pounding upwards as quickly as she could. The faster she got up, the faster she'd get back down again.

The sun had risen well into the sky, which was a lovely shade of blue with a hint of pink.

As she climbed, she sang a soft song in her head – not out loud, because she'd terrify the birds with her out-of-tune warbling. She just wanted to soak up the peace and quiet and listen to the birdsong, keeping the old memories submerged in the sea of turmoil swimming around inside her head.

The path was well trodden by hill walkers, and she took a right and began to trudge where there was no trail. Nothing like a little adventure. She grimaced. Walking was the only adventure in her life, if she was totally honest. I'm a freak, she told herself, reiterating the words that had hounded her through life so far. She had tried to overcome the bullies but instead had shrunk into her shell like a terrified snail. But out here she was free from all that. That was good, wasn't it? A chill breeze blew down the hill and wrapped around her shoulders.

Rounding a dead tree trunk, she noticed a sheep tugging at a branch at the foot of another tree up ahead. It looked like the fairy tree. This could be the place. Despite the sunshine, she felt suddenly cold. She had to look but she didn't want to. Too many memories.

Drawing closer, she saw that there was a mound of moss-covered stones next to the sheep. The animal raised its head, keeping a firm hold of the thin branch in its mouth, and stared at her for a moment before dropping it and scampering up the hillside.

'Naughty sheep.' She laughed nervously. Why was she talking to a sheep?

Wandering over to the tree, she picked up the branch. There were a few teeth marks in it – but it didn't seem to be a branch after all. A knobbly chunk at one end reminded her of her biology class years ago. A bone joint. A human bone joint.

'Don't be daft,' she chided herself.

She looked at the rocks at the foot of the tree. Maybe she'd found an undiscovered burial chamber. Had some ancient High King of Ireland been buried here? This hill was fabled in mythology to be the seat of High Kings.

She looked around quickly, but there was no one here except for bleating sheep keeping their distance. Dropping to her knees, she pulled off her light gloves and with bare fingers tore through the already disturbed reedy grass.

Nothing else visible. No way was she going to disturb the stones. She had enough bad luck without digging up a sacred burial ground. She knew all about Egypt and the curse that followed people once the dead were exhumed.

She sat back on her heels and picked up the bone again. It must belong to an animal. She felt disappointed that she hadn't the gumption to search some more. But it seemed to her that what she had been told had some truth to it. This was not the last resting place of an ancient High King, or High Queen for that matter. All the same, she pocketed the bone. She would have to think about what to do with it.

She tugged on her gloves and continued her hike.

But the higher she climbed, the heavier the bone weighed in her pocket. Not physically. Mentally. When she reached the summit, she sat and stared at the sprawling fields of her county, and some of the horror of her life took root in her heart. This place held no magic for her, only torturous memories.

She fished the bone out of her pocket. It had to be a human bone. A very small human.

Her whole body shuddered with the realisation that what she was holding in her hands could in fact be the bone of a little child.

CHAPTER FIFTEEN

Detective Maria Lynch was dogged when it came to analysing data, even if it meant phoning every number on the pages Lottie had given her.

She realised that most of the calls had been either made by Jack or were for him. Building supplies companies and possibly people who had hired him to do work for them. Back-and-forth calls. She quickly dismissed these as unlikely to have any significance at the moment. She made a note of the number of calls Jack made to his home: at least three a day, and sometimes five or six. Why was that? She'd mention it to Lottie later.

She started calling the outgoing numbers. On the ninth number, she found herself greeted by a soft but chirpy voice.

'Bubbles Day Care, Sinéad Foley speaking. How can I help you?'

At least someone was having a good day, Lynch thought.

'Hi, Sinéad. I'm Detective Maria Lynch from Ragmullin garda station. I just wanted—'

'Oh God, I hope there's nothing wrong.'

'Don't worry.' How to word her query? Be vague. 'Your number came up in the process of an investigation. Can you tell me, were you contacted by Isabel or Jack Gallagher last month?'

'Isabel called. She used to work here. She rang enquiring about my availability to take her baby for a few mornings a week. I got the impression she'd maybe found a part-time job, though I'd welcome her back here in a heartbeat.'

'Oh, right. Did you have any follow-up contact with Isabel or her husband?' Lynch was trying to be as diplomatic as she could. She didn't want to scare the woman.

'Actually, she was to pop in here after ten this morning, but she never turned up. We arranged it over the phone. I wanted to meet Holly, but she said she'd come alone.'

'How long ago is it since Isabel worked for you?'

'She took time off because she became very ill with her pregnancy. Her doctor advised it. Let me think. It was towards the end of last summer, or it could have been September. I'll check it and let you know.'

'Okay, that's grand.'

'She never officially left, but she didn't keep up contact. I wanted to discuss it all with her today. Is she all right?'

Lynch could hear children chatting in the background and ignored the query. 'If you think of anything else, will you contact me here at the station?'

'Sure I will.' There was a slight pause on the line. 'Please tell me, has something happened to her?'

'I'm not at liberty to say. Thanks again.'

Lynch hung up and made a note of the conversation. She needed to tell Lottie that Isabel Gallagher might not have had a doctor's appointment after all.

As she stood, McKeown arrived at her desk.

'What do you want?' she asked, sitting back down.

'Can we at least be civil to each other?'

'I've no interest in being anything to you except a reluctant colleague.'

'You started it.'

Her head shot up. 'The cheek of you.'

'Don't forget it was your idea. You came to me with the notion to get the boss in trouble. You actually convinced me and—'

'I don't want to talk about it, and especially not here,' she said through gritted teeth. 'Are you mad?'

'I must be, to be still working with you.'

'Why don't you piss off back to Athlone then?'

'Oh, I will, as soon as I can.' He went to move away, but stopped and lowered his head to hers, forcing her to look up.

'What now?'

'Don't try to double-cross me, Lynch. You really don't want to do that.'

'I've no idea what you're talking about.' She swished her hair like she always did when someone annoyed the life out of her. 'What do you want from me, McKeown?'

She watched as he ran his tongue along the inside of his cheek, and she knew he was contemplating admitting the real reason why he'd approached her.

Eventually he must have decided to err on the side of business.

'I'm having no luck tracing this Kevin Doran chap. I'm wondering if he turned up as a contact on Gallagher's website.'

'I know that's not what you really want to ask, but anyhow, I've passed that on to Gary in technical. Doran's number isn't on this phone bill and I don't think I've come across the name on anything I've searched.'

'Keep an eye out for it.'

Failing to come up with a smart reply, she said, 'I know how to do my job.'

He walked back to his desk and made a drama of sitting down, a smirk plastered to his face. That was it. She'd had enough of him. She shoved back her chair and marched over. Placing one hand on his desk and the other on the back of his chair, she leaned down to speak into his ear.

'I wonder what Mrs McKeown would think of your bit on the side.'

He turned round so quickly his nose brushed her cheek.

'You need to watch your mouth,' he hissed.

'And you need to be careful how you treat me, McKeown. Your wife wouldn't be too pleased if she heard what I've heard.'

'You're a bitch.'

Kirby entered the fray. 'Hey, watch your mouth yourself, McKeown.'

'And you need to get a wife and a life,' McKeown grunted.

'Yeah, like you. Everyone knows you slobbered all over Martina Brennan at the Christmas Party. You two have been nice and cosy since.'

'Shut up, Kirby.' McKeown buried his head in his work.

Kirby winked at Lynch as he opened a filing cabinet.

She smiled, stretched and walked back to her desk.

The phone rang. She took the call. A member of the public claiming to have seen a man running down Main Street with a bloody knife in his hand. By the time she'd calmed the caller down and ascertained that they had actually watched a horror movie the night before while downing a bottle of vodka and were most likely having hallucinations, she'd forgotten all about Sinéad Foley and Bubbles Day Care.

CHAPTER SIXTEEN

Anita Boland lived in a detached house in a mature complex on the outskirts of Ragmullin. The row of seven houses seemed to have developed its own sense of character. Anita's home had bay windows surrounded by a tangled mess of ivy. Rose bushes grew along the edge of the neatly mown lawn. Lottie thought everything blended well with the mint-green door.

She finished the sandwich Boyd had bought her at Milly's Garage and stuffed the wrapper under the seat. She was still hungry as she rang the doorbell.

In the sitting room, Anita offered tea or coffee. They declined. The room gave the impression of a family of seven living in it, though Anita lived alone. Books and magazines overflowed onto the floor from the large wooden bookcase. A dresser was crowded with Belleek china ornaments; the three-piece suite looked comfortable. The accessories associated with a baby added a touch of organised chaos.

Anita fussed, lifting baby blankets from the floor and stuffing them into a basket. Jack was seated in an armchair, his daughter asleep in his arms.

Lottie said, 'I asked an officer to bring your van. It should be here shortly.' Once SOCOs had given it the once-over, she thought.

Jack nodded. 'Thanks.'

Facing Anita, Lottie asked, 'Did Isabel often bring Holly to visit you?'

'Not often enough, really,' Anita said, tears falling one by one. 'I already miss her so much. I don't know how I'm going to get through this.'

Feeling the temperature in the room drop a few degrees, Lottie searched for somewhere strategic to sit. 'I'm sure you and Jack will find a way.'

'I'm going to put the kettle on.' Anita hurried out.

Lottie found space on the couch and sat opposite Jack while Boyd moved to stand by the window.

'I want to do a television appeal,' Jack said without preamble.

'A what?' She tried to stop her mouth dropping open, unsuccessfully.

'An appeal like you see when someone goes missing. I know Isabel isn't missing, but I could appeal for witnesses or someone to come forward who might know the killer or why she was killed.'

'Not really appropriate at the moment,' Lottie said. There was enough to do on the case without keyboard warriors clogging up her team's time. 'Jack, we're professionals and we will find who did this.' She hoped her words rang true.

'I have to do something,' he insisted. 'I can't be sitting here holding the baby while my wife's killer thinks he got away with it.'

His eyes were dry, she noticed, but his arm muscles flexed when he spoke, veins rising like tightened ropes in his neck, his polo shirt stretching across his chest as he breathed heavily. His little daughter remained sound asleep.

'You can help by answering a few more questions.' She moved to the edge of the soft-cushioned couch, sitting forward. 'I really need to know if you kept cash or valuables in the house.' She didn't think robbery was a motive, but she had to rule it out.

'No. We had feck-all money but we were happy.'

'Was Isabel happy having no cash or bank cards of her own?'

'Look, we had a single bank account and one bank card, which is in my wallet. Isabel agreed to that arrangement. We had to cut back. To save, so that she could get her dream extension to the house. Sometimes you have to make sacrifices to get what you want.'

'What about day-to-day expenses?'

'I never saw her go short.'

'For instance, how did she pay for petrol or diesel for her car?'

'I gave her a household allowance. Plus I've a business account with Wallace's Fuel Depot in Ragmullin. She charged her diesel to that. I can write off a percentage of expenses against my tax bill.'

'Right. Can I see your accounts?'

'For fuck's sake, what has all this got to do with her murder?' He jerked forward and Holly jolted in her sleep. Lottie noted that he didn't soothe her. It was like he wasn't used to holding the little girl.

'I'm getting the impression, Mr Gallagher, that you liked to keep your wife under your control.' She decided to be bold. 'Was Isabel threatening to leave you?'

'How can you say that? I loved her. She loved me. End of.'

'You said she had changed recently. What caused that change?'

'If I knew that, maybe she wouldn't be dead.' He shook his head and sniffed. 'I just want her back.'

She knew the importance of gaining information early on in an investigation, but Jack was in danger of disintegrating, so she parked that line of questioning.

'Do you have a life insurance policy on Isabel?'

'I don't believe where you are going with this.' He looked heavenward but returned his gaze having composed himself. 'No. We have no life insurance. You can check it out.'

'Okay, thanks, Jack. You say you left the house at six fifty this morning and arrived at work at seven ten. It's a ten-minute journey at most, so why did it take you that long to get there?'

'I took my time. Only part of the day I get head space. What difference does it make anyhow?'

'I need to pin down the timeline of events.' The approximate time of death according to Jane was between seven and nine. Lottie needed to rule Gallagher in or out.

'I did not kill my wife, if that's what you're insinuating.'

'I've had another look around your house. I know this will seem an odd question, but what do you use to shave?'

He answered immediately. 'Electric when I'm in a hurry; otherwise I like the old-style razor. Why?'

'Isabel had a razor blade in her hand when she was found. Any idea why that would be?'

'What? Why would she have that? I don't understand.'

She moved on. 'What can you tell me about Kevin Doran? Your handyman.'

'What about him?'

'I want to know who he is. Where he lives. What he does.'

Jack sat up straight in the chair and Holly cried out. He still did not comfort the child, but she went back into her slumber immediately. 'If that Doran bastard laid a hand on my Isabel, I'll cut his fucking balls off and stuff them down his throat.'

Anita walked in, a mug of steaming liquid grasped between her hands, her mouth dropping open on hearing Jack's last words. 'Oh God, do you suspect Kevin Doran, Inspector?'

'I'm just trying to trace him to have a word with him.'

Jack had calmed himself down. He said, 'Kevin is a bit of a waster, but he works cheaply. I suppose you get what you pay for.'

'What does he actually do for you?'

'A bit of bricklaying. Can hammer a nail too. Jack of all trades and slave to none.'

'What does he look like?'

'Ordinary bloke.' Jack shrugged one shoulder. 'Early forties, might be younger. Wore a beanie any time I saw him. Overalls and donkey jacket. Smaller than me, and skinny.'

'Where can I find him?'

'I don't know where he lives. I gave you his phone number, didn't I?' He shoved his hand down the side of the chair for his phone and scrolled through his contacts. Holly didn't like being moved, and cried out. Anita rushed forward, placed her mug on the mantel and took the child in her arms.

'You did, but there's no reply.'

'Hush, little one. Granny's here.' Anita rocked the baby, who smiled up into her face. At least someone loves the poor kid, Lottie thought.

Boyd came to life.

'Have you thought any more about who might have wanted to harm your wife?' he said, hands buried deep in his pockets.

'I've thought of nothing else for the last few hours, and unless that piece of shit Kevin Doran had something to do with it, I've no idea.'

'Why do you think it might be him?' Boyd pressed.

Hauling himself up from the armchair, Jack paced the compact room until he stood in front of Boyd. 'For starters, you two are asking about him. Then there's the fact that he was always hanging around the house.'

'Really? Why?' Lottie asked.

Jack turned to her, his eyes darker than before, his mouth a grimace, making his ears stand out like Boyd's did.

'I had no work for him the past few weeks. Didn't stop him knocking on the door annoying Isabel to see if she had jobs for him.'

'How did she react?'

'She felt sorry for him. Filled him with tea and biscuits. I told her he wasn't a dog.'

'So she was friendly with him?'

'I warned him not to come around when I wasn't there. You never know with his type …' He rubbed a hand over his eyes. 'I should have ditched him long ago.'

'Did he drive? A car, a van?'

'He had a battered red van. Not sure if it was his or not, and before you ask, I don't recall the licence plate.'

'That's fine.' Lottie hoped McKeown could trace the untraceable.

She glanced at Anita, who was standing with her back to the fireplace, softly threading her fingers through Holly's fine hair. The tenderness with which she was gazing at the child was in stark contrast to how Jack had held his daughter. Might be something, might be nothing, Lottie thought. But he'd been so keen to see the child that morning. Grief was a strange thing. She knew that all too well.

'How did you originally contact Doran?' Boyd moved into Gallagher's personal space. Too close for comfort, Lottie thought, but not close enough to be threatening.

'He contacted me. I'd put up cards with my number in a few places in town. Just to advertise that I was looking for casual help with the kitchen. He must have seen one.'

'How did you communicate?' Boyd asked.

'He gave me his number.'

'When was the first contact made?' Lottie took over.

'I don't know. Maybe less than a year ago.'

'Was that when you first met him in person?' she continued.

'It was a few weeks after that. He had no references, but he was eager, so I gave him a trial. He was a hard worker. Helped me renovate the kitchen.'

So his DNA would have a logical reason to be inside the house, Lottie thought.

'Did you trust him?' she asked.

'We weren't friends, if that's what you mean,' Jack said. 'He arrived, did a job, got paid and left.'

'But he remained in contact, so you said.' Boyd at last moved back a pace.

'Yeah, he hounded me for work. Turned up at the house at all hours.'

Anita had been silent for much of the conversation, but now she walked over to them.

'I need to prepare a bottle for Holly, and Jack needs to rest, so I think that's all for now, Inspector.'

They'd run out of questions anyhow. They moved to the hall.

Anita opened the front door, then turned to them, her hand on the latch. 'For what it's worth, I think Isabel felt sorry for Kevin. She told me that once. She said he was a good man. Shouldn't you be looking for someone else?'

'His name has come up,' Lottie said, 'so we need to interview him. Are you sure you never met him?'

Shifting from foot to foot, Anita darted her gaze towards the sitting room, where Jack was sitting with the baby. She lowered her voice. 'Come to think of it, I met him once. He seemed lost. You know those people with vacant eyes? People who've suffered? I honestly don't think he'd hurt my Isabel.'

She'd said the same about Jack, but Lottie wasn't convinced. Her words reminded her of Isabel's eyes in the photos. 'I noticed Isabel looked sad in the photos you gave me earlier. Was your daughter unhappy?'

Anita's shoulders shook as she broke down. Lottie put a hand on the woman's elbow to steady her.

'My Isabel was troubled. I thought it might be baby blues, but when I suggested it, she became angry with me. I didn't raise it again.'

'Was it anything to do with Jack?'

'Jack? He treated her well, but who knows what goes on behind closed doors?'

'Isabel didn't seem to have owned much.'

'That's just the way she was. She didn't like to spend, unlike me.'

'Did she ask you to babysit often?'

'Now and again,' Anita said softly. 'Usually during the day, when Jack was at work. They didn't socialise. Always saving. What good has that done them, eh? My little girl is dead and no amount of money can bring her back.'

In the car, Boyd turned to look at Lottie. 'I don't trust Gallagher one fecking inch.'

'What's got into you?'

'He's trying to steer us towards this Kevin Doran character.'

'It was me who brought up Doran's name first, not Jack.'

'Lottie, it's staring us in the face. Somehow Gallagher manoeuvred his movements this morning in order to return home and kill his wife. How could it take him twenty minutes to get to work? Once he gets down the lane from his house, it's a straight drive to Quality Electrical. And we only have his word that he left home at ten to seven. He's a liar, that's what he is.'

'Well, Isabel rang her mother around seven, so she was alive then. Anyway, Kirby should have news on Gallagher's movements when we get back to base.' She stared straight ahead. 'For a minute, let's say I agree with you about him. What's his motive?'

'He's a controlling son of a bitch and maybe Isabel had found the nerve or courage to leave him. He wouldn't like that at all. And I'd like to know more about where she went when she needed Anita to babysit.'

'All right. We'll talk to Anita again, but we need to let them grieve a little while we try to uncover what we can. Okay?'

He glanced at her. 'If you say so.'

As he returned his gaze to the road, he swerved the car unexpectedly.

'Will you watch what you're doing, for heaven's sake? You're making me nervous.'

He righted the car and continued driving more slowly. 'I'm making myself nervous.'

CHAPTER SEVENTEEN

Anita put Holly down on the floor, surrounded with cushions just in case, and laid out soft toys that she kept for the rare visits from her granddaughter.

'Jack, what are you going to do?'

'What do you mean?'

'About Holly.'

'I've just lost my wife and my heart is totally broken. I can't think about that now.'

'You can stay here, the two of you, as long as you like. You know that.'

'Thanks. Appreciated. But as soon as dumb and dumber let me back into my own house, I'm going home.'

'Dumb and dumber? The two detectives? God, Jack, don't be so disrespectful.'

'They were disrespectful to me, so they can fuck off.'

'Will you shush? Holly's listening. Babies pick up so much at that age. You don't want her first word to be a swear word.'

'She's just witnessed her mother's murder, so I think a few swear words are mild in comparison. Oh shite, what am I going to do?'

Anita turned away from her son-in-law as he buried his head in his hands. She stared out through the window and cried silent tears for her beautiful daughter. The image imprinted on her brain was the bedroom of blood, Holly crying in the cot, and poor sweet, kind Isabel lying dead at her feet.

She turned away quickly and moved to the sideboard, picking up a silver frame studded with diamanté. It held a photograph taken of Isabel on her wedding day. She was leaning against a tree, smiling with a smile so bright it was blinding. It was Anita's favourite image of her daughter. It radiated pure happiness. It was like Isabel felt she'd left her troubles behind, but she hadn't, had she?

She kissed the photo and vowed that this was the image with which she would replace the vision of savagery she'd witnessed earlier that morning.

Replacing the photo, she picked up little Holly and feathered her cheeks with kisses, holding her close so that the baby could hear her beating heart. She glanced at the photograph again. That had been the only time she'd seen Isabel in a state of unrestrained happiness. What had gone wrong before and after that marriage to make her daughter so sad?

She whispered in the child's ear so that Jack wouldn't hear. 'I hope this horror isn't all my fault.'

'I have to get out of here.' Jack stood up suddenly. 'I have to be doing something.'

'Please, Jack, you have to stay. At least until the family liaison officer arrives.'

'I don't need another face in mine. Not now. I need air. I'll be back.'

'What about Holly?'

'You seem to be doing okay with her.' He put on his coat and buttoned it to the neck.

'But that's not—'

'Enough, Anita. I won't be long.'

She followed him to the hallway just as he slammed the door behind him.

'Don't do anything stupid, Jack,' she whispered.

*

Kevin switched off the engine and shivered as the heat faded, but he couldn't keep it running in case he attracted attention. He unwrapped the Subway roll and stuffed his mouth with soft bread, salami and cheese.

When he was finished, he balled up the wrapper and threw it at his feet, where it joined a heap of detritus. It took him three attempts to open the can of Coke with his numb fingers, and when he finally succeeded, the fizz spouted up and spilled over the rim. He downed two good gulps and then sank into the seat to maintain his vigil.

Isabel's mother had to be inside the house, because her car was parked in the drive. He'd seen one of the guards driving it away from the Gallagher house.

The front door opened and he quelled the urge to leap up and press his nose to the windscreen. Instead he ducked his head and sank deeper into the stained upholstery.

Jack Gallagher came out, tugging a knitted hat from his pocket and pulling it down over his hair, almost to his eyebrows. Where was he off to? Kevin hoped his van couldn't be seen. Jack kept his head between hunched shoulders and turned left, headed for town.

Debating whether to follow him or to maintain his vigil, Kevin found it difficult to make up his mind. Surely little Holly was still inside with her grandmother? If so, Kevin needed to stay right where he was.

He watched Jack disappear around the corner. He desperately wanted to know where he was going, but he'd made a promise and he'd already failed once. He couldn't fail again.

Slumped in the mouldy seat, he felt the urge creep up on him. It wasn't unexpected, but the unbearable helplessness that washed over him in the darkest recesses of his mind was unforgiving and needed to be crushed. He fumbled, fingers numb in his coat pocket, and found the small tin box. Placing it on the greasy dashboard, he wondered if this would distract him or revitalise him. He had no control over his urges. None whatsoever.

'I'm so weak,' he told the box. 'Why do I need you so much?'

But Kevin had relinquished all power many years ago. He opened the lid and removed the rusted razor blade.

Lifting the flap of what was once a pocket on his grubby combat trousers, he stared at the bare skin on his leg. Silver crests marked the flesh like a bed of eels. He found an unblemished spot and lowered the blade, dragging it across the flesh until tiny blood bubbles rose to the surface. Deeper he went, and more blood crept up, flowing a little more freely now. He raised the blade and performed a similar action three more times, careful not to open any old wounds.

When he was done, he squeezed his eyes shut, allowing the pain to ease the anguish in his brain. Then he took an old brown-stained cotton handkerchief from the door panel and wiped the blade before replacing it in the box.

He slipped the box back into his coat pocket and returned to his vigil, watching the front door of Anita Boland's house through the ochre haze of the afternoon light.

CHAPTER EIGHTEEN

The office was buzzing with chatter when Lottie walked in. She had no time to absorb any of the reports on her desk, so she hoped the team were ready to impart all their information. Hopefully positive news, but she had a burning sensation in her chest telling her there would be little to report.

'Okay, quieten down. I want this over and done with in ten minutes. I've a post-mortem to get to and I'm already late. I haven't time for a full incident meeting. We'll go with who we have here. McKeown, you're up first. Anything on this mysterious Kevin Doran?'

'Blank wall, if you want the truth.'

'I want progress.'

'I've tried everything.'

'You can do better than that, McKeown.' Lottie paced around the cluttered floor.

'He must be using a false name.'

'Feck's sake, he can't be invisible. Everyone leaves a trace somewhere.'

'No one knows the licence number of the van. I've gone through every Kevin Doran in the county. None of them is our man.' McKeown ran his hand over his shaved head and stifled a yawn. 'He must be using an alias or living off the grid. Cash-in-hand jobs and the like. But I'll do some more digging.'

Lottie turned to Kirby. 'Did anyone at Jack's workplace know Doran?'

'I talked to a couple of his colleagues. Ciaran Grimes and Paulo Silva.' He flicked through his notebook. 'No one seems to have heard of him.'

'Someone better find him. What did you find out about Gallagher's movements this morning?'

'The boss man is a Michael Costello. He gave me Gallagher's job log. Tallies with what we were told.'

'It still took him twenty minutes to get to work,' Boyd said. 'And I know it doesn't take that long.'

'Agreed,' Lottie said. 'Once we get time of death, we can grill Jack about his timeline.'

She stopped pacing at the back of the room and leaned against a filing cabinet, which wobbled, causing a file to fall from the bundle perched precariously on top.

'This place is a mess. Can you people not put things away when you're finished with them?' She indicated the tottering files behind her, then realised she had left them there herself. After replacing the fallen file she resumed her pacing. 'We're the whole day at this and nothing close to a clue has been uncovered. Anything from forensics?'

'Too soon,' McKeown said.

'Kirby? Tell me more.'

The detective pushed out his chest with importance, causing a button to burst open. Hastily he tugged his sports jacket over it and related the gist of the conversations he'd had at Quality Electrical.

'Isabel worked there for a while. Well liked, but she left after meeting Jack. Apparently he convinced her she wasn't appreciated there, or some such shit, and the boss, Michael Costello, is a misogynist of the highest order.'

'Just what we need. Did you talk to the clients Jack was scheduled to be with today?'

'He was unable to access the first property, at Bardstown. Garda Brennan and I visited the second property.' He glanced at his scribbled notes. 'Spoke to Mrs Birmingham in Plodmore. She says Gallagher was there until he got my call asking him to return home. He left in an awful hurry, according to Mrs Birmingham.'

'Are the times tight enough to rule him out as a suspect?'

'Well, there's the forty-five minutes from the time he says he left the house, to clocking in at work, travelling to the first client, where he got no response, and then going to Mrs Birmingham's. No proof he was actually at Bardstown. So there is wiggle room there.'

'He remains on our list, then.'

'What list?' Boyd said. 'We don't have anyone other than Jack Gallagher and the invisible Kevin Doran.'

Lottie felt her chest constrict. 'If you were a bit busier, Boyd, we might have more suspects.'

'I was with you all day.'

Expelling a breath of frustration, Lottie turned to Lynch. 'What have you got for me?'

'Besides being contacted by a hallucinating member of the public, not much. I went through the phone bill you brought back from Gallagher's. It seems Jack had a habit of phoning home multiple times a day.'

'That supports my theory that he was a controlling bastard.' Lottie related her findings at the house. Or rather lack of findings.

'Doesn't prove he killed her,' Boyd said.

'You're changing your tune.' Lottie sighed in exasperation. 'We need to dig up everything we can on Jack Gallagher.'

'Maybe he hired someone else to kill his wife?' McKeown said.

Kirby butted in. 'Maybe he was having an affair and got his lover to do it. I saw this true-crime documentary and—'

'Now is not the time for speculation. I want a dossier on Gallagher on my desk first thing in the morning. Job for you, McKeown.'

McKeown yawned again, and she was tempted to shove a keyboard into his gaping mouth if she was boring him that much. He was saved by Superintendent Farrell storming in.

'I hope you lot are more efficient in here than out there.'

'What's up, Superintendent?' Lottie hadn't a clue what the woman was talking about.

'I'll tell you what's up.' Farrell tugged off her clip-on tie and tried to open the top button of her shirt, her face reddening. 'What lug gave the media a photo of the victim and her husband? It's been on some morning television show and repeated on the news.'

Lottie looked around at her team and was met with shrugging shoulders and shaking heads. 'We're professionals. There's no way on earth anyone would—'

'You better find out then. There were uniforms, SOCOs and God knows who else crawling around that house all morning. I want a head on a plate. You hear me? Head on a plate.'

She left as quickly as she'd arrived.

Lottie scowled. 'When I find out who leaked that photo, *I* will personally put their head on a plate.' Who would jeopardise an investigation like that? Not McGlynn, but she'd have to get him to check out his team, and that would not be a pleasant conversation. 'Kirby, will you speak to all personnel who were at the crime scene? Anyone who had access to the house. I'll talk to Jim.'

'Could be one of the neighbours, or a friend of the family,' Boyd interjected. 'Doesn't necessarily mean it's one of us.'

'I know that, but we have to clear our own people first,' Lottie spat.

McKeown said, 'The husband might have given it out.'

'But we had a media blackout in place until he arrived at the scene. He wouldn't have known why he was being called back home.'

Boyd said, 'Maybe one of his mates phoned him with the news that something bad had happened to Isabel.'

'He was Jack-no-mates, as far as Garda Brennan and I could discover,' Kirby pointed out.

'Maybe the television crew talked to him before uniformed officers got to escort him up the road,' Boyd said. 'They could have asked for a photo and he showed them his wedding photo from his phone. He did tell us he wants to do a television appeal.'

'Shit,' Lottie said.

McKeown turned the tablet screen to show them the photo that had appeared on *Good Morning Ireland*.

'Jack already knew she was dead,' Lottie said. 'He already knew because he killed her, or he knew because the media hacks told him.'

'But we don't know that yet,' Kirby said, trying to defuse Lottie's rising anger.

'Okay.' Lottie sat and stretched her legs, tiredness eating into her bones. 'Where were we? Anyone got anything else to add to this briefing?'

'I have something else.' Lynch waved the phone bill pages.

'Hope it's good.' Lottie glanced at the office clock. At this rate, the post-mortem would be over by the time she reached Tullamore.

'Isabel had a meeting arranged for ten this morning, but—'

'That reminds me, did anyone follow up with her doctor?'

'Boss, if you'll let me continue?'

'Carry on.'

'The thing is, the meeting wasn't with her doctor. A few weeks ago, Isabel Gallagher phoned Bubbles Day Care in Ragmullin. I spoke with

Sinéad Foley, the owner. Isabel used to work there until her pregnancy sickness got too much and she had to leave.'

'We know that.'

'She had an appointment with Sinéad Foley this morning after ten. But we know why she never turned up.'

'Why am I only hearing about this now?' Lottie slapped one fist into the other as anger quickly replaced her frustration.

'You were out most of the day.'

'I have a phone and radio in the car.'

'Sorry. Other things came up and—'

'And this day care owner never thought to inform us?'

'I'm sure she didn't even know Isabel was dead. I didn't inform her of the fact either.'

'Okay,' Lottie said. She grabbed her jacket and bag. 'Organise a meeting with Sinéad Foley for first thing tomorrow morning. She probably won't be able to tell us anything further, but all the same … Isabel worked there, so we might get a better handle on her, because so far all I'm getting is an isolated woman with no friends.'

'It seems odd that she'd want to leave the child in a crèche, though,' Lynch said. 'She had no current employment.'

'It's imperative that we find out more about Isabel Gallagher. Build up a picture of her as a woman, a real person. She was much more than the broken body on her bedroom floor. Something happened to put her in the sights of a killer. Keep digging. As deep as you can go.'

Lottie slung her bag over her shoulder and her jacket on her arm. 'Jane's going to kill me.'

CHAPTER NINETEEN

Walking along the lakeshore, the cool April breeze biting into her skin, Joyce kicked up pebbles, sidestepping the hungry swans as the water lapped at her soft leather pumps. She was despairing of ever being able to escape from her past. No matter which way she turned it over in her head, she could not see a logical conclusion to the mess. All she knew was that she had to act fast, but she'd wasted most of the day. Hadn't even gone into work, and now it was getting towards time to collect Evan. She hadn't even packed a bag.

The water soaked through her shoes and up the hem of her jeans as she stood immobile, staring out across the lake. A train shunted along the tracks behind her, picking up speed as it headed towards Sligo. If she drove away somewhere, her car would leave a trail. Toll roads and the like. But identification would be simple on a train, too, with CCTV. Could she leave without Evan? Her partner, Nathan, would care for him, of course. But no, she couldn't leave her son behind.

The envelope with the razor blade felt like an anvil in her pocket. She took it out and shivered at its unwritten message. Throw it in the lake, her internal voice told her. No, she had to keep it. A reminder that she would never be safe. Her tears fell unchecked. What was she to do?

Back in the car, she switched on the heater and watched a swirl of fog rise up on the water before realising it wasn't fog. It was a murmuration of starlings. Beautiful and free. Unlike her. She was shackled to her past, and the key might as well be at the bottom of the lake. It was all hopeless. Her heart was ugly and she would never be free.

Without a clear idea of what to do, the only thing she was certain of was that she had to do something. And do it fast.

She'd have to tell Nathan everything.

CHAPTER TWENTY

Lottie had sped along the motorway with the window down to try to clear her head. She couldn't fathom who would want to hurt Isabel, if not Jack. The best place to start was always the post-mortem, and she was lucky that Jane had helped her by moving it up her schedule. But she knew she was too late to observe. So be it.

Attired in gloves and mask, she listened to the state pathologist recite her findings.

'Isabel Gallagher was severely malnourished. Mastitis in both breasts. The inflammation would have caused her discomfort and pain.'

'Isn't that treatable?' Lottie asked, horrified.

'Of course it is. But both breasts were infected quite badly; she probably had to give up breastfeeding.'

'Oh, the poor woman. I did see tubs of formula at the house.' And perhaps Isabel was visiting her doctor those times Anita had to babysit.

'But that's not the worst of it.'

'Go on.' Lottie steeled herself for further shocking revelations.

'She had a womb infection. Post-partum endometritis. Severely painful when left untreated. She should have been on antibiotics, but I found no evidence of any having been taken, because the infection was still present.'

'Was she sexually assaulted?' Lottie hoped not, and didn't think so, because Isabel's pyjamas had still been on her body when she was discovered.

'I found no evidence of sexual assault,' Jane said. 'She had good personal hygiene.'

'Any evidence of old injuries? Broken bones, that kind of thing?'

'No broken bones.'

'Carry on.'

'Her stomach was virtually empty. A blood sample was taken from the baby in order to aid forensic analysis. And DNA samples were taken from the father and grandmother and various surfaces at the scene.'

'Go on.' Lottie knew this was leading somewhere. She hoped Jane wasn't going to tell her Jack was not Holly's father.

'I got all the DNA samples fast-tracked as I know how impatient you are and this is a particularly horrible crime.'

'Thanks, Jane. What did you discover? That Holly's not—'

'No, nothing like that. DNA samples confirm the family unit as presented. But two unidentified DNA samples were found. The sample lifted from the bar of the cot was male, not the father. Another was found in the kitchen. That presents as female, not Isabel or her mother. Samples are being cross-referenced as we speak. But find a suspect and we can then match the sample.'

'That's great work, thanks, Jane.' Lottie sighed. 'Which wound killed her?'

'I'll go through her injuries for you. She had a large haematoma to her forehead. I think it was caused by a gloved fist. Traces of black leather, but no DNA. That was enough to knock her out, but not kill her. Five stab wounds to her back, which would have been the last to be administered. The fatal wound was the cut to her throat, which was made after the knock to her head. The killer turned her over with a kick – see the bruise on her thigh?'

Lottie nodded.

'There's more,' Jane said.

Of course there is, Lottie thought. She was itching to get her hands on the full report and raging that she'd been too late for the post-mortem.

'Come with me.' The pathologist clip-clopped in her high-heeled shoes into the cutting room, as it was unofficially called.

The body of Isabel Gallagher lay naked on the stainless-steel table, all evidence of Jane's work invisible except for the stitched incision on the victim's chest. The dead woman looked so young she could be a child. Her body was thin, and her face, except for the large bump on her forehead, angelic.

'Poor pet,' Lottie said.

Jane stood at Isabel's feet and lifted one. 'See these?'

'Cuts?' Lottie peered closer at the silver lines. She recalled the fluffy socks. Had Isabel worn them for a reason other than warmth? 'Are they recent?'

'Maybe six months, or longer. Hard to tell, but they've healed well.'

'Self-inflicted?'

Jane shrugged. 'No way of knowing.'

'If she was self-harming, it might be one of the reasons why she didn't seek medical help for her infections.' But that didn't make sense. The woman had given birth in a hospital. Surely someone would have made a note of it and informed her GP. Then again, hospitals were so busy these days it might have gone unnoticed.

Jane moved to the side of the body. She lifted the left leg and pointed.

Lottie gasped. A criss-cross of raised silver scar tissue was evident on the inside of Isabel's thigh. 'It's been going on for some time,' she said. 'God almighty, what was she going through to cause all this?'

'It may have nothing to do with why she was murdered,' Jane offered.

Then again, it might have a lot to do with it. 'Thanks, Jane. Time of death?'

'Can't be conclusive, but if she was found at nine, I'd estimate she'd been killed within the previous two hours. Sorry I can't be more exact at the moment.'

'I look forward to your report.'

'I'll have it ready later on.' Jane regarded Lottie quizzically. 'You look troubled. Want to join me for a coffee when I'm done here?'

It was tempting, but Lottie shook her head.

'Sorry, Jane. I'd love to, but it will have to be another time. I need to bring this information back to the team.'

'You look washed out. You need to mind yourself, Lottie,' Jane said when they reached the corridor. 'I'm here if you need me.'

Whipping off her gloves and mask, Lottie dumped them in the hazard receptacle. 'I appreciate that. More than you will ever know.'

Outside the Dead House, she gulped in the cool evening air. Then she headed to her car and drove back to Ragmullin with all the windows down, trying to let the wind blow sense into her brain. It didn't work. Who the hell had killed a defenceless, damaged young woman?

She arrived at the station brimming with anger.

CHAPTER TWENTY-ONE

It was taking longer than he liked. His lorry was too visible. It was too bloody big. It stuck out like the proverbial sore thumb.

Nathan Monaghan lowered the window and leaned out into the evening breeze. He tried to get a look at what the delay was at the rear of the lorry. He couldn't see much, as it was shaded on both sides by high walls. He felt a chill on his bare bicep and watched the tattoo wrinkle and pulse with the cold.

'What's going on? Can't you hurry up?' His words were sharp, blowing back in his face.

'Shut up,' came the reply.

'I'm on the clock here. I need to be on the road.' This was ridiculous, he thought. 'It's the last time I'm doing this shite,' he muttered. He kept his arm on the ledge, trying to see in the wing mirror just what was delaying them.

'Five minutes, then you can fuck off with your complaining.' The voice now had a body attached. The short, squat man wore a black puffer jacket, the zip straining across a barrel chest. He had a full mop of greasy hair and a gold ring punched through his ear lobe. Chris Dermody was the name he'd given Nathan the night he'd offered him a grand to keep his mouth shut and make two extra stops once a month. One in France, the other in Dublin. A grand was a lot of money to Nathan Monaghan. It was easy money, if you weren't caught.

Something about tonight's event warned him to be extra cautious. The sting in the evening air, perhaps? Nathan didn't know, but he suddenly felt exposed in this industrial estate off the M50. Most of the units were offices, and one housed a television studio. Talk about doing things under people's noses.

'Come on, Dermody, hurry up. I have to go.' He pulled back into the cab and noticed a missed call from Joyce on his hands-free phone clipped to the dashboard. She must have called him while he was still at sea. He didn't trust himself to call her back. Not when his anxiety levels were scraping against the roof. She'd know something was wrong. Feck it, he'd better ring. Just as he went to tap her name, the phone died.

'Fuck,' he said, and rolled down the window again. 'Hurry the fuck up. I have to be back at base soon or questions will be asked.'

The fat man waddled around the side of the lorry and hauled himself up on the step, peering angrily in at Nathan.

'I don't give a flying fuck. I pay you to keep your gob shut. I do my thing. You do yours. Which is to stop here for five poxy minutes. If that doesn't suit you, mate, remember I know where your boy is.'

'Boy? What boy?'

'What's his name again? Oh, Evan, isn't it? Poxy name for a little scut, if you ask me.'

Nathan felt his muscles bulge as he clenched his fists. He wanted to land one right into the eye of stinking, greasy Chris Dermody.

'You touch him, I swear to God …' He stopped suddenly as he heard the rear doors clunk shut and the bars slide into place.

'God's no use to you, mate.' Dermody smirked, one tooth resting on his blistered bottom lip.

'Fucking bastard.' Nathan thumped the window frame as the fat man lit a cigarette. The flame lit his face in a ghoulish shadow. 'You touch a hair on his head, so help me I'll make a necklace out of your rotten fucking teeth, you fucker.'

He let the window up and gunned the engine, hitting the wrong gear and causing the lorry to stall.

'Fuck's sake.'

He got it going the second time and drove off without a glance in his rear-view mirror. He didn't want to see what they'd extracted from the back. What he didn't know wouldn't hurt him. It was an overused mantra, and he was beginning to wonder if it was just an old wives' tale or if it was true.

Once he hit the motorway, he searched around for the cable to charge the phone. Damn, it was in the footwell. He'd be home soon. Joyce could keep Evan safe until then.

But he couldn't shake the feeling that Dermody was way too dangerous to mess with.

CHAPTER TWENTY-TWO

Katie Parker couldn't find a space, so she had to park her car down the road. She jumped out without locking it and ran up the path.

Bubbles Day Care was on the side of town easiest for heading home. Katie felt happy leaving Louis here three days a week. Not that her wages covered the cost, but it gave her those few hours of freedom to work. When she'd come home from New York at the end of November, she'd intended returning, but decided Farranstown was the ideal place for Louis to grow up. Not far from the shore of Lough Cullion, it promised all the freedom she would not find living in New York City. That was when she realised that she'd been running away all her life. Since the day her dad had died. She made up her mind to stay at home and for once to act like an adult. And hopefully get a decent job.

She pushed open the gate and rang the doorbell. Ten minutes late.

'Sinéad, I'm so sorry. The traffic through town was mental and some gobshite got stuck at the lights and the cars were backed up to the Malloca Café.'

'Stop fretting, Katie. Louis is grand. He's been playing with Evan, haven't you, Louis?' Sinéad nodded towards the two boys, her swinging auburn curls shining under the light. Leaning closer to Katie, she said, 'Joyce, Evan's mother, is late too. She only works a few hours a day and is always here on the dot of four. So unlike her.'

In the two months since she'd secured her job at the coffee shop and enrolled Louis in Bubbles, Katie hadn't met Joyce, or Evan for that matter. She assumed the little boy was dropped off later than Louis in the mornings.

'Did you phone her?'

'Yes. Phone seems to be dead. No facility to leave a message or anything.'

'Where does she work?'

Louis clung to her legs.

'Home, Mama,' he whimpered.

'Just a minute, pet.'

Sinéad lifted up Evan, who had thrown a picture book across the floor. 'She works in Fayne's café. I tried there but there was no answer. They could be busy with the after-work office crowd. She's never been late before.'

'What about Evan's dad? Did you try him?' Katie picked up Louis and grabbed his jacket from a hook inside the door. It seemed he and Evan were the last two children waiting to be collected.

'Nathan Monaghan's a truck driver. Long haul. I think he's out of the country.'

'Do you have a number for him?' Katie didn't know Nathan or Joyce. This was not her problem. So why was she still standing here struggling to push Louis' arms through the sleeves of his jacket?

'I was holding off to see if Joyce arrived, but I'll give him a ring now.' Sinéad set the boy back down and went to get her phone.

'What age is Evan?' Katie said.

'Four. Nearly time for big school, isn't that right, Evan?'

'Not going to big school.' The child folded his arms defiantly.

'Sure you are, little man,' Sinéad said. She tapped her phone and held out the device towards Katie. 'Sounds like it's switched off, or a dead battery. He could be in France or Germany for all I know. You better head off. I'll hold on to Evan until Joyce shows up. I'm not going anywhere.'

'I'm sure she'll be here shortly.' Katie eventually got the zipper done up on her son's jacket. She hugged him close, inhaling the smell of cheese sandwiches and Play-Doh.

'I'm sure she will.'

'Try Fayne's number once more before I leave.' Katie noticed that Evan had tears gathering in the corners of his eyes. She got down to his level. 'Don't cry, pet. Your mammy will be here soon. Then you'll be home in your own house playing with your very own toys.'

'Want Mummy.'

'She'll be here soon, sweetie.' Katie looked around for Louis' little bag.

'That's weird,' Sinéad said, ending the call.

'What is?'

'Mrs Murray, the manager at Fayne's, says Joyce didn't turn up for work today.'

'Did she drop Evan here as usual this morning?'

'She did, but a bit earlier than normal. I thought she looked a little worried. I asked her if everything was all right.'

'What did she say?'

'Now that I think of it, she seemed distracted.' Sinéad ran her hand through her wild curls. 'I hadn't time to check the news all day, but one mother said she heard there was a murder outside Ragmullin this morning. Jesus, you don't think something might have happened to Joyce, do you?'

'Maybe she took the day off and headed up to Dublin to do some shopping, or something like that.'

'I doubt it. She would have told me. Gosh, I don't know what to do.'

'Has she any other relatives that can come pick up Evan?' Katie toed the floor, anxious to get home. Louis was beginning to fall asleep, his head resting on her shoulder, his body heavy in her arms.

'I don't think they have anyone close.' Sinéad seemed to pull herself together. 'Look, I'm sorry for moaning. She'll be here soon.'

Evan decided he'd had enough and started to cry in earnest.

'Shush, honey,' Sinéad said. 'Let's go into the kitchen and get some cookies. Would you like that?'

'I want my mummy.'

'I better go,' Katie said. 'You know my mother's a detective.' Now why had she said that? 'If there's anything we can do, let me know.'

'Sure. See you tomorrow, Louis,' Sinéad said, with a tired wave.

When Katie had her son safely buckled into his car seat, she looked over at Bubbles Day Care and wondered why Joyce had not arrived to pick up her son.

*

Once he was inside his own door, Kevin zipped up his jacket because it was colder inside than out. He appraised his knife collection, stuck into a piece of wood nailed to the wall above the sink. His routine whenever he came home was to take them down and clean them, polishing them one by one with Brasso and admiring the glistening steel. When he'd finished, he put away the cloth and tin, then set the blackened kettle on the cooker and lit the gas. His leg throbbed from the latest cuts and he rubbed it vigorously, kneading away the ache.

He got a loaf of bread from the cupboard.

'Little bastards!' It had been nibbled. Again.

The house was riddled with mouse holes. He'd abandoned all hope of eliminating them and dumped the traps out in the ditch. He couldn't be bothered with the hassle of setting them and emptying them and then setting them again and again.

He had no fridge, only an outdoor wooden unit with a mesh screen that he called his safe. In it he kept his perishables. He went outside and brought back a block of hardened Cheddar cheese. He cut the bread into thick slices and pressed in chunks of cheese he'd hewn from the block.

The kettle whistled. He switched off the gas and made tea in a blackened mug with the dust of tea leaves from the caddy. He'd need to fetch more supplies, but he couldn't risk entering a shop so soon after what had happened to Isabel.

Sitting at the wooden table, he shoved the bread and cheese into his mouth and washed it down with tea. He'd waited across the road from Anita's house for ages, but Jack hadn't returned. He'd have been better served following him rather than wasting his time in the van doing nothing.

But tomorrow was another day. He needed to plan for it.

He put down the crust, and belched as he watched a mouse scoot across the table. They eyed each other for a moment before Kevin brought the knife from his pocket and sliced right through the tiny animal.

'Gotcha!'

One down, he thought. He needed to be vigilant, because there were so many more.

He wasn't sure he was even thinking about the mice.

CHAPTER TWENTY-THREE

Farranstown House was abuzz with noise when Lottie eventually arrived home. She'd swung by the station and delivered the news from the post-mortem. Her whole team were run ragged, so she'd updated their tasks before leaving for the day.

Her mother was in command of the kitchen, two pots boiling on the stove, the aroma carrying out to the front door. Lottie stepped over two boxes that one of her kids had been searching, the contents haphazardly thrown back in. She hung up her coat on the old bentwood coat stand that had been there since God was a child. Picking up the plastic bag of Chinese takeaway that she'd purchased on the way home, she entered the warm kitchen, bracing herself.

'Hello, Mother. Something smells gorgeous. I wasn't expecting you, but thanks for coming over.' She slumped onto a chair, dumped the Chinese food on the floor under the table and picked up a pile of unopened post. Probably all bills. She groaned. Was she ever going to get her life on track?

'You can throw that in the bin,' Rose said.

'What?'

'That bag of nonsense food. I'm cooking spuds and cabbage with ham. Almost done.'

'Thanks,' Lottie said grudgingly.

Rose had a habit of interfering in her life, but this evening, after such a trying day, Lottie was glad of the home-cooked food. She didn't bother asking why Rose had appeared today of all days, because she knew the answer already.

With her back still turned as she lifted a lid and tested the potatoes with a fork, Rose said, 'I heard the news on the radio about the murder out at Cloughton.'

Lottie smiled to herself.

'I knew you'd have your hands full and you'd forget you had a home to come to.'

'That's unfair.'

'I know what you're like when a big investigation lands on your lap.' Rose spun round, waving the fork, her short silver hair gleaming in the steam rising from the saucepan, 'I can't have my grandchildren and great-grandson starving.'

Biting her tongue, Lottie opened her post. She was right. Bills. She heard Louis squealing with delight at something on the television in the front room, and it brought a smile to her lips.

Rose was still talking. 'And I don't know what you're doing living out here in the middle of nowhere. I was sure you and Leo had come to a monetary arrangement. How in hell did you end up agreeing to live here? It's ice cold and pitch black at night. My eyes are not great in the dark, you know, so I'll have to get on the road soon.'

Lottie decided to humour her mother. 'It suited me and it suited Leo once he realised he'd never get planning permission to demolish the house and build a hotel or a scheme of houses or whatever he'd intended. Anyway, it's only a lease arrangement until he figures out how to make money out of Farranstown.'

'And then what?' Rose brandished the fork furiously. 'You're going to be out on the side of the road with your children. Do you ever think about them?'

'For Christ's sake, I never stop thinking about them. Will you give me a break,' she muttered under her breath.

'Don't swear. No need for it. You'll give Louis choice vocabulary. But tell me what happened to that poor woman?'

Lottie groaned. Her mother's voice was like chalk grating on a blackboard. Her head already hurt and she'd been home less than five minutes. 'You know I can't discuss my cases with you.'

She heard the front door slam. Boyd walked into the kitchen, a big smile on his face.

'Rose, thanks for the dinner invite.'

'Oh, I know you love my cooking, and you need fattening up. Won't be long now until I have it on a plate in front of you.' Rose transformed into a different woman the second Boyd appeared.

Lottie felt him feather her hair with a kiss.

'How are you now?' he said.

'What do you mean, now?'

'You were narky as fu— as hell earlier. A good feed will put a smile back on your face.'

Lottie threw the post on the table. 'Boyd, you know I'm under pressure. All day working and not a single hint or clue as to who killed Isabel. It's so frustrating. There's a killer sleeping soundly in their bed tonight because we haven't a notion who they are or why they did what they did.'

She brushed past him. 'I'm having a shower. Be down in five.'

'I have yours on the plate!' Rose said. She tutted and placed the food in front of Boyd. 'You may as well have the first cut then, Mark. Eat up. Lottie, call Sean. I'll get Katie and Louis. Chloe headed out.'

'Sure.'

Upstairs, the bare landing was cold under her feet. She knocked on Sean's door and entered.

'Mam! You can't just waltz in like that.'

'I knocked.'

'You didn't wait for me to invite you in, did you?'

'Jesus, what are you now? Lord of the manor?' She sat on the edge of his unmade bed and glanced at the monitor, where he was deep in a game, his headphones now hanging around his neck. 'There's no way you could have heard me knock with those noise busters.'

'That's not the point. I need my privacy.' He laughed. 'Noise busters?'

'You're my son. I'm entitled to—'

'What do you want, Mam, seeing as you've burst through the *noise busters*?'

She closed her eyes. Why was everyone so hostile?

'I have a big investigation on, Sean, and I just wanted to say hello to my only son.' She reached out and squeezed his hand.

'Hello, Mam. Can I go back to my game now?' The sixteen-year-old swivelled his chair to face the screen. Two screens, she noticed.

'When did you get the second monitor?'

'Mark bought it for me.'

'Did he now?'

'Don't start, Mam.'

'I wasn't starting anything.'

'I know that look.'

'And what would that be?'

'Jealousy?'

'Give it a rest. Why would I be jealous of Boyd?'

'Because he gets me and you don't.'

That floored her. She ran her hands up and down her arms and tugged at the hem of her sleeve, unravelling a thread and pulling it hard around her finger. She counted to ten in her head and expelled a loud breath.

'Granny has your dinner ready. You better wash your hands and get downstairs.'

He rolled his eyes. 'I'll be down when I finish this game. Gran won't mind.'

She left her son in his dark room with clothes dropped everywhere like discarded props and went to the bathroom.

She stood under the shower for ten glorious, peaceful minutes, the tingle of the water drumming her skin, bringing some comfort to her tired brain.

When she stepped out onto the cold floor and found the already damp towel, she knew she had to make a decision about the house. It was tainting her relationship with Boyd. At the moment it was neither one thing nor the other. First, though, she needed to discover why Isabel Gallagher had been murdered, and by whom.

But before all that, she had to eat her dinner, or Rose would have a puss on her and life wasn't worth that hassle.

*

With Holly asleep upstairs in a travel cot loaned by a neighbour, Anita stood at the window and stared out.

'Where did you go, Jack?' she whispered. The curtain fluttered with her words.

Lost in his grief, he'd left the house that afternoon and she hadn't seen him since. She should have questioned him. But she'd given him space and now, hours later, she had no idea where he was.

Moving away from the window, she sat by the dying fire with no energy to bring in fuel from the shed. She should have asked Jack to do it. And that made her wonder what kind of man her son-in-law was. He'd been awkward with Holly, as if he'd rarely held his daughter in his arms. He had no idea how to feed her until she'd shown him. Had that been his fault, or had Isabel taken over those tasks?

A solitary tear fell from her eye and snaked down her cheek. She'd cried so much today, she was surprised she had any tears left to shed.

A sound. Outside the window.

She straightened her back and listened.

Nothing.

No. There it was again.

A knock. On the front door.

Not Jack – she'd given him a key. Oh God, I can't be doing with neighbours sympathising at this hour, she thought as she pulled on her slippers and straightened her jeans.

She opened the door and gasped when she saw the man standing on the step.

'What are you doing here?'

'Oh Anita, I'm so sorry about Isabel. Can I come in?'

And she let the man into her home.

A man she had first met over forty years before.

CHAPTER TWENTY-FOUR

Evan was sitting in front of the television eating a slice of toast, with a beaker of milk in his other hand. He was a sweet child, though at times prone to outbreaks of kicking and spitting. Just his age, Sinéad had told Joyce, but she felt it was something more deep-rooted.

'Where's my mummy?' he said, his mouth full of bread.

'She'll be here soon.'

Extracting her phone, she tried Joyce again. Not even a dial tone. She scanned the news app on her phone. The day had been so hectic, she hadn't had a moment until now.

'Oh my God!' she cried, reading about the murder. Isabel was dead. Murdered. And they'd been supposed to meet that morning to discuss Holly. She liked Isabel, who had worked for her for a few months last year. But now she was dead! That was why the detective had contacted her earlier. What was the world coming to? And now Joyce hadn't turned up.

Her anxiety grew as she watched the clock slip past eight o'clock. Something was definitely wrong. Her husband, Dylan, had a meeting after work and then he was going to the gym, so she couldn't talk to him about it. She needed to keep busy.

'Evan, honey, lie down on the couch when you've finished eating. I'm just getting Bubbles ready for tomorrow.'

In the room that had once been a garage attached to her house, she picked up the square peg boards with multicoloured designs the children had created earlier that day. A mishmash of colour. Various degrees of complexity, depending on the child's age. She popped the pegs into the little baskets and stacked the boards on a shelf. A shadow settled on the desk beneath the window. Looking out, she could see little with the light on above her. It was a quiet estate. No break-ins or disturbances.

Was that the front door opening? She paused her work and listened.

'Is that you, Dylan?' She peered through the window, but couldn't see his car in the drive.

She switched off the light and made her way back along the corridor that led to the house. No one in the hall. Her husband's coat was not hanging up. She glanced into the sitting room, where the inane chirping of some cartoon character punctured her eardrums.

Skirting around the couch to find the remote, she caught sight of the beaker lying on the floor, milk streaming across the deep-pile carpet. Crusts of toast squashed into the mess.

'Evan! You might be allowed to do this in your own home, but not in mine,' she shouted towards the downstairs bathroom, where a skein of light filtered under the door.

No reply.

Poor boy. She shouldn't have shouted at him. She picked up a pack of baby wipes she kept on the armchair for such emergencies and began to mop up the spilled milk. He was just missing his mum.

She threw the balled-up wipes into the fire and carried the beaker and plate to the kitchen.

'Do you need help in there, Evan?'

Maybe he couldn't reach the towel. The bathroom wasn't designed for kids. She and Dylan hadn't been blessed with a child so far, which was a pity because she loved children.

She went to the bathroom and pushed open the door.

Empty.

'Where are you, Evan?' she shouted as she ran upstairs and checked each room. No sign of the boy.

She raced back down and out the front door.

'Evan! Evan, where are you?'

Opening the gate, she looked frantically up and down the road. The street lights cast sepia shadows along the footpath, and leaves swirled in the evening breeze. Where was the boy?

She ran back inside and snatched up her phone. First she called Joyce, then Nathan. Still nothing. She tried Dylan's number. Same result. Where the hell was everyone?

After another full search of the house to ensure the child wasn't hiding, she slumped into an armchair, her racing heart the only sound in her eardrums. Should she notify the gardaí? Was it too premature? But where had Evan got to? Then a thought struck her. Hadn't Katie Parker mentioned that her mother was a detective?

Phone clutched tightly in her trembling hand, she dialled Katie's number.

CHAPTER TWENTY-FIVE

Boyd was asleep on the couch, his legs hanging over the end, a beige blanket across his chest. She couldn't help but love him. The blanket was dotted with flecks of white paint. Stretching as high as she could without falling off the stepladder, Lottie vowed this was the last ceiling she would paint. Ever.

'Mam, can I have a word?' Katie stood at the door, her face a mask of worry.

'Sure. Is it Louis? Is he okay?'

'He's fast asleep. No, it's just that I had a phone call from Sinéad.'

'Who?'

'She runs Louis' day care.'

'What's up with her?' Lottie climbed down the ladder, leaving the paint can on the top step with the brush lying across it.

'I've boiled the kettle. Want a cup of tea?' Katie said.

'I'd murder one.' Lottie found a rag steeped in turps and cleaned her hands as best she could before following her daughter into the kitchen. 'What was the call about?'

'It's weird really,' Katie said as she poured milk into her tea.

'You have my attention.' Isabel Gallagher had been supposed to meet Sinéad Foley, and now the Foley woman was ringing Katie. Might only be about childcare, but Lottie had an uneasy feeling it wasn't that at all.

Katie swallowed a mouthful of tea. 'When I picked Louis up earlier, Sinéad was worried because one of the kids there, Evan, his mum hadn't arrived to pick him up. Joyce Breslin. She works in Fayne's café on the other side of town. I explained about the bad traffic and all that, but it appears Joyce never arrived, so Sinéad was holding onto Evan while she tried to contact his dad.'

'Okay.'

'She couldn't contact either Joyce or Nathan – he's Evan's dad, I think. Then about ten minutes ago, Evan disappeared from her sitting room. She can't find the boy anywhere.'

The hair stood up on Lottie's neck.

'She should phone the station. The duty sergeant will send someone out to take her statement and organise a search. The boy might have been disorientated and wandered off.'

'The thing is, Sinéad was in the playroom part of the day care and she thought she heard the front door open and then a few seconds later it closed. Could someone have come in and taken the child?'

'It might have been his dad.' Lottie chipped off a pearl of dried paint from her knuckle. 'He might not have known where Sinéad was.'

'But how would he get into the house?'

'I don't know, Katie. What did you tell her to do?' Lottie was tired. The paint fumes were clinging to her nostrils and her throat felt raw.

Katie fiddled with her mug, swirling a spoon needlessly around the milky tea. 'I told her I'd talk to you and see if you could do anything.'

'I can't, Katie. I've this big murder investigation on my hands. She has to ring the station. They'll send someone out.' She saw the look on Katie's face. 'I'll call it in.'

'It's after half eight and Evan is only four. A little boy out in the dark on his own, Mam. You have to do something more than *call it in*.'

'Okay.' Lottie stood and fetched her jacket. 'I'll go round there.'

'Thanks, Mam. You're the best.'

*

Here he was, AJ Lennon, hardware supremo, sitting in what had been Fred's favourite armchair, his coat neatly folded on his knee. He'd aged considerably, and Anita wondered why the years hadn't been kind to him.

'I came to offer my condolences. Poor Isabel – I'm so sorry. How are you holding up, Anita?' His jowls sagged as he spoke, but she could still see the sparkle in his eyes that had enchanted her all those years ago.

'I know we've met in town from time to time, AJ, it's impossible not to bump into each other, but we haven't spoken for nearly forty years and now you waltz in here. Give me a break.'

'I just knocked on your door; you invited me in.'

'Always had a smart answer, so you did.' She held her arms tightly around her waist. Some things time could not change.

'Look, Anita, I'm just offering my sincere condolences.'

'You never appeared when Fred died.'

'Sorry about that. I'm here out of respect for your daughter, and to tell you that if you need anything, you should give me a call.'

'What on earth could I want from you?'

He sighed and folded his coat into an even smaller bundle. It would be a ball of creases, but feck him, a creased coat was less than he deserved.

'I'm sorry, Anita. Sorry for everything.'

'Bit late in the day for apologies.'

'I want to make it up to you.'

'This is not the right time, AJ.' She couldn't stop sobbing. 'I'm a broken woman. I've lost Isabel. I've lost everything I ever cared for.' She tried to wipe away her tears with the back of her hand. 'If it wasn't for Holly, I don't think I could go on.'

'Hush, woman. You're still young. You'll learn to live with your loss.'

'I've lived with loss all my life, but it's hard, AJ. Too bloody hard.'

'Tell me what I can do to help.' He rose from Fred's armchair and knelt beside her, taking her wet hand in his.

Fighting the urge to pull away, she said, 'When I truly needed you, you disappeared. I don't need you now.'

'I admit I was a coward. But I'm not the same person I was then. I'm no longer a coward.'

'What do you want?' Anger had replaced her sorrow.

'I met her again recently.'

Her head shot up. 'Isabel? She worked in your Ragmullin store for a while. Is that what you mean?'

'No,' he said. 'She came in one day; it could've been six months or more ago.'

'Is there a point to this story?'

'She didn't look well. Pale and drawn. I happened to be in the Ragmullin office that day. I'm not always there. I travel around a lot and—'

'For pity's sake, get to the point.' Anita knew she shouldn't be snappy, but AJ Lennon was the last person on earth she wanted in her sitting room right now, and she regretted letting him in.

'She almost fainted in one of the aisles. I saw it on CCTV. I went to help, but she said she was okay. She was pregnant.'

'Thanks for helping her, but where is this going?'

He knotted his fingers together until the skin turned white. 'She said that if anything ever happened to her, would I keep an eye out for you.'

'What?' Anita jumped up. 'Why would she say that? To you? She hardly knew you.'

'I have no idea, but it struck a chord with me then and again at lunchtime when I heard the news.' He unclenched his fingers and spread them out on his knees. When he raised his head, Anita felt herself wither under the intensity of his gaze. 'I feared for her that day. Her terrified little face, pale and drawn, and her bones holding up her baby bump.'

'I don't understand.' Anita wiped her eyes with a balled-up tissue and threw it into the dead fire. Had Isabel been afraid Jack would do something to her? Why would she say that? To AJ Lennon of all people.

With her back to him, she said softly, 'What do you think she meant?'

'I honestly don't know. She drank a glass of water and the colour returned to her cheeks, then she left.'

'Maybe she had a premonition, or something?' She couldn't get her head around what AJ was telling her. Maybe Isabel had suffered from baby brain or whatever. But she knew in her heart that her daughter had been frightened. Why? Of what? 'Why didn't you tell me? You could have come around as easily as you did tonight.'

'She was fine when she left and I was busy. I never gave it any thought until today. I'm so sorry.' He shook out his coat and tugged it on, then put a card on the arm of the chair. 'My number is on that. If you need anything, give me a call.'

'Thank you.'

He paused at the door. 'I'm so sorry for your loss. Take care.'

Holding a hand to her chest, she listened to him pull the front door behind him. The reality of his words sank in. Why did Isabel think something might happen? AJ's visit made her think of what she herself had been hiding all these years. Could Isabel have stumbled upon that? Had Anita's own tragic past been instrumental in bringing a murderer to kill her daughter?

'God, no!' she wailed.

Then she thought of her little granddaughter asleep upstairs, and sobbed into her hands.

CHAPTER TWENTY-SIX

Nathan Monaghan waited for the trailer to be unloaded at the Ragmullin depot, then parked the cab for the night.

He slipped into his car, his legs cramping with tiredness. A good healthy stew was what he needed, and a decent night's sleep. He should text Joyce to say he was on his way. Shit, he'd never charged his phone. Anyway, it'd be nice to surprise her. She wasn't expecting him until much later in the night, or even tomorrow. He was always vague. Suited him that way. The thought of hot food and his hot woman filled him with urgency. He floored the car and sped home.

The first thing he noticed was that there was no sign of Joyce's car in the driveway. He pulled up where her black Ford Focus was normally parked and marched to the door. The second thing of note was that there were no lights lit in the house. No curtains drawn. It was in darkness, with only the street lamp casting hues on the front of the house.

Inside, he switched on the light and waited.

Stillness.

Not a sound.

Not a breath.

'Joyce? Evan?' He marched into the sitting room, flicked the switch. Empty. Same in the kitchen. He plugged in his phone to charge and bounded up the stairs, a rush of fear propelling his feet. Evan wasn't in bed. Joyce was not in bed. He noticed the disarray in the bedroom, and the house felt like it had been abandoned.

He sat on the top step of the stairs. What was going on? Where was his family?

That Dermody idiot had mentioned Evan's name like it was a threat.

His heart stopped in his chest and he tried to catch his breath. The palms of his hands began to sweat.

As he made his way down the stairs, a finger of fear slithered down his spine like a bony hand nudging each vertebra. Surely this couldn't be anything to do with Dermody? No way. He'd done what had been asked of him. He didn't want to know what they were smuggling in the back of his lorry. As long as they did it quickly and stealthily, he should be beyond suspicion. There was no reason to harm his family.

As he reached the kitchen, he heard his phone ping with messages. He grabbed it, still charging, and gaped at the line of missed calls and texts.

He rang Joyce. Nothing.

Then he rang Sinéad.

Sinéad was frantic. That was the only word Nathan could find to describe her. Hair wild, face tear-stained, with a hand jammed into her mouth, she paced up and down the path in front of her house.

'What the hell is going on?' Nathan said, jumping out of the car.

She rushed to him, tripped on a paving stone and fell into his arms. He shrugged out of the impetuous embrace. Holding her at arm's length, forcibly clutching her elbows, he shook her.

'Sinéad, for Christ's sake, get a grip on yourself. I've a ton of missed calls. I was driving, my phone died … Where are Evan and Joyce? I've just come from the house and they're not there.'

'Where were you?' she cried. 'I called and called. No one picked up. I couldn't even reach Dylan. Now Evan is gone.'

'What are you talking about?' He shook her again, trying to make sense of her words while recalling Dermody's veiled threat.

'Joyce didn't arrive to collect Evan this afternoon. I kept him here all evening and then ... then he was gone.'

'Gone?' He tightened his grip on her arms. 'What do you mean, gone? Where? What are you talking about?'

'I don't know. You're hurting me, Nathan.'

He realised then that he was digging his fingers into her soft flesh and let her go. Evan was missing? No, that couldn't be right. And where was Joyce?

Sinéad walked inside. Her body deflated like a burst balloon, she slumped against the hall wall and slid down to the floor.

He rushed in behind her, drawing the door shut. Stepping over her outstretched legs, he flew through the downstairs of the house, calling for Evan. He glanced at the stairs, then, without waiting for permission, raced up them, running through every room, searching.

Back down again, his body trembling uncontrollably, he hunkered beside her. 'Sinéad, I want you to tell me everything. Absolutely fucking everything!' He clenched his fists between his knees in case he lashed out to stop her crying.

A sharp knock on the door forced them to look at it simultaneously. He was first to react, jumping up and hauling the door open.

'Mr Foley?' the woman said. Her tall frame was topped with a mess of unruly hair. Flecks of paint dotted her face and hands.

'Dylan's not here. Who are you?' he said.

'Is Sinéad Foley in? My daughter Katie got a call from her. About a missing boy? I'm Lottie Parker. Detective Inspector.'

'Nathan Monaghan. Joyce is my ... Evan is ... Oh God, I don't know where they are.'

'May I come in?'

135

He opened the door wider and watched her appraise Sinéad's slumped figure, sitting on the floor. Shit, he thought, this looks terrible, but he didn't care how it looked. He had to find Joyce and Evan.

Sinéad dragged herself to her feet. 'I'm Sinéad Foley. Thanks for coming.'

She led the detective into the sitting room and Nathan followed, his mind a jumble. This was the last thing he needed. A fucking detective in his face. But then maybe it was for the best. He was tired of all the lies.

*

Lottie stood with her back to the fireplace, where an earlier fire had burnt to embers. The room was warm and quiet. Sinéad sat on the arm of a leather chair while Nathan paced up and down, thumping clenched fists against his thighs.

'I don't understand what's going on,' he said.

That makes two of us, Lottie thought. She garnered the bones of the events from Sinéad before directing her question at Nathan.

'Joyce and Evan were definitely not at home when you arrived there?'

'No. There's no one there.'

'Sinéad, could Evan have opened the door and let himself out?'

'He's tall for his age, but I don't think so. I know he was bored and tired. Missing his mum. But I honestly think someone came in. I should have reacted sooner. I assumed it was Dylan – my husband. He had a late meeting after work before he went to the gym. He goes there every Monday, Wednesday and Friday. Regular as clockwork. He should have been back by now, though. I couldn't get him on the phone, but I can try him again.'

'Did you hear Evan scream or cry out?'

She shook her head, then her hand flew to her mouth. 'Oh God, do you think he knew who took him?'

'I don't know. Can you contact your husband for me, please?'

While Sinéad left the room to make the call, Lottie studied Nathan. Nerves flew off him in waves. Wired. He ground his fingers into his thighs. Eyes wide and edgy. Edgy? More like cagey. Was there something rumbling beneath his taut muscles? Something sinister? Or was it just her imagination running away with her after a day working on Isabel Gallagher's murder?

She sat opposite him. Took out her notebook. Leaned forward. Assumed her easy-to-listen-to voice.

'How long have you and Joyce been together?'

'What's that got to do with anything?'

'I need to have all the facts.'

'Why are you even here?'

'Sinéad asked me to come round. Once I've assessed the situation, I'm calling it in. Then it will be official.'

He kept his head bowed. 'No need for that. Evan must have run off.'

'Do you really think he did that at this hour of the night? He's only four, isn't he?'

'Did what?' He raised his face to her, eyes piercing, like steel bullets.

'Ran off.'

He moved towards her. 'I don't know what to think. I've been on the continent for two days, driving for hours on end, and I just came off the boat, delivered the load and picked up my car. Then I arrive home to this … mess. I don't even know where Joyce is.'

'Are you sure she couldn't have just arrived here and taken Evan?'

'How would she get in? I doubt she has a key. What are you even doing here? You should be out there searching for them. Someone might have taken them.'

Lottie straightened her shoulders. 'Taken them? Why would you say that?'

'I … I don't know what I'm saying. Look, I've only just arrived back in the country. I don't know where they are, but I want them found.'

'Okay.' Lottie folded her notebook closed and slotted it back into her mess of a bag. 'I'm calling in support, then we'll go to your house. A quick search.' A four-year-old boy was missing. His mother also. That was all she knew at this time. 'Once I have an officer here with Sinéad, you can show me the way to yours.'

Sinéad returned to the room as Lottie finished her call to the station.

'I eventually got hold of Dylan. He was delayed at the gym and has only just switched his phone back on. He's on his way home now.'

'Was your husband home at all this evening?'

'No, like I said, he had a meeting and went to the gym from there.'

'Where does he work?'

'He's in the health service.'

'Okay. Can you describe what Evan was wearing when you last saw him?'

'His jacket is still here. He had on his blue Bubbles sweatshirt, white polo shirt and navy joggers. I think he had his green dinosaur runners on.'

'Grand, thanks. Detectives and uniformed officers will be here soon.'

'I'm so sorry,' Sinéad said. 'I should have kept him by my side and not let this happen.'

'It's not your fault. We need to locate his mother. Have you any idea where she might be?'

The woman shrugged.

Nathan was wringing his hands into knots again. Lottie thought there must be no skin left. Sweat pulsed on his forehead. Was it only genuine worry bubbling under the surface of his skin?

'Nathan? Where might Joyce be?'

'I don't know. She's usually either at home or at work. She goes nowhere.'

She noticed he had tears in his eyes.

'I'm sorry,' he cried. 'This is surreal. I don't know what to do or say.'

A car screeched to a halt outside, followed by a loud knock on the door.

Sinéad went to let them in.

Lottie said, 'Garda Thornton and Detective Kirby will stay here with you, Sinéad, and take your statement. If you're ready, Nathan, let's go to your house.'

She turned to Kirby. 'Get as much detail as you can. By the way, where's McKeown?'

Kirby held up his phone. 'I've tried calling him six times and no reply. Had to bring old Thornton from the desk with me.'

'Okay, fine. I'll check in with you later.'

As she stepped over the threshold, Lottie noticed how clean and sweet-smelling the house was. Nothing out of place. No coats hanging on the banister. No shoes dropped by the door. She wished she could maintain a tidy house. As she moved further inside, the minimalism struck her as being similar to Isabel Gallagher's house. Was her tired mind playing tricks on her?

'She's not here,' Nathan said. 'I've already searched.'

'I want to see for myself. Does she drive?'

'Yes, and her car isn't here either.'

'Colour, make and licence plate number?'

'Black Ford Focus, 2007 reg. I'll get you the number.'

'Thanks. First let's see if any of her clothes are missing. Upstairs?'

His eyes widened. 'You really think she's run away?'

'I don't know what to think,' Lottie said, honestly.

She checked the kitchen and sitting room with a cursory glance before following him up the stairs. Three bedrooms and a family bathroom. So pristine as to be almost sterile.

'This is Evan's room,' Nathan said, a tremble in his voice.

She stepped over the threshold and sensed the energy. Baskets of toys. Shelves of colourful books. A single bed in the shape of a racing car, with a teddy bear resting on the pillow. Its ears were worn away from constant rubbing by little fingers. Its nose had the impression of having been sucked. To soothe Evan to sleep? If Joyce had taken him, Lottie was sure she wouldn't have left without her son's comfort toy. Unless she hadn't time to stop and think. No. She'd dropped the boy to day care with the intention of going back for him. Or had someone taken the mother and then gone to the day care and snatched the child? Her gut told her that was what had happened, but it could be totally wrong. There might be a reasonable explanation.

'Does it look like anything is missing?' she said.

'I don't know. His teddy is on his bed. He needs that to fall asleep.' Nathan opened the wardrobe and shrugged. 'How would I know what's missing? Joyce does all this stuff.'

'Let's have a gander in the main bedroom. You sleep together?'

'Of course we do.' He walked in ahead of her.

A suitcase lay open on the bed. Clothes had been dragged from the wardrobe; some lay on the floor, with more on the bed and very little in the suitcase.

'Looks like she was planning to leave,' Lottie said, staring at the clothing. All adult female attire.

'No, that can't be right. Why would she do that?'

'You tell me. Do you have more suitcases or holdalls?'

He dragged two empty holdalls from the wardrobe. Lottie wondered if Joyce had intended to run off and been interrupted while packing.

'Nathan, this looks highly suspicious to me. I'll need you to come to the station to make a full statement, and I'll need proof of your movements for the last twenty-four hours.'

'I've only been back in the country for a few hours. You can't think I did something to my family?'

'I'm not making any assumptions. I'll need a full description and photograph of Evan. The same for Joyce.'

'I can't believe this. Something serious has happened to my family and you're latching onto me without doing a proper investigation.' A muscle in his jaw ticked non-stop and his eyes darted around without landing on her.

What was he afraid of? What was he hiding?

'We have procedures to follow.'

'Okay, Okay. I've photos on my phone. I can send them to you.'

'Good. Now come with me.'

She shooed him out of the room. He didn't protest, and she pulled the door shut behind her. The only positive in all this was that there was no sign of a struggle, plus Joyce's car was not in the drive. Maybe the woman had abandoned packing and just fled. But why? And why abduct her own son? Lottie needed to peel away the layers of this family to find out just what the hell had happened.

Following Nathan down the stairs, she peered over the banister, and that was when she saw the speck of blood on the radiator.

CHAPTER TWENTY-SEVEN

'What was all that about?' Boyd said, following Lottie into the bedroom.

For once, she wished he'd gone home to his own apartment. She wanted to stretch out over her bed and sleep for a million years.

Pulling off her sweater, she said, 'It's possible Joyce Breslin ran off with her son. But the timelines don't add up.' She explained everything she'd discovered that night. 'If she scarpered after she dropped her son to day care, why wait until late evening to abduct him? Why not leave town, if that was what she was doing, without dropping him to day care? Why not finish packing and take her belongings? Where is she? Where is Evan?'

'Too many questions for this hour of the night. Why don't you get some sleep? It will all be clearer in the morning.'

'And then there was the blood on the radiator in the hall. Could have been there a long time, but I think it was fresh. McGlynn will examine it in the morning.'

'It is morning.'

She sighed and stripped off her jeans and shirt, and pulled on her old pyjamas. Boyd sat on the edge of the bed, fully dressed, as she rolled under the duvet. 'I've implemented procedures for finding the missing boy. Media outlets have been alerted. I sealed the house and left Nathan Monaghan in a cell.'

'You what? What have you to hold him on?'

'Nothing. He didn't argue. Said he had nowhere else to go.'

'That's a highly irregular move, even for you.'

'This whole thing is irregular. Plus, it's for his own safety. If someone did abduct Joyce and Evan, who's to say they won't go after Nathan as well.'

'What about Sinéad Foley? Didn't her name crop up in relation to the Gallagher murder?'

'Yeah. Isabel was to meet her this morning. Yesterday morning. God! Anyway, McGlynn appointed a SOCO to do a sweep of her house in the morning. Sinéad is staying at her mother-in-law's for the night.'

'Where's her husband?'

'He's with her now. He wasn't home when I left with Nathan, but Kirby filled me in. I need to check Dylan Foley's movements.'

'Why didn't you call me while this was going on?'

'Jealous?'

He laid a hand over hers and rubbed it gently. 'No, but I'm tired. Will I go back to my own place?'

'You're here, so you might as well stay.' She yawned and fluffed the pillow ready to sleep.

'That's the most half-hearted invitation I ever heard.'

'Boyd, I'm too tired to play this game. Get into the bloody bed, my feet are freezing.'

He didn't appear to need a proper invitation after all.

She gave him a tired smile, reached for his hand, then closed her eyes.

*

It wasn't an ideal arrangement, but it was better than being stuck in a B&B. McKeown stretched his arm across Martina Brennan's breasts and twisted the clock to see the time. Two a.m.

He lay back on the soft pillow. It was too uncomfortable for him, but Martina liked them plush and spongy. He was in no position to object, it was her apartment, after all.

She groaned and turned over, pinning his arm beneath her. He slid it out, wishing he could extract himself from the relationship just as easily.

He fumbled around on the floor until he found his phone under the bed. Seven missed calls from Kirby. Shit, he'd put his phone on silent earlier and switched off vibrate so as not to be disturbed. Must be a break in the Gallagher case. Well, he'd done his shift, so he was glad he'd missed the calls. Life was too short to spend it all at work. There were too many pleasures to be explored. Better ways to spend his time.

Should he phone Kirby all the same? To see what was going down?

'What are you doing on your phone at this hour of the night?'

Martina's voice was groggy with sleep and he felt her hand travel up and down his bare back, igniting a million electrons in his nether regions. Nether regions? He laughed.

'What's so funny?' she asked.

'I'm having bad thoughts about what I want to do with you.'

'I'm not objecting. Get back into bed.' Her hand travelled around his waist and she sat up in bed and kissed the back of his neck while her fingers reached further down and squeezed. 'You like that?'

'You know me too well.'

He threw the phone back under the bed, twisted round, hauled himself on top of her and, finding himself fully aroused, entered her with a groan.

He forgot all about Kirby and his blasted phone calls.

*

Anita lay on top of the duvet and covered her face with a pillow so that her uncontrollable crying wouldn't wake Holly. She couldn't stop feeling sorry for herself. It was all so unfair. Why hadn't she done enough to protect Isabel?

Her anguished cries saturated the pillow. She threw it to the floor and sat up suddenly. The baby was still asleep. Thank God.

Dragging herself from the bed, she went to maintain a vigil at the window. The amber hue of the street lights shining through the trees across the road caused the shadows to dance like spectres in the night.

She was sorry she'd let AJ into her home. Sorry to have ever laid eyes on him in the first place, but what had Isabel meant when she'd said those words to him? To look out for her mother if anything happened to her. Did she have a premonition of her death? And why talk to AJ? He had employed her at one time, but there was no relationship or friendship there. Not that Anita knew about anyway. After years keeping her past a secret, had *she* been found out?

As the night blurred, she wondered where Jack was.

She found a fresh pillowcase in the drawer and shoved the pillow inside. Men grieved differently from women, she supposed. But that didn't give him the right to abandon his daughter. Holly needed her father now that Isabel would no longer be around to care for her.

As she flung the pillow back on the bed, she heard the tiny cries of the little girl in the cot.

'Don't cry, sweetheart. Granny's here.'

She balled her hands into fists and thumped the pillow before going to pick up her little granddaughter.

*

AJ Lennon didn't feel like going home after leaving Anita's house, so he drove out to the warehouse distribution depot. He was proud of it. The largest in Ireland, if you didn't count Lidl. It had been a curse to get planning permission, but eventually, after wheeling and dealing with strategic economic plans, he had it in the bag.

He hadn't realised how long he'd spent inside, but it was late when he left by the main door. He stood in the car park, admiring his best accomplishment to date. A massive economic win for Ragmullin. The lights shone from the walls, highlighting the bays where lorries backed up their trailers. He smiled smugly. He was doing well for himself, thank you very much.

As he turned back to his car, he stopped. Two men were standing by a jeep.

'Damn it to hell,' he muttered as one of the men got into the jeep and drove off.

'Ah, the self-made millionaire himself.' Michael Costello's ginger hair shone yellow under the light and his beard bobbed when he spoke.

'What are you doing here?' Lennon felt small beside the well-dressed man. Well, he *was* small, but it was more than physical. Grinding his teeth, he added, 'I don't want you snooping around my business, Costello, stealing my ideas.'

'Jesus, man, lighten up. There's not one thing here that I haven't thought of myself. I could buy and sell you, you know.' He had the audacity to wink.

Lennon shoved his hands deeper into his coat pockets in case he had the urge to land a punch, knowing full well his hand would bounce right back. 'Well, I don't want you here.'

'Not to worry, midget man, I'm leaving.' Costello flicked a finger against the lapel of Lennon's jacket. 'And don't forget our arrangement. I'm counting on you to keep your side of the bargain.'

'I've never double-crossed anyone in my life! I don't intend to start now.'

'Good man. See you around.'

Lennon swallowed hard as Costello sat into his car and drove off, the engine a soft purr.

CHAPTER TWENTY-EIGHT

The little bone she'd taken from the hillside seemed to mock Dervla Byrne no matter where she went in her house. She'd placed it in a freezer bag and shoved it behind a tub of Flora. She'd shut the fridge door. Tried to forget about it. It was surely only an animal bone. If that was true, though, why had she brought it home?

It was the middle of the night and she was hungry. She slipped on a sweater and headed to the kitchen. She baulked at her reflection in the wall mirror. At thirty-five, she looked like a washed-up Hollywood icon. One of those who'd starred in the black-and-white horror movies. Her jet-black fringe was a straight line above unplucked eyebrows, and her only nod to non-conformity was that one side of her hair was longer than the other. Not by design, just a terrible haircut.

At the refrigerator door, her hand hovered on the handle. She opened it quickly, pulled out a packet of sliced cheese and the tub of Flora. Then she heard the crinkle of the plastic bag as it settled without the support of the tub.

With one hand balancing the cheese and Flora, she opened the door wide and stared at the little bone lying there in its see-through plastic coffin. Her breath came in sharp bursts and she flared her nose to take in the cool air, to calm her racing heart. Gulping loudly, she reached in and lifted out the bag. But just as quickly, she shoved it back in and slammed the door shut. She leaned against the cold metal and tried to restore her natural breathing using a method she'd learned a long time ago to help her cope with the darkness in her life.

When she was sure she could walk without collapsing, she moved to the table and took two slices of bread from its wrapper. She opened the tub and dug the knife in, then stopped as a thought fluttered in her brain. Kevin Doran. Why was she thinking of him? The breathing exercise? The past? No, it was because of the little bone lying in her fridge that she'd taken from Misneach hill.

Slumping onto a chair, she left the knife stuck in the tub. Her appetite had evaporated. She didn't want those memories to return. She wanted to get her life back on track and consign her miserable past to history. But was it his fault she'd been climbing the hill?

Without bothering to return the food to the fridge – she didn't want to see the bone again – she switched off the light and made her way back upstairs, knowing she would find little sleep.

Lying in bed, she kept thinking of the bone in her fridge. It could be ancient. But in her heart she knew it wasn't that ancient at all. She had to go back to the hill to find out if there were more bones buried there. It was something she could no longer fight.

*

Joyce knew she was being held inside some sort of steel container. A rag was tied around her mouth, but at least she could breathe. Her hands and feet were bound with something rough, possibly a rope. She moved her hands slightly, up and down in front of her. Definitely a rope. It was wrapped around her waist so she couldn't pull the gag away. There was nothing covering her eyes, but all she could see in the dark was the outline of walls.

She tried to think back over the events of the day. The terrifying ordeal. She'd been right. The envelope had been a warning. And it was all her fault. Hers and Isabel's.

She'd driven out to the lake to clear her head of the fear and foreboding. She'd needed time and space to think about what she could do. She needed a plan. She had to act. And fast. She'd go home and finish packing. Withdraw what she could from the bank, pick up Evan, then flee. She had no idea where to go, but once they were on the road, something would come to her. She'd also decided to tell Nathan everything.

She recalled now that she'd sat into the car and had been looking at the contents of the envelope. She'd taken it from her pocket and had it on her lap. The razor blade and an address to remind her that she would never be safe. With no clear idea of what to do, the only thing she was certain of was that she had to do something. And do it fast. She'd turned the car and headed up the narrow lane.

That was when she saw it. Coming towards her at speed. A dark SUV with tinted windows. She'd pressed her foot on the brake pedal, an automatic reflex when she should have kept going, rammed the other car or driven up on the bank and swerved around it. But no, she'd hesitated and it was enough.

The SUV's lights were on full, and even though it was daylight, they blinded her. There was nowhere for her to go. If she reversed, she was in the lake. She knew the other driver could reverse a little to give her room. There was something threatening in the way he just sat there. She couldn't make out his face through the tinted window, but it was possible he had a peaked cap and sunglasses.

The razor blade in the envelope burned a hole on her knee.

The SUV door opened.

He began walking towards her.

Frantically she looked around, hoping to see someone who could help. But there was no one else at this isolated location. She was on her own.

He had something long in his hand. Was it timber, or steel? Sharp pieces protruding at the end. Didn't look like nails; were they blades? Her hand went to her throat, a reflex caused by the fear coursing through her veins.

Then he was standing by her window. A gloved hand knocking on the glass pane. Her heart thudded like a train and her skull filled with blood. Her hand flew to the gearstick; she shifted it into reverse and was about to push her foot on the pedal when the window smashed.

Shards of glass had rained in on top of her. Stuck to her cheek and neck. Her hand fell into her lap. She felt the envelope there and quickly shoved it down the side of the seat, hoping someone might find it in the car and ask the right questions.

A hand thrust through the shattered glass, grabbed her throat. She wriggled and tried to twist out of the grasp, but she was restrained by the seat belt. She couldn't even bite through the leather glove. The engine died as her legs ricocheted around the footwell. His grip was getting tighter. She tried to gulp some air into her lungs, but nothing could get through the tightness.

The wind whistled through the branches overhead, rustling their budding leaves. A swan on the lake trumpeted, and the smell of something like sewage caught on the breeze. It would have made her gag, but she was already swimming into unconsciousness.

At least Evan was safe. No harm could come to her son.

That seemed like days ago, but it was still the same day, possibly night now. She was in some dark, cold, damp container with no idea of how she'd been brought here. Her head throbbed and tears slid from her eyes. She prayed that no matter what happened to her, her son would be safe. That was all she cared about.

A door opened. Something rattled. Footsteps pounded towards her.

She felt a presence loom above her. Her eyes widened as light fell through a narrow doorway behind the figure.

It was a ghost. Tall and white. All white, arms outstretched like an angel. No, she thought, it's the devil in disguise.

'Home at last.' A male voice. A laugh. Then a screech as he opened the lid of a box. 'I've brought your favourite toy. Now we can have some fun. Like the old days. You used to like this. Remember?'

She knew then what this was all about. She knew what was in the box. She knew the first cut would be the hardest. And after that, who knew what he had planned for her?

And Joyce wished she was dead.

Thirty years ago

At fifteen, he knew he had achieved ultimate control of his domain. His foster parents were eating out of his hand. He was able to keep the girl in check even though she was only five and already being spoiled by the 'parents'.

The newest kid wasn't so easy, though. He had already fallen through the cracks in the system. With nowhere else to go, the authorities had landed him here, in this house. Not fair, but fair enough; he just had to watch and wait, see what he was made of.

He discovered that the new boy was insular and quiet. Frightened and ashamed. What did he have to be ashamed of? It was the ones who'd abandoned him who should show shame. But one good thing worth noting: he never fought back.

In the words of the Bible, or some other book, it was like taking a lamb to the slaughter.

TUESDAY

CHAPTER TWENTY-NINE

The light cut across his eyelids. Kevin swiped a grimy hand around his face as he tried to wake up. He hadn't meant to fall asleep. He should have been out there, watching. Watching was his self-imposed job.

He'd been good at keeping a lookout. For the others. He'd always been the first to spot trouble and give the warning. That wasn't a gift; it came from the painful personal experience of sometimes being too late. He had vowed after one particularly bad episode that he would try to prevent it happening to others. So he became the lookout. He became the Watcher.

He half smiled at the memory, but quickly swiped it off his face. There was no reason to smile at the horrors that invaded his brain. Not now. He shook his head slowly. All bad. Very bad. Too bad, he thought, shaking his head so vigorously that flecks of dandruff fluttered around him like falling snow.

At the sink, he filled a basin with cold water. He had no running hot water and couldn't be bothered boiling the kettle, as he'd have to light the gas and he wasn't sure where he'd put the matches.

He splashed his face with the icy water before fetching the nail brush and a bar of carbolic soap from the shelf. He scrubbed his nails. Clean nails were so important. Didn't matter about the rest of his body, but nails were an extension of the self, and if they were clean, his soul was clean. He shivered at that particular memory but couldn't remember who'd said it originally.

When he was satisfied he'd washed away all the dirt, he dried his hands and face on the threadbare tea towel and searched for clean socks, knowing he didn't have any. He unrolled a pair he'd worn two days ago and pulled them on over the ones he'd worn yesterday, then stuck his feet into his old boots. Memories were flitting behind his eyes, blinding him to the present. What was wrong with him today?

Isabel. That was what.

He flattened his hair with fingers he'd dipped into the cold water, and tugged his beanie hat onto his head. He tapped his pocket to make sure he had the little box in case he needed it. Of course he would need it. And that thought filled him with nothing but anxiety. He hyperventilated before he brought his breathing under control. Calm. He had to be calm.

He left the cottage, slowly closing the door behind him. Though he had failed, he was still the Watcher.

*

Sunlight was peeking through a slit in the blinds when Dervla Byrne roused herself from a disturbed sleep.

After a warm shower, she felt life return to her skin if not her bones. She dressed in her comfort clothes of grey sweatshirt and pants. She slipped her feet into her grubby runners and debated what she was about to do.

As she swept the longer side of her hair into a knot on the nape of her neck, she caught a glimpse of her reflection in the wardrobe mirror. Her face looked as if it had depressed in on itself while she'd struggled to sleep. Hollows indented below her cheekbones and her eyes were like pits of darkness. She looked so much older than her thirty-five years, and that made her sad. She knew she didn't look like her foster parents – how could she? And she had no idea what her real parents looked like. She'd been unable to trace them. Doors refused to open and filing cabinets remained locked to her search. She tried to dislodge the resurfacing memories with a shake of her head, but the darkness was all-encompassing. Her hair fell from its loose knot and she set about tying it up again.

Down in the kitchen, she switched on the television and flicked the kettle switch to make herself a strong cup of tea. She noticed the hardened bread on the table and the open butter tub. Her eyes were drawn to the refrigerator, and an icicle of trepidation began its slow descent from the nape of her neck.

As the kettle hummed softly, she sat at the table and gazed at the television and its happy-clappy presenter with her perfect face of make-up warbling about some new lipstick or the must-have dress for summer.

She stood to turn off the offending show and stalled, hand in the air, as the screen changed to a photograph of a young woman, followed by another of a couple. The images dissolved as the camera returned to the doll-like presenter, who turned her body slightly, her tanned legs still delicately crossed at the ankles, to introduce her guest. The camera panned to the well-dressed man sitting there, his mouth a grim line and his eyes dark wells reflecting the studio lights.

Dervla was unable to move. The kettle whistled loudly until it switched itself off, but she could not drag her eyes away from the television. The sound was too low to hear what was being said, but when the woman's photograph came up on screen again, along with a garda hotline number scrolling beneath, she dropped to her knees.

'Isabel?'

Then she recognised the man on the couch.

She thought of all Kevin had told her, and knew she had to go back to the hill.

CHAPTER THIRTY

A shot of wind blasted through a crack in the tiny window high up on the wall. The muted light cast eerie shadows in front of her. A skein of cobwebs hung from the damp brickwork. Water tinkled in an old iron radiator, brown liquid staining the stone floor beneath it.

Lottie moved further into the basement cellar towards a shelf with empty paint cans lined up higgledy-piggledy. It'd take Ironman to open the lids, she thought as she ran her hand along the wall searching for the fuse box.

Feeling her fingers stick to the dampness, she pulled back her hand and shivered. The walls appeared to be bleeding with her dead biological mother's screams, anxiety-laden mortar holding the walls upright. Her mind was awash with memories that she knew she could not possibly possess. A stolen lifetime to which she'd never been allowed entry. She found the box, flicked the switch and a burst of light flooded the cellar.

'Lottie, what are you doing down there?'

She turned quickly, her breath catching in her throat before she relaxed. 'I was looking for the fuse box. I'll be up in a minute.'

'I've just put the kettle back on.' Boyd stood in the doorway on the top step, a worried crease in his brow, before he moved back into the kitchen.

'Coming,' she said.

Though she'd been exhausted and grumpy last night, she had to admit she'd enjoyed his company. She loved the heat of his body close to hers and was surprised to find it was the most natural feeling. It filled her with a giddy kind of warmth.

Mounting the stairs, careful not to fall through the old steps, she entered the kitchen, blinking at the brightness.

'You put in the new light bulbs.'

'I did. Cursed things to get into the old fittings.'

'You continue to surprise me, Boyd.'

He laughed and handed her a mug of tea.

'Thanks,' she muttered as his fingers brushed her grimy knuckles. A fizz sprang up, before nestling in the pit of her stomach. This was all so right.

'You really need to have this place rewired before you get electrocuted,' he said, letting his hand linger on hers before picking up his own mug.

'I need money in the bank to do that.' She kicked off her slippers and sat at the table. When he sat beside her, she rested one ankle on his knee.

'I don't like you going down to that basement. Too many bad memories there.'

'It's not the memories from the time I was held captive down there. It's just … I wonder sometimes. About her. About my real mother.'

'Rose Fitzpatrick is your mother. She raised you, loved you, cared for you. You're tormenting yourself with this fantasy about a woman you never met. A woman who is long dead. You have to stop beating yourself up about it.'

'Okay.'

Boyd grinned. 'Such an insincere agreement, Lottie Parker.'

'Did I tell you it means a lot to me having you here?' she said. 'But you don't have to stay every night.' Why did she say that?

The smile slipped from his lips. 'You make me sound like a lodger.'

He leaned back in his chair, and for a moment she thought he was going to lift her foot from his lap and drop it to the floor. 'I'm still figuring you out,' he said.

That makes two of us, she thought as she sipped her tea. He'd brewed it just the way she liked, the way Adam used to. What would it have been like to live here, in Farranstown House, with Adam? He'd probably have taken a few months off work to get stuck in. Adam had been like that. An all-or-nothing man. Boyd was a bit like that too, though his energy levels were depleted since he'd overcome a mild form of leukaemia, plus their last case had left him off work for a month, recovering from an incident at the quarry.

'What?' she said, when she drew herself up from the fug of her thoughts.

'Are you thinking about Adam? Wondering what it would have been like living here with him?'

She couldn't help the blood rushing up her cheeks. 'I should have remembered you can read my mind. Adam is … dead. You're here. I want you here.'

'So you say.' This time he did drop her foot.

She pretended not to notice and crossed her legs. 'I can't change the past, but I have learned to live with it. And I do love you.'

'The lady doth protest too much.'

Placing the mug on the table, she leaned in close to him, raised his chin with her fingertip and kissed him.

The door opened and Katie burst in with Louis by the hand. 'Can you two do that somewhere else? And what am *I* supposed to do today?'

'What do you mean?' Lottie said, drawing away from Boyd.

'Bubbles is closed. Sinéad phoned to tell me. God, Mam, I hope you find Evan soon. How am I supposed to work with no one to mind Louis?'

'Ask Chloe.'

'I did, but the witch said she was working late last night and needs to sleep. Some sister she is. I should have stayed in America.'

'What about Sean? He's on his Easter holidays.'

'And have him feed Louis Pot Noodles all day? Don't think so.'

'Then you'll have to ask Granny Rose.'

'Okay, I'll give her a call.'

'She adores Louis.'

'Yeah, for half an hour. She loves to be able to hand him back when she runs out of books to read him following the sixty-fifth episode of *Peppa Pig*.'

'She'll be delighted.' Lottie lifted Louis up and smothered him with kisses. 'Be a good boy for Granny Rose, won't you?'

'Stay with me, Nana Lottie.'

'Not today, sweetie. Maybe Saturday.' She put the boy down. 'See you later, soldier.'

Katie took his hand. 'He'll be in bed by the time you get home. I know what you're like when you have a big case.' She stomped out of the kitchen.

Lottie sighed loudly. 'Kids.'

'They keep you young,' Boyd said, and drew her into a hug. 'I better go. Might grab a shower here before I leave, if you don't mind?'

'Not at all. I hope there's enough hot water.'

Once she was alone in the kitchen, a feeling of loneliness hugged her body. She wanted to stay at home and mind her grandson. She didn't want to think about work. She'd made a resolution when she began the move that this was to be her home and the job was to stay in the office. But a tremor shook her as she thought of Isabel Gallagher's murder, and the missing child and his mother. Hopefully it was just a row between Joyce and Nathan. He'd seemed so edgy.

Definitely something wrong there. She needed to get her game face on. These cases were going to take every ounce of energy and focus.

After rinsing the mugs, she opened the refrigerator to stow the carton of milk inside. Boyd's bottles of Heineken lined the bottom shelf. She slammed the door shut. She was stronger than her temptation. But was she stronger than her addiction?

She tidied up the laundry and lifted his suit jacket from the back of the chair to leave it in the hall for him. As she moved it, she heard something crinkle in the pocket. Stop, Lottie. Do not snoop. But she had to.

She patted down the jacket. The tip of a white envelope peeked out from the inside pocket. Sealed. Boyd's name and his address on the outside. If she wanted to be sexist, she'd have guessed the handwriting was distinctly feminine. Who was writing to Boyd, and why hadn't he opened the letter? Who wrote letters any more?

Quickly she eased it back inside and hung the jacket on the chair the way it had been. She knew she'd be wondering about it all day. Then again, she'd be too busy to think about it at all.

She had a little boy to find.

*

She wasn't dead. Joyce knew that much at least. It was obvious because she could open her eyes and breathe, albeit with difficulty. Her face was sticky with blood, and through a dim haze she recalled a looming figure, dressed all in white, standing over her before he rained blows down on her crouched body. She had no idea what she'd been struck with, but the pain had been so intense, she must have passed out.

Now she was awake.

Her body silently screamed with each tentative breath she took and with every slight move she made. Trying to feel the floor with her feet, she held in the screeches she so wanted to utter. The blades. The soles of her feet were cut and bleeding. She welcomed the pain. It meant she was alive. What else had he done to her? Her face? He'd sliced her skin with the blades.

Slumping back against the steel wall, she wondered why she was still alive. In a way she wished she were dead, but she had Evan to think about.

Oh sweet Jesus! Had he taken her little boy? No! She couldn't handle that. She would gladly take whatever torture was meted out as long as a hair on her son's head wasn't touched. Surely he'd have been safe with Sinéad until Nathan arrived home from Europe? They'd know then that she was missing and the police would be searching for her. But would they find her in time? Before her abductor finished her off.

Recently Nathan had been tense and irritable, snapping at her and Evan for no good reason. Like having to wear the same shirt two days in a row because she hadn't dried the laundry. Then there were the long periods of intolerable silence, so profound you could almost hear it. And here she was trapped in some sort of container with only silence for company.

She cried. Big ugly tears.

This was hopeless. *She* was hopeless.

Then she stopped crying. She couldn't lose hope. She had a son. No one was taking Evan away from her or her from him. She was stronger than this. She'd come through worse circumstances, hadn't she? She had survived then, she could survive now.

She had to live for Evan.

She had to escape.

But how?

CHAPTER THIRTY-ONE

Sitting on the edge of the mattress, Larry Kirby coughed and coughed. Time to give up the damn cigars, he thought. He eyed the mess on the floor. Time for a deep clean, too.

When the coughing subsided, he yawned and waited. Running a hand under his nose, he wiped it on the sheets. They needed a good washing. He could tip into Primark and buy a new cheap set. Easier than washing and trying to dry them without a clothes line. He could always hang them on the radiators, but he was saving on oil and only put on the heat when it was absolutely necessary. Like when icicles dripped from his nose.

He found his trousers on the floor, with a handkerchief stuffed in the pocket. He blew his nose and tossed the snotty rag on top of the dirty laundry. Picking up his phone, he noticed he'd forgotten to charge it after coming home from the Foleys' house. It was dead as a dodo.

Shit.

Plugging it in, he waited for the juice to reach the target so that he could check his messages. Since Boyd now had Lottie, the people he called friends were at the grand total of nil. But he had long since given up feeling sorry for himself, so he hauled his arse into the shower.

When he was washed and dressed, he stood in the untidy bedroom and peered through the grimy pane of glass, ignoring the empty whiskey bottle on the floor between the bed and the wall. The reason he'd forgotten to charge his phone, perhaps.

He had to sort himself out. Get a life and a wife, like McKeown had told him in the office yesterday. Martina Brennan was wasting her time on McKeown. But Kirby was not one to cast aspersions aloud, so he normally kept his gob shut. Until yesterday. Maybe he shouldn't have said anything. Why had he? Perhaps he just liked Martina and didn't want to see her hurt. Shit, McKeown would be gunning for him now.

With two per cent battery, he checked his phone. Oh no! He saw the number he'd last called and hazily remembered making a drunken call last night. Holy Mother of God, had he really done that? He gripped his head and tugged at his hair. Fuck.

He had to stop drinking alone. And he had to get into work before Lottie ate him for breakfast. He hoped his late-night phone call wouldn't come back to haunt him.

*

The water was cold, but all the same, Boyd had a quick dip in and out, then ran his spare razor quickly over his chin before checking in the mirror and touching up the bits he'd missed. He paused. His skin was a pasty white, like dough left to prove, and the circles around his eyes were dark sacks. If his mother was still alive, she'd have him tucked up in bed with a glass of hot milk and a plate piled high with a sizzling fry and thick slices of brown bread. He smiled as he thought of the strong woman who'd raised him and his sister.

Maybe he and Lottie could head to the west to see how Grace was getting on. A weekend staring out at the wild Atlantic Ocean might help get some colour back in his cheeks. If they found the missing boy and Isabel Gallagher's murderer, they could take a few days off. This thought brought a smile to his tired face as he dressed in yesterday's clothes.

He tied his laces and tugged his trousers at the ankles, bemoaning the creases from Lottie having kicked his clothes from the bed to the floor. He'd have to stop by his own apartment and change his underwear and shirt. Damn. He'd stocked the fridge with lager, positioned his toothbrush and razor in the bathroom in a glass he'd brought with him, but he had no spare socks or boxers.

At the top of the splintered staircase, his eyes met Chloe's as she came out of her room.

'Morning, Boyd,' she said, her voice sombre, her eyes circled with dark rings. She pulled the knot tight on her dressing gown emblazoned with a large image of Winnie-the-Pooh.

'Hi, Chloe. Just on my way to work.'

'In that shirt? You're losing it, Boyd,' she laughed. 'My mother is having a bad effect on you.'

Was she sending him a message or just being jokey? He never would get kids. At least he and Sean got on.

'Are you okay?' Chloe's voice rose from a mist and he cleared his head with a shake.

'Yeah, just tired.'

'Oh-oh.' She winked.

'Not what you're thinking.' He grinned. 'I'm digging a hole for myself, aren't I?'

'You sure are. Wish I had my own place. I was working past two and my sister thinks it's okay to wake me at this ungodly hour. Much as I love Louis, I could do with another few hours in bed. Bathroom free?' She dragged a towel along the floor behind her.

Downstairs, he grabbed his jacket from the kitchen and his overcoat from the banister and left the Parker kids to their big old creaking house.

CHAPTER THIRTY-TWO

On the drive into work, Lottie brushed off thoughts of the letter she'd seen in Boyd's pocket. Whatever it was it was his own business. Today was going to be focused and productive. Nothing was going to avert her or her team from finding Evan and his mother, plus the bastard who'd killed Isabel.

She found a new sense of determination as she approached the station, but her resolve diminished on seeing the media scrum outside. She parked in the yard, found the rear door locked and had to make her way through the reporters to get to the front door. She uttered no comment to questions on the missing boy, and pushed inside, where she was met with more mayhem.

The woman was not for moving. Mid thirties, long brown hair swirling around her shoulders, a child maybe a year old sitting on her hip, a little girl not more than two or three holding her hand and a slightly older boy sitting on the bench inside the door threading beads onto a string. Steps of the stairs, as Rose would call them.

'I want to see him! I want to see him right now,' the woman ranted, swishing her hair this way and that.

'Can I help you?' Lottie said.

The woman swung around. 'I want Sam McKeown down here immediately.'

Lottie glanced at the duty sergeant and was met with a head shake.

'Detective McKeown isn't in yet. I'm his superior, Detective Inspector Parker. Maybe I can help you?'

The woman snorted. 'Might have known he'd have a woman over him.'

'I beg your pardon?'

'Forget it. He should be here. He told me he's working every hour that God sends.'

'Can I ask your name?'

'Melissa. His wife.'

Shite.

'Please, Melissa, it's more private in this office.' She indicated the small room used for form-filling.

'I'm not moving an inch until he talks to me. He told me he has a new case. Couldn't get time off to mind these. I have an appointment this morning.'

Lottie felt a growing sense of unease in her chest. 'If you wait in there, you can try ringing him.'

Melissa hustled the toddler onto her other hip. 'I'm blue in the face ringing him. He won't answer. Where is he?'

'Do you want me to leave a message on his desk?'

'I want you to get him in here!' The shout swerved into hysteria. 'I'm at my wits' end. Radio him or something. I'm not leaving until you find him.'

No way was she getting caught up in McKeown's marital woes. 'I'm sorry, Melissa, but as this is a personal issue, there's nothing I can do. Leave me your number and I'll make sure he contacts you.'

'He knows my bloody number.' She turned on her heel and sat on the bench beside the little boy. 'I'm not moving until I speak to him.' She rummaged in her large black leather bag, took out a bottle and began feeding the child in her arms.

Lottie relented. 'Okay. I'll see if I can ... locate him.'

She fled up to the office and phoned McKeown. It went to message. Kirby waltzed in. 'What's with happy families down in reception?'

'McKeown's wife and kids.'

Kirby blushed to his roots. 'His wife? What's she doing here?'

'Not moving until she sees him.' Lottie stared at the phone. 'Any idea where he could be?'

'Eh … I think he might be with Garda Brennan.'

'Have you a number for her?'

'Why would I have a number for her?'

'You're blushing, Kirby.'

'I'm not.'

Lottie pulled up the staff list on her computer and scrolled until she found the contact details for Garda Brennan. Kirby hovered at the door. 'What?'

'I think he's having an affair.'

'Really, Sherlock?'

'Look, boss, it might be best to let McKeown walk into his own fire. Don't get involved.'

The outer door opened, then shut. Lynch popped her head around Kirby's bulky frame. 'What's going on in reception? It's like a crèche down there.'

'McKeown's wife and kids,' Lottie said as she rang Garda Brennan's mobile.

Lynch gasped. 'Oh, this is going to get messy.'

Listening to the call go to message, Lottie stared at Lynch. 'Do you have any way of contacting him?'

'Did you try his mobile?'

'Good God, Lynch.' She couldn't help rolling her eyes. 'Why didn't I think of that?'

'Just trying to help.'

'This is all we need. A family crisis while we're swamped with work.'

'If I were you, boss,' Lynch said, 'I'd let him sort out his own mess.'

'Like it or not, McKeown is one of my team. I have to see what I can do.'

'Don't you at least feel sorry for his wife?' Lynch said. 'He's fucking around while she's stuck at home with three kids. I say let him sink.'

Holding the phone away from her, Lottie watched Lynch stride to her desk and shrug out of her coat. Kirby hopped from foot to foot before following his colleague. Maybe they were right. She put down the phone and sat with her chin on her hand. McKeown could sort out his own shit.

With that decision made, she began checking the night shift's reports to see if there were updates on the missing woman and child, or anything new on the murder investigation. Before she could fully concentrate, Superintendent Farrell rang.

'My office, Parker, and make it quick.'

The day that kept on giving, and it was only eight a.m.

'Sit down.'

No greeting, so Lottie sat.

Superintendent Deborah Farrell wore a stern face and a sharply ironed uniform shirt. She took her tie from the uncluttered desk and clipped it on. Trouble.

'What's the news on Evan and Joyce Breslin?'

'Sparse,' Lottie said. 'So far no witnesses to Evan's abduction and no sighting of Joyce or her car.'

'I'm taking control of the media and public appeals. I want all the information you have as soon as you have it. Photos of the child and his mother have been dispatched to every media outlet, Facebook and the like. We've set up checkpoints throughout the county.' She picked up a TV remote control. 'Now watch this, and no comment until it ends.'

Farrell pointed the remote at the flat-screen television on the wall. On the screen, a ticker tape flashed beneath the image of a studio in the form of a welcoming sitting room.

'What the—' Lottie began.

'Not a word.'

Lottie watched incredulously as Jack Gallagher leaned towards the young woman conducting the interview. Clean-shaven, his dark hair flopping over his forehead, he was dressed in jeans and white shirt. Face solemn. Hands rugged. Fingers interlaced.

'Welcome back. I'm Penny Campbell, and with me this morning is Jack Gallagher. As you might know, Jack's wife, Isabel, was found murdered in their home early yesterday morning. Our sincere condolences, Jack.'

'Thank you, Penny.'

'Can you tell our viewers why you've agreed to do this interview?'

His name popped up on the screen. He bowed his head and bit his lip.

Penny prompted, 'Your wife, Isabel, was brutally murdered in your own home, and this morning you have a message for the public.'

'The fucking cheek—' Lottie began, before Farrell cut her off again. Jack was speaking.

'My Isabel meant the world to me and Holly. Holly is our daughter. She's only three and a half months old.' He paused, choking back a sob, before continuing. 'Someone broke in to our home and stabbed my wife in front of our daughter's eyes. Who could do such a thing?' He wiped his eyes, though Lottie couldn't see any tears.

The presenter leaned forward and placed her hand on his, an intimate gesture to resonate with her viewers. Lottie scowled. This woman was the ultimate professional. Wagon.

'This is difficult for you, Jack. Take your time.'

He raised his head, nodded. 'Whoever carried out this awful … horrific crime is out there and someone knows who they are. I'm pleading with your viewers to help me find whoever murdered my wife.'

'Isn't that a job for the gardaí?'

'Yes, but I can't sit at home and do nothing. I need to be actively involved. The gardaí do things their own way, which is way too slow for me. I'm imploring your viewers to take a long, hard look at those around them. I believe Isabel was murdered between seven and nine yesterday morning. The killer must have been covered in her blood. The scene … it was an awful sight to behold.'

Lottie fumed. 'For fuck's sake, he hasn't even been inside the house.'

'Unless he committed the crime,' Farrell said quietly, pausing the screen.

'Shite in a bucket.' Lottie couldn't contain her anger. 'He's a dangerous bastard. And he's relishing this limelight.'

She looked at the time on the bottom right of the screen. The interview had been broadcast over half an hour ago. The phones would be hopping soon. 'I need to bring him in. I have to find out why he's jeopardising our investigation.'

'Why wasn't he already in custody?' Farrell asked calmly. Too calmly.

'He was nowhere near the crime scene when his wife was murdered. We have witnesses who place him nearly twenty kilometres away at the time.'

'You've confirmed time of death, then?'

'It was between seven and nine, according to the pathologist. Unless he's a magician, it'd be physically impossible for him to be in two places at once.'

'Unless … he orchestrated the whole thing. Got somebody else to carry out the murder.'

Lottie stared at her superintendent. Was Farrell watching too much Netflix? Real crime never turned out to be as fanciful as fictional crime. Then again …

'Play the remainder of the interview.' She leaned forward, elbows on knees, as the screen unfroze and the presenter continued.

'Did the investigating officers allow you into the house?'

'No, but I can imagine what it was like. They said Isabel was stabbed. There must have been a lot of blood. Whoever did it would have bloody clothes. Someone knows who did this.'

'Bloody clothes?' Lottie said. 'What is he now? An amateur detective? A forensic analyst? Making a laughing stock of us, that's what he's doing.' She shut up and listened to the presenter with her fake concern, relishing her ratings hitting the roof.

'Do you want to speak directly to the killer if they're watching this morning?'

Gallagher straightened his back on the low couch and held up his hands. 'Isabel was my whole world. Why have you taken her from me? You've left a little baby without her mother. Please, give yourself up.'

'Thank you, Jack.' Penny turned to face another camera, her mourner's mask in place.

'Rewind it a few seconds,' Lottie said, standing. She moved towards the screen. 'There. Stop. Start it again.'

She watched as Jack straightened himself and held out his hands. 'Pause it there.'

Farrell came and stood beside her.

'See his hands,' Lottie said.

'Okay. What am I looking for?'

'Those marks. They're like cuts.'

'Don't seem to be fresh.'

'I know, but Isabel had cuts to her feet and thigh. Not recent, but all the same ... Why didn't I notice them yesterday?' Lottie turned and headed for the door. 'Where is that studio?'

'Dublin. He's probably on his way back by now. Where is he staying?'

'His mother-in-law's. I'll be waiting for him, and I'm bringing him in.'

Farrell switched off the television. 'I advise you to tread very carefully. If he is the killer, he's slick. He'll be two steps ahead of you at all times.'

'I know. Thanks. Even if he's innocent, what sort of grieving husband does a television interview the day after his wife was murdered, and without informing us first?'

'An extremely clever one.'

CHAPTER THIRTY-THREE

The office was in uproar when Lottie returned from Farrell's room.

'You can fuck off, McKeown,' Lynch screeched. She was backed up against a filing cabinet, McKeown, towering ogre-like, reaching across the desk trying to grab her. His hand just missed but snatched a fistful of hair.

Lottie roared, 'McKeown! Back off. This instant.'

'She's a bloody weasel, that's what she is.' He rubbed his hand over his pate, which was as red as his cheeks. 'A snitch. A rat. A—'

Lottie caught his arm and dragged him away. She flashed a look at Kirby, who was standing by the door, ready to run. 'What are you doing just standing there? Why didn't you intervene?'

'It got out of hand quickly,' he said.

'I'll say it did.' Lynch flopped onto her chair, pointing a finger at McKeown. 'Stark raving lunatic, so you are. I don't care what's going on in your life, but I'm owed an apology and an explanation for this obnoxious outburst.'

'You'll get no apology from me, bigmouth.' McKeown curled his hands into fists, tight by his sides.

'Calm down.' Lottie pushed him onto his chair. 'Is this to do with your wife and kids downstairs?'

'So *you* know about it and all. A room full of squealers. I should have realised it'd come to this. Just because I'm an outsider, you all think you can do the dirty behind my back.'

'Hey!' Kirby said. 'The only one doing the dirty behind anyone's back around here is you, buster. Everyone in the station knows about your carry-on. It was only a matter of time before it got back to your poor wife.'

'It's my business. Not yours, you fat fuck.'

'Cool it!' Lottie stepped in between the two men before rounding on McKeown. 'Take your wife home and sort it out. And when you return tomorrow, you better apologise to your colleagues. This is your mess, McKeown, yours alone, and you need to fix it.'

He shunted back his shoulders defiantly. 'I'm not going home. I've a job to do here.'

'Not in this state, you don't. Leave before I suspend you.'

'Suspend?' Lynch shouted. 'Fire him!'

Lottie groaned. Where the hell was Boyd? His calm head was needed for this spiralling mess.

'Okay, okay,' McKeown conceded. 'I'm leaving. But don't expect any apology from me until whoever told Melissa owns up.' He glared at Lynch, grabbed his coat from the floor where he'd flung it and stomped out of the office, jabbing his fist into the door for good measure, leaving behind a dented arc.

Lottie exhaled a breath of relief. 'Now who is going to tell me what the hell is going on here?'

Boyd stuck his head around the door. 'Did I miss something?'

*

With things relatively calm and Lynch sulking, Kirby raced through the reports that uniforms had collated about the missing child and his mother. Nothing relevant jumped out at him. As he munched through a bag of crisps, wondering if it was too early for a smoke break, a call came through.

'Kirby,' he said, picking crisps out of his teeth.

Garda Martina Brennan sounded confident on the line, and he wondered if she had been spared the McKeown debacle.

When he hung up, Lottie was prowling around his desk.

'Got a report in, boss,' he said. 'There's a car abandoned in a ditch, close to Lough Cullion. Side window smashed.'

'Did you get the make and colour? Licence plate?'

'Black Ford Focus. Reg number matches Joyce Breslin's car.'

'What are you waiting for? Get out there. Make sure there isn't a body in the lake. Anything further on the whereabouts of the boy following all the alerts we issued?'

'Nothing so far,' Kirby said, looking guiltily at the reports piled high on his desk.

Lottie slapped a hand on the files. 'This shite should have been written up. I've reports and spreadsheets coming out of my ears, and do you know something?'

'What, boss?'

'You're slacking.' She sniffed the air around him.

'I haven't been drinking,' he lied.

She pulled back and laid a hand on his shoulder. 'Yeah? And I'm your mother.'

'I'm fine, honestly.' He hid a yawn, conscious that she had a nose like a Rottweiler and would definitely smell the stale stench of alcohol. 'Are you serious about searching the lake for a body?'

'Assess the scene first. Broken window suggests foul play. Do the usual checks and arrange to get it out of the ditch.'

'I'll take Lynch with me.'

'I need Lynch for FLO work. Take Garda Brennan. Traffic will be there, so why are you still here?' She smiled, but Kirby could see it didn't reach her eyes. Stone-cold green emeralds this morning, and he wondered if all was not as rosy as it could be at Farranstown House.

'Okay, I'm gone.' He grabbed his coat and left her mooching through the unfinished reports on his desk.

Rather you than me, boss, he thought.

CHAPTER THIRTY-FOUR

Lottie checked the overnight updates. Not a thing had been reported about Evan's whereabouts. The house-to-house enquires had yielded no clues or witnesses to the alleged abduction. Checkpoints had been set up around the county, and she perused the data but found nothing to lift her mood. She followed up with everyone who'd been tasked with finding Evan, fervently hoping that he and his mother were not at the bottom of the lake.

Because Superintendent Farrell had taken command of the missing persons media briefings and alerts, Lottie turned her thoughts to Jack Gallagher. He had refused the presence of a family liaison officer yesterday, and now she suspected she knew why. He was turning out to be a cunning individual who didn't want to be beholden to anyone. She was sure Isabel had been totally under his control. Domestic abuse by denying her money. His television appearance gave that scenario added weight. He was a bloody control freak. But did that make him a murderer?

She grabbed her jacket and nodded to Lynch to follow her out to the car. Sitting into the passenger seat, she waited for the detective to get behind the wheel.

'Thought we'd be having a recap meeting this morning,' Lynch said, 'but it looks like I'm driving. Where are we off to?'

'Wisteria Villas. Anita Boland's house. I'll fill you in. I'm too angry to drive. I'd probably knock someone down on the way.'

*

Anita greeted them at the door, little Holly asleep on her shoulder. The woman looked decidedly older than yesterday, her trendy clothing replaced with baggy tracksuit bottoms with a floaty white T-shirt, and her feet shod in black Ugg slippers.

'Sorry, the place is a mess.' She led them into the kitchen at the back of the house. 'I'm not used to caring for a baby, and the neighbours have been calling all morning with food. You can take some home if you like.'

Every available surface was full of Pyrex dishes and trays of sandwiches.

'Where is Jack?' Lottie said.

'I don't actually know.' Anita sat by the table, cradling the child to her chest.

'Did you watch *Good Morning Ireland* earlier?'

'Are you joking me? I hadn't time to brush my teeth or make a cup of tea, let alone switch on the television. Why?'

Lottie motioned to the kettle; Anita nodded.

Lynch filled it and flicked the switch. 'Mugs?'

'Shelf to your right.'

'Where is Jack?' Lottie repeated.

Anita patted her granddaughter's head. 'I haven't seen him since yesterday. He left me here all alone with Holly. Just walked out. I hope he didn't go back to their house. It'd break him altogether.'

'The house is sealed off and under guard. SOCOs are still working there. It could be a week before it's released back to Jack.'

Anita shrugged a shoulder. 'I honestly don't know where else he would go.'

Lottie believed her. 'Jack appeared on television this morning, making a plea for Isabel's killer to come forward.'

'He what?' Anita paled and her hand shook so violently that Holly opened her eyes momentarily, before drifting back to sleep. 'Why would he do that?'

'I thought you might know.'

'I … I have no idea. He never said anything. Perhaps the TV show contacted him?'

'I phoned the producer. Jack contacted them.'

'Is he still there?'

'No. I've put an alert out on his van.'

'Surely you don't suspect Jack …?' Anita's mouth dropped open as she realised the enormity of what she was about to say. 'You think he did that awful thing to my daughter, don't you? And this is his way of deflecting attention.'

'Everyone is a suspect until they're not.' Lottie trotted out her old adage.

Anita's eyes flashed with anger. 'Why didn't you lock him up yesterday, if you thought he did it?'

The kettle whistled. Lynch said, 'Would you like tea or coffee?'

'Tea would be good,' Anita said. 'I don't understand any of this.'

'Neither do I,' Lottie said.

Lynch began opening the lids of canisters in search of tea bags.

'The cupboard beside the one where you found the mugs.'

'Detective Lynch will be here as your family liaison officer. You need to have someone with you at all times.'

'This is my worst nightmare.'

'I know,' Lottie said. 'It's a terrible time for you. Is there any other family who could stay with you?'

'It's just me and Isabel … I mean, it's just me now.' Her eyes were wild with fear and her voice trembled. 'I have to keep him away from Holly.'

'Don't worry, once he returns, we'll be taking him to the station to interview him.'

Lynch poured the boiling water on top of the tea bags and fetched milk, then set a mug in front of Anita.

The woman lifted it to her lips before putting it down again. 'That's the front door.'

Jack Gallagher sauntered into the kitchen. 'What are you two doing here? Are they annoying you, Anita? Will I take Holly?'

'Where were you, Jack?' Anita said coldly, holding the baby tightly.

Lynch and Lottie stood.

Lottie said, 'Jack, we have further questions we'd like you to answer. You need to come with me.'

'I'm going nowhere with you or anyone else for that matter. I need to be with Holly.'

'Didn't stop you disappearing yesterday, did it, leaving her with Anita. Or driving up to Dublin and plastering your face all over the television.'

'That's my business.'

'No, Jack,' Lottie said. 'Everything you do and everywhere you go is our business while we are investigating your wife's murder. From what we know so far, you were the last person to see her alive.'

'You know nothing then, because the killer was the last person to see her alive. If this is the way you want to play it, I'm phoning a solicitor.'

'You do that. Then you're coming with us.'

He yanked his phone out of his pocket and moved out of the kitchen. Lynch followed close behind.

Placing a hand on Anita's shoulder, Lottie said, 'Have you got everything you need for Holly? Baby formula, nappies?'

'I think I'm okay for now, but all I can really give her is love and the reassurance that I'll protect her with all my heart. I failed my daughter, Inspector, I'm not going to fail Holly.'

Lynch returned with Gallagher. 'Solicitor will meet him at the station.'

'Let's get going,' Lottie said.

'Bring a tray of sandwiches with you,' Anita said.

CHAPTER THIRTY-FIVE

It had been an awkward and silent drive out to the lake with Garda Martina Brennan. Kirby had come to the conclusion that keeping his mouth shut was the best option after the earlier McKeown debacle.

He mumbled to himself as they approached the two traffic gardaí standing by the abandoned car at the end of the lane to the lake. Doors open. Side window smashed.

'The keys are in the ignition,' Martina said.

Kirby slouched around the rear of the car, his shoes slipping in the damp reeds. 'Any sign of the occupant?'

'No.' Garda Fuery shook his head. He was tall and scarecrow thin, his hat sitting like a sleeping black cat on his narrow skull. 'My colleague walked the shoreline. I've called for support to trek through the woods.'

'Good. Did you open the boot?' Kirby stuck the stub of an unlit cigar in the corner of his mouth.

'Yeah. Found a few reusable shopping bags. All empty.'

'Licence plate has the number Nathan Monaghan gave the boss last night.' Kirby glanced inside. 'No blood visible.' That was good, wasn't it?

He pulled on nitrile gloves and opened the back door first. A child's booster seat with a bundle of picture books on it. He paused before running his hand along the seat and down behind it. Searched through the pockets on the back of the seats. Nothing.

In the front, he flicked open the glove compartment. A packet of chocolate buttons and a child's hat. He crouched down and searched under the passenger seat and in the footwell, followed by the driver's seat. Same result. Then he tried along by the handbrake. His fingers touched something. An envelope. He glanced inside. Shit.

Hauling himself out of the car, he asked for an evidence bag. Brennan fetched one and Kirby spread it out on the bonnet of the car and laid the envelope on top.

Brennan leaned in beside him. 'A razor blade.'

'Isabel Gallagher was found with a razor blade in her hand.' Kirby glanced at her. 'Could mean her murder and the disappearance of Joyce and Evan are linked.'

'There's a piece of paper, too,' Brennan said.

Kirby teased back the flap and read the words on the scrap of paper. 'The Occupier, 14 Castlemain Drive.'

'That's the big estate on the west side of Ragmullin,' Brennan said. 'Over two hundred houses.'

'I know where it is.'

'Joyce Breslin doesn't live there.'

'I know that too.' He put everything in the evidence bag, then signed, dated and sealed it before handing it to Brennan. 'SOCOs can have a look at these.'

Lighting a cigar, he inhaled deeply before coughing and spluttering in the cold air. The lake looked as rough as he was feeling. The waves, tossing white froth over the stones, made his stomach churn.

'What do you suggest we do?' Garda Fuery languished by the rear of the car.

'I'll get SOCOs to check it first, then you can make yourself useful. Call Hartnett's Recovery to bring their off-loader and take the car to wherever SOCOs want it. Can you do that?'

'Sure I can.' The guard sloped back to the squad car.

Kirby extinguished the cigar between his fingers and inspected the broken glass on the road. He circled the car slowly. Standing behind it, he glanced down at the lake, then back at the glass. It looked like it had been smashed with a hammer or something similar.

'Why break the glass?' He stood beside Brennan. 'What does it look like to you?'

'Well,' she said, tapping the radio clipped to her hi-vis vest, 'it could be a carjacking.'

'But why was she out here, and where is she now?'

They moved away and sat into their car.

'You don't have to keep giving me the cold shoulder,' she said.

'Don't know what you're talking about.'

'I know there's gossip behind my back about Sam and me. I heard his wife appeared at the station this morning.'

'What do you want me to say? I'm not the one who dirtied his bib in public.'

'I thought you at least would be different to the others. My mistake.'

He ran a hand through his bushy hair. 'What are you talking about?'

'You seemed more human. I thought you'd be on my side. After all, you and Gilly O'Dono—'

'Stop right there. Gilly and I were two single people. Neither of us was involved in an affair. Not like McKeown.'

'I meant the difference in rank.'

'That's bullshit and you know it. McKeown is a cheat. When did you find out he was married?'

She blew out a long sigh. 'This morning, when I heard about his wife and kids turning up.'

'Don't give me that crap.'

'All right.' She slouched down in the seat. 'I suspected it. Didn't know for sure.'

'But you went ahead and fucked him anyhow.' He regretted he'd said it when he saw the hurt in her eyes.

'You don't have to be so crude,' she said softly.

'Sorry. What you and McKeown do is your own business. But when it impacts on working relations in the station, then it's everybody's business. Do you get me?'

'Think so.'

Tears were streaking mascara down her cheeks. Brennan had always been fun, and like Kirby, she loved her food. They'd often shared a McDonald's together. He resisted the urge to push a wayward strand of her fair hair behind her ear.

'Give him the boot,' he said. 'That's my advice, for what it's worth. He has a wife and three kids.'

'I know, but—'

'There's no but in this situation. Ask yourself, where is he now?'

'He followed her home to Athlone.'

'See?'

'No, I don't bloody see anything.' She folded her arms awkwardly over the seat belt, which strained across her stab vest and hi-vis jacket.

'Martina, you're not naive. McKeown didn't rush to you when this blew up earlier. He went to his wife. Tells its own tale.'

She wiped her nose with the back of her hand, like a sad child. 'Suppose so. But I think I love him.'

'Listen to what you're saying. You only think it. What does anyone know about love anyway? I was married and thought I knew all about it. I met Gilly and thought I knew then. But now, with all that I've lost, I really don't know what the hell love is. Overrated, if you ask me.'

She laughed then. 'You're a tonic, you know that, Kirby.'

'That's good to know. Now all we need is a strong drink.'

'Care to help me drown my sorrows?'

'What do you mean?'

'Come for a drink with me.'

Kirby felt a smile break out on his face. 'That's the best offer I've had in ages.'

'Is that a yes?'

'Don't you think you need time to get over McKeown?'

'I'm not asking for a shag, just a drink.'

'I'm not sure about a drink, sweetheart.'

'And I'm not your sweetheart.'

'Sorry.' Shit.

'Not yet, anyhow.'

'Fine so.' He let his grin spread from ear to ear.

'Kirby, I'm just lonely.'

'So am I, so am I.' He shook himself back into work mode. 'We better get out of here, or they'll start talking about us.'

He glanced in the rear-view mirror to see Garda Fuery standing in the middle of the road, smirking.

'For fuck's sake.'

He gunned the engine, then raced up the lane and onto the road, away from spying eyes.

CHAPTER THIRTY-SIX

For the second day in a row, Jack Gallagher sat before Lottie and Boyd in the interview room. This time he had a solicitor by his side. She seemed too young to have sat her Leaving Cert, let alone to have qualified as a solicitor.

Lottie watched mesmerised as the black-haired woman's fingers fluttered through a file of paperwork before thumbing a diary and marking off notes with a bitten-down Bic biro. She knew all about looks being deceiving, so she'd have to be alert.

After the formalities were dispensed with for the recording, Jack folded his arms and set his mouth in a thin line. Lottie could hear the 'no comment' before it was even uttered.

Lilian Regan opened her mouth and a set of glistening teeth glared across the table. 'My client, Mr Gallagher, is extremely upset by your actions today. He has cooperated fully with your investigation into the murder of his wife. He does not see any reason to be in here, once again.'

'It's just an interview; he hasn't been charged with any offence,' Lottie said.

The solicitor opened her mouth again, then shut it. Flicked a few pages in the file and closed it. Her file was thicker than the murder file being compiled by Lottie's team. Time to cut to the chase.

'Mr Gallagher, earlier today you appeared on *Good Morning Ireland*. What was your reason for doing that?'

'I want my wife's killer found and you lot are sitting on your arses doing nothing except harassing me. I had to do something.'

'You could be hindering our investigation.'

'There's nothing to hinder, because you're doing fuck all.'

Regan laid a demure hand on his arm. 'Please, Mr Gallagher. Don't answer unless I say so.'

He brushed off her hand and laid his on the table.

Lottie noticed how scrubbed his skin looked. Was she reading more into him than necessary? She saw the little cuts on his fingers.

'Why didn't you ask us for permission first?'

'I'm a free citizen last time I checked.'

For now, Lottie thought. 'We're trying to eliminate you from our investigation, so I'd like your permission to check your phone and to triangulate its whereabouts between six a.m. and nine a.m. yesterday.'

A deep puce flushed up his cheeks and settled in the rings under his eyes. 'You what?'

'You heard me.'

Regan butted in. 'My client has no wish to—'

'I can speak for myself,' Gallagher said.

'Please do,' Lottie said.

'My phone is my own private device. You have no business checking it. I've given you a full statement on my whereabouts yesterday morning, and I know you've checked with my colleagues and my boss. So why the hell do you need my phone?'

'Covering all bases. Doing a proper investigation.'

'While the scumbag who killed my wife is running around free?'

'There are procedures to follow.'

'Procedures my hole.'

'So can we have your phone and permission to—'

Her words were cut short by the smack of his phone on the table. 'Here. Take it. Check all you want. I've nothing to hide.'

In that instant, Lottie knew they'd find nothing incriminating.

Boyd bagged the phone.

She said, 'I need you to tell me why Isabel wasn't allowed a phone of her own and why she was kept a virtual prisoner in the house.'

'You what? You're losing your marbles, missus.' He bunched up his hands before loosening them and placing splayed fingers downwards. 'How many times do I have to repeat myself? Isabel didn't want a phone. She had a car, didn't she? So you can cut that prisoner crap.'

'I still can't understand the rush to do a television interview.'

'I'll do what I need to do to find who murdered my wife. And if I find him before you, which seems highly likely, I won't be responsible for what I do to him.'

'Did you really love her?' She tried to wrong-foot him.

'What?' He dragged his hands from the table to his lap, where Lottie couldn't see them, but she did notice a tic gathering pace at the side of his mouth. 'What do you mean?'

'Did you love your wife, Mr Gallagher?'

'Course I did. What kind of a question is that?'

'You've hardly shed a tear. The only emotion I sense is anger.'

The solicitor leaned forward. 'What are you trying to prove, Inspector?'

Lottie ignored her, keeping her focus on Gallagher. 'What type of marriage did you have? Happy? Sad? Volatile?'

'Volatile?' He straightened his back but his chin jutted forward. 'Who's been talking to you?'

'I'm asking the questions. So it was a volatile relationship, then?'

'You're twisting my words.'

'Sometimes words don't have to be twisted to get to the truth.'

'I'm telling you the truth now. Me and Isabel, we were happy until some lunatic decided to stab the life out of her.'

Time to wrong-foot him again. 'What happened to your hands?'

'What?'

'The cuts on your hands. How did you get them?'

He spread his fingers out flat and stared at them.

'You don't have to answer,' Regan said.

Raising his head slowly, he eyeballed Lottie. 'I cut my hands empty-ing the dishwasher. Isabel had a habit of putting the knives pointing upwards. Plus, I'm an electrician, a job that comes with its own dangers. Satisfied?'

'No,' Lottie said, but his words rang true. 'Your fingerprints and DNA were secured yesterday, and I'll get SOCOs to check your hands.'

'Yeah, do that and waste more time.'

'Where were you last night?'

'What?'

'Is "what" your favourite word?' Boyd couldn't help himself, and Lottie glared sideways at him.

'I was at Anita's.'

'She says different.' Lottie watched for a change in expression and was rewarded as he bit his lip and stared at a point on the wall above her head.

'I … I went for a walk. To clear my head. She was asleep when I got in, and then I left at five this morning to get to the television studio.'

Lottie picked up the bag with his phone. 'I'm sure this will help us pinpoint where you were and if you're telling us the truth.'

He bit his lip again.

'Do you know Joyce Breslin and her son Evan?'

His nostrils flared. 'Are they suspects?'

'They're missing. A mother and her four-year-old son.'

He shook his head. 'Heard something on the car radio this morning, but I don't know them.'

Regan tapped her closed file with the end of her chewed biro. The hum of the recording equipment was the only other sound breaking the silence.

'Is there anything you want to add, Mr Gallagher?' Lottie said eventually.

'I have nothing else to say to you.'

'If you're not charging my client with anything, we are leaving.' Lilian Regan stood and gathered her voluminous file, dark hair flying like a blackbird's wings in flight. 'Superintendent Farrell will receive a complaint about your treatment of my client.'

'I'm sure she will add it to her list.'

Lottie waited while Boyd opened the door and watched them exit.

When they were alone, he said, 'I'll get this phone to Gary in technical.'

'I want to know everywhere Gallagher's been and everyone he's been talking to or texting,' Lottie said. 'Do you think he's innocent?'

'If he's innocent, why can't he tell us where he was last night?'

'Another woman? We need to find out everything we can about him.'

'And we still have a missing child and his mother to find.'

Yes, they had. 'Get onto the lab and find out about the blood we found on the radiator at Joyce's and if SOCOs found anything else there. Ask them about the cuts on Gallagher's hands. Dishwasher? I don't know any more.'

CHAPTER THIRTY-SEVEN

If anything, the day was growing colder. An east wind blew around the side of the house and hit Kirby in the face. For what seemed like the tenth time, he pressed the doorbell of 14 Castlemain Drive, the address found in the envelope in Joyce's car.

Martina had decided to stay in the car to make a phone call. He didn't envy McKeown, if that was who she was calling.

He pressed the bell again.

Stepping back, he took another look up at the detached two-storey. The blinds were down and the white PVC door had faded to a sickly yellow. A rotting pumpkin wilted in the corner of the porch and a plastic skeleton hung from a flower hook on the wall. He had to scratch his head to remind himself how long it was since Halloween. Six months at least.

'You won't get an answer there.'

A woman stood at the gate with a buggy, a well-bundled-up child glaring at him from behind a clear rain cover.

'Oh, and you are?' Kirby went to join them.

'Who wants to know?'

'Detective Larry Kirby. Ragmullin garda station. I'm looking for whoever lives here.'

'I'm Meg Collentine. There's been no one in or out of that house for must be a couple of years. Gosh, maybe longer.'

'But someone put out Halloween decorations.'

'I don't pay much notice, but I'd say they've been there two years at least.'

'Good God,' Kirby said, thinking there was someone lazier than him after all. 'Any idea where the owner is now?'

'Nope. This is a large estate, as you can see, but it's a quiet community. I think Neighbourhood Watch has been on the case. Apparently the house is bought and paid for. No outstanding mortgage or rent. Nothing anyone can do. I just wonder where they went, is all.'

'They?'

'No one really knew them. They never interacted with the neighbours.'

Kirby scratched his head, vowing once again to get his hair cut. 'Them? They? Who are you talking about?'

'Never saw a husband or partner, but what do I know? I saw the woman in the supermarket one day. Young, pale thing she was. She looked terrified, if you want my opinion. But as I say, you make your bed, you lie in it. There was a little girl. I'd say she was maybe two, and I'm sure she had a baby with her that day. Not that I saw much of them.'

Kirby digested this information. 'Can you give me descriptions?'

'Sorry, that was a few years ago. A good while before they left.'

'And you have no idea where they are now?'

'Nope.'

'There's a black Ford Focus car associated with this house.' There wasn't really, except for the letter he'd found down the side of the seat. 'Did you see it here at any time?'

'I wouldn't know one car from the next. Maybe the family took it with them.'

'And no one reported their disappearance?'

'What was there to report?'

Kirby scratched his head again and glanced up at the house. It was in need of serious maintenance. The gutters hung off the roof, moss clung to the edges, weeds sprouted upwards. The walls were green from the weather. The grass at his feet was scraggy and overgrown.

'Can I have your phone number? Just in case I need to follow anything up.'

'What have they done?' Meg said, and recited her number automatically. 'They haven't been murdered, have they?'

'Just routine enquiries.'

She looked at him dubiously. 'I live around the back, two roads over. Number 171. I'm in the semis. Couldn't afford a detached. And I honestly know nothing about this house or who lived here.'

He scribbled her details into his notebook. 'Thank you.'

When she ambled off with her buggy, he walked around the side of the house. There was no gate, and two wheelie bins stood against the wall. He eased past them and rounded the corner. A concrete pathway bisected the overgrown back garden. No shrubs, flowers or toys. Graffiti on the rear wall.

He depressed the handle on the back door; it was locked. The upper half of the door had frosted squares of glass. He moved further along to the window. Arching his hands over his eyes, he peered through a gap where the blind hadn't reached the sill, but he couldn't make anything out. Maybe the family had emigrated. Wherever they'd gone, Kirby felt it was very odd. And why was there a scrap of paper with this address in Joyce Breslin's car?

He'd have to do more digging if he was to locate the missing woman and her son. It all might just be a wild goose chase.

*

Lottie postponed the team meeting until later. Jack Gallagher had crawled under her skin and nested there. She had to find out more about him. She headed off in the car. Alone.

It only took a few minutes to get to Quality Electrical, where she had to press an intercom at the gate to be admitted. Kirby had interviewed Mr Costello yesterday, but she wanted to hear for herself what he thought of Jack. Plus Isabel had worked here.

The compound was huge. A large unit with rolling doors to her left, and to her right, a bland two-storey building. The office. She headed inside and up the stairs.

'Thanks for seeing me, Mr Costello.'

'Not at all. I'll help any way I can. Tea, coffee?'

'I'm grand.' She took the chair in front of the desk while he seated himself behind it.

His eyes were clouded behind spectacles that seemed to dim in the light, and his ginger hair and untrimmed beard lent him a homely look.

'How is Jack holding up?' He leaned forward, his hands clasped on top of paperwork.

'What can you tell me about Jack Gallagher?'

'I hope this doesn't mean he killed his wife.'

'We are investigating all possibilities. So, what is he like?'

'As I told your colleague yesterday, he's a great worker. I've no complaint in that department.'

'But you have in others?'

'I'm sorry, that came out wrong.'

'Mr Costello, tell me what it is that's worrying you.'

He stretched back and ran a hand over his hair. 'It was more the way he was with Isabel. You know she worked here for a while?' Lottie nodded. He continued. 'That is, until he made her give up work.'

'Why did he do that?'

'I don't know. He was in and out of the office like a fly on shite. Pardon me.'

'It's fine.'

'He was round here as often as he could manage. Once he'd finished work for one client, he'd be back here with an excuse to pick up supplies for another, even though the rule is you stock your van the night before for the next day. Time is money and I don't tolerate waste.'

'What did you do about it?'

'I called him out on it. Accused him of checking up on his girlfriend all the time and said he was out of order.'

'And he didn't like that?'

'He apologised and said it wouldn't happen again. The next day Isabel handed in her notice.'

'It sounds like she was under his control.'

'Exactly what I thought.'

'How did she seem to you?'

'She was a lovely young woman. Friendly, smiling. A real hit with the lads and gals here. No job was too small for her. She'd make tea for anyone.'

'Was that her role?'

He paused and bit his lip, thinking. 'To be honest, she was employed as an office administrator, but it was too much for her. I ended up giving her light duties.'

'Why didn't you let her go if she couldn't do the job she was hired for?'

'Isabel brought sparkle to this dull place. I liked having her around.'

'Are you married, Mr Costello?' Lottie glanced around the office without spotting any family photographs.

'What has that got to do with anything?'

She donned her stony face and kept silent.

'No, I'm not married at the moment.' He grinned. 'I didn't fancy Isabel, if that's what you're implying, but I was sad to see her leave.'

'Did you hire another administrator?'

'I reckoned it wasn't worth the hassle of training someone else. I spend long hours here; a few extra hours at night and I save myself the cost of office admin.'

'A workaholic, like myself,' Lottie said.

'Doesn't leave much room for anything else. Are *you* married?'

'Widowed.' Why the hell had she said that? 'Let's get back to Jack.'

'Of course.' He was once again leaning forward, his scent warm and fresh.

'Jack got on well with everyone, is that right?'

'Well enough. But he didn't socialise with the crew. Kept to himself.'

'Did you tackle him about Isabel leaving?'

'I did. He told me it was none of my business. And he was right. If she wanted to leave, whether from coercion by her boyfriend or not, I had no right to interfere. But between you and me, I think he was insanely jealous of her being here all day.'

More proof of what Lottie believed to be Jack's controlling nature. 'Where did he work before he came here?'

'Your colleague queried that yesterday, and I told him it comes under data protection.'

'Jack Gallagher is only talking through his solicitor at the moment. It would help if you could tell me.' She had no idea why she was flirting with this man. Where Jack worked previously had absolutely nothing to do with anything, as far as she knew.

'Okay, but you didn't hear it from me.' He tapped the keyboard and read from the screen. 'He worked at AJ Lennon's hardware company.'

'Thank you. By the way, do you know a Kevin Doran?'

He shook his head slowly. 'Can't say I do.'

'Or Joyce Breslin?'

'Have these people anything to do with Isabel's murder?'

Lottie set her mouth in a thin line and didn't answer.

'I heard the woman's name on the news this morning. Odd that she disappears the day Isabel was murdered, don't you think? Perhaps she had something to do with it.'

The thought had crossed Lottie's mind. 'Thank you, Mr Costello.'

'Oh, it's Michael, Inspector. Is there anything else I can do for you?'

Since she'd entered the office, she'd been thinking, so she blurted it out. 'I've just moved into a really old house. Electrics are terrible. How would I find out the cost of rewiring it?'

'Leave your address with me. I'll have it assessed for you.'

'Oh no, that won't be necessary. I'm a bit broke anyhow.'

'No charge to have a look. I insist.'

Despite her misgivings at mixing work and home, she wrote it out for him. 'Thank you so much. I'll see myself out, Michael.'

As she made her way out of the office, she was sure his eyes were plastered to her denim-clad legs. And for some reason, she didn't mind. It made her feel good about herself.

CHAPTER THIRTY-EIGHT

AJ Lennon's hardware company had been in business for thirty-five years. So AJ informed Lottie when she came to see him straight from Quality Electrical. She trusted her team to be working hard on finding Joyce and Evan Breslin. She just had to tick these boxes and hopefully find something to lead her to Isabel's killer.

Lennon's was well known across the length and breadth of the country. On a clear day, the company logo could be seen from Lacy's Bridge on the western side of Ragmullin. Lottie had googled the company and found it had started out as a small family-run shop. When AJ took over from his father, he transformed the business, and during the Celtic Tiger era the company had boomed with the surge in the house construction market. It was rumoured Lennon was worth millions. Sitting across from him now, she didn't get that impression.

His office was small but tidy. Two filing cabinets and a large desk. No window. AJ was in his early sixties but could pass for ten years older. His hair was thinning; grey with an orange tinge, like he'd attempted to dye it at some stage but it had faded. Over a cream shirt that might once have been white, he wore a grey crew-neck jumper with a hole in the cuff, as if he was constantly poking a finger through it. She recognised that nervous twitch. She hoped she had overcome it, because watching Lennon, she saw how irritating it was.

'Detective Inspector Parker, it's an honour to meet you in person.' His jowls sagged onto his shirt collar as he spoke, and his narrow eyes looked like they didn't belong on his face. She shook his hand. Firm but sweaty. 'You're a legend in Ragmullin.'

'I doubt the criminals would agree.'

'Ah sure, feck 'em, the lousy bastards. How can I help you? Are you doing home renovations?'

'If only. No, I'm here on official business.'

'Oh, the murder. Awful business. That poor young woman and her family. I hope you catch the lousy bastard.'

Must be his catchphrase. 'Jack Gallagher worked here before he moved jobs. Can you tell me about that?'

'His move, or about when he was here?'

'Both.'

'Oh, let me think.' He tore the hole in his cuff a little wider. 'It was a good few years ago now. He worked as a retail assistant, but I learned he'd studied to be an electrician and found it hard to get a placement. He punched in a couple of years on the shop floor, but I knew he was wasted here. I put in a word with Michael. He took him on.'

'Michael Costello?'

'Yeah. He does business with me on a wholesale basis. My company is a lot more than retail, you know.'

'Do you recall having any trouble with Jack while he worked for you?'

'I don't remember much about him at all, so that means he kept his nose clean. I've no idea how he got on at Michael's place. Why don't you have a chat with Michael?'

'I already did. So you haven't had any interactions with Jack in recent times?'

'He's doing up that house of his and I set up an account for him. He was in and out a good bit, ordering stuff. His little wife even came in when they were doing the kitchen. Picked out a new sink and taps.'

Lottie didn't know why his words 'little wife' made her cringe, but they did. 'Her name was Isabel.'

'Of course.' He scrunched his eyes, and his hair moved at his ears. 'Tragic.'

'I was told she worked here at one time. Did you know her personally?'

'God, not personally. She was an employee for a while, a few years ago now. I have a very large staff all over the country, Inspector.'

'Right. Did you know her family – her mother, say?' They'd be close enough in age, she thought.

He bit the side of his cheek. 'What's her name?'

'Anita Boland.'

'Let me see.' He closed his eyes for a moment. 'She might be a customer. Has she renovated her house?'

'Not that I know of. Had you any interactions with Isabel in recent times?'

'I met her when she was debating over kitchen taps. I advised her to get the single-handed nickel-plated faucet. Tried to get her to go for the Quooker, but she said it was too expensive and they'd a lot more to do with the house and were saving.'

'It must have been an unusual conversation for you to remember it so clearly.'

'I remember the sales I lose.'

'It seems odd to me, Mr Lennon, that as the head of this successful company you would be on the shop floor selling kitchen taps.'

He laughed. 'I like to know what's going on, then I can make executive decisions on customers' needs. I try to get around most of my stores at least once a month. Keeps the staff on their toes, too.'

'Did Isabel pay cash for the taps she settled on?'

'Charged them to their account, I imagine.'

'When was the last time you saw either of the Gallaghers?'

'Couldn't rightly say, but Jack got a few bags of cement around Christmas, I think it was. I can check the account and email it on to you, if it's okay with him. I wouldn't like to go behind his back.'

'Grand, ask him. He'll probably tell you to contact his solicitor.'

Lennon's chubby cheeks paled. 'He's not … God, no. You can't suspect he killed his wife, can you?'

'I suspect everyone until I don't.'

'That must be tough on the family.'

'Do you know Jack's family?'

'God, no. I meant his wife's family.' He tugged at his cuff again.

'Thought you didn't know them either?'

'I meant in general, like.'

Lottie picked up her bag from the floor making ready to wind up the conversation. This was a complete waste of her time. She noticed that Lennon appeared to relax as she stood.

'Do you know Joyce Breslin?'

'The woman who's missing with her son? Heard about it on the radio earlier. Awful.'

Lottie stared at him, waiting.

'Name doesn't ring a bell,' he said, 'but I can check the accounts.'

'Does the name Kevin Doran ring any bells for you?'

His face looked like it was frozen with his mouth half open. Slowly he shook his head. 'Kevin … who?'

'Doran. That's the name we have, but it could be anything, if I'm honest. He worked on the Gallaghers' house with Jack. A handyman from what I've gleaned so far.'

'Sure anyone could be in and out of the shop and I wouldn't know. I told you I'm not here all the time.'

'Can you see if he has an account with you, then?' She doubted very much there would be any Kevin Doran on Lennon's books. 'Or he might have signed something for Gallagher.'

'I'll check it out.'

'Any way of doing that now, is there?'

'No, I have to ask Carmel in Finance. I'll get back to you.'

She dropped her card on his desk. 'My number and email are on that. I look forward to hearing from you.'

At the door, she turned, pushed her bag to her shoulder and arranged her jacket over her arm. 'Did anything happen here to force you to put in a word for Jack with Michael Costello?'

He shook his head slowly. 'Well, I found out he was an electrician.'

'You said that, but I'm wondering if there was something else …'

'It must be five years ago or more, but I'll—'

'Check it out. Thanks. I look forward to hearing from you.'

She left him in the silence of his stuffy little office, worrying the hole in his sleeve.

CHAPTER THIRTY-NINE

A fog hung low on the hillside. Dervla climbed quickly but had to stop once or twice to find the trail she'd taken the day before. After fifteen minutes or so, she came to the tree shrouded in mist, its branches stretching out, calling her. Terrifying her.

She shrugged off the old memories and talked down her fear. There was nothing here to hurt her any more. Still she glanced around furtively to make sure she was alone.

Taking the little trowel from her parka pocket, she fell to her knees, the dew from the soft grass seeping into her joggers. She felt around at the base of the tree. Searched for a mound formed unnaturally. Disturbed earth. Her fingers glided over the grass and she noticed soil sneaking through. Had the sheep come across it just before she scared it away? Or had another human been searching?

She began to dig. *What am I doing?*

She thought she heard a sound behind her and swung round, her heart beating into her eardrums. A blackbird took flight from a branch, flapping its wings loudly and cawing like the fires of hell were burning its feathers.

'Stupid bird,' she said, but a cold sliver of fear glided over her skin, pushing up goose bumps. Like the times she'd been here when she was younger.

No, stop, Dervla.

She had to find more bones. She needed proof so that someone in authority would believe what she'd found. No one had ever believed her about anything she'd spoken about before, and that weighed heavily on her narrow shoulders. Well, she supposed she was apt to lie now and again, but this was different. This was someone else's truth.

She heard a soft thud as the trowel hit something. Dropping the tool, she flicked away the soil with her hands.

It looked up at her. A little eyeless skull.

Dervla screamed and stared.

Tears streamed down her face until she wiped them away with muddy fingers. She couldn't take it in, but she realised that what she'd been told before was true. There was something buried here. A child. She shook her head slowly.

'Poor little thing,' she cried, knowing she should have searched long before now.

There was no way she could take it away from its burial site. It might bring her bad luck or something. Quickly she scooped up the clay and covered the little skull. Tugged at the grass around her knees and spread it on top of the mound. She stood and broke a branch from the tree and stuck it in the soil. A marker to remember where she'd found the last resting place of a child, though she knew she would find this spot in the dark. And it would haunt her dreams for eternity.

She made her way back down the hillside, her mind a jumble of confusion. If she spoke about this, she was betraying a trust. If she didn't, no one would ever discover what had happened to this little child. She weighed up her choices. This was evidence. Of a crime? She didn't know. Was Kevin responsible? She didn't know that either, but someone had concealed the body and that was enough for her.

By the time she'd reached the foot of the hill, she had made up her mind.

CHAPTER FORTY

Maria Lynch made up two bottles of formula for Holly and stood them on the counter to cool. She'd sent Anita to lie down after she'd rocked the crying baby to sleep in her buggy. Bored silly, she wandered into the sitting room, lifting ornaments, opening drawers, flicking through books, quietly snooping, but found nothing to inform the murder investigation.

Jack Gallagher eventually returned from the station, blowing out smoke from a cigarette he'd dropped outside the front door.

'You still here?' His elbow thrashed into her arm as he pushed past her. Lynch tottered before righting herself. Unable to say if it was accidental or not, she followed him to the kitchen, where he noisily opened and shut cupboard doors.

'Where the fuck are the mugs?' he yelled.

'Anita and Holly are resting. Keep it down.'

'Piss off.' He mauled one of the plates of sandwiches before stuffing a dainty triangle into his mouth.

The kettle began to whine.

'You need to put in water.'

She leaned against the door jamb, arms folded, watching him. His agitation increased with each step he took, from the wall socket to the sink and back again. He found a mug, and grudgingly offered it to her. She shook her head. No way was she sharing a cuppa with him and his foul humour.

'I can make it if you like?' She approached the counter.

'I can make my own tea in my own house, thank you very much.'

'It's not your house.'

'Whatever.'

'Did you do much to help Isabel at home?'

'Like what?'

'Cooking, laundry. Hoovering, bathing Holly. That sort of thing.'

'Listen here.' He moved into her space. 'I work every hour God gives me. She was the one at home all day with only a baby to occupy her.'

Lynch stood her ground. 'Isabel never asked you for any help?'

'Why would she? She was well able to mind a house and a baby, so she was.'

'It must've been hard for her, all the same. Isolated out there on the side of a windy hill, all day, every day, with no friends and only a baby for company.'

He slammed the empty mug on the counter. 'What are you trying to say?'

'I'm trying to get a picture of what life was like for her.'

'And how will that help you find who killed her?'

'It's like doing a jigsaw puzzle. Eventually we find a piece that doesn't quite fit, and that gives us a lead.'

'Sounds daft to me.'

The kettle whistled and he made his tea, filling the mug to the rim with milk. He sat at the table, sloshing the liquid without wiping it up.

'What was Anita's relationship with Isabel like?' Lynch stayed by the counter.

'Now you suspect Anita as well?' He shook his head wearily. 'You haven't a clue, do you?'

'Did she visit your home often?' Lynch said, unperturbed.

He slurped tea and put the mug down. 'Not that often. Don't think Isabel talked to her much.'

'Oh, why not?'

'How would I know what goes on between women? The way I saw it, Isabel couldn't wait to get married to get away from her mother. I never asked why because I was happy to have her with no strings, aka no mother-in-law, attached.'

Lynch had formed the impression from Anita that she and Isabel had enjoyed a good relationship.

'Surely Isabel must have said something about it. I know I tell my husband about every little argument I have with my family. A problem shared and all that.'

'You didn't know Isabel. She was quiet and intense. One of those women who found it hard to express her emotions.' He stared at Lynch. She tried not to look away from his gaze, eyes dark enough to drill a hole in her soul. 'But she was my wife and we loved each other.'

'Why would someone kill her, though?'

'I wish I knew.'

'You should have asked us about the television interview before doing it.'

'I knew you'd stop me. You don't know how hard it is to see things move so slowly and not be able to make an impact. I had to do something.'

Lynch pushed away from the counter just as he suddenly stood.

'You believe me, don't you?' He grabbed her arm. 'That I didn't kill my wife.'

She shrugged off his hand. 'I look at where the evidence brings me.'

He seemed about to say something else, but a sound vibrated from the deep pocket in his jacket on the back of the chair. A flush brought heat to his cheeks and he turned, grabbed the jacket and went out the back door.

Lynch watched him from the window. He was holding a small, narrow tablet, tapping the screen.

The doorbell sounded.

Garda Thornton had arrived to relieve her. Lynch was wanted back at base for a team meeting.

She was glad to flee the claustrophobic house.

CHAPTER FORTY-ONE

The team gathered in the incident room while Lottie checked over the photos on the board, her eyes drawn to the missing boy, Evan. She'd ordered divers to check the lake after the car had been found there, and a search of the woods had found no one.

Where are you, Evan? She hoped to God he was alive and well cared for. So far the superintendent's media briefing, the social media and news alerts and the checkpoints had had no success. No witnesses to the boy's abduction or his current whereabouts, and so far, no sighting of his mother. Except for her car.

She turned to face the room and the muttering hushed.

'First of all, I want to discuss the disappearance of Joyce and Evan. Leaving aside for the moment the fact that we found her car, can we trace her movements yesterday?' She paused and glanced at the fairly naked board to her right. 'What type of mood was she in when she dropped Evan off at Bubbles Day Care?'

Kirby said, 'Sinéad Foley didn't notice anything out of the ordinary. Evan was in good form and she said Joyce didn't delay or chat.'

'And she didn't turn up at work at all?'

'No. I checked that with Fayne's café manager.'

'So if she didn't go to work, did she return home?'

'I looked over the house-to-house reports from Loman Road, her estate. Her next-door neighbour was in her back garden most of the day, planting bulbs. She noticed nothing unusual. Still, it's possible Joyce went home at some stage.'

'There were signs there she'd started to pack,' Lottie said. 'And less than twenty-four hours after she was last seen by Sinéad Foley, we find her car. All traffic cams and CCTV are being checked to see if we can find where the car had been before that. But who's to say how long it was abandoned at the lake. Any witnesses come forward?'

'Traced a couple of fishermen, but they used a different lane.'

Lynch said, 'Why not take her son that morning and leave then, if that was what she was doing?'

This was what chewed at Lottie's brain. 'See if you can find out if she was followed, Kirby. Is there CCTV at the lake?'

'Are you joking me?'

'Does it look like I am?'

'Sorry. I'll check with the council. There might be hidden cameras to catch illegal dumping and antisocial behaviour. Can't promise anything.'

'I don't want a promise, I want results.'

'Sure.' Kirby busied himself making a note.

'It seems logical,' Lottie said, 'that Evan was taken by someone other than his mother. Have we traced the partner's movements? Nathan Monaghan. What's the exact time he arrived back in the country, and what time did he arrive in Ragmullin?'

'I've been on to the port and the ship had docked by six p.m.,' Boyd said. 'Nathan Monaghan's lorry was at the warehouse in Ragmullin by nine.'

'What warehouse?'

'AJ Lennon's Hardware.'

'What? I've just been talking to Lennon. Jack Gallagher used to work for that outfit years ago, and so did Isabel for a little while. By the way, why would it take Monaghan that long to drive from Dublin on a Monday evening?'

'Have you seen the traffic on the M50?' Kirby said.

Boyd said, 'Here's another interesting thing.'

'Go on.' Lottie folded her arms, waiting.

'I checked out the car found at the lake. It's not registered to Joyce Breslin. It's registered to a company. Lugmiran Enterprises.'

'Really? What link has she to this company?'

'I couldn't find anything about them online, but I'll check further. It might have something to do with Nathan Monaghan. Will I bring him in?' Boyd asked.

'Phone him,' Lottie said. 'He was here last night, fingerprinted and DNA sample taken, but he wasn't held under caution. He seemed glad of somewhere to put his head down. He left this morning. I got word that SOCOs are finished at his house.'

'Here's some news,' Kirby said. 'I did a quick search of the car at the lake and found an envelope down the side of the driver's seat.' He held up the evidence bag. 'There was a scrap of paper inside with a typed address. The Occupier, 14 Castlemain Drive.'

'In Ragmullin?

'Yeah, it's that enormous anonymous estate down by—'

'I know the one. Continue.'

'Well, I swung round that way. The house is as empty as a beer keg after Paddy's Day. All closed up. A neighbour, Meg Collentine, told me it could be over two years since anyone was seen around.'

'Did this Collentine woman know anything about the car?'

'She didn't remember it. She thought it was a family who lived there. She remembered seeing a woman and a couple of kids.'

'Probably nothing to do with Joyce, then. She only has Evan. Where are this family now?' Lottie felt Kirby was building up to something. She wished he'd get on with it.

'God only knows. Australia or Timbuktu. Want me to follow up further?'

'We're short-staffed and under pressure, but see if you can find anything about the ownership of the house, and the car.'

'The motor tax is over six months out of date. Insurance the same,' Kirby said.

'Any sign of Joyce's phone?'

'No.'

'Get on to service providers. I want a log of her calls and texts. I'll ask Nathan if he knows anything about it.'

'Right, boss.' He waved the evidence bag again. 'There was a razor blade in the envelope too.'

'What? Show me.'

Kirby pushed the desk forward to extricate himself and ambled to the front of the room. He handed her the bag, dramatically.

She glanced in at the blade. 'Looks new, but get it to the lab straight away.'

'Will do.'

'Isabel Gallagher had a blade in her hand. Jesus, this could tie the two cases together.'

Kirby took the evidence bag, puffing out his chest, delighted with himself.

Lottie said, 'Isabel used to work at Bubbles Day Care, where Joyce had Evan cared for. That's another link.'

'A coincidence?' Boyd said.

'Possibly, but let's see if the lab can match the blade to the one found in Isabel's hand.'

'Sure.'

She continued. 'I found a speck of blood on a radiator at Joyce's home. Any results back on that?'

'The lab is running a DNA check against a hairbrush and a child's toothbrush. Be a day or two.'

'I need to know now.' She slumped down on a chair. 'Was there anything found at the Foleys' house to lead us to the identity of who might have taken the boy?'

'Maybe he just wandered off?' Lynch said.

'Didn't I leave you at Anita Boland's house?' It had only just struck Lottie that Lynch wasn't where she should be.

'You asked Garda Thornton to take over for a couple of hours because I was required here.'

'So I did.' Lottie clapped a hand to her forehead. 'Okay. But I want eyes on Gallagher at all times. Monitor his movements. We don't want any more impromptu television appearances. Which reminds me, did his TV debut elicit any noteworthy response from the public?'

Garda Brennan scanned pages spread out on the desk. 'The usual crackpots with conspiracy theories. It's distracting from the appeal to find Evan.'

'I could swing for Jack Gallagher. Do you have anything concrete to report, Garda Brennan?'

The guard shook her head slowly. 'Nothing.'

'We still need to follow up each call. We might hear something about Mr Gallagher himself.'

She filled in the team on her conversations with Michael Costello and AJ Lennon. 'Jack moved from Lennon's to Quality Electrical five years ago. I heard no evidence of any wrongdoing, except that he likely got Isabel to leave her job at Quality Electrical. What else have we got?'

'We need to pin down the timeline for Isabel's murder,' Boyd said. 'We only have Gallagher's word that she was alive when he left for work.'

'What if he killed her the previous night?' Garda Brennan sat forward, her face alight with enthusiasm.

Lottie shook her head. 'She rang her mother around seven yesterday morning. Jack might still have been there then. The post-mortem confirms she died within the two hours before her body was discovered. The pathologist can't be more accurate than that. It's still possible he had time to kill his wife before he clocked in at work.'

'It took him twenty minutes to do a ten-minute drive,' Boyd said. 'He had a window of opportunity there, or he could have doubled back home after clocking in and before he reached the second property on his calls.'

'There is no one to confirm he was actually at the first property.' Lottie thought for a moment. 'But would he have had time to clean up and dispose of his bloody clothing? And if he did, where did he do it? And where is the murder weapon?'

'A man who can stab a woman to death in front of his own child is capable of doing anything in any timescale.'

Lottie considered that. 'Triangulate Jack's phone to confirm he actually went to his first job yesterday morning.'

Boyd said, 'His phone is with tech now, so the GPS should let us know where he went. If he hadn't switched it off, that is.'

Lottie stared out at her team and wished she had more bodies to help.

'Wait a minute,' Lynch said. 'I saw Jack Gallagher with a tablet earlier. He was on it in Anita's garden before I left.'

'The sly bastard,' Lottie said.

'Who was he communicating with?' Boyd said.

'Haven't a clue.' Lynch shrugged. 'I'll see if I can get my hands on the device and check what app he was using.'

'Do it, Lynch,' Lottie said. 'Keep a close watch on him. And if he leaves the house, I want him followed. Radio for support if you need it. Okay?'

'Sure thing.'

Lottie took a few deep breaths to restore her equilibrium.

'We have two investigations running concurrently. My main priority at the moment is finding four-year-old Evan Breslin and his mother. Alive. The razor blade found in Joyce's car might well be a link to Isabel's murder, as Isabel had one in her hand. The women may have been acquainted via the day care, because Isabel worked there for a few months. I want to know everything about both of them.' She knew Lynch was the ideal person for this work but she had to use her as FLO. Shit.

As if Lynch had read her mind, she said, 'If I had a decent laptop and mobile internet at Anita Boland's house, I could make myself useful while keeping an eye on Gallagher.'

'Organise it. And remind me to send a few others on the next FLO course. I can't be wasting good detectives while real work is necessary.'

'I can help out,' Garda Brennan said.

'Right. Send Thornton back to base.' She looked at Kirby. 'Was Sinéad Foley's house and day care checked thoroughly?'

'I can confirm the kid isn't hiding in the attic or the garden shed.'

'Any security cameras?'

'One inside the day care unit itself, and another in the garden where the kids played. Nothing of interest on them.'

'Jesus, a kid doesn't just disappear into thin air.' But she knew they did, all the time. 'I need to confirm Sinéad's husband's movements, and I'll have another word with Nathan Monaghan. Do you all know what you have to do?'

Heads nodded, chairs screeched across the floor and mutters grew into chatter. She checked her phone and found a notification from McGlynn.

'SOCOs have found a razor blade beneath the hall radiator in Joyce Breslin's house!'

The chatter died away.

'Kirby, fast-track that blade you found in her car.'

'Will do.'

'Has anyone traced Kevin Doran yet, the handyman?' Blank faces stared back and Lottie remembered it had been McKeown's job. 'Someone take it on, and don't lose sight of the fact that our priority is finding Evan alive.'

The noise in the room rose again, and above it all Lottie heard the tentative voice of Martina Brennan.

'What if he's already dead?'

She groaned. The young woman had a lot to learn.

CHAPTER FORTY-TWO

Jack felt like he had a shadow stalking him; no matter which way he turned in the house, there was a pair of eyes stuck to him. The detective was back and she was like a leech he couldn't shake off.

He knew he'd made a mistake with the tablet. Goddammit. How could he have been so stupid? Lottie fucking Parker would know by now that he had it. That wasn't good. Not good at all. The FLO, Lynch, had left for a meeting shortly after, leaving a big hulk sitting there drinking copious amounts of tea, talking non-stop to Anita about the good old days. Give me a break, Jack had yelled in his head. And just when he had decided to escape, the detective was back. Nothing for it but to be brazen.

He pulled on his jacket and had the zip halfway up his chest when she came into the hall behind him.

'Where are you off to?'

'Out.'

'You should stay here with your daughter. You can't leave everything to Anita.'

'She loves caring for Holly. I'm suffocating in here. I need fresh air.' All of that was true, but it was not all of the truth.

'Just the same, you should stay here.'

'Why?' He stepped closer. 'To look at the four walls?'

'Who were you communicating with on that tablet?'

'None of your bloody business.'

'Why didn't you hand it over to Inspector Parker at the station?'

'She asked for my phone and I gave it to her. A tablet isn't a phone last time I looked.'

'Why do you need to carry around a tablet plus a phone?'

God, she was persistent. 'I need it for my freelance electrical work.' He moved to the door.

She was behind him in one step. 'Are you prepared to hand it over?'

He paused, one hand on the latch, the other on his pocket. 'Unless you have a warrant, I'm keeping it. And if you insist on harassing me, I'll call my solicitor.'

Lynch wasn't to be deterred. 'Where are you headed to?'

'What are you? My jailer? I'm a free man, so I'm off out to get some air. Tell Anita I'll be back later.'

Opening the door, he stepped outside, ignoring her calling him back. She could piss right off and leave him alone.

*

The day warmed up and Kevin was sorry he didn't possess a light jacket, because he was sweltering. Standing under the trees across from Anita's house, he watched with interest as Gallagher burst out the front door, followed by a woman with her hair in a short ponytail. She was calling him back, but he walked out the gate, turned for town and kept on going.

Stepping out from the trees, Kevin caught sight of the woman going back into the house. He dipped his head and quickened his pace. He had to talk to Jack at some stage, and now seemed as good a time as any, when there was no one else around.

At the corner by the pharmacy, Jack paused and Kevin held back, watching. Jack turned right, up by the canal. Perfect. Kevin followed, his breathing laboured. When he was right behind Jack he put out a hand to touch him.

The big man whirled round, fist raised. Kevin ducked.

'Why are you sneaking up on me like that? I might have landed you in the canal.'

'Sorry, Jack. I'm scared. After what happened to Isabel and all—'

Jack clutched a handful of his jacket at the shoulder and dragged him to his chest. Spittle landed on Kevin's face as the big man's voice raged. Maybe this was a mistake. Maybe he should keep his mouth shut. Say nothing, a voice warbled in his brain.

'What do you know about what happened to my wife?'

'I swear to God, I don't know a thing. The guards, they're everywhere. I'm terrified they might think I did it.' Kevin couldn't breathe as Jack slid a hand around his throat and pulled him up to his face.

'They're asking about you. Why do you think they're doing that? They must think you killed her.'

'I swear I'm telling you the truth. I'd never hurt her.' Kevin couldn't stop the snot running down his nose. Jack made him feel like a useless kid. 'She was good to me.'

'Oh yeah? And wasn't *I* good to you? Making up jobs for you to keep her happy. Now that I think about it, there might have been some sort of kinky business going on between the two of you.'

'Don't say that. Don't disrespect her like that.'

'Disrespect? I'll give you disrespect, you little weasel.'

Kevin almost fell to his knees as Jack released his grip on his throat. The relief was only temporary. A thump landed on the side of his head and a fist punched him in the chest. He heard a thunderous splash and realised he was in the rancid water.

'Help!' he yelled.

'You can fuck off if you think I'm going to help you, you piece of shit. And stay away from my daughter!'

Kevin flailed around in the canal, trying to get his feet on the bottom, but there was nothing there. Water gushed over his head and he swallowed a mouthful. That was when he remembered he couldn't swim.

*

Maria Lynch stood on the step, seething with rage. She thumped the door jamb as Jack hurried away. That big hulk was as guilty of murdering his wife as McKeown was guilty of cheating on his. She was about to turn back inside when she saw a man step out from the trees across the road and set off after Jack.

Who was he?

She ran inside and fetched her coat and phone. 'Be back in five, Anita.'

'Where are you off to?' Anita sat by the buggy where Holly lay fast asleep. For a moment Lynch wished her youngest was as good.

'Won't be long. Don't open the door to anyone until I get back.'

'You're scaring me now.'

Lynch forced a smile. 'Absolutely nothing to worry your head about.'

The anxiety leaped from Anita to settle on her own shoulders, but she kept going.

Walking quickly, she tried to spot Jack or the man who had come from the trees. At the pharmacy, she glanced towards town and then up the canal path. There they were, seemingly embroiled in a heated argument. Should she approach or remain where she was? She hesitated, but the decision was taken from her when the man toppled into the water. Jack stepped back before setting off at speed.

'Feck.' She broke into a run.

Reaching the bank, she saw the man's hands shoot up from the water before submerging again. Bubbles formed on the malodorous mess. She tore off her coat, kicked off her shoes and, without stopping to think of the danger, jumped in.

The ice-cold water swallowed her breath, and she gasped. She waded towards where the bubbles were decreasing in intensity. Her feet were losing their grip on the muddy bottom the further she moved away from the bank, until there was only water beneath her. Grappling around in the mess of weeds and reeds, she tried to locate him. Nothing. She inhaled a deep breath, held her nose and ducked underneath.

It took a second to see through the silty haze. There he was, his face contorted, hands flapping. She grabbed hold of his coat and began to haul him upwards. He was a dead weight, and fighting. She had to get him to the surface quickly.

Bringing her face close to his frantic one, she indicated upwards. He seemed to relax, and she flipped her feet wildly and began to ascend. Her head broke through the water and she gulped huge gasps of air.

'You got him!' someone yelled.

A small crowd had gathered on the bank. Thanks for the help, she thought, dragging the man towards them. Arms reached out and he was hauled through the thick reeds and up onto the path. Another pair of hands found hers and she gladly let them take her weight until she was on solid ground. She lay looking up at the blue sky, gulping air.

'You okay? We called an ambulance.'

'Thanks,' she mumbled.

Turning onto her knees, she watched as a woman wrapped her coat around the shivering man. He would live. Now she had to find out all she could about this person for whom she had risked her life.

He lay shivering in a foil blanket while paramedics took his vitals. Lynch peered down at the face she did not recognise.

'Hello? Can you hear me?'

His eyes remained closed as he was lifted onto a wheeled stretcher and pushed along the narrow towpath. Two ambulances had reversed onto the entrance to the path, rear doors open, a small crowd huddled beside them.

Once the stretcher was hoisted inside, one of the paramedics slipped an oxygen mask on the half-drowned man.

Lynch allowed herself to be bundled into the other ambulance and a blood pressure cuff was wrapped around her arm. When the paramedic was satisfied she wasn't about to die on him, she called Lottie and told her where she was headed and why. The door closed and she heard the engine jump to life. She lay back on the plastic-covered pillow and closed her eyes.

CHAPTER FORTY-THREE

Boyd watched as Lottie fled the office. Where was she off to?

He went to the door to call after her, but she'd already disappeared around the corner at the end of the corridor. He turned back and sauntered to Kirby's desk. The smell of fried food wafted towards him. 'What are you at?'

'Accessing the National Driver Vehicle files to trace who owned Joyce's car before Lugmiran Enterprises, because I can't find anything on that company.'

Boyd drummed his fingers on the desk while Kirby worked.

'Right, I have a name and address,' Kirby said triumphantly. 'Frank Maher.'

'I'll go with you if it's not too far. He might help us find Joyce and her little boy.'

'Right.'

'On condition that I drive,' Boyd said quickly. He was sure to end up with grease in his lungs if he went in Kirby's car.

'On condition I can stop at McDonald's. I'm starving.'

'No way I'm letting you eat in my car. Come on. We won't be long.'

Frank Maher lived down a narrow road at the side of the canal, not far from the convent school. Four old terraced houses lined the lane. Further down, over the supply bridge, Boyd saw the shimmer of ambulance lights flashing. Someone must have fallen in, he thought. Once the sun came out, the silly season started.

The door opened.

The man looked to be in his eighties, tall and willowy, with a slight hunch probably formed from having to constantly bend his head to enter doorways. He seemed genuinely happy to have someone other than his dog to talk to. The old collie raised its head, then, finding its master's guests uninteresting, returned to soak up the heat from the Aga stove with its door wide open.

It was positively boiling in the house.

'I'm Frank, and he's Bosco.' The man cleared newspapers from one chair while Kirby lifted a basket of folded laundry from another.

'Frank,' Kirby began once they were uncomfortably seated, 'we're here about a car you used to own. A black Ford Focus.' He recited the licence plate number.

'That's long gone. I haven't driven anything this five years. Didn't pass the eye test so couldn't renew my licence. Stupid rules and regulations. I only ever drove to Tesco. Now I have to be waited on hand and foot by my poor niece. Not that she minds, though what would I know? Youngsters are used to putting on a face in more ways than one.' Frank chuckled.

'Did you sell the car?' Boyd said.

'Aye, lad, I did. On one of those websites. Best Deals, I think.'

'Have you any record of the buyer?'

'You've got me there.' The man scratched the side of his head. Boyd was afraid he would lose his few remaining grey strands if he scratched any harder.

'Ever hear of Lugmiran Enterprises? It's currently listed as the registered owner of the car.'

'Can't say I have.'

'Did you get information from the buyer in order to complete the transfer of ownership?'

'Sure didn't the lad say he would take care of it. All I had to do was bank the five thousand yo-yos he paid me.'

'He paid you in cash?'

'He did right enough.'

'Did you meet him in person?'

'Just for the few minutes it took to hand over the car and take the money, but you needn't ask me what he looked like, because I can't remember much about him.'

'Any little thing would help,' Kirby pushed.

'What's this about, if you don't mind me being nosy? If he didn't do the paperwork and I'm still the registered owner, I hope the bastard hasn't crashed it and gone and killed some poor unfortunate soul. God, I couldn't live with myself if that happened.'

'Nothing like that at all, sir,' Boyd said.

'Sir? A boy after my own heart. I was in the army, you know. You have respect for your elders, not like some of the youngsters nowadays.'

'If you can remember anything, it would help us.' Boyd found he had to work hard keeping the old man on the subject.

'Let me think. He was a tall man. But sure everyone is tall now that my back is fecked.'

'Was there a woman with him?' Boyd asked.

'A woman?' Frank closed his eyes for a moment.

'Yes, sir. Did the buyer have anyone with him?'

'Can't say that he did. The deal was done out the front. He must have walked here, because he drove away in my car and there was no car left outside. Unless someone dropped him off. Maybe that's it.' He pointed a finger like a schoolteacher.

'He might be from the town, then?' Boyd probed.

'He might be from Mars for all I know, lad.'

Boyd leaned back in the chair. This was getting them nowhere.

'Bosco hadn't much time for him, if I recall correctly. Howled like a banshee the whole time we were out front.'

'And is Bosco a good judge of character?'

'He didn't lose his rag when you two came in, so that tells you something.'

Kirby guffawed and Boyd smiled awkwardly.

Frank added, 'I'll ask my niece if she kept anything. She did the ad for me. I have one of those smartphones, but I'm not as good on it as I could be.'

'If you give me her phone number,' Boyd said, 'I can follow it up.'

'Ah, lad, I don't want to be worrying her. She's an anxious pet. Leave your number with me. I'll call you if she kept anything.'

Boyd supposed this was better than nothing. He put his hand in his jacket to take out a card, and his fingers touched the letter he'd put there yesterday. He'd forgotten all about it. He'd been too distracted and busy. Finding his card, he handed it to Frank.

The old man walked them to the door, Bosco remaining in the kitchen guarding the heat. 'Any news on that murder? Poor lass. Awful business altogether.'

'We're working on it night and day,' Boyd said.

'Why are you here asking about my old car then?' The old man's eyes bored into Boyd. 'I'm not too senile yet, so it must be something to do with her killing.'

'No, it's in relation to another case. I meant to ask, do you know a Joyce Breslin?'

Boyd couldn't be sure, but he thought the old man's eyes flickered as he shook his head.

'Don't recognise the name. But the battery goes a bit flat in here betimes.' He tapped the side of his head.

'Ask your niece about her too, if you don't mind.'

'Don't mind at all.'

'Thank you, sir,' Boyd said.

'Thanks, Frank,' Kirby said.

About to step outside after Kirby, Boyd noticed a framed photograph hanging on the hall wall.

'Jolly bunch,' he said.

'Aye, lad. That's my niece and some of her friends. Years ago now. She's a bit of a loner really. It was taken on some summer camp or other, I think, though it might be something else entirely. Feel sorry for the lass. That was a happier time for her.'

'What happened?'

'If I knew that, maybe I could help her.'

Boyd could see the old man was getting upset. His cue to leave. 'Good day, sir.'

*

Frank stood at his front door for a long time after the car had disappeared from view. Then he shut the door and stared at the photograph before he went to join Bosco. Sitting by the table, he searched under the mess of newspapers for his phone.

CHAPTER FORTY-FOUR

'What the hell is going on?' Lottie said when the ambulance doors opened.

Lynch knew she must look like a drowned rat, her hair matted to her scalp and her clothes sopping wet beneath the blanket. 'I'm fine, thanks for asking.'

'Sorry. I hope you're okay, Maria. What happened?'

Taking the paramedic's hand, Lynch stepped down, her foil blanket flapping in the breeze. 'The man I rescued from the water is in the second ambulance. I don't know who he is, but it looked to me as if Jack Gallagher pushed him into the canal.'

'Where's Gallagher now?'

'Don't know.' Lynch shrugged her shoulders wearily.

'We best get you inside,' the paramedic urged.

The second ambulance pulled up. The doors opened.

'I'm not letting him out of my sight,' Lynch said, indicating the man on the stretcher, oxygen mask clamped to his face.

Once inside A&E, the man was taken to a cubicle. A nurse showed Lynch to an empty treatment room so that she could take off her wet clothing, and handed her a towel and a gown.

'Stay with him,' Lynch told Lottie, and shut the door for privacy.

It took her some time to peel off her wet clothes. She felt awkward in the gown, unable to tie the strings at the back. She towelled her hair and glanced at her reflection in the glass door of a cabinet. She turned away quickly – she looked like nothing on earth.

A knock on the door before Lottie entered.

'Are you decent?'

'Half decent. How is he?'

'He's being assessed.' Lottie paused. 'The nurse says you need a tetanus shot.'

'I'm up to date on my shots.' Lynch sat on the bed, the bundle of wet clothes on her knee.

'Give those to me.' Lottie took the clothes and found a roll of plastic bags on top of the cabinet.

'Thanks,' Lynch said.

Lottie placed the clothes in the bag. 'So what happened?'

Lynch explained how she'd followed Jack Gallagher and had seen the man fall into the water. 'It was obvious he couldn't swim. For a second I considered following Gallagher, but instinct made me stay to try and help the man.'

'You think Gallagher knew him?'

'I was some distance from them, but they appeared to be arguing. I didn't recognise him.'

'I've been told he could be suffering from hypothermia, so we can't interview him yet. Once you've been checked over, I'll drive you home.'

'Thanks. I just want a hot shower and fresh clothes, then I'll be back on the job.'

'Take some time off. You've endured a traumatic experience.'

'No, we're short-staffed, with too many critical investigations.'

'Are you sure?'

'Dead sure.'

Lottie smiled, and Lynch hoped this was a turning point in their working relationship, though with Lottie Parker you could never be sure of anything.

'Once I get you home, I'll come back here to see what this man has to say and if he wants to press charges.'

'And I want to interrogate Gallagher.' Lynch was looking forward to that.

*

Kevin opened his eyes to a glaring light. He tried to raise a hand as a shield but found it linked to a trail of tubes and wires. Sounds of chatter and machines beeping flitted in and out of his clogged ears. It felt like his head had been dunked in a bucket of water. Water. The canal. That bastard Gallagher.

He should have known it could only end in drama. Jack might not have intended pushing him in the canal, but Kevin knew the man liked to exert his control over others. Isabel had told him that.

Trying to adjust his eyes to the blistering overhead lamps, he took a few breaths, alarmed at the gurgle coming from somewhere deep in his chest. At least he was alive, but he had to get out of here before someone found him.

'I know nothing,' he muttered to himself over and over.

He lifted his head and forced himself to sit up. Swinging his legs to the side of the bed, he examined the myriad of lines twisting around his arm. He shuddered to think someone had undressed him and clothed him in a gown. They would have seen his scars. Questions would follow.

'I know nothing,' he repeated.

If he pulled out the tubes, would an alarm ring? Probably. Plus, he needed clothes. Easing to his feet, he stood for a moment and let the dizziness pass. He shuffled to the curtain, trailing the thin lines behind him, and peered through the slit. Should be easy enough to get out, but he still needed clothes. Turning back, he saw a blue plastic bag tucked under his bed. Bingo.

It was easy to move once he'd found his balance, but his breathing was laboured. What would it be like once he took the lines out? He hoped he didn't bleed to death. Deciding it was best to get dressed elsewhere, he tugged out the bag, heavy with the wet clothes, and hastily detached himself from the monitors.

A high-pitched wail brought a nurse to swipe back the curtain.

'You can't just pull them out. Get back into bed until I fix you.'

'I need the bathroom. I'm bursting,' Kevin croaked.

'We don't even know your name. I have to take your details.'

'When I get back.'

She made to take the blue plastic bag from him. 'You won't need this.'

'Please, I feel safer with my stuff.'

'I'll put back your drip. You can bring it with you. It's on wheels.'

He didn't argue. No point. When she was done, she pointed him in the direction of the bathroom.

'Through that door, you'll be on the corridor. Turn left and it's the second door.'

'Thanks. Be back in a tick.'

*

Joyce had shouted until her voice was as hoarse as a chicken's squawk. She remembered chickens in the back yard of one of her foster homes. The neighbours were up in arms over the noise, and one night someone crept over the fence and choked three of the birds. That thought brought her memories crashing into reality. The horror when she saw the little feathered bodies lying in the shit-covered grass.

Her throat, torn and raw, felt worse than the cuts to her face and feet. She stopped shouting because she couldn't stand the pain any longer, and the silence fell around her like a cold sheet of steel.

She shivered uncontrollably from the cold. What was this place? She was sure she was in a container, but where was it? In some yard? Or out in the middle of a field? She had no idea.

Would she ever see Evan again? Her fervent hope was that he was safe. Nathan would have picked him up and given him his tea, put him to bed and got him up this morning. She hoped he'd had a good night's sleep.

'Oh God, help me,' she cried in a whisper, realising that her hopes were futile. Of course they'd taken her son. 'Please, God, show us mercy.'

But there was no God to help her. She was all alone.

Then she heard a soft skittering noise and a scratching behind her. No!

Feeling entirely hopeless, she shrivelled her body up into a ball and cried into her hands cradling her knees.

CHAPTER FORTY-FIVE

Lottie sent Garda Brennan to Anita Boland's house with instructions to make contact as soon as Gallagher returned. After she'd dropped Lynch home to shower and change, Jim McGlynn called to say they'd finished the examination of the Foley property. No evidence of the lock being damaged on the front door. If Evan hadn't left of his own accord, which was unlikely, how had the little boy's abductor gained access?

Back at the hospital, she was met by a flustered nurse, who told her the mystery man was no longer in A&E. Dammit. Well, she had enough on her plate without chasing ghosts. Brennan or Lynch could follow up with Gallagher to find out what the altercation by the canal was all about and unearth the name of the man he'd dumped in the water.

She fumed the whole way back to the office, where she picked up Boyd and headed to Sinéad Foley's house. He filled her in on his meeting with Frank Maher.

'Make sure you get the details from his niece. It might lead us to this Lugmiran company. It's very odd. Has ANPR or traffic cams thrown up anything on Joyce's movements yesterday?'

'No, and Kirby contacted the council. They've no cameras at the lake.'

'The super has ramped up the checkpoints around the county, and further afield, to see if someone's memory can be jogged.'

'Time is moving on,' Boyd said. 'We need to find Joyce and her son before it's too late.'

Lottie squirmed. She didn't want to think about that. 'This man in the canal, he'd had an argument with Jack Gallagher. Could he have had something to do with Isabel's murder?' She parked the car outside Bubbles Day Care.

'He likely has something to do with something, if he annoyed Gallagher that much. Come on, let's see what the Foleys have to say for themselves.'

Sinéad Foley opened the door, her eyes bleary. She wore a creased white blouse over jeans. Her feet were bare.

'Sorry. I look a state. Didn't get much sleep last night. My mother-in-law talks incessantly and I'm worried about Evan.'

'I'm glad you're back in your house so quickly,' Lottie said.

'Your forensic team were very professional. There's no place like home, as Dorothy said.'

'*The Wizard of Oz*,' Boyd said, redundantly. Lottie glared.

They were led into the sitting room, where a man sat tapping a slim laptop. He rose to greet them, extending a long, muscular arm. His hand was smooth.

'Dylan Foley,' he said. 'It's a horrible business about poor Evan. Any news on his whereabouts?'

'We're working on it,' Lottie said. 'I'd like to ask a few questions.'

'Ask away.'

She declined the offer of a seat and stood with her back to the empty fireplace. Dylan closed the laptop and slid it down the side of the cushion, while Sinéad sat on the arm of his chair. He laid a hand on her thigh. Comforting or controlling? Lottie wondered. Then she shook herself. Sinéad didn't seem perturbed or uncomfortable. She was reading too much into the slightest show of affection. God, she needed to get a grip.

Boyd remained by the door, leaning against the wall, hands deep in his coat pockets.

'Before I ask about Joyce and Evan,' Lottie said, 'can I ask you, Mr Foley, if you know Jack Gallagher?'

'Call me Dylan, please. No, sorry, I don't. Saw on the news last night about Isabel's murder. Any leads?'

'I can't talk about that investigation at the moment. You were at the gym yesterday evening when Evan disappeared, is that right?'

'Yes. I had a meeting at work and it ran over, so I went straight to the gym.'

'Which gym is that?'

He shifted on the chair and removed his hand from his wife's leg. 'Why are you asking all this? I had nothing to do with Evan going missing.'

Lottie sighed. 'Everyone has to account for their movements. We're at a critical time in the search for Evan. With each passing hour—'

'I'm sorry.' He held up his hand in apology. 'Just tired. My mother talks for Ireland and—'

'I told them that,' Sinéad said snappily, and stood. 'Would either of you like a drink? Water, tea?'

'No thanks,' Boyd said.

'We won't be here long,' Lottie added.

Sinéad nodded, moved away from Dylan and sat on the couch.

Lottie returned her attention to the husband. 'You work in the health service, right?'

'I'm in therapy.'

'Oh?'

'No, that came out wrong.' He laughed, a little too high-pitched for comfort. 'I'm a social worker at a community-based therapy project. Mainly for foster children. A very demanding job, but to me it's a vocation.'

He was full of his own importance. Lottie straightened her shoulders. 'Why is that?'

'I feel it's my way of giving back to the community, and I like helping people.'

His words sounded rehearsed. He was smiling affably, his hands relaxed on his lap.

'I need to verify your whereabouts yesterday evening.'

'No problem. Sheefin Park gym. My work base is at the Ragmullin Community Project Centre.' He sat forward and dug out his wallet from his back pocket, handing her a business card. 'The office number is on that. You can check with my supervisor.'

'Great. Thanks.' Lottie glanced at Sinéad. 'You've had time to think since we last spoke. Do you recall anything else? Anything out of the ordinary or unexpected?'

'I've racked my brain, but no. Sorry.'

'Do you have any idea why Joyce would go missing, and then her son?'

'No.'

'She ever talk to you about worries or fears she might have had?'

'Not a word. We're not really—'

'Where are you going with this?' Dylan fixed his eyes firmly on Lottie's. Dragging her attention away from Sinéad? She couldn't tell.

'I'm trying to get a picture of Joyce's state of mind.'

'She seemed okay whenever I met her,' he said.

'You've met her?'

'Of course. Joyce and Nathan were friends of ours. We've had them round for dinner. Isn't that right, darling?'

Lottie glanced at his wife, who kept her head down, studying her hands on her lap.

'When was the last time they were here for dinner?'

'A few weeks ago, wasn't it?'

'Something like that.' She didn't look up.

What was she missing here? Lottie looked over at Boyd, and he raised one shoulder. He wasn't sure either.

'What's Nathan like?' she asked.

'Grand fellow,' Dylan said.

'Sinéad?' Lottie lowered her head, forcing the other woman to look up at her.

'He … Nathan's a good man.' Sinéad stood suddenly, gripped her arms around her waist.

'How did you all become friends?' Lottie said.

Dylan said, 'I met him at the gym and we got talking. Realised then that Sinéad was minding Evan a few days a week. After that we met up for a pint now and again. I invited them for dinner. Sinéad and Joyce hit it off.'

'How long ago was this first dinner party?'

He shrugged. 'Last summer. We had a barbecue.'

'And neither of you noticed any odd dynamic between Nathan and Joyce?'

'They were a pleasant couple and we became friendly with them as we got to know them,' Dylan said. 'I don't see how this is helping you find Evan.'

Lottie turned to Sinéad. 'When Nathan didn't return your call, what did you think was going on?'

'Nothing. I mean, I knew he was abroad. Joyce had told me that. And when she didn't answer, I tried his phone. That's all.'

'Do you think Nathan could have abducted Evan?' Boyd said.

'God, no, why would he do that?' Sinéad paled and looked horrified.

Why indeed? Lottie felt they were being stonewalled and she knew she was losing valuable time in the search for the little boy. 'So neither Joyce nor Nathan gave you any cause for concern?'

'None at all,' Dylan said.

'Is Nathan a regular at Sheefin Park gym? I believe you go three times a week,' Lottie said.

'Three times a week and the odd Saturday. But I haven't seen Nathan there in a while. He drives a lot. I can ask around if you—'

'Won't be necessary. We'll follow it up, thanks.'

'If that's all, I have to make it to a client consultation.'

'Sure,' Lottie said, and stepped towards the door.

Boyd opened it but didn't move into the hall. 'Was it usual for Evan to be left here after hours?'

'What do you mean?' Sinéad said.

'Had there been other occasions when Joyce didn't pick him up at the allotted time and you had to call Nathan?'

Lottie noticed a bright flush creep up Sinéad's pale face. Dylan placed an arm around his wife's shoulders and pulled her to his chest.

'I think that's enough for now. You're upsetting my wife.'

'Answer the question, Sinéad.'

The woman looked up from beneath her long lashes, eyes watery. 'Once before. Around Halloween last year. The next day she told me that she got held up at work, but she didn't ring or anything. Luckily Nathan was home and he came for Evan. Joyce never even apologised.'

'I suppose she thought because we were friends she could take advantage,' Dylan said, 'but I soon let her know that this is Sinéad's business and she had to respect it.'

There went that friendship, Lottie thought. 'Okay. Is there anything else unusual you can share with us?'

'Nothing I can think of at the moment,' Sinéad muttered.

'If you do think of anything else, let me know. I will most likely need to question you both again at a later date.'

'We will help you in any way we can,' Dylan said, his fingers now white from gripping Sinéad's shoulder.

'That's good. We need everyone to cooperate so we can bring this little boy home alive.'

'Oh God,' Sinéad cried, burying her face in her hands.

'Another thing. There's no evidence of the front door being damaged or the lock interfered with. How could someone have gained access to your house?' She looked from one to the other. Sinéad shook her head, clutching her elbows, but Dylan seemed uneasy, dropping his eyes.

Sinéad said, 'Tell them.'

'Dylan?' Lottie pressed.

'I didn't think it was important,' he said.

Dear God in heaven. Lottie braced herself for whatever stupidity was coming her way. 'You better tell me.'

'When I got back to my locker at the gym last night, the door was open. But I'm sure I locked it, or maybe I forgot.'

'Anything missing?'

'I only keep three keys on my key ring. The car, the office and the house key. And now I'm realising the significance of it …'

'Spit it out, Dylan.'

He took a key ring from his pocket. There were only two keys on it.

'My front door key is missing.'

'You should have informed us immediately.' Bloody hell, another headache. They'd have to check out everyone who was at the gym last night. Scrutinise the security footage – that was if they even had cameras in the changing rooms. Probably not.

'I didn't notice until we got back to the house this morning after your forensic guys had finished. Sinéad had to use her key. Mine was gone.'

'Could you have lost it anywhere else before or after the gym?'

'It's possible, but I didn't notice it was gone because after my session my phone exploded with Sinéad's calls.'

'Did you notice anyone different at the gym last night?'

'It was just the usual crowd. I'm sorry.'

'That's okay.'

The couple retreated into each other's arms.

'One more thing,' Lottie said, turning back, feeling like Columbo. 'Do either of you recognise the name Frank Maher? He's in his eighties, lives down by the harbour. Used to own Joyce's car.'

Sinéad remained silent, her head buried in her husband's shoulder, but Lottie could have sworn Dylan's smooth face twitched.

'Can't say that we do,' he said.

'You sure?'

'Absolutely.'

Lottie knew that was all she would get from him, for now.

CHAPTER FORTY-SIX

Back at the office, Lottie sat at her desk trying to clear the headache that was pounding in her forehead. If someone had stolen Dylan Foley's front door key and used it to gain access to his home, that proved Evan had been abducted. It was also clear, if that was the scenario, that planning was involved. The abductor had been aware that neither Joyce nor Nathan was around, and had known Dylan Foley's movements. Unless it was Nathan himself who had been involved in the boy's disappearance.

She buried her head in her hands.

Boyd appeared around the door with a bottle of water and two paracetamol. 'You need these, and then you need to eat.'

'I need a strong drink.'

'Come on, Lottie.'

She took the pills and swallowed half the water.

Screwing on the cap, she said, 'We haven't one hint as to where Joyce and Evan are. A stolen key. A car that once belonged to an old man. And then we have the Foleys. What were those shenanigans all about? Was there something going on between Sinéad and Nathan? She looked fairly shifty or am I reading too fecking much into people who are just uncomfortable in my presence?'

'You need to relax.'

'God, Boyd. We haven't one clue as to who murdered Isabel Gallagher. Nobody out in that arsehole of nowhere has cameras; it's like a fucking free-for-all in the countryside. They don't even lock their doors, for fuck's sake. House-to-house enquiries brought us nothing bar the price of a cow at mart. No weapon found at her home. Nothing from DNA yet. Kevin Doran is the invisible man. It's all going backwards and I'm turning into a basket case.'

'Take a breath.'

'Don't tell me to take a bloody breath. I need a break in these cases. One tiny bastard clue. That little boy could be dead, is probably dead, because we can't sort an arse from an elbow. Help me out here, Boyd.'

'Perhaps you should call in reinforcements. Split the two investigations. There's little to tie them together except the fact that Isabel had arranged a meeting with Sinéad Foley yesterday morning.'

'Isabel had a razor blade in her hand and one was found in Joyce's car and another in her hallway.'

'True.'

'Boyd, I'm tired, but I know the two women are connected. At Isabel's post-mortem I saw with my own eyes the cuts to her feet and thigh. Probably made with a razor blade. Maybe I'm stretching credibility, but there's a thread there that I just can't catch. Yet.'

She drank more water and wiped dribbles from her chin.

'We have to find Evan.' She looked over at him. 'You should write up that Foley interview. See if you can pick holes in what they said, and confirm Dylan's whereabouts last night. Check with the gym; get their security footage if they have any cameras. Also I want any footage you can find from the surrounding businesses or whatever is located there. I need names of members and a list of who was on the premises while Dylan was there. Talk to everyone. And find out when Nathan works out there.'

'Who's to say the key didn't disappear earlier in the day?'

'Don't even go there.'

'Righto.'

He whipped the door shut behind him and Lottie let out a sigh of relief. She wanted to savour the quiet of her office for a few moments. It didn't last long before Kirby bustled in the door.

'Boss, there's a woman downstairs. You should have a word with her.'

'Should I now? Kirby, I'm drowning in work as it is.' She waved her hand over the mountain of budget reports, overtime claims and court files, and the growing pile of door-to-door reports with nothing to tell her where Evan was. 'If she can't tell me anything about either the Gallagher case or the Breslin case, I don't want to see her.'

'She says she has something important to show you. Asked for you specifically. There's something about her. I don't know what it is, but I really think you need to talk to her.'

Her headache refused to ease. She drained the remaining water.

'Oh for God's sake, Kirby, where is she?'

The room off the reception area wasn't much bigger than a pantry, and it was like a mini furnace when Lottie entered.

She squeezed in behind the desk and appraised the visitor. Aged somewhere between twenty and forty, she was swimming in a full-length black parka. Her hair was an untidy mess at the nape of her neck, her forehead indented with deeply ingrained furrows, puddled with perspiration. Her eyes were pools of something Lottie couldn't decipher. Pain or fear? One or the other, if not both.

'You can take off your coat if you like,' Lottie said. 'It's hot in here.'

'All right.' The woman struggled to tug the sleeves down before letting the coat rest around her waist.

Lottie scanned the name on the form. 'Dervla, you wanted to see me? I'm told you have something to show me.'

'I shouldn't have come.' Dervla made to stand, but was restrained by her jacket.

'You're here, so you must have a good reason. I won't bite. How can I help you?' If only her damn headache would disappear.

'I'm afraid.'

The eyes widened, dark and worried. Crow's feet ingrained around them from way too much stress for one so young. But now that Lottie looked at her, the woman might be nearer the forty mark. It was hard to pin down her age.

'Why are you afraid?'

A shrug. A sniff. A hand rummaged for her pocket but came up empty. 'It's all so weird and I know I shouldn't have come, but I didn't want it in my home any more. It follows me around, you see.'

God preserve me, Lottie implored. The thought was interrupted by images of what she'd do to Kirby for landing her with this woman.

'What follows you? Something in your home or out in the street?'

'It was in the fridge. All night. I couldn't sleep properly. And when I did fall asleep, I had nightmares about it.'

Sweet Jesus, help. 'Oh, and what is this thing in your refrigerator?'

'A bone.'

'A bone?'

'I knew you'd think I was loopy.'

'Not at all.' Lottie kept her fake smile in place, but it was beginning to hurt worse than her headache.

'I found it yesterday. On the hill. I brought it home and put it in a bag. But I think I should have left it where it was. It's bad luck to disturb the dead.'

'What hill would that be?'

'Misneach.'

'I didn't think the public were allowed there. Isn't it a sacred site?'

'It's more open nowadays. For hikers and hill walkers. Oh, and there's the Sun God festival.'

Lottie hadn't time for this. 'This bone you took, it has you worried, has it?'

'Yeah. I think … no, I'm sure it's human.' Dervla rolled up the sleeves of her shirt as a bead of perspiration dribbled between wild eyebrows.

'How can you be sure?'

A shrug. 'Just know.'

'Is it still in your refrigerator?'

Dervla dug around in her pocket and eventually extracted a freezer bag. She laid it reverently on the desk between them.

'It's very small,' Lottie said, examining the bone through the plastic. 'It could be from an animal.'

But she knew. She knew just by looking at it that it had come from a very small human. It was far too weathered to belong to Evan.

'It's like it came from a little child.' Dervla swallowed a loud sob. 'Shit, I'm sorry. It has me rattled.'

'That's understandable. You did the right thing bringing it to me.'

'Really?'

'Of course you did. I'll send it to the lab for examination. After that, I'll know exactly what I'm dealing with.'

'There's more.'

'What?'

'More bones. I went back up the hill. This morning. Dug around a bit. It was so small. A tiny skull.'

'A skull? Did you take that too?'

'God, no. I felt guilty enough taking the bone. I'll have nothing but bad luck for disturbing a grave site.'

'Dervla, I need you to tell me exactly where you found these bones.'

Dervla ran her sleeve under her nose and sniffed loudly. 'It's hard to explain. I'd have to bring you up there to show you the exact spot, and I … I'm not sure I ever want to go there again.' She looked up into Lottie's eyes. 'Too many bad memories.'

'Don't worry. I'll get someone to take the details of where you made the discovery and you can leave the rest to us.'

'When it was just the one bone, the first time I was there, I thought maybe the sheep had just dragged it from somewhere else, but—'

'We'll deal with all that. I'll have the site examined and get this bone tested and dated.'

'It could be ancient, couldn't it?'

'It could be.' But Lottie knew it wasn't that ancient at all.

Dervla took a few deep breaths, her face puce in the airless room. She fanned a hand in front of her nose.

'I think you need some air,' Lottie said.

She placed the bag with the bone in an evidence bag she found in the desk drawer, then sealed and dated it, adding her signature with a flourish.

A phone buzzed somewhere in the depths of Dervla's coat.

'You can answer that out in reception. It's airier there. I'll get someone to take a full statement from you.'

'Thanks. You're very kind.'

'Just doing my job.'

As the young woman rolled her sleeves back down, Lottie caught sight of a zigzag pattern of healed cuts on her left forearm. Just like a bed of eels.

CHAPTER FORTY-SEVEN

Frank Maher rubbed Bosco's neck, wrapping his fingers around the dog's soft coat. He'd pulled a chair over to the stove and was stirring a pot of soup with his other hand.

'Oxtail, lad,' he said to the dog. 'My favourite.'

Bosco moaned in agreement.

The front door opened and shut.

'Hello, missy. I was trying to ring you. Damn phone. You'd think I'd be used to it by now.'

'Ah, don't worry, Uncle Frank. I heard it but couldn't answer it. How are you doing today?'

'Sit down there and I'll make us a cup of tea.'

'No, you have your soup. I don't need tea. I'll be having my dinner soon.'

'How was your day?'

'Same old, same old. How was yours.'

'Same old, same old.' Frank stopped stirring. 'No, something different happened. That's why I was ringing you. Two detectives were here asking questions.'

'Really? What did they want?'

Frank watched his niece as she moved the newspapers from one side of the table to the other.

'They were asking about my old car, the one you sold for me.'

'What about it?'

'It must have been used in a robbery or something. Bastard who bought it never registered it in his own name. Put it in some dummy company name. Are you okay, lovey? You've gone white in the face.'

'If you don't need anything from the shop, I'll be off. Have to cook my dinner. I had a busy day today and I'm tired.'

'Oh, and what were you doing? Hill walking again?'

'Are you okay if I leave?'

'I'm fine, lovey, but I'm worried about you. Maybe you should have a word with Kevin.'

'Kevin?' She shot up out of the chair like she'd been fired from a cannon. 'Why on earth would I want to talk to him? I'm so over all that. I'm off. Ring if you need anything.'

Frank had never seen her so put out about anything. The car. Was it to do with the car? Surely not.

'When you get home, will you see if you can find the details of who bought that car? Don't want those guards around here again.'

'Details?' She was by the door, her lips trembling. 'Why?'

'Didn't I tell you? They want to know who bought it.'

'Sure how would I know that?'

'You did the Best Deals thingy on the computer. Got me five grand. Remember?'

'Oh. Right. Not sure I kept anything, but I'll have a look.'

'They asked if I knew Joyce, too.'

She paled and gripped the door jamb. 'What did you tell them?'

'Nothing at all.'

She hurried out.

Frank rose slowly, noticing the thick scum on the soup. Damn it to hell. He should have kept stirring. He pushed the saucepan to the back of the stove and followed his niece.

'What's wrong? You can tell me, Dervla love.'

But she was already gone.

'Youngsters nowadays, Bosco. I'll never understand them.'

*

Why did he still think of her as a teenager? She was thirty-five, for God's sake. She didn't want to worry him, but when he'd mentioned the car, Jesus, she thought she'd have a heart attack right there in his stifling kitchen. And then Joyce. Why were the guards asking about her?

She hung up her coat, opened the refrigerator and whistled with relief. Thank God the bone was gone. She wouldn't be able to spend another night in the house if it was still there.

One good deed done. She'd been anxious about visiting the garda station, but the inspector had been nice. She'd read about her in the local paper a while back. Seemed like a decent sort. And the burly man who'd taken her statement was like a teddy bear. She smiled, recalling his pudgy face and wild curly hair, and the constant tapping on his shirt pocket. She'd forgotten his name, but she wouldn't need to see him again so it didn't make any odds. Once she'd described the tree on Misneach, he'd said he knew exactly where she was talking about, so she wouldn't be needed to go with them.

There was little to eat in the fridge, so she got a bowl of cornflakes. Water would have to do, as she was out of milk. She used cold boiled water from the kettle and sat at the table spooning the soggy flakes into her mouth like a child.

As she ate, her arm itched. She didn't want to scratch it or it would bleed again. That made her think of Kevin. Damn Frank. Why had he to go and mention Kevin? Maybe she should contact him. Bad idea. This was partly down to him, and there was no room for Kevin, or anyone like him, in her life.

She switched on her iPad and scrolled through the news to see if there was anything about a robbery or a car crash. Why hadn't he filled out the forms for the change of ownership? The dumb fool. But she knew he was no fool. She shivered, hunching up her shoulders to hide the chill, and kept scrolling. Her finger hovered over the screen as she saw the wedding photograph under the headline *Mother of one slain in her own bedroom.*

She tapped the screen to bring up the full story that she'd seen on the telly, then squeezed the photograph to make it bigger, zooming in on the dark eyes of Jack Gallagher and the happy eyes of Isabel.

She scrolled to the next article, about a missing boy and his mother.

Now she really must talk to Kevin.

CHAPTER FORTY-EIGHT

Maria Lynch was well and truly pissed off by the time she returned to Anita's house.

Garda Brennan took one look at her and said, 'If you don't mind me saying, you look like shit.'

'Thanks for the vote of confidence, Martina.' Lynch headed for the sitting room. 'Where's Anita?'

'The little one wouldn't settle, so she took her upstairs. I think they both fell asleep. Poor woman is overwhelmed.'

'I don't blame her. Any sign of Jack?'

'Not a dicky bird.'

'Did you hear from McKeown?'

Martina blushed. 'Why would I hear anything from him?'

'Give me some credit. Everyone and their dog knows you two have a thing going.' Lynch eased her aching body into one of the more comfortable armchairs.

Squirming, Martina said, 'Will I make a cup of tea? Something to warm you up?'

'Ben filled me with coffee, thanks,' Lynch said, thinking of her husband's fussing. He hadn't wanted her to return to work, but she was glad of the excuse to escape the bedlam of their house.

'Honestly, in the beginning I didn't know Sam McKeown was married.'

'But when you found out, you didn't end it, did you?'

'No, I didn't. Big mistake.'

'We all make mistakes; the trick is to learn from them and not make them again.'

'I'm trying,' Martina said. 'I love my job and don't want to balls it up over a married man. Was it you who phoned his wife?'

The front door opened and shut.

'Jack's back,' Lynch said.

Gallagher walked in with a large brown bag stained with vinegar, oozing the smell of a chipper.

'You two look mighty comfortable,' he said. 'Shouldn't you be out hunting the prick who killed my wife?'

Lynch glared.

Martina stood. 'I'll put on the kettle.'

As she disappeared, Jack slammed the bag down on Anita's good coffee table and stood in front of the fireplace.

Lynch didn't care for him towering over her, but in all honesty she hadn't the energy to stand. 'Where were you?'

'None of your business.'

'It is when a man ends up in the canal after you pushed him in.'

'Don't know what you're talking about.'

'I followed you. I saw it with my own eyes. Who was he?'

He seemed to relax, as if he'd made up his mind about something, and sat down. Lynch looked longingly at the brown bag.

Leaning back on the cushions, he ran a hand over his forehead. 'Kevin Doran. The guy who did odd jobs for me around the house. I told your inspector about him yesterday. Don't know why you haven't brought him in.'

'We couldn't bloody well find him!' Lynch raged. 'What went on between you?'

'He followed me. Must have been watching the house.'

'You should have called me.'

'I wanted to know what he was up to. I told him you were asking about him. Lost my head for a minute and grabbed him. Next thing I know, he's flailing about in the water, so I cut my stick out of there.'

'And left me to fish him out.'

'Really? Sorry about that.'

Was that a smirk? She thought it was. 'He might press charges for assault.'

'No he won't.' He looked at her then, as if seeing her discomfort. 'You look a bit pale.'

She wasn't buying the fake nice guy act. 'What was the conversation about?'

'Are you listening to me? There was no conversation. Where is he now, anyhow?'

'He left the hospital before Inspector Parker or I could interview him.' Shit, she shouldn't have told him that. 'Tell me what you two were talking about.'

He stuffed a handful of chips into his mouth. 'You saw us, so you know there wasn't time for a conversation. He was fixated on Isabel. You need to find him. Arrest him.'

'Where can we find him?'

'I gave your inspector his phone number. That's all I have. Can't you get him that way with all your technical wizardry?'

'Where does he live?'

'If I knew that, I'd be there wringing his neck.' He stood and picked up his chipper bag. 'Damn, these are gone cold. I'm putting them in the microwave. Would you like a few chips on a plate?'

'No thanks.'

He left her alone. Lynch thought about the tea that Martina was taking ages to make. And then she recalled how casually Gallagher had mentioned wringing Kevin Doran's neck. He was one cold customer.

*

Kevin made his way back to his van, walking in his wet clothes along the canal from where he'd been plucked earlier. She must have been a detective, he thought, the woman who'd saved him. Had she been following him, or Jack? It made his leg itch thinking the gardaí were asking about him. Shit. If they knew who he was, did they know where he lived? And if they knew all that, had they discovered his role in everything?

He shivered, his damp clothes sticking to his skin. He still had a cannula in his hand.

Fuck Jack Gallagher. He should never have approached him. It was stupid. Almost fatal.

The van was where he'd left it, under the trees across the road from Anita's house. Though he'd lost his keys in the water, he found the spare set taped behind the front wheel. He opened the door and slid inside. His phone was on the dash and he was glad he wouldn't have to buy a new one. They were cheap anyhow, not going to break the bank. He laughed, thinking how he'd never had to use a bank when he had plenty of hidey-holes for his cash at his cottage.

He drove home, his head dizzy, forcing his eyes to focus on the road. No point in getting pulled over for tax or insurance by an overzealous garda. Not now.

At the cottage, he parked under the oak tree before making his way through the long grass to the front door. He had a spare key hidden beneath a tuft of earth, and he congratulated himself on this pre-planning exercise he'd devised when he'd first felt the fear.

'I know nothing,' he whispered, and entered the darkness.

A sense of loneliness hugged his shivering skeleton as he stripped off his clothes and searched for something to wear. After finding an old tracksuit, he dressed and set about taking the cannula from his hand.

With a grubby roll of plaster beside him, he tugged the needle from his flesh and swallowed the pain. The blood streamed down his hand, so he held his arm aloft and wound the plaster round, tearing it with his teeth. He wrapped a tea towel around the mess.

His vision blurred and his hands trembled when he'd finished. He should lie down, but he had things to do. What had he to do?

He shook his head from side to side. Think, Kevin. A shiver raced up his arm and across his shoulder blades, and his whole body shuddered.

The blurriness refused to fade. He rested his head on the table among the bloody cloths and plasters and closed his eyes. He was fast asleep when his phone vibrated with a message, scattering the mice from the floor into the walls.

It was hours later before he awoke.

CHAPTER FORTY-NINE

The little bone was dispatched to Jane Dore at the Dead House. Lottie knew it could not belong to Evan. There was no way, if the boy was dead, he'd be reduced to bone so quickly. Jane told her they might need an anthropologist to take a look at it. That cost money. The super would have a coronary with an already overrun budget. At least get me DNA or something, Lottie had implored the pathologist.

Kirby had filled her in on Dervla's statement. He knew the area. She sent him off to check it out, telling him to bring Garda Brennan with him.

*

Kirby picked up Garda Brennan from Anita's house and headed out to Misneach.

'Do you walk a lot?' Martina asked.

He wasn't sure if she was mocking him, but giving her the benefit of the doubt, he said, 'I'm able to climb a hill on my own; don't know why the boss wanted you along.'

'I think it's because I did a CPR course.' She grinned.

'Ha ha. Very funny. I was up here a couple of times for the Sun God festival.'

'Didn't know you were into that lark.'

'There's a whole lot you don't know about me,' Kirby said. 'Is Detective Lynch babysitting Gallagher again?'

'Yeah. I made them tea and escaped.'

'Correct move.'

'I might have been better off there than having to climb a bloody hill. It'll be getting dark soon and I'm not sure I like the prospect of being stuck up here all night.'

'Not even with me for company?'

'Those SOCOs scare the shite out of me, the way they can deal with all that blood and gore.'

Kirby threw a glance over his shoulder to see the two technicians and another uniformed garda bringing up the rear.

'This is a waste of time and effort,' he said.

'But it could be Evan buried here.'

'Boss says the bone is old.' He pointed. 'Up there. That's the tree Dervla Byrne mentioned. Come on.'

He tried not to huff on the last leg of the climb. It wasn't that high really, but he was overweight and unfit. Why had he tried to be bloody Joe Wicks in front of Martina? Though now that he looked at her, she was struggling a bit too.

The branches of the tree, with their flowering buds, stretched outwards like they were protecting a special treasure buried beneath the roots. The stone wall encircling the tree was falling down in places, rocks spread around with moss and grass growing over them.

'I can see where she was digging,' Kirby said. 'Bad attempt at replacing the soil. We're lucky the sheep haven't been back.'

'How do you know they haven't?' Martina said.

'Well, I don't, but … feck it.'

He indicated the site to the SOCOs and stood back to let them begin. Dervla had said she hadn't to dig down too far. The SOCOs unpacked their tools and got to work.

'It's sad and horrific to think someone buried a little kid here,' Martina said quietly.

Kirby glanced at her, surprised to see tears gathering.

'Abandoned a little body and walked away,' she whispered. 'What type of monster does that?'

'The world is full of monsters, and unfortunately most of them look just like you and me.'

'Found something,' the shout came.

Kirby moved forward. 'What is it?'

'A tiny skull.'

'That's what the young woman found. Anything else? Clothing? Something to give us a clue.'

He watched as the SOCO slowly brushed the soil from the skull. He felt Martina move closer, her body shaking with emotion. Or maybe it was just the chill that blew around the side of the hill.

'Yeah, there's more bones, possibly a full skeleton. Ah, Jesus Christ.'

'What is it?' Kirby hunkered down, still keeping a little distance so as not to compromise anything they might find.

'It looks to me like a disposable nappy. They can take two hundred years to decompose. This poor little thing wasn't even potty-trained.'

A cry from behind Kirby made him turn around, and he saw Martina sink to her knees in tears.

*

Joyce had no real idea of the passage of time. She was hungry and thirsty, with a weakness eating into her muscles. Her knees and shin bones creaked when she tried to move. How much longer would she be kept here, trussed up and immobile? Her mouth was dry; she felt all the mucus in her throat had turned to sand. With the tight gag, the skin around her mouth and jaw was cracked.

She must have dozed, because her eyes flew open as the gag was being removed. Gulping air, she wobbled even as she leaned against the wall, her legs trussed. She could smell him. Something familiar tingled at the back of her brain. A trace of dust lined her lips where his finger had lingered while he loosened the rag.

Then he spoke.

'Missing your little boy?' He tugged her hair at the nape of her neck, drawing her head backwards. Still in darkness.

'What did you say?' Her voice didn't sound like her own. A frog's croak, no longer a chicken squawk.

'Your little shining light, is that what you call him?'

'Don't mention him. He's just a child.'

A bottle was held to her lips. At last! She gulped greedily, spluttered, and the water spurted out of her mouth.

'Fine, if you don't want it, I don't care.' He let go of her hair and her head fell forward like an unsupported puppet.

She coughed. Tried to speak. On the third try she formed a hacking sentence. 'You better not touch a hair on his head.'

'His head doesn't concern me. He's a bleeder too. Just like you.'

Her mind raced. No. Was he winding her up? Evan was with Nathan. She mustn't fall into this trap.

'You're wondering if it's possible for me to really have taken him. Let me tell you this for a fact, you will die without knowing.'

Why was he such a cruel bastard? And how could she think about anything when he held her life in his hands? Her son's life too.

'Help me.'

The blade glinted in the narrow shaft of light that sliced through the crack between the door and its hinges. She felt in the weariness of her bones that her life was nearing its end. She would welcome the release from years of torture and pain. The only light in it all had been her son. She had to believe he was safe and unharmed.

Her captor was still talking. She tried to concentrate on his words. To find some little hope to cling onto. Somehow, through the haze of pain, she felt she knew him.

'I often wondered what motivated you to keep on living. Anyone else in your position would have strung a rope around their neck and ended their miserable existence.'

'I never give up.' She was surprised at the steel in her voice, and in that instant she vowed she wouldn't beg for her own life. She'd only beg for her son's.

'That's obvious,' he laughed, 'or you'd be long dead. Sorry I didn't think of this sooner. Would have saved me a lot of trouble.' The sound of his laugh drove a spear of fear into her chest. He wasn't human. He didn't care about life, only pain and death.

She squinted, trying to see his face, but it was sheathed in darkness. His voice, though? She was sure she knew it, though it was obvious he was trying to disguise it. She tried to add a face to it, but the ringing in her ears blocked out all recognition.

'You're going to kill me?'

'Course I am.' He laughed again, a sinister twang lacing the sound. 'I relish the prospect of lifting pieces of your skin, bit by bit, and watching your blood seep down the blade and fall to the ground.'

'Who are you?' He must surely be deranged. But hadn't she known that all along?

'Oh Joyce, darling, you know who I am.'

'I … I don't,' she lied, trying to delay the inevitable. Trying to drown her terror in words. The fact was, she did know him and she knew exactly what he was capable of.

'Doesn't matter to me whether you do or you don't.'

'How did you find me at the lake?'

'A tracker on your phone. But don't get your hopes up. The phone and the tracker are now dust. No one will find you.' His breath washed over her. She turned away, just as he added, 'What will it be like to die not knowing if Evan is alive or dead?'

The blade nicked the skin at the centre of her throat. She felt a sting.

'You can do what you like to me, but please … don't hurt my son.'

Where was this bravado stemming from? She had lived so many years in absolute trepidation that this day would come, and now all of a sudden she felt strangely calm. Once she knew Evan was safe, she'd gladly succumb to whatever final torture this maniac had in mind.

'Oh dear,' he mocked, 'I don't think you are in any position to bargain. I can do what I like and you can't stop me.'

Another nick, deeper this time. Her body spasmed. It was going to be slow and painful. She could handle that. She welcomed it. Closing her eyes, she breathed through her nose, trying to transport herself to a different place. To believe that her son was safe and well, because the alternative was too cruel to imagine.

The knife was lowered from her throat to her breast and the blade forced into her flesh.

That was when she screamed.

CHAPTER FIFTY

'Will someone stop that snivelling brat? He's getting on my tits.'

'I want my mummy. I want my mummy!'

'Shut the fuck up, you little shite.'

Evan cowered like he'd seen animals do on television. He loved animals, but his mummy wouldn't let him have a dog. He'd like a dog. A small one, because they had a tiny garden. Small dogs were more cuddly anyhow. He liked thinking about the dog, because thinking about nice things kept him from thinking about not so nice things. His mummy had taught him that. Mindfulness, she'd called it. A big word for a small boy, she'd said. Keeps the monsters out of your head. But now the scary monsters were out of his head and they were here with him.

He wanted his mummy. He missed her. He started to cry again. No, he couldn't do that. He would make the bad man angry, and his arms were already sore from being shaken.

'What is wrong with that fucking kid?'

Evan shrivelled into himself. The man used bad words all the time. It wasn't nice.

'Will you stop? He's only four years old. He's terrified.'

That was the woman. She gave him juice and crisps. His mummy would be cross if she knew how much rubbish he was eating. But there were no cooked dinners here. He had to eat whatever he was given.

Thinking of food made him feel hungry all over again. Roast chicken and mashed potatoes would be lovely. No, he needed to think of nice cuddly animals. Maybe a cat. A cat was small, and wouldn't bite the furniture like a dog might do. A black one. Sooty. That was a good name for a black cat. That made him smile.

'What the hell is he smiling about? Jesus, but the kid is giving me the willies. How long do we have to keep him here?'

'Stop bloody moaning,' the woman said. 'It will be worth it.'

'You're impossible, do you know that? Make yourself useful. Get me another can. I'm parched.'

Evan didn't know if he should keep smiling or cry again. It was hard to know what to do to keep them from hurting him. He didn't like being hurt. No one had ever hurt him before. That thought seemed to poke at a memory deep in his brain. He *had* been hurt before. Shadows floated behind his eyes and he tried to make the vision materialise.

A phone rang somewhere.

The grumpy man answered it, listened, said, 'Yes, okay, if that's what you want,' and hung up. 'Hold that can.'

'Why? Who was that?' the woman said.

'The head-the-ball. About the kid. Move your arse.'

'What?'

'You heard me.'

'Ah no. I never signed up for violence.'

Evan crouched further into himself, wrapping his arms tight around his knees, squeezing as tight as he could, but he couldn't stop the tears nor the wail that broke from his throat.

'No, no, no. I want my mummy.'

'For fuck's sake,' the man's angry voice said. 'At least I won't have to listen to that shite for much longer.'

And Evan cried all the harder.

CHAPTER FIFTY-ONE

Lottie took the call informing her that a body had been discovered in a pool of stagnant water behind a newly constructed house at Bardstown. Kirby had just arrived back with news of finding the skeleton on the hill. He'd told her that SOCOs thought it might be a toddler. They'd cordoned off the site and the pathologist had been and left.

Lottie's heart felt crushed. Who would bury a little child on a windy hill under a fairy tree and leave it there without ceremony or recognition? It had to be murder. She hoped to God it wasn't connected to her current investigations.

Leaving Kirby behind, Boyd fetched the car and they made their way out to Bardstown, ten kilometres from Ragmullin and not far as the crow flies from Gallagher's house.

She entered through the hoarding surrounding the new building, Delaney Construction emblazoned on the green timber. This had been the location of Jack Gallagher's first job on Monday morning, but he'd been unable to gain access.

Walking up the shingle driveway, kitted out in her white boiler suit, she kept her head down, barely conscious of Boyd's steps behind her. She speeded up, wanting to run, to take off, to be on her own when she viewed the body. How had she failed so badly?

'Lottie, wait up.'

She heard his voice like it was in the distance. She didn't answer. Single-mindedly, she continued towards the lights that SOCOs had erected behind the two-storey new construction. It was only eight o'clock in the evening, but the light was fading as the sky darkened with rain clouds. She noticed the absence of birdsong in the trees surrounding the site.

'The body isn't going anywhere.' Boyd's voice broke through her brooding. 'Take your time.'

'It's my fault.' Her words were carried off with the breeze.

She could have done more if she hadn't been consumed by the murder of Isabel Gallagher and her mindless search for the ghostly Kevin Doran. Wasting time when she should have been looking for Joyce and her son. She felt a shudder travel the length of her body. She walked around the side of the house and approached the blue tent. Eerie shadows moved around inside, body shapes looming larger than normal on the canvas.

Boyd gripped her elbow.

'Listen to me, Lottie. It's not your fault. It's the fault of the murderer. You don't have to feel any guilt and you certainly don't have to look at the body.'

She swung around on the ball of her foot. 'Of course I've to bloody well look. It's my job.'

He pulled her close, lowered his head to lock his eyes with hers. She wanted to look away, but she also needed to feel his reassurance.

'I know it's your job,' he said, 'but I can do this.'

'It's just … I might have been able to prevent this happening. I should have spent more time and resources on the missing rather than the dead.'

'You did all you could.'

His hand dropped away and she thought she might fall over with the suddenness of his release. He was staring over her shoulder.

'What is it?' Turning around, she caught sight of Superintendent Farrell striding in their direction. 'Ah, shit, this is all I need. A bollocking.'

Farrell strode into their space. 'This is a right fuck-up.'

'I beg your pardon?' Lottie said, willing authority into her tone.

'It wasn't like looking for a needle in a haystack, was it?' Farrell's voice barrelled around the yard. 'The body dumped right where Jack Gallagher was supposed to be working on Monday morning. God grant me patience.'

'We don't know how long the victim has been dead or how long the body has been here.'

'But it is *here*! That's the bloody point. And this place gives us a connection to Gallagher. What have you been doing at all?' Farrell stamped her feet as if to incite heat into frozen feet, but it wasn't that cold. Lottie thought it was an avoidance measure. Perhaps it was her Farrell really wanted to thump.

'I'm about to look at the body,' she said, inching away from her superior officer.

'Cause of death?'

'I don't know yet, as I haven't seen the body.'

'Why are you standing here then? I need the information on my desk in one hour. I'll have to organise a press release. The media will be rabid. All of Ragmullin will be up in arms over this incompetence. Get to it.'

Farrell turned on her heel and was being driven away down the driveway before Lottie could utter an expletive.

'Don't let her get to you,' Boyd said.

'Everything she said is true. Why is the body here if it's not a link to the Gallagher killing?'

'Someone playing mind games with us?' Boyd said.

'The killer is clever.'

'I agree,' he said. 'It's a clear message and we need to decipher it quickly. We still have one more missing person to find.'

She watched as he abandoned her and strode towards the tent. Attaching her face mask, she threw back her shoulders and, with a confidence she didn't feel, followed him in.

The smell of early decomposition was rife in the air. With sombre eyes, McGlynn glanced up at the new arrivals.

'I don't need an audience,' he grumbled. 'It's too cramped in here.'

The tent had been erected over a section of a pond. Green algae lay like grease on the surface.

'What can you tell us?' Lottie folded her arms, determined not to be pushed around.

'Looks like this area was excavated for future landscaping. The rain we had last week filled the hole and the water festered. It's rancid.'

Lottie couldn't take her eyes off the partially submerged body.

Glynn continued. 'From what I can determine, there are multiple stab wounds. They appear similar to Isabel Gallagher's on first glance, but there are differences.'

She forced herself to look down at the body.

Joyce Breslin lay naked in death, her dignity stripped away. Her feet pointed to Lottie's own. The dark hair on her head, where McGlynn was stooped, fanned out like a floating basket, tarnished with green slime. Stab wounds were visible on the torso, and Lottie could see what McGlynn meant. A series of cuts traversed the body, particularly on the face and chest area. Skin was lifted as if it had been first poked, then sliced. A deep wound gaped on the neck.

Lottie fought the urge to find a blanket and cover the woman's nakedness. To restore some humanity to her. You wouldn't dump a dog like this.

'What in the name of God happened to her?' Boyd said, rubbing his forehead as if he could erase the vision.

'She's dead,' McGlynn said. 'And not being smart, but that's all I can tell you at the moment. No way of knowing which wound was the fatal one. There's no blood here that I can see, but the pond will have to be drained. I believe she was killed elsewhere.'

Lottie noted that the skin had a corpse hue. 'Wherever she was killed, there must be a lot of blood. How long do you think she's been dead?'

She braced herself for McGlynn's mantra of him not being God and all that. But he just shook his head. 'Not long. A few hours, I'd guess. The pathologist will have a more accurate estimate.'

'We need Jane to get here as soon as possible. I want the body removed and the pond drained. The boy … Evan, he could be in there.' She held a gloved hand over her mask. The thought of the four-year-old's body somewhere in the water turned her stomach.

'I'm working as quickly as I can. If I had no interruptions, I'd be a whole lot quicker.'

'Sorry. But thanks, Jim.'

She glanced at Joyce's feet. Hunkering down, she cocked her head sideways. Slivers of raised flesh coursed across the contours of the soles. Some old, most new.

'See that, Boyd? Isabel Gallagher had similar marks on her feet.' Standing, she drew her eyes up along the body, but was unable to see any further evidence of old wounds. Jane should be able to tell her.

Outside the tent, she approached a group of three men huddled together. One was smoking and another was biting his nails. The third was staring into space as if wishing he was somewhere else.

'Who found the deceased?' she asked.

'I did.' The space-gazer. Mid thirties. Small build. Navy overalls and a hi-vis donkey jacket emblazoned with the Quality Engineering logo.

A black woollen beanie covered his hair and ears. 'Ciaran Grimes is the name. This is awful.'

'Why were you here?'

'Mr Costello sent us to see if we could get access to the site, to start the wiring in the morning. I called to Delaney, the builder, for the key. Jack could have done that the other morning, but he didn't as far as I know.'

'The body is way round at the back of the house. What brought you down there?'

'Wanted a smoke and wandered about, so I did. That's when I saw the feet poking out. Nearly chucked up my tea.'

'And did you?'

'My stomach is a bit stronger than that, so no.'

'What time was it when you found her?'

'I told the guard over there.' He pointed to Garda Brennan, who was busy taking notes from another man, tall and well dressed, with a pair of spectacles plonked on top of his head holding his ginger hair in place. His beard looked like he'd run his hands through it multiple times. Michael Costello.

Grimes caught her gawking. 'That's the boss man.'

'I know who he is.' Returning her attention to Grimes, Lottie said, 'When did you find her?'

He shifted from foot to foot. 'Can't be sure. Maybe around seven. I phoned Mr Costello and he told me to call the guards. I knew she was dead, so there was no need for an ambulance.'

Lottie glanced back at the tent. 'From where was the body visible, and what did you do exactly?'

He shook his head, the beanie bobbing. 'I didn't see it until I was right up close. A fucker of a rat scampered up from the water when I threw the cigarette butt in. Sorry for the language.'

'Go on.'

'Right. Sure doesn't another one run out after the first. I nearly stood on the bastard. Jesus, I can tell you I jumped. Not that I'm afraid of them or anything, but I really don't like the dirty buggers.'

'So you saw her feet. Did you go any closer?'

'I went in a bit to investigate. Sorry I did that now.'

'Don't be sorry. If you hadn't gone to look, God knows how long she'd have lain there undiscovered. How did you know she was dead?'

'The stab wounds … it was obvious. I didn't touch her.' He dug his grubby knuckles into his eyes. 'This is terrible.'

Lottie looked around and noticed a container unit further down the site. 'Do the builders have security cameras here?'

'Nah. No need out here in the sticks.'

'Okay. Has Garda Brennan taken your statement?'

'She did that before she moved on to more important people.'

'Mr Grimes, you are very important to this investigation. We'll need your consent to take a sample of DNA and your fingerprints. Will that be okay?'

He shunted from foot to foot. 'Do I have to?'

'I can get a warrant.'

'Suppose it's okay, then. I was wearing gloves anyhow.'

'Thought you didn't touch her?'

'I … no … I mean …'

'It's okay.' She walked off, leaving him staring after her.

CHAPTER FIFTY-TWO

At the station, Kirby washed his hands. Then he washed them again. Not that he'd touched anything while out on Misneach Hill, but he felt the evil of whatever had happened to that child eating under his skin. He dried his hands on a paper towel and went to the office.

The bones had been removed to the morgue and there was no more he could do about them for now. He pulled up his chair and got to work checking the security footage from the gym where Dylan Foley claimed his key had been taken.

'Shit,' he groaned as the images loaded on the screen. There were no cameras in the locker rooms, just those mounted high up on the wall outside the premises.

Hard as it was to admit it, McKeown was the best at the CCTV stuff, and he wasn't here. Kirby found it hard to focus on the grainy outdoor images, but with Joyce Breslin's body discovered and still no sign of her son, he needed to work quickly. There was a chance the boy was still alive. He scanned the fuzzy footage, finding nothing noteworthy. After a while, he gave up and began painstakingly reviewing his notes, focusing his concentration on the dead woman, Joyce.

They had little or no background information. She was as elusive as Kevin Doran. If he could find out nothing about her past, he had to think about more recently.

Where could she have been held? Sinéad and Dylan Foley's house and Bubbles Day Care had been searched the night Evan went missing. So strike that out. Joyce and Nathan's house on Loman Road had also been searched, with few results except for the spot of blood on the radiator and the razor blade beneath it. And the kid's teddy bear was still on his bed. He scratched his head with a biro. Think, Kirby, think, he willed himself.

He drew his biro down through the list of interviews in his notebook. Frank Maher. No way that old man had it in him to abduct and hide Joyce, let alone murder her, transport her body out of town and dump her in a pond at the back of a newly constructed house. Not that it would be any different if it was an old house. Then it struck him.

Feverishly he flicked through his notes. The vacant house at Castlemain Drive. The address they'd found in the envelope down the side of the seat of Joyce's car. The car registered to Lugmiran Enterprises. So far they'd found out that Lugmiran was a shell company registered in Jersey. He'd contacted the Criminal Assets Bureau to investigate. CAB had told him shell companies were near difficult to link to any individual.

He couldn't help thinking that it had to have something to do with Joyce's death. Why register a car to a shell company if there wasn't something dodgy going on?

He grabbed his keys and shuffled out of his chair. Looking around for someone to bring with him, he realised everyone was at the Bardstown crime scene. A few minutes was all it would take, and then he would feel like he'd done his best. After all, he was certain the house was empty.

Number 14 Castlemain Drive was like a creature with blacked-out eyes. Switching off the car engine, Kirby lit a cigar and cracked open the window, watching and listening as he smoked. The estate was silent in the dusk. No children about, except for a couple of teenagers hanging out by a green electrical substation box located beside a wall at the turn in the road.

He coughed, breaking the stillness. Stubbing out the cigar, he left the car.

At the front door, he automatically rang the bell. Not waiting for a response he knew wouldn't come, he walked to the rear of the house and peered through the slit at the bottom of the window. It was dark, with only the hue of street lights casting shadows. The wooden Venetian blind was almost down to the windowsill. Not a thing moved.

At the back door, he shaded his eyes and pressed his nose to the glass. Beyond the six small frosted panes he saw the outline of appliances, but no movement. It was well and truly empty. The door looked like it hadn't been opened in years. All the same, he felt a nagging urge to get inside.

By his feet he spied a red brick covered in moss. It might have been used to keep the door open during hot weather, or maybe not. Picking it up, he debated what he was about to do. There was no reasonable cause to force entry. No reports of antisocial behaviour. Nothing to prove the necessity to commit an illegal act.

'Fuck it.'

He smashed the block into the bottom corner pane, and listened. No alarms. No lights flashing on. No running feet. No shouts from neighbours. Just the hum of traffic from the main road and the scuttling of a cat through the grass. He hoped it was just a cat.

Dropping the brick, he pushed in the remaining few shards of glass. After donning a pair of nitrile gloves, he eased his arm inside and depressed the handle. Exhaled a long relieved breath as the door eased inwards.

'This is a wild goose chase,' he muttered. But in he went.

Stepping over the broken glass, he paused in the dimness to find his bearings. He was in a utility room. Washing machine, dryer, cupboards. A door hung open. He tried the light switch, but there was no electricity. Figures, he thought, seeing as whoever lived here had abandoned the place years ago. He flicked on his pencil torch and proceeded further inside.

A kitchen. Shadows screamed up and down the walls as he shone the torch around. Leaning over the sink, he pulled the cord, raising the blind to let in a little more of the dying evening light. But the dusk had painted the sky a sad pink, and it added only a sliver of illumination.

What was he hoping to find? It didn't seem plausible that Joyce had been held here. Obviously no one had been inside the house in years.

He trained the torch to his feet and swept it outwards. The linoleum appeared to be stained, but it could be his imagination. He cast the light over the kitchen cabinets and countertop. A few drawers hung loose, and one cupboard door was open. A dresser stood by the wall behind the table, doors shut. Nothing else caught his attention as he did a quick inventory.

The refrigerator, with no electricity, contained rotting food, and the smell caught at the back of his throat. Worse than an autopsy, he thought as he held a hand to his nose and shoved the door shut with his foot.

The table was covered with broken crockery. More beneath it. He was about to right an upended chair when he stooped to see better. A brown stain had hardened into the linoleum. Blood? If it was Joyce's or Evan's, it would not be presenting like tanned leather. They'd only been missing since yesterday. This stain was not recent.

Pushing further into the house, he glanced into the living room. Nothing struck him as unusual. He grabbed his chest as it tightened, and cursed the cigars. But he knew the tightness was in apprehension for what he might discover.

Upstairs, he felt totally spooked.

A watery drip, drip, drip bored a tunnel into his brain until he found the offending tap in the en suite situated off the main bedroom. Luckily the plug wasn't in the sink, but the smell of stagnant water was in the air. He turned off the tap, but still it dripped. Glancing around, he noticed the shower tray was coloured brown, a slow, intermittent trickle from the shower head. It too looked like dried blood. What the hell had happened in this house?

Backing out, he scanned the bedroom. King-sized bed, unmade, with sheets trailing to the floor; wardrobe doors open, clothes hanging off hangers and more scattered on the floor.

Main bathroom next. The smell from the toilet churned his stomach. A trail of dried liquid led down the side of the bowl and across the floor. The bath was empty.

Kirby steeled himself. Two more rooms.

The first one surely belonged to a child. Perhaps a little boy. A model plane hung from the light shade; bedclothes with a dinosaur print. A young child, though, because it wasn't a bed. It was a cot. Fuck.

His brain pinged with warning. Unless he was totally mistaken, he had walked into an old crime scene. He'd check the final room, then call it in.

Outside the next door, the smell was unmistakable. Stale and musty. Like stagnant metallic water. Blood? His torch beam revealed a little girl's room. One corner stacked with cuddly toys. A colourful unicorn mobile hung over the pink cot. He stepped closer, his heart thumping like a high-speed train. There were no blankets. But the mattress ...

'Oh no,' he groaned.

The torchlight picked up the dark brown stains of dried blood. He trained the light along the floor. A brown trail from the cot to the door, staining the pink fluffy carpet. No mistaking it.

'What the hell happened here?'

Out on the landing again, he listened, looked towards the ceiling at the loft hatch. Not a sound; only the thumping from within his own chest. There was no way he'd fit up there, but it was obvious no one had been in this house for a long time.

Down in the kitchen, he assessed his surroundings in a new light. Something awful had happened to the occupants of this house. Something that had caused the survivors to disappear. At least one of them had been badly injured or killed. The baby from the cot with the pink unicorn mobile?

With his heart breaking, he called it in.

CHAPTER FIFTY-THREE

Four-year-old Evan was still missing.

Lottie knew they were rapidly running out of time to find the boy alive, and she prayed that his little body wasn't at the bottom of the pond where they'd found his mother.

She waited on site while SOCOs used industrial-sized pliers to break the chain lock on the yellow steel container behind the house. She stood behind them as they shone torches inside. Blood. She knew instantly that this was where Joyce had been held captive and murdered.

Leaving them to do their forensic examination, she got Garda Brennan to drive her to Michael Costello's office, as he'd told her it might be the best place to talk. She'd formed the impression he was rattled by the discovery of the body.

Costello was as accommodating as he had been when she'd spoken to him before. He pulled out a chair for her and poured her a generous mug of black coffee. She welcomed the caffeine hit, gulping it down. Not too bad. She noticed he hadn't offered coffee to Garda Brennan, or a chair to sit on.

Boyd had insisted on staying on site, wanting to be the first to know if anything was found there in relation to the missing boy. She hoped he was making progress with the builder, Trevor Delaney. He then had to interview the owner of the house. She'd sent uniforms to the station with Ciaran Grimes and his colleagues to record formal statements, along with taking DNA samples and fingerprints.

'I'm totally shocked by all this,' Costello said, his eyes gleaming from behind his spectacles. She had to admit he looked upset.

'When was the last time anyone had access to the site?' she said.

'The builders had been pulled onto another project while we were to do the electrical work. There was a mix-up over gaining access, and because of Isabel's murder, I only followed up with Delaney today. I was anxious to get the job started tomorrow, so I sent Ciaran out this evening to make sure we could enter the site.'

A text came from Boyd. None of Delaney's crew had been on site since the previous Friday. Uniforms were conducting interviews. The house owner was in Dublin for medical reasons.

'Do you think Jack could have gained access somehow?'

'He said he couldn't on Monday morning; that's why I sent him on another job.' Costello tugged at his beard, which gleamed under the tube lighting. 'Do you think he's involved in this woman's murder too?'

'I don't know what to think right now, Mr Costello.'

Her phone vibrated in her pocket again. She slipped it out. Glanced at the caller. Kirby. He could wait.

'You trust all your staff?'

'I do. I've never had to question their honesty or loyalty.'

'Emergency services were called at seven ten p.m., after Ciaran Grimes discovered the body. Why did he call you first?'

'He wanted to know what he should do. He's not the sharpest knife in the drawer.' He tapped the edge of his spectacles.

'And where were you when he called?'

'I was here. Haven't been home yet. I told him to call 999 then I drove out to Bardstown. Poor Ciaran was in an awful state.'

'I'd say he was.'

'Inspector, I can assure you he had nothing to do with this.'

'You're probably right, but right now two of your employees are connected to two murders. Isabel worked here. Has Joyce Breslin any connection to you or your business?'

'Is that the victim's name? The woman who was missing with her son.'

She still had to inform Nathan. 'I just want to know if you know her.'

He shook his head slowly. 'I saw her photo on the news. Oh God. Her little boy. What is he? Four? Awful to think what might have happened to him.' He stopped and stared intently at Lottie. 'You don't think he's in that pond, do you?'

She held his gaze. 'I'm exploring all possibilities, but I believe and hope he is still alive. Thanks for your time, and if you think of anything that might help us, please call me.'

She stood. Garda Brennan opened the door.

'Of course,' Costello said. 'And I've not forgotten about giving you a quotation for that rewiring job.'

'Thanks,' Lottie said, though it was the furthest thing from her mind right now.

She followed Brennan down the stairs.

Outside Quality Electrical, Garda Brennan waved her phone. 'Inspector, I think you need to check your messages. Detective Kirby is trying to reach you.'

'He can wait.'

'It's important. He's at the house on Castlemain Drive.'

'What house?'

'The address that was in the envelope with the blade. The one in Joyce Breslin's car.'

'Oh, right. What about it?'

'He thinks it's a crime scene. He's waiting there for SOCOs to arrive.'

'Evan?' Lottie was afraid to breathe.

'It's not recent, according to Detective Kirby.'

Lottie tugged her hair as if the stinging of her scalp could make her think straight. She phoned Boyd. 'You're sure Delaney Construction have nothing to do with Joyce's body?'

'Positive,' he said. 'Trevor Delaney has an airtight log system for his employees. All accounted for. His crew are in the clear.'

'Who does that leave us with? The house owner?'

'He's in a Dublin hospital. Not him.'

'Get uniforms to canvass the neighbours.'

'Being done as we speak. No one lives too close, but there's a few further down the road to be called to yet.'

'Okay. What about the container?'

She could hear Boyd flipping pages of his notebook. 'It was used for storing the builders' tools and equipment. It's likely Joyce was held and murdered there. It will take SOCOs some time to examine. They've called for more lights.'

'Talk to Jim McGlynn. Tell him to send someone, anyone, to 14 Castlemain Drive. Kirby thinks it's an old crime scene.'

'Really? SOCOs were out on Misneach Hill, too. McGlynn will blow a gasket.'

'Can't be helped. Evan is still missing. When you're done there, you'd better go see what Kirby has found.'

'What about you, Lottie?'

'I've to tell Nathan Monaghan we've found his partner. Then I want to shake the truth out of Jack Gallagher. He's been conjuring up disappearing acts, and right now, with very few people to put in the frame, getting the truth out of him might help me find Joyce's missing son.'

'Monaghan could be involved, or Dylan Foley.'

'Tell me something I don't know, Boyd.' She hung up before he could reply.

CHAPTER FIFTY-FOUR

Lottie could see that Nathan had been crying even before he opened the door.

She stepped inside and followed him to the kitchen, where he sat on the nearest chair. The room was cold. Curtains open. She drew down the blinds, swished over the curtains and eyed the tearful man. Garda Brennan made herself comfortable leaning against the door.

'I'm afraid I've some bad news,' Lottie began.

He sniffed loudly and ran a hand under his nose. 'He's dead, isn't he? You can tell me. I've been preparing myself all day for bad news.'

'Bad news about whom?'

'Evan. They killed him, didn't they?'

'I'm afraid you're confused,' she said. 'I'm here about Joyce.'

'Joyce?'

'You thought I was talking about Evan. Why?'

'He threatened me with Evan. He never mentioned Joyce.'

He looked up then. His eyes widening and his mouth drooping as if realising he'd made a mistake but couldn't figure out what he'd said wrong.

'Care to tell me who you mean by *he*?'

He seemed to gather himself when he saw the look on her face. Straightening his shoulders, he said, 'No comment.'

On guard, Lottie thought.

'I'm sorry to have to inform you, Nathan, that earlier this evening we found the body of an adult female. We'll need you to make a formal identification, but unfortunately, I'm in no doubt that it is Joyce's body.'

'Joyce? Dead? I don't understand.' He gulped. 'How did she die? Where is she?'

'I can't give you much information at this time, but it's clear she was murdered.'

'Murdered? How?'

He was like a bloody robot, and her head ached. 'I can't tell you at the moment. We need to make contact with her family. We haven't been able to trace any relatives. Is there someone we should call?'

He shook his head. 'I've no idea. We never really talked about her past or family. I don't think she had anyone.'

'You sure? Think, Nathan.'

He gazed at a point above her head, trance-like.

She coaxed, 'What is it?'

'You could try locating Evan's father.'

Lottie felt like the floor had capsized beneath her. She glanced at Garda Brennan, whose eyes bulged incredulously.

'Are you telling me you're not Evan's father?'

He shook his head, tears flying, lips quivering.

'Who is, then?'

'Joyce never said. She got upset when I broached the subject. Said I was Evan's dad now. I was happy with that.'

'Christ almighty, why didn't you tell us before? *He* could be involved in their disappearance.'

'How was I to know it was important?'

'Of course it is! You sure you don't know the name?'

'I don't, honest.'

'Right.' She wasn't convinced, but decided to let it go under the circumstances.

'I think someone else might be involved, though.'

'Who? Talk to me, for pity's sake.' Her tolerance levels deserted her and she had to push her hands deep into her pockets to keep from throttling him.

'Now is the time to be honest with me, Nathan. Did you have anything to do with Joyce's death? Why did you think Evan was dead?'

His whole body deflated as he hugged his waist, arms tight around each other. 'He … he threatened me over Evan. Oh God, it's all my fault.' He opened his mouth to let out a shriek before folding into himself, sobbing.

Sitting forward, Lottie felt every hair on her arms rise to attention, as if a bugle had sounded. 'You have to calm down and tell me what you know. Look at me, Nathan.'

He raised his red eyes and stared vacantly.

'Who made threats?' she said.

'Dermody.' Another sniff.

'Who is Dermody?' She looked over at Brennan, and the young guard shrugged at the new name in the mix. Two steps forward and ten back.

Nathan rubbed his elbows, nails digging into bone. 'Chris Dermody. I don't know who he is, but sometimes I have to … I suppose you'd say I do jobs for him. You know, like when I'm driving. Secretly.'

Lottie began to draw the picture in her head. Nathan was smuggling something into the country for this Dermody character. 'When did you last see him, and what did he say to you?'

'Yesterday evening. I met him at an industrial estate outside Dublin. Whatever was stowed in the back of the lorry was taken out. Then he said he knew Evan. It was a threat to keep my mouth shut.'

'What were you smuggling for him?'

'I don't know what it was. He pays me well, so I don't ask.'

'Who is your main employer?'

'AJ Lennon.'

That name, cropping up again. 'Does Chris Dermody work for him too?'

'I don't think it's anything to do with Lennon, to be honest. Dermody pays me to make unscheduled stops on the continent, and when I stop at the designated location – that's what he calls it – something is packed into the back of my lorry under a false compartment. I stop off at another designated location in Dublin, and that's where it's unloaded. Then I return to Ragmullin with my normal load. I don't want to know what I'm transporting for him. I just take the money, because I need it. Joyce doesn't make much, and there's day care costs and all that. Oh God! Poor Joyce.'

He stared at Lottie, his eyes pleading for understanding. You can fuck right off, she thought, and sat back, trying to make sense of this new information. It was obvious Nathan had got himself involved with criminals.

'How much do you get paid for this smuggling?'

'A grand a time. He pays without argument, but last night when I stopped off in Dublin, he mentioned Evan. I took it as a warning in case I was having second thoughts.'

'And were you? Having second thoughts?'

'I suppose I was.'

'Why is that, if you needed the money?'

'Joyce mentioned one night recently that she might soon have a substantial payday. I grilled her about it, but she kept tapping her nose and smiling. Maybe she found out I was smuggling or thought she was going to win the Lotto. I really don't know.'

'Right.'

'Then when I got home last night, Joyce and Evan were missing.'

'And you didn't think it important enough to tell me all this before now?'

'I'm sorry. I was scared.'

'And how do you think an innocent four-year-old boy is feeling?'

He began to sob loudly.

'Pull yourself together. Joyce is dead and I have to find Evan. When did you last see Chris Dermody?'

'Yesterday evening.'

'So the evening Evan went missing,' Lottie said, thinking aloud. 'The day Joyce was abducted. How could this Dermody know she wasn't around to pick her son up if he was in Dublin?'

'I don't know.'

'Who does he work for?'

'I don't know. I don't think it's Lennon, because if he was involved, the stuff could be unloaded at the warehouse without me having to make an unscheduled stop in Dublin. But I could be wrong.'

'How did you get involved in this mess, Nathan?'

He sniffed and ran a hand over his eyes. 'Met Dermody in Fallon's one night. The pub.'

Lottie cringed, thinking of Chloe working there. 'Go on.'

'He seemed to know I was a truck driver, that I was making regular runs to Europe collecting products for Lennon. He made an offer I found hard to refuse. This was about six months ago. Believe me, I don't know who he works for. Maybe he's a lone wolf. And I swear to you I have no idea what I was smuggling.'

If Nathan was capable of smuggling, Lottie wondered if he was capable of being involved in his family's abduction. 'Dylan Foley said he originally met you at the Sheefin gym. Did you ever take one of his keys?'

'Why would I do that?'

'Maybe your friend Dermody threatened you and you stole it for him. He then used it to slip into Foley's and abduct Evan.'

'You're crazy! I'd never do that. Fuck's sake, I don't even go to the gym any more.'

Nathan sat with his hands held out, palms upwards. He could plead the innocent victim all he liked, but he was implicated, either unwittingly or intentionally. And now she'd have to get the DOCB, the Drugs and Organised Crime Bureau, involved.

She could arrest him for smuggling – he'd admitted it – but she had no hard evidence and she had not put him under caution. Shit. And she was still no closer to finding Evan.

'Get your jacket. I'm taking you to the station. You may need to contact a solicitor.'

The threads of the investigation were snaking out all over the place instead of being wound into a spool. It was turning into a logistical nightmare.

'What about Joyce?' He fetched his jacket from a hook on the back door and turned to face her. 'Will I have to see her body?'

'If I can't find any other next of kin, yes.'

He held the table edge to steady himself. 'I'm not sure I can look at it.'

Lottie rubbed her head in confusion. 'Nathan, did you love her?'

'Of course I did. And Evan was like a son to me. I thought of him as my own flesh and blood. Oh God. I hope he's not dead.'

'You and me both,' Lottie said.

As Garda Brennan followed Nathan out to the hall, Lottie took a quick look around the kitchen. The wall calendar snagged a memory in her brain. She scrutinised the dates. Evan's childcare days were marked with a felt-tip pen. A large red bubble. It was obvious that Joyce had intended to be around for the rest of the month. Some days were highlighted with *Nathan away*. She leaned in closer. A small x marked on Friday this week.

'Nathan, what had Joyce planned for Friday?'

'Don't know.'

'Did you not share your plans for the week ahead?'

He sighed. 'Not really. Joyce has always been kind of secretive. It never bothered me. She has her life and I have mine. Live and let live. Oh God …' He began to cry again.

'By the way, her car was registered to a Lugmiran Enterprises. Who are they?'

He dragged his jacket on over trembling arms. 'Never heard of them. That's the truth.'

'Yeah, and I intend to find out the real truth.' Lottie had no idea what that was any more.

'I just want you to find Evan.'

'Evan is my main priority, but you should have told me he wasn't your son. We've lost vital time.'

As Brennan led Nathan out to the car, Lottie went back to the kitchen. She took the calendar from the wall and closed the door as she left.

CHAPTER FIFTY-FIVE

Katie Parker led the man into the half-painted hallway.

He stopped behind her, staring at the walls. 'Your mother said the house was old, but I didn't realise it was actually this old.'

'It's ancient,' Katie said. 'What can I do for you, Mr Costello? Mam won't be home until later. She's working on a huge murder case at the moment.'

'I know. The murdered woman, Isabel, used to work for me. Her husband still works with my company and I believe he's in the frame for it.'

'Oh, that must be awful for you.'

'It is, but I still have to work. I apologise for calling so late, but your mother mentioned the house needed rewiring and I told her we could assess the cost for her. Is it okay if I have a look around?'

'Would it be better if you waited until she was here, Mr Costello?'

'Oh, that's fine then. I was just passing on my way home, and thought I'd stop by. I'm Michael, by the way.'

'Right then, Michael, my granny is here if you want to have a word with her?'

'That would be perfect. Does she live here too?'

'No, she has her own place. Don't think she needs any electrical work done on her house, though. Come on. She's in the kitchen.'

Katie admired the good-looking man as he stood back to let her walk in front of him. A real gentleman. She thought his beard and ginger hair made him kind of cute – for an old guy. She noticed Louis sitting on the bottom step of the bare wooden stairs and scooped him into her arms.

'And who is this little man?' Michael said, leaning over to ruffle the boy's hair.

Katie smiled. 'Louis is my son. He was asleep earlier but then he woke up crying, and now he refuses to go back to sleep.'

'You're lucky to have him.'

'Thank you. I am lucky.'

His comment was a change from people telling her she was too young to be a mother, which usually made her squirm. Louis' dad had been murdered before she even knew she was pregnant. She'd missed out on college and a whole load of stuff, but she loved her son too much to have regrets over what might have been.

'God, that's dangerous.'

'What is?' She turned to see Michael staring up at the chandelier hanging from the cracked hall ceiling. 'Oh, that. Granny says it's an antique.'

'More like a dangerous relic. And it could crash at any minute. Tell your mother it needs to go. I can see this house needs a complete overhaul. In the electrical department, I mean.'

'It needs an overhaul full stop,' Katie said with a laugh. 'Have you eaten? Gran has made the most delicious cottage pie. I'm sure she'd be delighted with your company.'

'You know what? I have no idea when I last ate a proper meal.'

'Let's see what's left in the dish then.'

She walked on ahead, feeling an urge to put on a show for him. His manners were old-school but his face was classy; his beard in fashion. His eyes were something of a mystery. Granted, he was maybe twenty plus years older than her, but you never knew …

CHAPTER FIFTY-SIX

People huddled together in silence on the green area across the road from where Kirby stood smoking a cigar. A strip of garda tape hung loosely between the pillars of the house. Boyd took two packets of overalls from a SOCO and signed in with the guard at the gate.

'You look as wrecked as I feel,' he said, handing one packet to Kirby and tearing the other open.

'Yeah, well it's a bit of a mess in there, I can tell you.' Kirby put the pack under his arm, topped the cigar and placed it in the yellow-stained pocket of his shirt.

The night air was chilly and Boyd had promised to help Sean paint his room, but now he was bone weary. He didn't think he'd be able to hold a paintbrush let alone put a foot on a stepladder.

'You look yellow around the gills,' Kirby said struggling with one leg in the overalls.

'Just tired.'

'I know what'll fix that. A creamy pint of Guinness in Cafferty's after we're done here. What do you say to that?'

'Sounds good, but maybe another time. Let's have a look inside. Who did McGlynn send?'

'A young lassie,' Kirby said. 'All business. I mean, she's very profes-sional. Might not even let us in.'

'Bollocks to that. I didn't come here to be left hanging around.' Boyd zipped his overalls and waited while Kirby wrestled with his.

'They'll kill me for traipsing all around first without the proper gear.'

'If you hadn't gone in, you wouldn't have found the scene.'

'At least we don't have to wait for the state pathologist. We don't have a body.'

'Unless you haven't yet found it.' Boyd pushed in the back door and entered the house.

SOCOs had set up a small generator to run their halogen lights.

'We need to get the electricity reconnected,' Kirby said.

A stale, fusty metallic smell hit Boyd in the face once he stepped into the kitchen. He sidled out of a SOCO's way while another white-suited figure stood directing operations from the hall.

He approached her and smiled behind his mask. 'Detective Sergeant Boyd.'

'I'm Gráinne, and please don't touch anything until I've had a run-through first. I've carried out a quick inventory of the kitchen. Look in there if you have to.'

'Grand, thanks,' Boyd said. 'I won't upset your apple cart.'

'I'm serious. I've had my fair share of bullying, bungling detectives leaving traces of themselves all around my crime scenes. You seem too nice to add to that ignominious list.'

Boyd thought of the lecture Kirby would get when she found out he'd been inside without a protective suit. 'I assure you, I am the consummate professional.'

Her silver-blue eyes carried her smile. He noticed a line of freckles on her forehead. Her eyebrows were fair and he imagined her hair hidden beneath the hood was a mane of wild red curls.

'I'm sure you are, but that's what they all say. Now if you'll excuse me, I've to go upstairs to oversee the cot with dried blood, then I'm shutting up shop for the night. Our generator is shite and we need daylight to do a proper job, unless you can magic up electricity for me tonight. Would that be possible?'

'I doubt it.'

'Then have your cursory look. I'll be back at dawn for a proper inspection.'

When she'd marched up the stairs, Boyd felt a void left in her place. He shook himself and joined Kirby in the kitchen. 'Don't think I'm allowed to see your crime scene yet. She wants to do the full examination in the morning.'

'It will give you nightmares. Best to wait.' Kirby began opening and closing drawers. 'Whatever went on here, it occurred a long time ago.'

Boyd said, 'You thought Joyce might have been held here before her body was dumped, didn't you?'

'That was my initial reasoning,' Kirby said. 'This address was on the scrap of paper I found in her car, and because of the scene upstairs, it must have a connection. But the house was locked up tight. I've found no blood trace that's recent. No evidence that anyone has been here in the last few years, never mind days.' He wheezed as he talked. 'I need to give up smoking.'

'Not the first time I've heard that.' Boyd crossed to the table and chairs. A dresser stood against the wall, glass doors on the top section with wooden doors beneath.

Behind the glass, with one pane cracked as if something had been thrown at it, there was nothing much of interest. A shelf of cookery books. Another held a mismatched collection of mugs, and on the bottom shelf, a mess of different-sized plates.

'Thought I might find something to match the page you found in the car. Or something to tell us the identity of the owners,' he said.

'And my name is Santa Claus,' Kirby said from beside the sink.

Hunkering down, Boyd opened the wooden doors. The cupboard held four baskets filled with hats and gloves and scarves.

He went through each one. A pink Peppa Pig hat with satin ribbons felt sad in his hands and he shoved it back quickly. More hats, some embroidered with Superman and Batman images. Adult mittens and gloves. He picked up a pair of gloves and felt something stuffed inside.

A blue silk scarf.

He asked a nearby SOCO for an evidence bag.

Placing the bag on the floor, he set the bunched-up scarf on top and carefully unfolded it.

'Jesus Christ, Kirby.'

'I've been called worse.'

'This is serious.'

Boyd sat back on his haunches as Kirby joined him.

'And you found those inside the scarf?' Kirby said.

'I did.'

Lying on cool blue material with a splash of yellow were three razor blades, rusted and bloody.

CHAPTER FIFTY-SEVEN

With Nathan Monaghan waiting in a cell for his solicitor to arrive, Lottie returned to her office. She was overcome with a sense of helplessness. Her gut was telling her she wasn't doing enough to search for Evan, and now that his mother had been found dead, it was increasingly unlikely the boy would be discovered alive. No, don't think like that, she cautioned. He is alive, that's what I have to believe in.

She ordered a search warrant for AJ Lennon's warehouse, with little hope of getting it signed by a judge before morning, if at all. She contacted the DOCB informing them about Nathan and Chris Dermody and an alleged smuggling operation. They told her they would locate Dermody for her as quickly as possible.

In her mind, it was likely that Dermody was responsible for taking Evan, but what reason could he have for brutally murdering Joyce? Surely that would push Nathan away rather than embed him further into the smuggling operation.

And then there was Isabel. Nathan had said he didn't know Isabel or Jack Gallagher. Nothing was adding up.

To occupy her mind while she waited for word from the bureau on Dermody, she checked the multitude of missed calls and texts. Besides Kirby's, the rest were from Lynch. She opened the earliest message.

'Holy shit,' she exclaimed, rushing out to find Garda Brennan. With Kirby and Boyd at Castlemain Drive, she was floundering for staff.

'What is it?' Martina said.

'Get the car. Now.'

Once they'd cleared the station gate, Lottie said, 'Siren and lights. We need to talk to Gallagher before he does a disappearing act again.'

'Isn't Detective Lynch at the house?'

'Yeah, and according to her, Gallagher claims the man he pushed into the canal was Kevin Doran.'

'The handyman we've had difficulty tracing?'

'One and the same. Hurry.'

Brennan obliged and floored the accelerator. Lottie sank into the seat as their speed picked up on the short journey across town. Traffic was light at this hour of the evening, and it was comforting to know they could be there in three minutes.

Anita opened the door, a dejected droop to her mouth. Lottie pitied the grief-stricken woman but had no time for platitudes as she made her way into the sitting room.

The space seemed more cluttered than the last time she'd been here. Empty baby bottles stood on a stack of books on the floor, coats lay abandoned on the couch, baby clothes were drying on the radiator, and the buggy had blankets piled high.

Anita must have caught Lottie's glance in that direction. 'Holly is asleep upstairs. Poor little pet.'

Jack Gallagher stood with his back to the roaring fire. 'Have you found Isabel's killer?'

'Why don't you tell me, Jack?'

'How many times do I have to say, I had nothing to do with it.'

Lottie planted herself squarely in front of him. Lynch was by the window, her face etched with tiredness and agitation. 'Head on home, Detective Lynch. Garda Brennan will take over for now.'

Lynch's weary eyes lit up. 'Thanks.' She gathered her belongings and left.

Garda Brennan stood by the door. Anita flopped onto the couch without lifting the jackets flung there. Lottie envied the woman being able to sit down in her own home, as tiredness trekked slowly up her leg muscles. But she didn't envy the sorrow-creased lines etched around the woman's eyes.

'Have you found the bastard?' Gallagher said.

'Will you sit down, please?' Lottie indicated the armchair to his right. When he was seated, she sat opposite, relieved to take the weight off her feet and doubly glad of the coffee she'd had earlier in Costello's office to keep her head clear.

'Jack, I want to know all about Kevin Doran.' She went straight to the heart of her visit.

'What's this about?' Gallagher rubbed the knees of his trousers to a shine.

'Earlier today at the canal, you had an argument with Doran and he ended up in the water.'

'So what? I told the other one, Detective Lynch.'

'Oh my God. You pushed him in the canal?' Anita cried. 'How could you, Jack?'

Lottie kept her focus on Gallagher. 'What did you talk to Doran about?'

'He was following me.'

'Why? What did he want?'

'Said he was afraid your crowd were going to pin Isabel's murder on him. It was him, wasn't it? I should have drowned him when I had the chance, but I'll kill the bastard yet.'

'You are not going to kill anyone else.'

He looked up, eyes wary. 'What's that supposed to mean?'

Lottie pressed on. 'Where did you go after you argued?'

'Nowhere.' Gallagher shrugged. 'I walked. Needed to clear my head. My wife's been murdered, in case you've forgotten.'

She ignored his sarcasm.

'I'll put the kettle on,' Anita said, rising.

'Stay here,' Lottie ordered. Anita flopped back on the pile of coats. 'Jack, are you going to tell me what's going on?'

Jack kneaded his hands into each other, his eyes troubled.

She knew she was close to uncovering something crucial. She could feel it in her aching bones. 'Where did you go after you left Kevin in the canal? This time, I want the truth.'

'How many times do I have to tell you? I just kept walking.'

'Detective Lynch informed me that you have a tablet and I think you received a message from someone. Who was it?'

'What message?'

'I can find out myself, but I'd rather you told me now.'

He seemed to reconsider, maybe thinking he'd been backed into a corner. 'It's not connected to Isabel's murder.'

'My team has spent nearly two days trying to find Kevin Doran and you can walk out the door and meet him. I want that tablet.'

'The tablet has nothing to do with Doran.'

'Hand it over.' This was ridiculous. Techie Gary could access the tablet remotely if she asked him.

He glanced at Anita, his face pumping purple. Please don't let him say he has a woman on the side, Lottie thought.

'I … I was seeing someone.'

Lottie groaned. Anita gasped.

'Not like that,' he said quickly. 'She's just a friend.'

'Why the need for a secret device, then?'

'I didn't want Isabel to get jealous. She might have checked my phone.'

'Jack!' Anita cried.

Lottie said, 'I'm sure you had your poor wife under so much control she had no way of checking anything.'

'That's a lie!' Jack roared.

'You need to start telling me the truth.'

'I am. Fuck's sake.' He ran his fingers through his hair, then his face relaxed and his hands dropped to his knees in defeat. 'Her name is Tanya Cummings. And she *is* only a friend, no matter what you think.'

'What is this about, Jack?' Anita said, her eyes boring holes through her son-in-law.

'I'm sorry, Anita, but it's nothing for you to worry about.' He turned, glaring at Lottie. 'Go on, check her out if you want.'

Anger like molten lava threatened to consume Lottie. 'You can't go picking names from a hat for an alibi.'

'We met for a few hours this evening. Just went for a drive. Nothing else.' Then it seemed that her words dawned on him. 'Why do I need an alibi?'

'We found the body of Joyce Breslin earlier at the Bardstown property you were supposed to be working at yesterday morning. Care to tell me about that?'

'What?' A nervous tic twitched his lips. 'I don't understand what you're getting at.'

'Did you know Joyce Breslin?'

The high purple hue on his cheeks faded and Lottie thought he was about to pass out.

'I … I don't think so.'

She brought up Joyce's photograph on her phone. 'Will this help you to remember?'

Anita leaned over to glance at the photo. 'Isn't she that missing woman? God, is she dead? What about her little boy?'

Gallagher barely glanced at the photograph. 'Don't know her.'

'I think you do,' Lottie insisted, ignoring Anita trembling by her side.

'You're making this shit up,' Gallagher growled. 'My wife's body is lying in some steel drawer in the bowels of a mortuary and I thought you'd come to tell me you'd found her murderer. All you're doing is throwing out accusations. You're a fool.'

He stood up, his bulk towering over Lottie where she sat. She wasn't about to be intimidated. She rose suddenly, stepping into his space.

'Where were you this evening from the time Detective Lynch saw you leave the canal until just before eight p.m.? And don't dare lie to me.'

'I told you. I was with Tanya. You can ask her if you like. I needed to talk to someone who wasn't family. That's all.'

Anita cried out. 'Jack! What have you done? You persecuted my daughter and all the time you were shagging someone else.' She drew her hand back and slapped him so hard, the sound reverberated around the room. 'You're a bastard.'

He caught her wrist. 'Anita, you need to understand. I'm sorry, but I found it hard to cope with Isabel's moods. Especially after Holly was born. I just needed a friend.' Releasing her, he made for the door.

Garda Brennan made herself fill the space. 'Stay where you are, Jack.'

Anita choked back a cry. 'I hear Holly. I'll be in my bedroom if you need me, Inspector.'

As she ran out, Jack turned back and slumped onto a chair.

Lottie had had enough of this shite. 'You're coming to the station and we will continue this conversation under caution. Do you wish to call your solicitor?'

'At this hour of the night?'

'Up to you.'

'I can't believe this is happening to me.'

He was pathetic. 'I have a job to do. And I intend to do it no matter what you or anyone else thinks of me.'

'I want to say goodnight to Holly first.'

Was this the first time he'd displayed any interest in his daughter? No way was Lottie letting him out of her sight.

'There's no need to disturb her.'

'Right then. You win. Let's get this charade over with. I'll fetch my coat.' He marched towards the door, and fair dues to Garda Brennan, she stood her ground once again.

'Your coat is on the couch,' she said.

Both women escorted him out of the house. As Lottie stared at him in the back of the squad car, she hoped she was making the right move at the right time.

CHAPTER FIFTY-EIGHT

With Jack waiting for his solicitor, Lottie phoned the DOCB and was informed that Chris Dermody was not at his Dublin address. She emphasised the importance of finding him – Evan's life could be in the smuggler's hands.

Divers had continued their search of Lough Cullion, where Joyce's car had been found, without success. They hoped to resume at first light. Woods and forests were being meticulously combed, farms and sheds throughout the county being checked. It was increasingly likely that the little boy could have been whisked off to Dublin, if Dermody was their man. The Ragmullin force had been flat out, and now she had to trust in the bureau.

Nathan Monaghan's solicitor was unable to make it in to the station until early the next morning, so he'd agreed to spend another night in the cells. Lottie had to admit he was being very cooperative. Or maybe he was just terrified of Chris Dermody.

Jack Gallagher was another kettle of fish altogether.

His solicitor, Lilian Regan, arrived and promptly conferred with her client in the interview room. Lottie had a feeling this was going to go belly-up.

'My client is prepared to give you the contact details for Tanya Cummings,' Regan said.

'I have that information, thanks.'

The solicitor continued. 'He will also consent to remaining at the home of Anita Boland until such time as you have evidence with which to charge him or release him from suspicion of his wife's and Joyce Breslin's murders. Seems to me you're on a fishing expedition, Inspector, trying to hook in my client with no bait. To clarify, you have absolutely no proof of any wrongdoing.'

'He pushed Kevin Doran into the canal. The man ended up in hospital.'

'Is he pressing charges?' The solicitor smirked.

If I knew where to find him, Lottie thought, then maybe. 'Detective Lynch had to jump in and save Mr Doran. We will be pressing charges, Lilian.'

'This is bullshit,' Gallagher said.

'I asked you this at Anita's house and I'll ask you again. Where were you this afternoon up to eight p.m.?'

'With Tanya Cummings. Have you not spoken with her yet? She works in Lennon's in case you don't know.'

Lottie sighed. Lennon's again! There was only one of her, and her team was stretched. She'd sent a uniform to Cummings' home address, but he'd come back with the news that she was not at home.

'Do you know Joyce Breslin?'

'No.'

'Her son went to Bubbles Day Care, where Isabel used to work.'

'How does that mean I know this woman?'

How indeed? What was she missing? Perhaps she was totally wrong in her conviction that Jack was involved in both murders.

'I am holding your client for further questioning, Miss Regan. His DNA and fingerprints will be run against those found at the Bardstown site where the body of Joyce Breslin was discovered this evening. His van will also be forensically examined.'

'Get a search warrant,' Lilian said.

Jack threw his arms in the air and let them fall heavily on the table. He glared at Lottie. 'You're trying to stitch me up.'

She walked slowly from the room, leaving both of them staring after her.

In her office, Lottie fetched her jacket and bag. Her agenda for the night was simple. Home. Eat. Sleep. Hopefully tomorrow her brain would be clearer and things might fall into place. Her heart contracted as she thought of Evan. The little boy was still missing, despite the force doing everything imaginable to find him. It was not looking good. She despaired for the poor little mite, but she was no good to him if she was dead on her feet.

Kirby and Boyd bustled into the office just as she was escaping.

'Thought you two had absconded.' She hid a yawn with her hand.

'Don't go anywhere yet,' Kirby said. 'Not until you see this.'

'It's late. We've all had a curse of a day. Can't it wait until tomorrow?'

'Won't take long.'

'That's an evidence bag,' she said, noting the bag in his hand.

'From the house on Castlemain Drive.'

'Ah, Kirby, you know I've enough cases on the go. Bones found on a hill, two murdered women and a missing boy.' She glanced from one man to the other. 'In case you've both forgotten.'

'You'll want to see this,' Boyd said.

He took her by the elbow and led her to his desk. Refusing the chair Kirby pulled out for her, she remained standing.

'Get on with it.'

Pulling on gloves, Boyd proceeded to open the bag. Carefully he extracted a folded blue silk scarf.

'Don't tell me you took this from a potential crime scene?'

'Gráinne okayed it.'

'Who the hell is Gráinne?'

'The lead SOCO on site. They've packed up for the night. Said they'll be back at first light. Kirby will try and get the electricity company to reconnect the house. We left two uniforms in a car outside it.'

'SOCOs have generators and all that jazz, don't they?' Her head buzzed with exhaustion.

'Most of their equipment is where Joyce's body was found. Gráinne's team decided it was best to commence a full examination of the scene tomorrow.'

'Do you know how much all this is going to cost? We even had SOCOs and uniforms out on Misneach. The super will blow a gasket. I'll be filling out reports and balancing budgets until kingdom come.'

'Sorry,' Boyd said, looking anything but.

'Right.' She eyeballed him. 'Did you examine this crime scene Kirby found?'

'I didn't go up the stairs. I'll head back in the morning. Gráinne says they'll be there at seven.'

'You will be *here* at or before seven, Boyd.'

'Right, whatever. Now, look, at this.'

She rocked on her heels while he unfolded the scarf. Then she stood still. 'What the hell?'

'Yeah.'

She stared at the blades. 'A razor blade was found in Isabel's hand. Another under the radiator at Joyce's house and one in the envelope in her car.'

'That led us to Castlemain Drive, where we found these. Another connection,' Boyd said.

'Now all we need is to find a blade with the bones on Misneach Hill and we have a complete puzzle with no answers.' She was so tired and hungry, she wasn't sure if she was being sarcastic or serious.

'The bones have been removed from the hill,' Kirby said, 'and sent to the state pathologist. Regarding the Castlemain house, I was looking into its ownership, so I'll get back to that now.'

'No, Kirby, go home and get some sleep. Do it first thing in the morning.'

He didn't need any further encouragement.

When Kirby had shuffled off home, Lottie explained to Boyd what had happened in their absence.

'Listen to this. Nathan Monaghan is not Evan's father,' she said.

'Why didn't he tell us before now?' Boyd said. 'That's vital information. It means the boy could have been abducted by his real father.'

'If we only knew who he was. I've tasked the night shift with trying to find out. Might be on his birth cert, if they can locate it.'

'Why haven't the bureau found this Dermody character? They have more resources than we do.'

'They will find him.'

'Do you believe what Monaghan said about Dermody's threats towards Evan?'

'It has a ring of truth to it,' Lottie said. 'The bureau say Dermody has been in Mountjoy on two occasions. Once for armed robbery and another time for possession of Class A drugs.'

'Could he have taken Joyce?'

'Possibly, or someone from his clan. If they did, they'd have known Evan would still be at Sinéad Foley's late in the evening.'

'But how did they gain access to the house?'

'Dylan Foley says that someone must have taken his door key at the gym. Apparently that was where he first met Nathan. Could Nathan have taken the key? Or is Dylan somehow involved? Hell, is Sinéad involved too? It's a mess of questions without answers.' She yawned, feeling sick. 'Our main focus of attention must be getting Evan home safe.'

'Home to what?' Boyd said. 'His mother is dead. Nathan, the man he called Dad, will be locked up for his involvement in smuggling. Evan is an orphan, for all intents and purposes.'

Lottie's heart broke for the little boy. 'Child protection services will care for him until we find his real father.'

'We need more resources, Lottie.'

'Of course we do. Would you ring McKeown? You're the most amiable of the lot of us on the phone. I want him here first thing tomorrow. He can sort out his personal life later. And tell him to stay away from Lynch. We have enough drama without inviting it into the office.'

'Will do. You don't see Nathan Monaghan as the killer, do you?'

She clenched her teeth and thought for a moment before saying, 'We checked his movements for when Isabel was murdered and Joyce disappeared. There's no way he could have been directly responsible for either. He was back in the country when Evan was abducted. We need to talk to Chris Dermody to see how or if he is involved.'

'It's late. Everyone is working flat out to find Evan. We're even searching the lake. But you have to admit, Lottie, it's looking very bleak for the boy.'

'That's why I won't be able to sleep.

'Come on. Out of here.'

'Just a minute,' she said as her desk phone rang. 'Hello. Yes. Go on.'

She listened, pen poised to take notes. 'That's brilliant. Thanks a million. Make sure you get a full statement.' She hung up.

'What was that about?' Boyd said. 'You look excited.'

'That was Garda Fuery. He was talking to a farmer about a kilometre from where Joyce's body was found who saw a navy van come down the road earlier this evening, around six o'clock. He hadn't seen it head up there. But he took the licence plate number. And guess what?'

'It belongs to Jack Gallagher?'

'We have him, Boyd! At last, some good news. He's being held for the night and we should have something more substantial to wave in his face in the morning, once we have the search warrant for his van.'

As Boyd pulled on his jacket, Lottie saw the edge of the envelope peeking out of the pocket. It was on the tip of her tongue to ask him about it, but she decided now was not the time for personal issues.

'I'll stay at mine tonight,' he said, 'even though I promised Sean I'd help with the painting.'

'Rose texted at some stage to say she'd made her special cottage pie. "The one young Boyd likes", she said. You better come and eat it.'

'At this hour?'

'I know you'd eat Rose's cottage pie at any hour. Come on.'

CHAPTER FIFTY-NINE

When he woke up, Kevin saw the message from Dervla and was instantly alarmed. There was no need for her to be contacting him. He checked what time she'd sent the message. God, it was hours ago. He hoped she hadn't done anything stupid. Staring at his small black phone, he tried to think of his next move.

'I know nothing,' he recited over and over.

But that wasn't true at all. He knew a lot of things. Things he should not know. Things that frightened the life out of him. Things Isabel had told him when he'd been preparing the foundations of her new extension, before Jack ran out of money.

He went to the chest of drawers and pulled out the broken bottom drawer. It wasn't a good hiding place but he'd needed to keep it close at hand in case she needed him. Taking the flip-top phone from the drawer, he switched it on, relieved to see it was fully charged. Like Isabel had told him to do. He smiled at how good he was at following orders, and then felt the smile drift from his face. Isabel was dead. There was no way around that. He had failed to keep her safe. Failed to watch her. Not that she'd asked him to exactly, but he'd felt duty-bound to take on the role of her protector. Everything came back to him, didn't it? Always his fault. That was what had been drummed into his head for years. He had no idea how to make things right any more. And then he wondered about his blackouts. Surely he hadn't hurt her? Hadn't killed her?

He glanced at the screen. Isabel had given him her secret phone to mind the day before she was killed. She'd known, hadn't she? It was clear to him now. She'd always told him danger was close. Just how close she hadn't been sure. But now Kevin was one hundred per cent certain she had known.

There was a missed call, and then a text message alert on the screen. Unopened and unread.

He pressed the key and read the message, and after that he read it again.

Who could he trust to tell about it?

He wandered around his small kitchen, the phone in his hand, reading the message over and over again.

The birds nesting in the chimney cawed loudly and the mice scratched inside the walls and scampered across the floor around his bare feet. He ran a hand over his thumping forehead. There was no one he could trust. He was alone in the world. Like always.

A loud knock sounded on his door.

He stalled, but opened it to a little gap.

A young woman stood on the stoop, shaking like a leaf.

It wasn't that cold out, was it? Not that he knew, because he hadn't been outside since late afternoon. Or was it longer? It was hard to mark the passage of time.

She was shivering uncontrollably, her eyes wide and wild, her face streaked with tears.

'Can I come in, Kevin?'

Still he stood with the door barely open. No one came into his house. Ever.

'What did you do?' he asked.

'Me? Nothing.'

'You don't look like someone who did nothing.'

'You're a pain in the arse, Kevin. A bastard, do you know that?'

'I do. That word was beaten into me years ago. I'd no father that I knew of and a mother who didn't want me, so I was told. So yeah, I think I qualify as a bastard.'

It looked like she laughed, but it was only her teeth chattering.

'Are you going to let me come in?'

Still he held the door between them. 'What do you want?'

'Oh, for fuck's sake, we need to talk. There's something going on and people are getting killed. Murdered.' Her dark eyes narrowed and she leaned against the door, his arm taking all the weight. 'We know why, don't we, Kevin? We have to do something about it.'

'No, Dervla, I don't want to be involved. I've enough shite in my life. Look where I live, for God's sake.'

She wasn't taking no for an answer. 'I still want to come inside. I'm frozen solid. I had to walk from the top of the road.'

It was pitch dark outside, and in the miserable light he noticed mist settling on her hair like raised crystals.

'You better not make me sorry about this.'

He dragged the door in over the stone floor and ushered her inside. She walked past him, and with a final look at the night, he shut the door. Bolted it.

'Could you make me a cup of strong tea?' She was sitting at the dirty table. He hoped the mice stayed out of sight.

'This is not some fancy café.'

'I only want something to warm up my blood.'

'I don't have any tea. Why are you here?'

'Kevin, a little manners would go a long way to making a woman feel safe around you.'

'Cut the shite, I need to know what brought you out all this way.'

He sat opposite, nervous energy making his knee jig against the roughly hewn table. She was still shivering, her eyes deep pools. Nothing reflected in them.

She lowered her head for a second before it shot up, a curve on her lips he couldn't read. 'I found a bone yesterday.'

'A bone?' He'd tried to keep his fake anger set like wax on his face, but he couldn't stop his open-mouthed surprise.

'I think it's a baby's bone. Like from an arm or a leg. Then today, I went back and found a skull. I think there's a whole skeleton there.'

'Jesus, Dervla. What the fuck?'

'Yeah.'

'Where did you find the bones?' Inching back into the chair, he felt the need to be further away from her and her black eyes.

'On the Misneach Hill. I remembered what you said about that night ... out there. I'm not as dumb as I look.'

He held his breath. No, it couldn't be that. He tried to remain calm, to ease the drumming in his ears. 'It's probably an ancient sacrifice.'

'No, Kevin, it's not.'

'I hope you left them where you found them, or you'll have nothing but bad luck.'

'I left the skull, but I took the bone to Ragmullin garda station.'

'You what? Why would you do that?' Oh hell, now it was a terrible mess.

'I had to get rid of it and it didn't seem right to just throw it in a bin.'

'You could have brought it back to the hill.'

'Those little bones are somebody's child.'

'So?'

'Why would someone dump a child on the hill?'

'To make a sacrifice?' he chanced. He had to get her out of here. Dervla Byrne was dangerous. Why had he ever trusted her? But he'd told her the tale as a mythological fable, never thinking she would take him seriously.

'I think someone put a little body up there to hide a crime.'

'I haven't a clue what you're on about.'

'Listen to me, Kevin. I remember what you told me once. Do you? Probably not, with that fucked-up brain of yours.'

'That's not nice.'

She smirked. 'I think someone murdered a little child and tried to bury its body up on that hillside. But I found it! I might get a medal or something, do you think?'

He thought she was high on something, and tried not to allow her words to swim inside his skull, tried not to be distracted by the two phones sitting on the table where he'd left them. His and Isabel's. He hoped Dervla wouldn't ask about them.

Then he saw her eyes follow his. 'Why have you got two phones?'

He squirmed. She definitely wasn't as dumb as she liked to let on.

'Safety in numbers,' he laughed hoarsely.

But she wasn't laughing. 'What are you up to, Kevin Doran?'

'Nothing. What are *you* up to? Why come all the way out here to tell me about some stupid bone?'

'I sent you a text, but you didn't have the manners to reply. I thought maybe you were dead out here and no one would find your body for years and years. You'd be lost like that baby's bone, which was lost until I found it.'

'Are you drunk?'

'I wish.' She turned up her nose and it gave her face an ugly expression. He didn't like it. She continued, 'What's that smell? It's like something died in here.'

'It's the mice. They get stuck in the walls and die, then their little bodies rot.'

'That's gross. Can't you get the bodies out or something?'

'I wish they'd all get bloody well stuck and die and leave me alone, and that goes for you too.' The thought took hold so quickly he had no time to halt his words. But they didn't seem to register with Dervla.

'You always were a bit weird.'

'Takes one to know one.'

She laughed then, and the laughter brought light to her cheeks as they puffed with the movement of her lips. Her eyes lost some of their darkness. He wondered if he should put a match to the oil lamp. No, it was bad enough that *he* could see the state of his home; he didn't want her seeing it. So they sat with only the shadows waltzing around them.

'I can't understand what you want me to do about this bone of yours.'

'I don't need you to do anything with it. I gave it to the guards.'

'Right. Okay.' He scratched his stubbly jaw. 'Why are you here, Dervla?'

'I saw the news. She's dead.'

'Who? Christ, Dervla, explain.'

'Isabel Gallagher. She's dead.'

'I know all about Isabel,' he said slowly, his voice trembling. 'I … I was there, yesterday morning, when her mother found her.' He held his head in his hands. 'The wails of that poor woman.'

'You were there?' Dervla reached out and grabbed his sleeve and the words flew out of her mouth. 'At their house? Where she was murdered? Oh God, Kevin. This is so exciting, but a nightmare too.'

'Suppose it is.'

'Did the guards interview you?'

'They don't know about me. Well, that's not true. According to Jack, they do know about me. But they don't know much because they haven't found me yet. You're the only one who knows where I live.'

'This is serious shit. Jack is dangerous. I've heard … You just need to know he'll hang you out to dry and then twist the noose.'

Kevin kept his head down, his arms crossed over each other, tugging on his sleeves, his body rocking on the chair. 'He pushed me in the canal earlier today.'

'Oh my God! That's awful, Kevin. Are you okay?'

'I'm here, amn't I?'

'What happened?'

'Some woman pulled me out and the ambulance brought me to the hospital. I left before anyone could talk to me.' He looked over at her from under his eyebrows.

She grinned awkwardly. 'You're a lunatic, so you are.'

'I know.'

'The guards know about the car.'

'What car?'

'Remember a few years ago, Uncle Frank sold his black Ford Focus on Best Deals? I had to do the online stuff for him. Well, I know who bought the car, so I do.'

'Who?'

'Jack Gallagher, that's who!'

'Really?' He scrunched up his eyes. 'I don't remember Jack driving that.'

'It was before he got involved with Isabel. He probably sold it or something.'

'Then what's that car got to do with anything?'

'I haven't a clue, but the guards were asking Frank about it. He wanted me to get the details for them.'

Kevin shrugged, a bony shoulder nicking his jaw bone. 'So give them what they want. It's nothing to do with Isabel.'

'Maybe not, but why are they asking now, after all this time? After she's been murdered. Kevin, something doesn't add up.'

'None of my business.'

'Isabel is dead and you told me you were watching out for her. That makes it your business.'

Pushing back the chair, he filled a mug with yellow water at the sink. He'd need to check the well and the pump. The bog was seeping again.

He faced her. 'Do you think Jack used this car to get to their house and kill her and then hid the car afterwards or something?'

She chewed on her thumbnail and Kevin thought how childlike she looked.

'I don't know what to think,' she said. 'I just think he is dangerous as hell. Kevin, we need to go to the guards and tell them what we know.'

He slammed the mug on the table. The itch in his leg yearned for a blade. Physical pain to ease the torment crawling like mice around his soul.

'No way. I'm staying out of this. I almost drowned today. You can go to them if you want, because you sold the car for Frank, but keep me the fuck out of it. I know nothing. I know nothing.'

She stood and gripped his trembling arm. 'We are in this together, no matter what. Remember. We swore we would look out for each other.'

'We were kids then.'

'We still are kids in most ways. We're both alone, Kevin. Damaged goods. But others helped us when we needed it, and I think it's time to return the favour.'

'But Isabel is dead now. Look at me, I can't even look after myself, let alone anyone else. I failed Isabel.' He glanced at the secret phone on the table.

'It's hers, isn't it?' Dervla said. 'Isabel's.'

He nodded. 'I was doing my best to watch out for her. I failed, Dervla. I failed.'

'How come you have her phone?'

'She gave it to me the day before she was killed. "Mind it for me, Kevin," she said. "Tell no one about it, no matter what happens." That's what she said.'

'What's on it that she wanted no one to see?' Dervla went to pick it up, but he made a grab for it and held it to his chest.

'Can't tell you.'

'You have to.'

'No I don't.'

'You're acting like we're in a schoolyard, but you must be forty if you're a day. Come on, it might be important. It might help the guards to arrest Jack for Isabel's murder.'

'I don't think there's anything about Jack on it.'

'Did you look?'

'I saw a message. It was flashing.'

'What did it say?'

'I'm not sure what it means.'

'Show me.'

Should he trust her? He'd been through so much that he'd learned to trust no one, maybe only Isabel. But she was dead, and whoever murdered her could be after him. Was it Jack? Maybe.

'Okay.' He flipped open the phone and showed her the message.

'Kevin, that's just telling her she had a missed call.'

'I can't do a lot of things, but I can read.'

'Whose number is it that called her?'

'I don't know. There's no name.'

'I'm sure she didn't keep a contact list in the phone, in case *he* found it.'

'We could ring the number and see who answers, I suppose,' Kevin said dubiously. His hand shook and the phone almost fell.

'No, I don't think that's clever. We need to bring it to the guards. I was talking to a lovely detective today. Lottie Parker. She'd be a good one to go to.'

'I can't.'

'Give it here. I'll bring it in.'

'What would you say? I don't want my name mentioned.'

'I could put it in an envelope and leave it at the desk in the station. I could put the detective's name on it and write something like "For Your Eyes Only".'

'Or you could just say "Private and Confidential" like a normal person.'

'Neither of us is normal and well you know it, Kevin Doran.'

He sat heavily on the chair. He knew it all too well.

'Okay. I read the last message she got, before that missed call.'

He knew she saw the fear flit across his face, because he found it difficult to mask. He might as well show her. He turned the phone for her to read the text.

He is going to kill us. Be careful. J

'It's a warning,' she said, scrunching her eyes, her eyebrows meeting in a fuzzy black line. 'Who is J?'

'I don't know, do I?'

'Could it be Jack?'

'No way. He didn't know she had a phone.'

'Jesus, Kevin, could it be Joyce? Shit, I clean forgot to tell you. Joyce is missing. I saw it on the news. And her little boy is missing too.'

'Oh God, no. Not Joyce.' Kevin's jaw tightened and his brow furrowed. 'If she sent this message to Isabel, it means he could have killed her and her boy too.'

'What will we do?'

'Here, take the phone. I don't want it any more. Give it to your detective, but leave me out of it.'

'You look half handsome when you beg.' She smiled, and it was the second time since she'd arrived that her eyes lost their darkness.

'Get out of here.'

She laughed, more like a little girl's hysterical giggle, and he realised it was a long time since anyone had laughed inside these walls. If there ever had been laughter here in the first place. He felt a tear at the corner of his eye for all he'd never experienced, and even though Dervla sat down beside him and held his hand, he felt more alone than he ever had in his life.

'Kevin, how did Joyce know Isabel? And what were they doing that someone was after them? Who could it be?'

He shrugged, afraid to speak.

She filled the silence. 'Do you think it might be to do with all that happened to us, years ago?'

'Isabel wasn't part of that.'

'This J might not be Joyce at all. Oh, I'm all confused now.' She palmed the phone. 'It could be Jack.'

'You better go, Dervla.'

'Right, I will, and I'll take this to the guards. Let them figure it out.'

'Remember,' he said, his voice cracking, 'I know nothing.'

Six months previously

He shovelled the gravel to one side half-heartedly. He knew Jack hadn't enough money to do the extension, but he'd still insisted on clearing the site. It was a warm October day, the sun making a rare appearance, and he heard a car pull up out front. He leaned on the shovel and craned his neck to peer around the side of the house, but he was unable to see Isabel's visitor.

The car was familiar, though.

Joyce's car.

He froze, his body a silhouette in the glare of sun behind him. What was Joyce doing at Isabel's house?

Chatter carried from the open kitchen window and he heard the splash of water pouring into the kettle. Inching forward, he moved to the right of the window and pretended to work there as he listened to the conversation.

Joyce was speaking – he'd recognise her voice anywhere.

'I really think we should do this, Isabel.'

'But if he is as dangerous as you say, I'm not sure.'

'Look around you, for Christ's sake. Living here as poor as a dormouse. Think of what you could do with the money. A new life for you and your baby, if that's what you'd like. Or something as simple as a warm coat. Hell, girl, you haven't even bought a buggy yet.'

'I know, but—'

'No buts. He introduced you to self-harm. He played on your insecurities, degraded you without you knowing and destroyed your self-worth. He did

the same to me. This way we can both get back at him, take some of his money and in the process maybe destroy him for good.'

'Oh God, Joyce, I couldn't kill him.'

'Neither could I. That's not what I mean. But I don't think he'd be able to live with the fact that he was outsmarted by two women.'

'I'm not sure.'

'Isabel, I know my partner is involved in smuggling, even though he thinks he's being careful. I'm not stupid. He's being secretive about the extra money he has, and I know his wages are the same as always. You overheard a conversation about it too. So it all points to the one man. It has to be him. He has to be making a fortune and squirrelling it away somewhere the law and the taxman can't get at it.'

Kevin moved closer to the window as cups clattered on the table. The tea was being made. He heard Isabel move to the fridge and open the door. He had to strain to hear as she talked into the cool air.

'Joyce, sometimes I wish I'd never met you.'

CHAPTER SIXTY

Rose was still at Farranstown when Lottie and Boyd arrived home.

'Mother! Have you seen the time?' Lottie said. 'What are you doing here at this hour?'

'Waiting for you. You missed him, you know. Lovely man. He took loads of notes and photos, but he thinks it will cost you an arm and a leg. Said he'll do his best.'

'Who?' Lottie threw her jacket over the back of a chair and sat at the table beside Boyd. 'What are you talking about?

Rose heated a plated dinner in the microwave. 'If you'd been home at a reasonable time you'd have met him and you wouldn't have to be eating a nuked dinner.'

Lottie felt Boyd squeeze her hand, warning her not to rise to the bait.

Rose was still in full flow, her silver hair standing rigid. 'Michael, he said his name was. Electrician. Probably has a ten-letter degree. He told me you spoke with him today and wanted a quote for rewiring this house.'

'Who are we talking about?' Boyd said.

'Now I get it.' Lottie relaxed her hand under his. 'Michael Costello. I asked if he'd get someone to call in sometime to give me a quote. The electrics are dire here. I'm fed up going to the basement in the dark, flicking fuse switches. Did he look down there?'

'He did. Very efficient. I have to say, he made quite an impression on Katie. Can you believe this? He offered her an office job.'

'That was nice of him,' Boyd said dubiously.

'It will be good for her,' Rose said, putting the plate in front of him. Lottie was ravenous but said nothing. 'Well, I'll be off now. I hate driving in the dark, but needs must. Your dinner is ready to go in the microwave, Lottie. Goodnight.'

The door shut softly, and Lottie exhaled. 'That woman riles me at every opportunity.'

Boyd shoved a forkful of mashed potatoes into his mouth. 'Stop cribbing. She didn't have to stay this late. She was being kind.'

Lottie went to tap the timer on the microwave. 'She wanted to see how late home I'd be. She stayed to give me a dig for not being back early. I wonder how much the rewiring will cost?'

'You probably shouldn't have asked Costello for a quotation.'

'The work needs to be done and he offered. God, I'm starving.'

'Well, I hope you know what you're doing, Lottie.'

'Not really. Do you think I should put this in for three or four minutes?'

*

Tiredness was probably the cause of their stilted conversation over dinner. Boyd knew Lottie was trying her best, but he couldn't help the cloud that had descended on his mood. When he'd taken off his jacket to sit and eat, he'd remembered the damn letter he'd received yesterday.

While she was having a quick midnight shower, he took out the envelope and laid it on the table. It was from his ex-wife, Jackie. She'd been a lying bitch every day of their married life and he'd thought he was rid of her once the divorce was finalised. And now here she was, derailing his life once again, just when he thought he might be able to keep it on track. And that was before he'd even read the damn letter.

He hadn't had a minute all day, and when he eventually unsealed the envelope, he felt his heart tug at the sight of Jackie's clearly scripted words. He still had some feeling for her, even after all she'd done to him. Some things were never irretrievably broken, no matter how much the other person hurt and betrayed you. Or maybe he was just a dumb eejit.

Her words were like a knife in his chest. There was no way on earth what she'd written could be true. It just couldn't be. She was a cheat and a liar. That was all there was to her. He couldn't believe a word that came out of her Botoxed lips, nor from the tip of her pen. But somehow, despite all that, he knew it *was* true. But what was her motive? Why tell him now? Why try to break his heart like that?

He crumpled the letter and was about to throw it in the trash, but for some mad reason, he decided to keep it as a reminder of the scheming she was still capable of. He pushed it deep into his inside pocket, hoping it would disintegrate.

He went upstairs with his ex-wife's words playing like an out-of-tune orchestra in his brain.

*

Lottie had tried her best to lift Boyd's mood. She'd attempted banter over their late dinner, but he seemed too tired to engage. And he was annoyed about Michael Costello having been there earlier. But she wasn't one to look a gift horse in the mouth. She hoped Costello would give her a good deal. Maybe she could pay by instalments.

She wasn't much company for Boyd either. Evan was still missing, and after the discovery of his mother's body, she knew the likelihood of finding the little boy alive was minimal. She felt powerless.

After her shower, with Boyd lying on the bed, she went to the kitchen and ran water over the dishes then stacked them in the dishwasher. Unable to find the detergent tablets, she switched on the machine anyway. It would have to do.

She searched the fridge for a Diet Coke. Hadn't she put a few right at the back, behind yoghurts, to hide them from Sean? He was always scoffing her soft drinks. She caught sight of Boyd's lager. Sensing her throat drying up, she gulped, her thirst like an addiction. She grabbed a can of Diet Coke, knocking down four yoghurts in the process. They exploded on the floor. Swearing loudly, she slammed the door shut. She wiped up the mess and threw the containers in the bin.

At the table, she cracked the tab and swallowed the cold liquid. It cleared her head a little.

She argued to herself in Boyd's defence. It was the pressure of the last few months. Time in hospital, the cancelled wedding, helping her with the house move, the murder investigations, the missing boy. All that combined would send any sane person into a spiral. As she rationalised Boyd's disposition, her eye fell on his jacket hanging on the back of the chair. He'd never mentioned the letter. She glanced at the door and listened. All quiet. Easing her hand into the pocket, she inched the crumpled envelope out with her finger.

'None of my business,' she said, drawing back. Normally he shared everything with her, but not this. His secrecy was making her skin pulse with curiosity.

Everyone was in bed and Chloe was still at work in the pub. Should she do it? Feck it. Not one to shy away from doing things she shouldn't, she flattened the envelope on the table.

His name and address on the envelope. The writing looked feminine. Not Grace's – she knew his sister's scrawl. Who, then? She held it to her nose, and a flowery perfumed scent made her gag. Feck. Shite.

Her mind suddenly went into overdrive, concocting scenarios with no basis in reality. Was he hooking up with someone else? No, that couldn't be it, could it? He had no time for another woman. But wasn't McKeown juggling a wife and three children in Athlone while fooling around with young Garda Brennan in Ragmullin? The logistics of that must be a nightmare. No, there was no way Boyd would do that. Would he?

Her curiosity increased, a series of waves rippling within her stomach. Each more overpowering than the last. Each one bringing her closer to betrayal. Was she really that person? Was Boyd that person? If so, what had she to lose?

Her fingers fluttered over the envelope and she bit down hard on her lip. A tiny glimpse wasn't going to kill her. But it might kill their relationship. She'd been through worse with Adam, death being the ultimate betrayal.

She had to know who was writing to Boyd.

As she took the sheet of paper out of the envelope, the stairs creaked. Shit. She bundled the envelope back into his jacket and grabbed her drink. She blew out a nervous breath, and even though her hands were shaking like feathers, she donned a demeanour of nonchalance.

Boyd walked in, still dressed. 'I was waiting for you. I need a glass of water.'

She stood up too quickly, knocking over the can of Coke. Dark liquid streamed across the table to the floor.

'Need a cloth for that?' he said.

'Thanks. There's one in the sink.'

He threw her the cloth. 'What's up?'

'I was half asleep. It's so late. You startled me, that's all.'

'It's been a long day.'

She silently mopped up the Coke and went to squeeze out the cloth in the sink.

He stood there eyeing her. 'What is it, Lottie?'

'Nothing.' She threw down the cloth. 'I'm going to bed. I need my head straight for tomorrow.'

He caught her arm. 'Something's up. You know I can read you. Tell me what it is.'

'Why don't you tell me?' she snapped.

'Tell you what?' He dropped her arm. 'You've lost me, Lottie.'

She handed him his jacket. 'Who is the letter from?'

'What letter?'

'The one in your pocket.'

His face flushed. He picked up the jacket and shrugged his arms into the sleeves.

'Where are you going?' She stood flustered by the kitchen door, not knowing what else to say.

'Back to my apartment.'

'Because you don't want to tell me who is writing love letters to you?'

'You read it, so you know.'

'I'm not that bad.' Shit, she'd nearly been. 'I didn't read it.'

'Why should I believe you?'

'I swear I didn't, though now I'm sorry because I bloody well should have.'

At the door, he turned, and her heart melted into smouldering pieces. His hazel-flecked eyes looked so sad. What had she just done?

'Honestly, Boyd. Stay. Let's talk about it.'

'We can talk tomorrow. I'm shattered. Goodnight, Lottie.'

She couldn't let it go. 'Tell me who it's from.'

'If you don't trust me, Lottie, we have nothing.'

The sound of the front door closing echoed like an angry symphony through the walls of the old house. She hadn't even the energy to cry. She hauled her body up the stairs and fell into bed.

But sleep didn't arrive until the birds were chirping the dawn of a new day.

*

Anita lay in bed waiting in vain for Jack to return from the station.

Even if he hadn't murdered her daughter, how could he have pushed a defenceless man into the canal?

And the more she thought about it, the more she believed he *might* have killed her daughter. Always another woman involved. She should have known. Isabel should have known.

She sat up in bed abruptly. Had Isabel found out? Was that why Jack killed her? She'd seen her slashed body. A jealous rage resulting in a brutal murder?

But why hadn't her daughter confided in her? Anita answered herself in the dark of the night. Because she hadn't been a good mother. She had tried so hard, but her secret past seeped into her everyday life. Her existence was strangled trying to keep the truth buried.

Now her past had been resurrected to haunt her even more. And she had done absolutely nothing to right the wrong. It was too late.

Fishing around in the dark so as not to wake Holly, she found her phone on the floor by her bed. Two a.m. Too late to call? He worked all hours. He might be awake. And if he wasn't, she would wake him.

She scrolled through her contacts until she found the name she'd entered at one time, hoping she would never have to make the call.

It rang and rang. She hung up. Not long after, he called back.

'Do you know what time it is?'

She ignored that. 'We need to talk.'

*

Michael Costello looked out of his office window. He'd just spent an hour trying to finish last month's VAT returns. It would be good to have an assistant again. Isabel hadn't worked out, but maybe Katie Parker would be a beneficial addition to his payroll. She seemed like a bright girl. And if he could calculate a reasonable quotation, Lottie

Parker might hire his company to do the work. Always good to have the gardaí on your side. And boy could her mother cook! The cottage pie had been delicious and Rose Fitzpatrick had filled him in on the history of the house. Good to have that knowledge in his back pocket.

His head hurt from squinting at the columns of figures. He should get his eyes tested. He might need new spectacles. He needed to go home. He didn't want to go home. He also needed to check that his plans were being adhered to. He didn't want to do that either. Everything was going a little bit pear-shaped. Fucking melon-shaped, if truth be known.

He twirled his mobile phone around on the desk with one hand and pulled at his beard with the other. He'd risked jeopardising everything when he'd employed Jack Gallagher on AJ Lennon's recommendation. It had been a necessary move at the time. But then Gallagher, the bastard, had convinced Isabel to leave. Now Jack was in trouble.

He pulled Jack's employment contract out of the filing cabinet. He wanted to feel it in his hands. If memory served him right, he would find something in the small print, and then he'd have the ammunition to fire the man.

He'd just found the pertinent clause when his phone rang.

*

Two kilometres outside Ragmullin, in his monstrous glass-walled house, the only nod to his wealth, AJ Lennon twisted and turned. Not a wink of sleep. He'd hoped Anita might contact him. But what reason would she have? He had nothing to offer her now that Isabel was dead.

He heard his dog bark downstairs. The golden retriever was more of an ornament than a pet. Most of the wealthy people he knew had dogs, so AJ had taken him from the pound. Saved him from certain death. And somehow he'd grown to love the poor dejected animal. The only friend he had in the world.

Rex barked again.

'What's up, boy?'

AJ hadn't the patience to deliberate over a name, so he'd settled on the most common one from his childhood. Rex was a good name for a dog, better than some new-fangled, unpronounceable word.

He dragged a dressing gown on over his cotton boxers and headed slowly down the marble staircase, flicking lights on as he moved. He hoped nothing would interfere with all that he had planned. The expansion he'd worked so hard for could not falter. He would not stand for that.

In the kitchen, he grabbed a knife from the block while watching the dog growling in his large basket.

He hoped it wasn't a burglar. He had a security system that even he couldn't understand, so it was doubtful someone had gained access to his glass prison.

'What's disturbed you, Rex?'

As he patted the dog's ears, he noticed what had roused the animal from his slumber.

His phone was dancing around the counter on vibrate. He hadn't brought it up to bed with him. A conscious decision. His bedroom was his sanctuary, free from work and technology. He didn't even have a television up there, just a bookcase full of easy-reading titles to help him sleep.

As he glanced at the screen before he lifted the phone, the call died. He checked the caller ID and pressed callback.

Thirty years ago

He'd never hurt an animal in his life. Of course he wanted to, but why would he slice and dice the neighbour's pet when he had his own little colony of lab rats to work on?

Rats of the human kind.

They were easy to manipulate. Especially the damaged ones – they were the easiest to break. And his ingenuity was in watching them hurt themselves. He didn't even have to lay a hand on them, and he still got the rush of excitement as they drew blood through their own skin.

This mound of Mother Earth was perfect for the rituals. Each of his experimental fold had a mother who'd abandoned them, himself included.

Lugh, the Celtic Sun God, was a warrior king, master craftsman and saviour. He had magical weapons including an invincible spear. At that time the boy didn't have a spear, but he'd found razor blades. They were just as good. A spear might kill. He didn't want to kill, not yet. A blade could cut, cause pain and raise blood. The act itself was addictive. Especially to those already broken.

WEDNESDAY

CHAPTER SIXTY-ONE

As dawn broke, Lottie dressed quickly and vowed to have a proper breakfast before heading into work. When she switched on the light in the dark kitchen, a bulb flickered then died. Not again!

Down in the basement, she found the fuse box and flicked the offending trip switch. She hoped Michael Costello would come up with an affordable quotation, otherwise she'd spend the rest of her life climbing up and down these steps and likely fall and break her neck.

Back in the kitchen, she was surprised to see Katie sitting at the table. Her daughter's hair was piled in an untidy bun on top of her head and her face was streaked with mascara trails.

'Why are you up at this hour, hun?'

'Couldn't sleep.'

'It's difficult to get used to this old house.'

'It's not the house, Mam.'

'Is it Louis?' Lottie pulled out a chair and sat. 'You can talk to me, you know that.'

'Whatever.'

'Listen to me, Katie, I'm up to my armpits in multiple investigations and I have to get to work, but I'm not leaving here until you tell me what's upset you.' She realised that despite everything that was going on, she had to put her family first, even though she hadn't always managed to do that.

'I should be happy. That friend of yours, Michael, he offered me a job in his company.' Katie tugged at a strand of flyaway hair and twirled it around her finger like a child.

'That's good, isn't it? You never really liked working in the café. You'll probably make more money, too.'

'But what about the day care costs for Louis? Five days a week. I won't be able to afford it.'

'Don't worry. We can figure something out. I'm sure Chloe will help.'

'You're joking me! Look, forget about it. You've enough to be doing without worrying about me, Mam. Go to work. I'll be fine.'

'You're not fine. You've got more shadowy circles under your eyes than I have, and that's saying something.'

Katie grinned lopsidedly, like her dad, and Lottie reached for her hand. Her daughter looked out from beneath her long lashes, where tears had caught on the fine hairs like dew drops.

'I miss Dad.'

It was as if invisible fingers had caught Lottie's heart and squeezed until it threatened to burst. 'We all miss him, sweetheart. But we have to live our own lives now. He would have wanted that.'

'I know all that. It's just … if only I could talk to him. Dad could make things seem all right even when they weren't. He was like a magician.' Tears escaped her lashes and fell softly to her cheeks.

'If you give me a chance, I can try too.' Katie had gone through so much in the years since Adam's death, and had come out the other side. Or was Lottie deluded in thinking that?

'It's just … sometimes I feel I don't deserve this luck. I mean, that man just walked in here and offered me a job. Why?'

'Maybe he sensed you weren't happy. And he has a vacancy in his office.'

'I know all that, but I've messed my life up so much. I don't want to mess this up.'

'You won't, and I'll help any way I can.'

'Mam, you're the best, but you have your own life.' Katie snatched her hand away. 'I have to stand on my own two feet and grow up.'

'I really want to help you.' Lottie was at a loss to know what else to say.

Katie stood and flicked on the kettle. 'Tea or coffee? I'll put some toast on. Did Boyd not stay last night?'

The conversation was over. But not quite. She'd give it one last shot. 'I have to go to work, but I'll be home early this evening and then I want you to tell me what's really bothering you.'

Katie's eyes flashed with anger. 'Mam, you will not be home early. Here, have a slice of toast. Eat it in the car.' She slapped the barely toasted bread onto the table and left the kitchen.

What in the name of God was all that about?

CHAPTER SIXTY-TWO

Deep in his tiny little heart, Evan knew his mummy wasn't ever coming back, and it made him cry and cry. Last night he had felt a cold shard of ice slip down his back and it reminded him of something he had blocked out. His mummy had told him to forget all about that time, that it never happened, but Evan knew it had happened and it made him so scared.

And now she wasn't around to tell him not to be scared any more. She would have come for him if she could, so something real bad must have stopped her.

He didn't like it here with no proper food. He missed going to day care. He missed seeing all his friends. He even missed Louis, though Louis was really only a baby and could be so annoying. He missed Sinéad but he didn't miss Dylan. *He* was a bit scary with his big muscles always moving under his shirt. And he missed Nathan, and his bed and his teddy. It was so hard to sleep without Teddy.

It was too dark. He forgot what it was like to be outside, even though he thought he'd only been here a few days. Maybe it was more. He didn't know.

The space where he was kept at night was too small and tight, though he was tiny. It was like a cupboard under the stairs because he heard footsteps go up and down some of the time. Other times it was so quiet he thought he must be alone.

'I want you, Mummy. Come and pick me up …'

She had to be on her way.

But at the same time, Evan knew she wasn't ever coming for him.

He missed his teddy.

CHAPTER SIXTY-THREE

Driving to the station, Lottie made a call to AJ Lennon's hardware shop and got confirmation that Tanya Cummings' shift had started at seven. She swung the car in a U-turn and headed there. If Cummings was indeed Jack Gallagher's bit on the side, she might prove to be a pivotal cog in his innocent plea or else confirm his guilt. It was imperative Lottie talk to the woman before tackling Jack again.

She entered the same small office with the jowly man sitting behind his desk. He got up and smiled, holding out his hand. She shook it quickly and sat, biting her tongue because it was too soon to accuse him of smuggling. She needed evidence.

His hair was distracting her and she itched to tell him to cut out the faded orange dye. He wore the same navy jumper with the hole in the cuff. How the hell could this man be a millionaire? His shirt looked clean, with a starched collar biting into his thick neck.

He indicated a chair, his hand shaking nervously. 'Don't mind this place. I like being in here. Helps me think. Some people expect me to have a big luxurious office, but I'm not one for all that malarkey. I still have to do the same job, no matter what the trappings are.'

'Your shop opens very early.'

'Seven on the dot, every day Monday to Saturday. Sunday, ten until six. I'm sure you're not here to learn all that, though. What can I do for you?'

'Did you ever check out if Kevin Doran was on your accounts?'

'Who?' His eyes narrowed.

'You were to ask your finance department if he had charged anything to the Gallagher account.'

He slapped a hand to his forehead. Pure dramatics. 'Clean forgot. I'll get on to it this morning.'

'Do that.'

He half rose from the chair. 'Is that all?'

He seemed anxious to get rid of her. Feck him.

'I'd like to have a word with one of your employees. Tanya Cummings.'

'Oh. Right. Tanya. Right. Quiet young one, as far as I know. What has she done to warrant someone as important as yourself needing to talk to her?'

'She hasn't done anything that I'm aware of. It's in relation to a case. Could I use your office to talk with her? Won't take long.'

'No bother. I'll get someone to fetch her. Give me a minute.'

Alone, Lottie felt the air relax around her, Lennon having brought his nervous anxiety out the door with him. She looked around his office. It was indeed below the level she'd expect from a millionaire businessman, but at least it wasn't a faux banker's look.

He bustled back in. 'Tanya will be with us in a minute.' He sat, and the space was once again suffused with an uneasy silence.

'Is this the location of the original Lennon's?' Lottie said, making conversation.

'No, that was a small shop on the edge of a housing estate. First place I sold. Too many sad memories there.'

'Oh?'

He laughed. 'A-ha! I can spot the way your detective's brain is working. Imagining a crime in everything, no matter how innocuous it might seem to the man in the street. Or woman, for that matter.' He laughed, and Lottie shifted awkwardly. 'My father was a hard taskmaster, and the first chance I had, I transformed the company from groceries to hardware. When that took off, I sold the old place and opened up in a bigger premises. All over the country now. Ah, here she is, the woman herself.'

'You were looking for me, Mr Lennon?' Tanya Cummings looked not much more than twenty, and only came up to his shoulder, her wild fair hair held back from her face by a hairband. She wore a yellow short-sleeved T-shirt and navy trousers.

'I'm Detective Inspector Parker and I'd like a word, Tanya,' Lottie said, standing. 'Could you give us a few minutes alone, Mr Lennon?'

'Sure. Unless Tanya wants me to stay. Moral support, you know.' He winked and Lottie felt her skin crawl. The man was only trying to be polite, wasn't he?

'It's fine, Mr Lennon,' Tanya said.

'If you're sure?' He patted her bare elbow as he left, and Lottie thought she saw the woman flinch.

'Take a seat.' She indicated the visitor chair.

'I'm really nervous, talking to a detective. What is this about?'

Lottie leaned against Lennon's desk, and crossed her legs at the ankles, getting to the point straight away. 'You know Jack Gallagher?'

'Who?'

'Jack told me to talk to you. Gave me your contact details.'

'Why would he do that?'

'So you do know him?'

A one-shoulder shrug. 'A little, I suppose. Just to talk to. He comes in here now and again. Buys electrical materials and stuff for his house. He said he's renovating it.'

'When did you last see him?'

'Haven't a clue.'

'Could it have been yesterday?'

'I was working yesterday.'

'You mentioned he comes in here to buy stuff. Did he come in yesterday?'

Tanya sat up straight and seemed to make herself taller on the chair. 'His wife was murdered, so I doubt he was in buying anything for his house.'

A smart mouth, Lottie concluded. Two could play that game. 'He doesn't seem particularly grief-stricken to me.'

'Why would you say that?'

'Because he was messaging you yesterday.'

Her eyes widened and she had the grace to blush. 'It's not what you think.'

'And what do you think I think?'

'That we're having an affair.'

'Are you?'

She bit her lower lip and twirled the silver stud in her ear. 'I know Jack from when he used to work here.'

'That's over five years ago. You couldn't have worked here then?'

'I'm twenty-five. I know ... I still look like a teenager. My mam says it will stand to me when I'm sixty.'

'Tell me about Jack.' Lottie hadn't time for Tanya's small talk.

'He's a lonely man. We like to chat. That's all.'

'Really?'

'Yeah, really,' she sneered. 'His wife doesn't ... didn't understand anything about the materials needed to renovate a house. I know everything there is to know, having worked in this dump since I left school.'

'Don't you like it here?'

'It's a job, isn't it? Pay isn't bad. Almost makes it worth having to put up with creepy jaws.'

'Who?'

'AJ. The boss.' She froze, then looked around the office. 'Shit, he could have cameras in here.'

'I doubt that.' All the same, Lottie scanned the room too, glad she was blocking the computer, as it seemed to be the only thing that might be filming them.

'He's a bit of a perv,' Tanya whispered. 'You know I once—'

'Let's get back to you and Jack Gallagher. Did you contact him yesterday?'

More twirling of the stud before she said, 'I did.'

'And did you meet him?'

'I did.'

'Where?'

'He walked up the canal line. I met him under the bridge. I'd taken a late lunch break.'

'He wasn't driving?' Lottie asked.

'Not then.'

'But later on he was, is that what you mean?'

'Yeah. He went back to his mother-in-law's house to fetch his van and then he picked me up after work.'

'What time was that?'

'Four thirty.'

'And where did you go?'

She shrank her neck into her shoulders and dropped her eyes. 'Around.'

'Come on, Tanya. I haven't all day.'

'We drove out to his house. He wanted to show it to me. I'd never seen it.'

'He brought you to the scene of his wife's murder?' Lottie gasped, appalled.

'What's wrong with that? Gee, the man's grieving. It was his way of dealing with it.'

'And did he bring you inside the house?'

Tanya shook her head. 'He wanted to, but there was crime-scene tape and guards at the wall. He parked down the road and we just sat in the car. We could see the house from there. We talked. That's all.'

'What time did you leave there?'

'I don't know. He dropped me back here so I could get my car. Said he had to put his little girl to bed.'

That was a lie. 'Did he drive by Quality Electrical, where he works?'

She shook her head emphatically. 'Not when I was with him. But he drove by the house in Bardstown where he was supposed to be working when Isabel was killed.'

'Why did he bring you there?'

'He said that if he'd had access to the site Monday morning, then he'd have an airtight alibi and you wouldn't be thinking he killed his wife.'

'Did you stay long at that location?'

'A few minutes. Couldn't see much of the house with the hoarding around it.'

Damn, Lottie thought, that was the sighting the farmer had had of Jack's van. Did that rule him in or out? Or was Tanya complicit in his actions?

'Did either of you get out of the van and enter the site?'

'No, like I said, he wanted to show me his own house. Bit weird, I know, but it seemed to calm him down.'

Lottie felt her head swim. She didn't know what to make of this development. 'How long have you been having this affair?'

'I told you, it's not an affair.' A flash of temper lit up Tanya's eyes. Lottie wondered if the young woman could have been consumed with jealousy and decided to get rid of Jack's wife herself. It wasn't outside the realms of possibility. Or maybe she helped him cover his tracks.

'The relationship, then. How long?'

'Maybe nine months or so. He seemed to be unable to fathom Isabel out after she got pregnant. So he said.'

'Where were you on Monday morning from seven a.m.?'

Tanya's mouth hung open. 'You can't be serious!'

'I only asked you to account for your time on Monday morning.'

'You think ... God, I've heard it all now. It's true what they say.'

'And what's that?'

'You try to pin things on people. Force things to fit where they don't.'

'Monday morning, Tanya. Where were you?'

'I could refuse to answer.'

'I could arrest you for impeding a murder investigation.'

Turning up the corner of her mouth, Tanya nodded. 'I met Jack for ten minutes before he went into work, and I was here for my shift at seven fifteen. Creepy jaws can show you the timesheets. Happy now?'

'I'll ask Mr Lennon for them. Thank you.' It pained Lottie to be nice, but she had a job to do. 'Where did you meet Jack on Monday morning?'

'Pulled up in a lay-by, talked through the windows. Didn't even get out of our cars. Happy?'

She wasn't, as there was no way to prove it. 'Do you know Joyce Breslin?'

'The woman who's missing with her son? I know of her.'

'And how is that?'

'She was in here one day and there was a bit of a scene.'

'A scene? Explain.'

Tanya sighed, and was silent, as if debating whether she should tell or not.

'Come on, Tanya, I haven't all day.'

'I suppose you'll hear eventually anyway. You see, Isabel somehow found out that Jack was messaging me. She marched in here, brazen as you like. I was on the paint counter that day. I actually thought she was going to hit me with a can, she was that mad.'

'But she didn't?'

'No, she just mouthed off stuff about Jack being her man and I could fuck off and all that. I was so embarrassed.'

Lottie contained the urge to roll her eyes.

'Then this other woman comes up and starts talking to her. I heard Isabel call her Joyce, and when I saw her on the news, I knew it was the same woman.'

Lottie unfurled her arms and leaned forward. 'What happened?'

'They got talking. Hugged each other at the door as they left.'

'Did you overhear the conversation?'

'Are you joking me? I fled to the other side of the shop once Isabel was distracted by the other woman.'

'Did you hear any of it?'

'No.'

'But you saw them leave.'

'I escaped over to the bathtub section. I saw them from there. Mr Lennon came over to see what the fuss was about, but I told him it was just a misunderstanding about an order.' Tanya held a finger in the air, her eyes wide. 'Wait a minute. I seem to remember him being interested all of a sudden when he noticed Joyce and Isabel together.'

'Did Joyce have a little boy with her?'

'I don't think so – I'd remember something like that.'

'And there's nothing else you can recall about either of them?'

'Nope.'

This was another link between Joyce and Isabel. It proved they'd met outside of the day care setting. 'When exactly did this happen?'

'Must be six weeks or more ago. I'm not rightly sure. Can I get back to work now?'

'You'll have to make a full statement. You'll need to come with me.'

'I'm not in any trouble, am I?'

'Not at all.'

'Will you square it with Mr Lennon without making me look guilty of something I didn't do?'

'Of course. I'll get those timesheets, too.' Lottie wasn't going to take Tanya Cummings' word for where she was on Monday morning while Isabel Gallagher was being stabbed to death in front of her baby daughter.

After Tanya left to fetch her coat, Lottie walked out of the office, straight into AJ Lennon.

'All okay?' he said. 'Hope my star employee hasn't been dirtying her bib.'

'It was just a few questions. I need her to come to the station to make a formal statement. Okay with you?'

'Certainly. Always willing to help the law, that's my motto.'

'Good. Can I ask you something, Mr Lennon?'

He stuck out his chest, full of his own importance. 'Anything I can do to help the law, I will do.'

Jesus, such shite. Did he have to keep saying it? 'Do you have security cameras throughout the store?'

'I do. People nowadays would put a toilet in their arse pocket and bring it home if they could. My stats are—'

'How long do you keep the footage?'

'It's all backed up. When exactly are you interested in?'

'There was an incident about six weeks ago. A woman came in and approached Tanya at the paint counter. There was some shouting, then another woman arrived and the two of them left together. Can you remember that?' She wanted evidence to prove Joyce and Isabel were acquainted, and that Isabel knew about Tanya. His hail-fellow-well-met demeanour disappeared in a flash.

'Can't say that I do.' He shook his head way too many times. 'I move around the stores from week to week. Do you have an exact date?'

'Tanya said you were present at the time. Said you were over at the bathroom section.'

He shook his head again. 'No memory of it at all.'

'She also said you seemed interested in the two women.'

'If I knew who they were, it might help jog my memory.'

'One was Isabel Gallagher. And you knew her because she worked here at one time.'

He pulled at the hole in his sweater sleeve and moved around Lottie to enter his office, before stopping quite close. 'Was that incident anything to do with why Isabel was murdered?'

She sidestepped his query, because she didn't know the answer. 'The other woman appears to have been Joyce Breslin, and she was found murdered last night.'

'What? Gosh, that's awful.'

'You sure you don't remember the incident?'

'I'm nearly one hundred per cent sure.'

'I'll send round one of my team to collect the security footage. Is that a problem?'

'No problem at all.'

Lottie followed him into the office.

'Do you know Chris Dermody?'

'Never heard the name.'

We'll see about that, she thought. 'While you're here, can you print off Tanya Cummings' clock-in data for Monday last?'

'That I can do. Give me a second.'

She waited while he tapped the keyboard. She took the page when it printed and hurried out of the office, shutting the door firmly behind her.

As she walked through the store to wait for Tanya, she ignored the shiny new appliances she'd love to have in Farranstown. She was too busy wondering why AJ Lennon, who had originally fawned over her, had scuttled into his shell once she'd mentioned the two dead women. And she still had to interview him about Nathan Monaghan and the smuggling. She needed airtight evidence before she cracked that whip.

CHAPTER SIXTY-FOUR

The trees outside were black stalks in the dark when Kevin awoke, so he turned on his side and went back to sleep. When eventually he got up, it was still early. He had no job to go to. He could stay here all day. Or not. Something crept across his face and he swiped his hand, giving himself a clout on the nose. 'Damn you, little bastards.'

Splashing cold water into a basin, he thought of Dervla's visit the previous night. He hoped he'd done the right thing handing over Isabel's phone. Isabel wouldn't be pleased with him. But she was dead, and he missed her, and he'd broken his promise to her.

When the cold water had sufficiently awakened him, he ran a finger around the corner of his eyelid and removed the clot of sleep that had been stuck there for a few days. He scrunched the corner of a tea towel tight and cleaned his ears. Good God, they were black. Bunching up the cloth, he threw it into the basin and tugged on his boots over yesterday's socks. He'd drive to town and watch Isabel's mother's house for a bit. See what Jack was up to. Maybe he'd catch a glimpse of the baby. He missed seeing little Holly.

But Kevin had greater problems now. He'd have to move away from here soon. There was no one left whom he'd made a promise to. That was if he didn't count Dervla, and no one really counted Dervla. It made him a little sad, because she wasn't all bad. Not all of the time. He shivered as he buttoned up his jacket. Isabel wasn't all bad either, was she? And then he remembered Joyce.

Maybe he should have kept Isabel's phone.

Too late now.

CHAPTER SIXTY-FIVE

Boyd was on the phone, sullen and grey-faced, when Lottie entered the office. His hair was still damp from his shower, his skin dull from lack of sleep. She wondered what was in the letter and if that was what was worrying him, but didn't ask. Best to give him time and space. She was good at giving people space even when they needed her close. Katie could testify to that, though conversely, Lottie felt weary because her daughter wouldn't talk openly with her. Did that make her a failure as a mother?

'What did you say?' Boyd said, hanging up the call and pushing back his chair.

'I must be losing it if I'm voicing my thoughts out loud.' She attempted a joke.

'Nothing new there.'

'I brought in Tanya Cummings. Jack Gallagher's alibi. She's making a statement.'

'Is she involved in Isabel's death?'

'Her timesheets tell me no, but who knows.' She put the pages on Boyd's desk. 'Have a look and see if you agree.'

'What about Joyce's murder?'

Lottie told him about Jack's tour of the countryside the evening before, which would account for the farmer's sighting of his van. Still, he could be involved.

'But if he killed Joyce,' Boyd said, 'did he also abduct Evan, and if so, where is the boy?'

'I don't know.'

'Was there something else?' A note of impatience in those few words. He drew his chair in tighter to the desk and clicked the mouse. A dismissive act? Stop! She needed to cease super-analysing everything he did and said.

'Who was on the phone?' she asked.

'The front desk,' he said. 'They're bringing up Jack Gallagher. His solicitor has arrived.'

She glanced at her watch. 'Already?'

'Bright-eyed and bushy-tailed, according to the duty sergeant. Interview Room 1.'

'You're with me for this.'

She dumped her bag and coat across her desk, disregarding the slap of files hitting the floor. She grabbed a notebook but couldn't find a pen. Damn.

They headed down the corridor. McKeown appeared at the top of the stairs.

'Sam McKeown!' Lottie said. 'You're a sight for sore eyes. Glad you're here.'

'Really? You're the one who threw me out.' He leaned against the wall as if he had the weight of the world on his shoulders, ready to keel over.

'You're here now. We're up to our gills. There's a shitload of security footage to be analysed. Kirby made a stab at it. Do that first, and I'll catch up with you when I'm done with Gallagher.'

'Sure thing.' He pushed away from the wall.

She eyed Boyd at the bottom of the stairs, waiting. Lowering her voice, she said, 'McKeown, sort out your personal life. And stay the hell away from Lynch.'

He dipped his head and disappeared into the office.

'The Prodigal Son returns,' Boyd said. 'Have you absolved him of his sins?'

'I sent him home yesterday because the situation between him and Lynch was volatile. He's a good detective and I need him. Concentrate, Boyd. We're up against Jack Gallagher. I need you alert.'

'Yes, ma'am.' He gave her a mock salute.

'Smart-arse,' she said with a smile.

She walked on ahead, contemplating the real smart-arse she was about to interview.

Jack Gallagher sat close to the table, head lowered, fingers knotted, hands resting on the surface. His solicitor looked sharp in a black suit over a white shirt buttoned to the neck. Lilian Regan was growing in confidence, Lottie figured, though the bitten biro was still in her hand.

After Boyd concluded the formalities, Lottie leaned over the table and stared directly at Gallagher. He must have felt her scrutiny in the awkward silence, because he raised his head sharply.

'What are you looking at?' he growled, spittle settling at the corner of his mouth.

'I have a warrant to seize your van. Officers are taking it in as we speak.'

'My van has nothing to do with anything. What are you doing to find my wife's killer?'

'Mr Gallagher,' Regan said, placing a hand on his arm. Gallagher shrugged her off.

Lottie proceeded. 'Tell me about your affair with Tanya Cummings. When did Isabel find out?'

'What?' He widened his eyes incredulously. 'Isabel didn't find out because there was nothing *to* find out.'

'Tanya says that a few weeks ago, Isabel came to AJ Lennon's hardware store spoiling for a fight. So she did know.'

'Why don't you stop wasting your time with me? I didn't kill my wife.'

'Did you know Joyce Breslin?'

He shook his head and twisted his hands into each other. Hiding something, she thought.

'Answer the question for the tape,' Boyd said.

Gallagher glared. 'Okay, okay. I heard on the news about her going missing with her son, and that's that. Did you find the boy?'

'Do you know where he is?'

'You're having a laugh now.'

'I'm not laughing,' Lottie said, stony-faced.

'I know nothing about him or anyone else,' Gallagher said, emphasising every word. 'I never met nor knew Joyce Breslin.'

The angrier he got, the more Lottie felt he was covering up something.

'Know anything about the car Joyce Breslin was driving the day she disappeared? Black Ford Focus.' She reeled off the licence plate number.

There, she saw it. She nudged Boyd's arm. Did he catch it too?

'Black Ford Focus,' she repeated.

'Means nothing to me,' Gallagher mumbled.

'The car was sold by eighty-three-year-old Frank Maher. Lives at Harbour Place Cottages. Best Deals. Any bells ringing?' She was grasping at straws. Frank's niece still hadn't contacted them with the information about who had bought the car. 'What about Lugmiran Enterprises?'

A quick twitch of his eye. 'Never heard of it.'

The solicitor piped up. 'My client has answered your question, Inspector. Please carry on, or we are walking out of here.'

'He's going nowhere until I get to the truth.' Lottie was growing weary of the cat-and-mouse antics. She was throwing everything at him, waiting for a reaction. 'What about number 14 Castlemain Drive?'

'Never heard of it.'

'Did you kill Joyce Breslin?'

'No, I did not. I don't even know her.'

'Did you kill your wife?'

'Do I have to repeat myself? I told you I didn't.' Spittle landed on the table in tiny round dots. 'This is a waste of time. You know I was at work and nowhere near my house when she was murdered.'

'She was killed before nine, when Anita found her body. You were the last person to see her alive.'

Lilian Regan butted in, waving her half-eaten biro. 'You don't have to say anything, Jack.'

'I made my statement, and other than that, it's no comment.' Gallagher folded his arms, but Lottie could see the tendons trembling beneath his cotton shirt.

'Did you pay someone to kill your wife?'

He unfolded his arms so quickly, lashing out across the table, that Lottie had little time to react. His hand caught the side of her face and her head snapped back. Boyd was around the table in two steps, holding Gallagher down. Lilian jumped up and stood with her back to the door, trembling.

'That's assault, Jack.' Lottie felt her face sting but she knew it would ease in a few minutes. 'Consider yourself charged.'

'My client and I request a recess,' Lilian said, tentatively retrieving her chair, which had fallen over in the melee.

'Granted.' Lottie gathered her notebook while Boyd signed off the recording. 'But he wears handcuffs.'

'Are you okay?' Boyd said once they were outside the interview room.

'Takes more than a slap on the jaw to rattle me.'

'He has some temper on him.'

Lottie rubbed her cheek. 'That may be so, but I don't think he killed his wife.'

'The number of stab wounds points to a crime of passion in my book.'

'But what if someone else wrote the book and wanted it to look like that?'

'What do you mean?'

'We have witnesses to prove Jack was nowhere near the house Monday morning. Tanya confirms meeting him before work and the post-mortem puts the death two hours before nine a.m. I know it's tight, really tight, but I don't think he did it. There's nothing forensically tying him to Isabel's murder, and I can't find a reason why he would kill Joyce and abduct her son. It makes no sense for him to be involved. But he flinched when I mentioned Joyce's car and Lugmiran. I can't fathom it.'

'He's after slapping you across the face and you're standing up for him?'

'I know, but it feels all wrong. It's as if we are being led away from the truth. Boyd, is someone trying to frame him?'

'Why would anyone do that?'

'I don't know. Let's see what SOCOs say about his van.'

'If we go with your logic, then evidence could have been planted in it.'

'If there's any evidence in that van, it's because Jack Gallagher had Joyce Breslin's body in it. We have an eyewitness who places his van at the Bardstown house.'

'But Tanya gave a logical explanation for that.'

'Okay, agreed. Humour me just for a minute. Let's say someone wanted to frame him; they might not have counted on Anita being the first to discover Isabel's body. They might have expected Jack to be the one to find her.'

'You've spun into the realms of science fiction, Lottie. Why would someone want to frame him?'

'I don't know. He knows something about Joyce's car and that in turn means he is possibly aware of the house on Castlemain Drive where Kirby discovered an old crime scene. The address was found in Joyce's car along with a razor blade. What's the significance of the blades, and who took Evan? Where the hell is he?'

'If you're throwing everything into the fire,' Boyd said, 'what about Sinéad and Dylan Foley? There's no footage from inside the gym, and so far Kirby has found nothing on the tapes from the adjacent businesses. Who took his key, if it was even stolen at all?'

'It might have been taken earlier in the day. At his work or somewhere else.'

'Stretching it again, Lottie.'

'Or Dylan Foley took the boy.'

'So where is he?'

Lottie sighed. 'Evan could be dead, Boyd. I've failed him.'

'The kidnapper, who is probably our murderer, is extremely clever. The entire country is on alert and we as a force have been doing everything.'

'But it's not enough, not near enough. And we still haven't found a motive for any of it.' She thought she might cry if she spent any longer thinking of their futile search. 'Any word from the DOCB on Chris Dermody?'

'He hasn't returned to his home. They've called in all their known contacts and snitches. Nothing so far.'

'Why was I expecting that answer?'

Back at her desk, Lottie noticed the calendar she'd taken from Joyce's house last night. An x marked for the coming Friday. It bugged her. Joyce had written notes for every other appointment, but nothing for Friday save the small x. Why not?

Her mind was swamped with questions. What was the relationship between Isabel and Joyce? What was with the razor blades? One in Isabel's hand, another in the envelope in Joyce's car – or rather Lugmiran Enterprises' car – and one in her hallway. And then the ones found at the house at Castlemain Drive, the scene of an old crime. The blades had to be the key. But were they the key to finding the boy alive? No ransom demand had been made, so why was he taken? The motive still eluded her on all scores.

She went to see if McKeown had made any progress. A fresh pair of eyes was always welcome.

'McKeown?'

He raised his head. It seemed as if he'd shrunk into himself in the last twenty-four hours.

'Find anything on the footage from around the gym?'

'I concur with Kirby. Nothing. As there's no footage from inside, I've checked every business camera close to the facility. Nothing out of the ordinary. I can see Foley parking his car; he goes in and comes out. I checked all the clients for the relevant time and all are clear. No reason to suspect any of them of being involved.'

'Another dead end.'

'Then I got to thinking that maybe the key was taken from Dylan Foley *before* he arrived at the gym.'

'He claimed he had his keys with him going in and he put them in his locker,' Lottie said.

'I carry around a bunch of keys and wouldn't know one was missing until I went to use it.'

'Point taken. Ask him for his client list and CCTV from his office building.'

'I phoned him and he was dubious about letting me have the list. You might have a word with him. I've asked for the Community Project Centre security footage. No guarantee we'll get it.'

'Ring him back. Tell him he's putting the life of a four-year-old boy at risk if he doesn't inform us of his clients for Monday. All the information will remain confidential.'

'Will do.'

CHAPTER SIXTY-SIX

Kirby made sure Gallagher's van had been brought to the yard for forensic analysis, then headed to the incident room to work in peace.

He was still reeling from last night's discovery at the house on Castlemain Drive, with the child's cot covered in dried blood. It was obvious a family had disappeared. The boss should be prioritising it, but he supposed she was already dealing with two murders and a missing four-year-old.

He began trawling through databases to find who owned the house, and had just made a significant discovery when Lottie and Boyd walked in.

'Boss, I've found something interesting about 14 Castlemain Drive.'

'Kirby, I told you, it can't be a priority at the moment,' Lottie said. 'Wait until forensics give us an idea of what happened there. It appears to be historical.'

'But it has a tentative connection to Joyce Breslin,' Kirby said. He puffed out his chest, then, realising a button might pop on his shirt, drew it in again. 'The house is owned by Lugmiran Enterprises. Same company that owns Joyce's car!'

'Interesting, but you've been unsuccessful in finding out anything about that company.'

'I'm going to keep working on it,' Kirby said. 'The Castlemain address was in an envelope down the side of the seat of Joyce's car. I think someone sent it to her as a threat, and then just before she was abducted, she shoved it down there hoping we might find it and delve into its significance.'

Boyd said, 'We still need names.'

'The Criminal Assets Bureau is investigating it as well as the DOCB,' Kirby said. 'The owner is entombed under layers that have to be individually peeled back. Takes time.'

'Anything come in from Frank Maher about his niece who set up the car sale for him?'

'I'll get back to him when I have a minute,' Kirby said, scribbling a note on a file cover. 'Will you listen to what I'm trying to tell you? CAB should be able to find out if the car and house are linked to drug money.'

'Good work in any case, Kirby,' Lottie said.

'But how can this help us find Evan?' Boyd said. 'Especially now that his mother is dead.' A hush fell over the room.

'What about her background check? Any news on who Evan's father might be?'

Kirby and Boyd shrugged.

'I need it yesterday. Whatever happened in that house could turn out to be something Joyce was threatened over and ultimately murdered for. What about your friend in forensics, Boyd? Any update?'

'Gráinne? No news, but they were only going back in this morning.'

'Call her once we've finished here.'

McKeown walked in holding his iPad, his head between his shoulders like a cracked boiled egg. 'Where's Lynch?'

'She's safer with you not knowing where she is,' Kirby said.

Garda Brennan arrived, carrying a bundle of manila folders, papers slipping from their binding. 'I've got all this copied. Will I …' Her mouth hung open, the words lost, as she noticed McKeown at the far wall. 'Shit,' she muttered. Placing the folders on the nearest desk, she turned, ready to escape.

Kirby put out a hand to halt her. 'You're needed here, Martina. Team meeting.'

She shrugged off his hand. 'I can go to Anita's house to replace Detective Lynch. You don't really need me to be here.'

'Guys, calm down and sit down,' Lottie said, waving a hand. 'Things are gathering pace, so leave your personal vendettas outside the door. A little boy is still missing and his mother has been found murdered. Isabel Gallagher and Joyce Breslin knew each other. Are we all on the same page?'

Kirby flicked through the folder Brennan had passed him. 'What page is that?'

He cringed when Lottie rolled her eyes. 'I'm speaking metaphorically.'

'Will I explain that big word for you?' McKeown sneered.

'Screw you,' Kirby said under his breath.

'Christ almighty!' Boyd exploded.

As Kirby turned away so that he wouldn't have to be looking at McKeown's bald head, he caught sight of Superintendent Farrell entering the room.

'Boss.' He indicated the super's arrival.

'Hope I'm not interrupting at a crucial time in your meeting.' Farrell's tone was laced with sarcasm and a large dollop of anger.

'Joining us, Superintendent?' Lottie said.

'I'm here as an observer. I want to see how such an efficient team operates. A team, let me remind you, that failed to find an abducted woman before she was brutally murdered; failed to track down another woman's murderer, or indeed a motive for said murder; that continues to flounder around in the dark, unable to find a four-year-old abducted child.' She marched to the top of the room and inched into Lottie's space. 'What's the meaning of this shit show? Can you explain it to me, Detective Inspector?'

'Superintendent,' Kirby said, 'during the course of exhaustive detective work, we have uncovered another crime scene.'

Farrell's cheeks flared bright red. 'Have you not enough crimes to be dealing with? Wait till the media get wind of this incompetence. I won't be held—'

'It's linked to Joyce Breslin,' Kirby blustered.

'What do you mean?' Farrell's anger deflated.

'I found evidence of a crime having occurred at a house in Castlemain Drive. The house and Joyce's car are owned by a company called Lugmiran Enterprises. I'm waiting for CAB to come back to me, but it takes ages to unmask the names of those involved in this type of corruption.'

'Why isn't anything simple any more?' Farrell said.

'Forensics are at the house as we speak,' Kirby continued. 'There was a lot of blood in a baby's cot and—'

'Stop right there. Is it a recent crime?'

'Appears to be historical.'

'Then park it until you find the missing boy.'

Lottie said, 'Superintendent, this company may have some connection to Joyce Breslin.'

'Right. I want full details on my desk in fifteen minutes.' Farrell marched back down the room. 'That gives you fifteen minutes, Detective Inspector Parker, to sort out this mess and devise a plan to bring all these investigations to a successful conclusion.' Papers fluttered on the tables as she made her way out. 'And find the boy. Alive!'

*

When the air had stilled after Superintendent Farrell exited, Lottie said, 'I'm heading over to that house to see for myself.'

'Wait. The forensic report from the Gallagher house is just in,' McKeown said, tapping his tablet. 'Should be on your computer.'

'Tell me some good news without me having to dig a bloody trench for it.' Lottie was finding it hard to believe it was only two days since Isabel's murder. Forensics must have prioritised it to have results this quickly.

McKeown said, 'A partial boot print was found in the bedroom. Too disintegrated by other footprints stamped over it. All those are returned as Anita Boland's. But SOCOs discovered another boot print by the back door.' He turned the screen around for all to see.

Kirby craned his neck to have a look. 'That looks like a work boot,' he said. 'The ridges might help identify a brand.'

'Caterpillar. Size thirteen.' McKeown's mouth slid into a wide smile.

'How do you know that?' Kirby's cadence was more than disgruntled.

'From one of McGlynn's team. Only problem is, they say it's the most popular brand of safety boot.'

'Kirby, get on to Jack Gallagher's boss, Michael Costello, and see what footwear they supply to their workers.'

'SOCOs have Jack's boots. Size thirteen. They are currently cross-referencing them against their findings,' McKeown said. 'We have the report from Joyce's house too.'

Lottie skimmed her eyes over the forensic report.

'If you read on a bit,' McKeown added, 'there's a preliminary analysis of the razor blade found beneath the radiator in the hall.'

'Go on.'

'They've lifted prints from the blade. One set belongs to Joyce but the other isn't a match for anything on the database. Doesn't match Jack Gallagher or Nathan Monaghan.'

'When we find a viable suspect, we can try to match it. I'm still waiting on results of Joyce's post-mortem.' Lottie's shoulders sagged with the weight of all they didn't know. 'We also need to find out what she had scheduled for this Friday.'

'Maybe she was meeting Isabel,' Boyd said.

McKeown said, 'Might be an affair.'

'You'd know all about that.' Kirby spoke before he could stop himself.

'You're a Class A gobshite,' McKeown spat, standing so quickly his chair flew backwards.

'If you don't sit the fuck down,' Lottie said, 'I'm going to lock you in a cell until you do.'

Once order was restored, McKeown continued. 'I got Joyce's phone records. A lot of texts to an unknown number. Pay-as-you-go. Trying to chase it up.'

'Anything on the day she went missing?' Lottie asked.

'One text to the same number around ten that morning. Nothing since.'

Lottie said, 'See if you can get a script of that text. I've to interview Nathan Monaghan again, so I'll ask him about it. Once DOCB succeed in tracking down Chris Dermody, we might have a clearer picture as to who was actually paying Monaghan to smuggle drugs. They might yet be responsible for Evan's abduction.'

'Or it might have nothing to do with anything, just like Kirby's house of horrors,' McKeown said.

Lottie's mouth flatlined. 'A little boy's life is in danger, so we're not taking any chances.'

'Sorry, boss,' McKeown said. 'I get it.'

Kirby said, 'Whatever happened in the house at Castlemain Drive could have something to do with the bone found on the hill.'

Lottie stared at him. 'Forensics should tell us that. McKeown, did you find out anything about who Evan's father might be?'

'His birth cert only states the mother's name. Nothing entered for the father. And I'm finding it difficult to discover anything about Joyce herself. She appears to have no employment history before she began work at Fayne's coffee shop. Odd for a woman in her late twenties.'

'Nathan Monaghan could be the mastermind behind everything,' Boyd said. 'Even though he wasn't in the country when Joyce was abducted, he might have had her killed and has little Evan hidden away somewhere. He seems to love the boy, and maybe she threatened to take him away from him. Oh, I don't know.'

'I don't buy that. Nathan is a wreck.' Lottie folded her arms and leaned against the wall, thinking.

'We've all seen wrecks of people do the unthinkable before,' Boyd said.

'I know. But I believe he's just a pawn caught up in a dangerous game.'

'What about AJ Lennon's Hardware?' Boyd wasn't giving up. 'We've seen that name pop up a good bit. Nathan drives for them, and Jack Gallagher and Isabel used to work there. Plus Jack's new girlfriend Tanya Cummings works there now.'

'Something else to be mindful of,' Lottie said.

Martina put up her hand.

'Go on, Garda Brennan,' Lottie said.

'I've only just thought of this, but when Detective Kirby and I spoke to the neighbour on Castlemain Drive, she mentioned two children. I'm thinking it could have been Joyce living there and one of the kids was Evan.'

'That's what I was thinking,' Kirby said.

'Anything is possible,' Lottie said. 'Once SOCOs have DNA and fingerprints from the scene, we can run them against Joyce's.'

'The thing that bothers me … sorry …' Garda Brennan stopped speaking as all heads turned towards her.

'What is it?' Lottie said.

'I was just thinking …'

'Dangerous,' said McKeown with a wink.

Brennan blushed but continued. 'If Chris Dermody threatened Nathan with taking Evan to force him to continue smuggling, how did he know the boy would still be at Sinéad Foley's house that evening? He had to have known about it in advance, and the only way to know that is if he was involved in abducting and killing Joyce. There could be a whole network of people involved.'

This kid was good, Lottie thought. She glanced at McKeown. 'Have another hard look at Dylan Foley to see if he's involved with Dermody in this smuggling racket. Boyd, you're with me.'

'Where are we going?'

'To talk to your friend Gráinne.'

CHAPTER SIXTY-SEVEN

It bugged Dervla that there were no contact names saved in the phone Isabel had given Kevin. She'd spent the night going over the messages and she still had no idea who Isabel had been communicating with. Just the one number, over and over again. And the texts appeared to be in some sort of childish code mostly signed off by someone called J. It had to be Joyce. The last one was the scariest.

He is going to kill us. Be careful. J.

Well, that had come too late for Isabel, hadn't it? Dervla thought it odd that first she'd found the bones on the hill and then this phone had fallen into her lap. Perhaps the gods were planning for her to become some sort of saviour. Or was Kevin behind it all? After all, he was the person who had told her about the late-night burial on Misneach.

'Is it you, Kevin?'

She paused, phone in hand, standing in the middle of her pitiful kitchen. No, Kevin was a dope. How had she ever thought he'd be able to understand what she meant when she'd told him about Jack Gallagher and the car? Kevin's idea of danger was only when it concerned his dear, sweet Isabel. Tough luck. Isabel was dead and she hadn't been so sweet after all. Not that Dervla felt it was her place to burst Kevin's naive bubble.

She'd found the bone, hadn't she? She'd brought it to the guards. *She* would be the hero. Once Uncle – ha, that was funny; he wasn't even her uncle – Frank had mentioned the car, she knew the significance of her find. Oh God, did she know!

While she debated what to do about the phone, she gave it the same treatment as she'd given the bone. Freezer bag and into the fridge. Shut the door and forget about it for a while.

She had the day ahead of her to consider her options.

If she wasn't so afraid of him, she'd tell Jack about the bone and maybe about the phone. She'd tell him she knew he'd bought the car. Would he actually pay her to keep quiet about it? She could do with a few bob. Being on social disability was a bore. Living like a pauper. If it wasn't for the euros she scavenged from Frank's shopping budget, she'd be destitute.

Was it too late to approach Jack with her blackmail plan? The guards already had the bone and had excavated the site on Misneach. Shit, why hadn't she thought up this plan before going to the gardaí? But she knew about the car and they didn't. Bingo!

She scanned through the news app on her phone and read about poor Joyce's body being found in a pond beside a new house. Hmm. It wasn't a million miles from where Jack lived. Was he a double murderer? She shivered at the thought. This shit was getting too real. Dervla knew she should feel some sort of sorrow for the dead woman she'd once known, but her heart had turned to lead a long time ago.

She leaned back in the chair.

She needed to plan this out carefully before she did anything rash. No point in making two mistakes. She had to get Kevin on board. That was the easy bit. Then she had to talk to Uncle Frank – twice as easy. The hard part would come next. That was when she would call the man who had caused them all so much pain.

Why wait?

He would pay for her information now.

She forgot all about making a plan.

She made the call.

CHAPTER SIXTY-EIGHT

'You're so frustrating at times.'

'Could say the same about you.' Boyd turned his head from the road to look at her.

'Watch the road,' Lottie said.

'Why do you think I'm frustrating? I'm doing my best here.'

'I know you are, but I also know you're keeping secrets from me.'

He reddened.

She pushed on. 'The letter you refuse to talk about.'

His knuckles turned white, tightening on the steering wheel, and the car took off as he pressed the accelerator.

'Slow down, for feck's sake. You'll kill us both.'

'I don't know why you had to snoop in my personal stuff.'

'I wasn't snooping. I just saw the letter. What's it about?'

'The letter I can't quite get my head around? The one where my ex-wife is up to her scheming again? That one?'

'Jesus, Boyd, I'm sorry. You know I'm a nosy cow at times.'

'All the time.'

'Okay, but why didn't you tell me it was from her?'

He slowed to within the speed limit. 'I couldn't, not until I figured it out for myself. I still don't know what she's up to.'

'I didn't read it, if that makes you feel better. But it made me wonder why you kept it secret.'

'It wasn't intentional. Look, we've been so busy, and anyway, Jackie is up to no good. Let's not talk about it now. Tonight. We'll discuss it then. Okay?'

Lottie zipped the white suit tight to her neck, making sure her mask was secure before she tugged up the hood. The house on Castlemain Drive looked worn out and dead, except for the ant-like work of the scattering of SOCOs flitting in and out with evidence bags.

Stepping into the kitchen, she immediately felt assaulted by a sense of evil lurking in the air. Every hair on her skin prickled. She sensed nothing good had ever happened in this house.

'Which one is your friend?' she said, trying to shake off the sensation of doom.

'She's not my friend. I never met her before last night.'

'Lighten up, Boyd.' She noted the work being done by SOCOs. 'Looks like there was a fight here.'

'Blood is spattered in patches,' he said, 'as if someone got a broken nose.'

A voice behind them said, 'Don't make assumptions. Let the evidence speak to you.' The woman was tall and imposing. 'Forgive me if I don't shake your hand, Inspector. Cross-contamination. I'm Gráinne Nixon.'

'What can your evidence tell me, Gráinne?' Lottie said.

'A fight took place down here. Upstairs, well, it's a different story.'

'And what does that story tell you?'

'Two children, a girl and a boy, if we take it that the colours are traditional. They both slept in cots. The boy appears to have been younger than the girl.'

'Besides the colour schemes, anything else to tell you it was a boy and a girl?'

'Their clothing is still in the wardrobes and drawers. The girl was maybe three years old. Her cot was saturated in blood.'

'From the child?'

'It's likely. I don't know how long the blood has been there, and it may be difficult to draw any DNA from it, but I never say never. I'll keep you up to date.' Gráinne's eyes penetrated Lottie's own. 'There are no bodies here, Inspector.'

'Tell me about the second child's room.'

'No evidence of any violence there, but it's possible both kids were in the one cot for some reason or other. Time will tell.'

'And you say you've no idea how long ago this crime happened?'

'It wasn't recent, and currently that's all I know for certain.'

'And definitely no bodies?'

Gráinne shook her head, a curl of red hair escaping from under her hood. 'We did a grid search of the property. No bodies.'

'The blood in the cot … Do you think the child died?'

'It depends on the age, weight, height, all that, but to my experienced eye, I'd say no child could have survived that amount of blood loss without medical intervention.'

'And it's definitely historical?' She was hoping it had nothing to do with Evan. Much as she feared the boy was already dead, she hoped she could still find him alive.

'That's what I said.'

'Nothing to do with Evan so,' Lottie said, glancing at Boyd, relieved but unsettled. She looked back to the SOCO. 'Any idea of the weapon used?'

'From the series of lacerations and slashes to the mattress, my guess is a knife. But further analysis of the mattress is needed.'

'Thanks, Gráinne. This is a long shot, but can you send impressions of the slashes to the state pathologist? Just in case the weapon used here can be matched to our current murders. May we take a look upstairs?'

'Work away. We've a lot to do, so don't touch anything.'

'I know the drill.'

She edged into the hall, relieved to hear the muffled thud of Boyd's footsteps behind her. Areas on the stairs had been marked out by SOCOs. Blood drops. She braced herself on the threshold of the pink bedroom.

'Go on,' Boyd said softly.

'It's so unfair. A child with her whole life in front of her … It doesn't bear thinking about.'

She stepped inside and her heart filled with sadness at the sight of the cot, its bars lowered, a little unicorn mobile above it.

'I can't go in any further,' she gasped.

'That's okay,' Boyd said. 'We can leave.'

'Okay, but I better look into the other rooms.'

The little boy's room was really a baby room, evidenced by the bottles still standing on a small locker, their liquid congealed. It reminded her of Holly's bottles in Anita's house. So much had happened in the last few days, she didn't know which way to turn next or how to form a cohesive thought. She felt tears prick her eyes at the sight of the model aeroplane hanging from the light fitting. She stepped towards the cot and stalled.

'Come on, Lottie, let's go.' Boyd's voice sounded like it was trapped in a bubble. Her brain filled with white noise and her heart constricted.

'Look,' she said.

'It's a kid's cot.'

'On the pillow.' She moved closer and dared to breathe. 'A teddy bear.'

'So?'

'It's the same as the one I saw on Evan's bed.'

'Lottie,' he said, 'I'm sure there are a million teddies like that one.'

'It's too much of a coincidence. The letter in Joyce's car had this address on it.' She pushed out past him and flew down the stairs. 'Gráinne? Can you fast-track a DNA test on the teddy bear in the boy's room? Plus anything else from which you might be able to extract DNA.'

'Sure thing. Straight away.'

'Get the lab to run the sample against Evan and Joyce Breslin. Compare any DNA or fingerprints you find with those we've gathered from our active cases. Talk to McGlynn.'

'Is there something I should know?' A deep crease grew between Gráinne's eyebrows.

Breathless, Lottie said, 'Our missing boy might have been in this house at one time. And it seems another child might have been injured, even murdered here. I need to know if it was Joyce's child and …' She found it hard to go on.

'What is it?' Gráinne said.

'The bones of a child were discovered on Misneach Hill. They've been removed to the mortuary. Make sure all samples are run against those too.'

'How old are those bones?'

'Almost everything else was decomposed except for a nappy, so they're not recent.'

Once outside, Lottie paced the small garden, trying to find something to indicate who had lived here.

Nothing. All they knew was that it was registered to Lugmiran Enterprises.

Another bloody mystery.

And Evan was still missing.

*

'Swing by Frank Maher's house before we head back to the station,' Lottie said.

'What for?' Boyd said.

'The car Joyce was driving had the letter with the Castlemain address, and that car was once owned by Frank Maher.

'Frank still hasn't contacted us with information from his niece about the sale of the car,' Boyd said.

'Another piece of evidence we need to nail down.'

Boyd parked outside the small gated garden of the house close to the canal.

'He has a dog,' he said.

'I like dogs.'

'Sean said you wouldn't let him have one.'

'I have enough mouths to feed already.'

She knocked on the door and it opened almost immediately. It was obvious the man had once been tall, but now he had a hump on his shoulders. His hair was thin and his face weathered.

'Mr Maher?'

'That's me.'

Lottie introduced herself.

'Nice to meet you,' he said, 'and it's a pleasure to see your good-mannered friend again. Come in.'

Lottie squinted at Boyd as he returned a helpless expression.

'Did you tell your niece we needed to speak with her?' Boyd asked.

'I did. Has she not contacted you?'

'No, and we really need that information.'

'Hold on a minute.' Frank stood and knocked loudly on the wall by the stove. 'If she's home, she'll be here in a minute or two.'

'She lives with you?' Boyd asked.

'Next door.'

Lottie turned when the front door opened and a young woman walked in. The surprise caused her mouth to hang open.

'Dervla,' Frank said, 'these detectives want to have a word with you.'

'With me?'

'Yes, you,' Lottie said, unable to mask her surprise on seeing the woman who'd brought the little bone into the station.

'Oh, hello, Inspector. I hope you found the skull on Misneach like I told you.'

'Dervla, you know something about the car your uncle sold five years ago, and you haven't provided us with that information as yet. Care to explain?' She indicated for the woman to sit.

'I ... I ...' Dervla stood frozen in place.

'Talk to me,' Lottie said through gritted teeth.

'No need to get angry,' Frank said. 'I'm sure Dervla has a good reason for not contacting you. That's right, isn't it, pet?'

'I ... I ... It totally slipped my mind. I'm so sorry.'

The old man slapped his hand on the table. The dog jumped with a howl. Lottie looked at Boyd. His shoulders rose in a question. What the hell was going on?

She stepped into the tension-filled void. 'I think we should have this conversation at the station.'

'No, no,' Dervla said, her hands waving. 'I can tell you now. I advertised the car on Best Deals and I was contacted by a man called Jack Gallagher. He picked up the car and paid cash. Five grand. He promised to make the necessary changes with the car registration office. Did he not do it? Is it still in Frank's name?'

'Jack Gallagher bought the car? You're absolutely sure?'

'That's the name that was on the message on the website. And I've seen him on the television. His wife was murdered. It's the same man.'

Lottie bit down on her lip, thinking. Jack Gallagher had bought the car that Joyce Breslin was driving. The car was registered to Lugmiran Enterprises. Just like the house where they'd discovered evidence of an older crime.

'Boyd, check with the station. Make sure Gallagher is still there.' Of course he was still there, she thought, and returned her steely gaze to the woman childishly biting her fingernails. 'How do you know Jack Gallagher?'

'I don't know him. Swear on the Bible. I only ever met him that one day and then I saw the news about his murdered wife. That's it, you have to believe me.' Blood seeped around her nails.

'Why didn't you tell us this straight away? Your uncle told you we wanted to know about the car.'

'I … I was bothered by the bones I found. They really scared me. I'm sorry.'

'Come on.' Lottie wasn't buying her innocent plea. 'You discovered bones and a skull buried on a hillside. You've been instrumental in selling a car to a man whose wife was murdered. The car was in the possession of another woman, who is also dead. What else are you involved in?'

'Me? Nothing. I swear to God. You can ask Kevin if you don't believe me. Listen, he's the one who told me about the body on the hill. He was terrified. I was terrified. I don't like that hill. It has something to do with ancient rituals or something like that. It scares me, but curiosity got the better of me and I went up there for a snoop. It's Kevin you need to talk to, not me.'

'Kevin?' Lottie asked, her eyes widening. 'Are you talking about Kevin Doran? He works as a handyman.'

'Yeah, that's him. Kevin Doran.'

'What? Bloody hell! We've been trying to find him. Where is he?'

'At home, probably.'

'Where's that?'

'I can bring you there.'

'Tell me the address. You're going to the station to make a full statement. I advise you to hire a solicitor, because whether you know it or not, you are in shit up to your ears.' It wasn't fair to be so crass, but fuck it. Dervla Byrne had withheld critical information, whether deliberately or not.

'A little boy is still missing, and if you've concealed information that could have helped us save him, you're going to jail.'

Dervla surprised Lottie by breaking down in a wash of tears. She cried and sobbed like a baby. Frank put his arm around her and held her to his chest.

'No need to be going off at her. She's just a child.'

'She's a grown woman, for feck's sake.' Lottie felt Boyd nudge her elbow in warning.

'You know nothing about her,' Frank said as he soothed his sobbing niece. 'She's had it tough and knows no different. She and Kevin are friends. I know them. Take it from me, they're harmless.'

'I'll be the judge of that.'

'Look, Inspector,' Frank said, rising to his full height, surprising Lottie. 'They were all troubled kids. Myself and the wife took them in, God rest her soul. We fostered them, along with … along with a lot of others. The truth is, I'm not really Dervla's uncle, but we bonded like family, and I rented the house next door for her so she would have her own place. She was a fragile child and needed taking care of, but I'm sad to say she's ended up caring for me.'

'Jesus Christ,' Lottie said.

'You could have told me this when I was here yesterday,' Boyd said.

'You never asked, son.'

Lottie steeled herself to keep her anger submerged. She turned to Dervla. 'Tell me where Kevin lives.'

'You'll need to write it down. It's complicated.'

'Go ahead then. Boyd, ring for a car to take her in.'

*

When the detectives had left, Frank patted the dog's head, and felt sad for Dervla. It wasn't really her fault. None of this. No. He knew exactly who should be behind bars, but he was family and there was no way he could turn him in.

Dervla was a little simple, and so was Kevin. Too simple to be mixed up in all of this. He took out his phone, unlocked the screen and made the call.

'The guards were here,' he said. 'They know about the car, and they know about Kevin.'

There was no reply. Just an irritating dial tone. After a minute, Frank realised they had hung up on him, and he went to fix his lunch.

CHAPTER SIXTY-NINE

'Hello, Kevin, did you think I'd never find you?'

Kevin froze in his doorway. 'What … what are you doing here?'

'I'm coming in to talk with you. Be a good boy and go back inside.'

Kevin cowered before his visitor and cupped his hands around his ears to keep out the sound of that voice.

'Don't hurt me. Please. I know nothing. I did nothing. Please.'

'You are still pathetic. Get inside.'

He couldn't see any way of escape, so he did as he was told.

'This is such a dump, I'm surprised you haven't died in your own filth before now. You could have saved me a lot of bother.'

'What … what are you talking about?' Kevin felt himself shrivel up against the wall. 'I don't understand.'

'You never did. Now sit down there and we can have a chat.'

'I don't want to sit. I have to go out. I have to be somewhere else.'

'Sit. The. Fuck. Down.'

The words pierced his head like metal skewers; even his hands over his ears couldn't keep the noise out. His brain thrummed and his heart was ready to leap out of his chest, but years of coercion had taken their toll, so he did as he was commanded.

'Put your hands on the table where I can see them.'

He placed his hands palms down and hoped the mice stayed away.

'Now, what's this I hear about a phone Isabel gave you?'

'I know nothing, about anything. You're scaring me.'

'Answer the fucking question. You know what I'm capable of.'

Kevin bowed his head so that he didn't have to look at the placid face in front of him. He knew what evil lurked beneath the facade of normality.

'I d-don't know about any phone.'

A long sigh filled the room before the visitor continued. 'I admit she was clever hiding a secret phone. I had no idea that one so dumb could be so crafty.'

Kevin kept his mouth shut. He knew Isabel was not crafty at all. Secretive, yes, but then what did he really know about her, in truth?

The visitor's voice filled the silence. 'It was you, Kevin. That night. On Misneach. You saw us there, didn't you? Burying the child. Admit it.'

His body stiffened and he held his breath. The skitter of mice vied with the sound of his visitor's harsh breathing. And Kevin knew he wasn't getting out of this situation alive. He began to cry.

'Good God, you're still a sniveller.' Disgust distorted the voice. 'You told Dervla all about it. You might say little, but you couldn't keep that nugget to yourself. That's why the guards swarmed all over the hillside yesterday. What else did you tell her?'

Realising he had to say something, Kevin blurted, 'I told no one nothing.'

'Oh, but I think you did. How did you get Joyce involved?'

'Joyce? I ... I h-haven't s-seen her in years and years.' A seed of bravery rooted in his heart and he looked up. Mistake. His visitor held a knife pointed directly at him. 'I ... I d-don't know what you w-want from me.'

'I want you to never breathe another word to a living soul again. Remember what I taught you about pain?'

Kevin nodded, and immediately craved his little box of blades. 'Yes, I remember.'

'Well hear this, Kevin boy, I'm going to let you experience the ultimate ecstasy.'

The knife. Kevin could stomach the blades, but not the knife.

With a spurt of energy, or maybe carelessness, he shoved back the chair, leaped up and ran for the door.

His visitor was quicker.

He felt his hair being tugged. He kicked back, suddenly free. He ran to his bedroom, tearing through the curtain he used as a door. Mistake. Trapped. No way out of his home. No way out. He sobbed and slowly turned to face his attacker, who was holding aloft the large stone Kevin used to sharpen his own knives.

As it crashed into his skull, Kevin saw the world fragment, before he fell back on his bed and the light in his eyes went out.

CHAPTER SEVENTY

The clouds had darkened considerably as Boyd drove them from Frank Maher's house, and by the time they reached the townland of Cornerstown, five kilometres outside Ragmullin, the sky was a pewter-grey canvas.

Cornerstown was no more than a scattering of farms and houses, no one living close enough to call a neighbour. Having followed Dervla's instructions, Boyd parked the car at the entrance to a narrow lane.

'She said we should continue from here on foot or we'll wreck the car,' Lottie said.

'Beats me how Doran gets his van down there.'

Lottie tugged her jacket collar around her throat and shivered with the wind swirling from the east. 'Looks deserted.'

Boyd buttoned his coat and stretched his cramped legs. 'You know what they say about looks?'

They made their way down the overgrown lane, grass growing like a moustache up the centre. In places, she could see crushed hedges, as if they'd been constantly battered by something. A red van, most likely. At the end of the curvature, she came to the cottage, no more than a ruin, surrounded by a crumbling stone wall.

'He could be inside with a shotgun pointed through the keyhole,' Boyd said.

'You really know how to instil confidence in a woman.'

'Maybe we should call backup,' Boyd suggested.

'We'll be grand.'

'Famous last words.'

'Shut up, Boyd. It's possible he's holding Evan in there.'

'I don't see how he could—'

'Kevin Doran has been an elusive thread in all this. Keep an open mind.'

She pushed through the long grass lining the perimeter wall, briars snagging on her jeans, and popped her head around the pillar. The gate was no more than a piece of corrugated iron, hanging open from a rusted hinge.

The tumbledown cottage was situated at the end of a short path badly constructed from mismatched paving stones. Moss, thorns and nettles grew indiscriminately between the cracks and crevices; the wild weedy grass on either side stormed upwards. Trees and bushes surrounded the abode, their branches like cupped hands.

'It's like being in the middle of a bloody forest,' she whispered, ducking down with a finger to her lips. She waved her hand for Boyd to crouch behind her, then raised her head and scanned the cottage. It looked empty. Was it even Kevin Doran's home? Had Dervla lied to them? Lottie was taking nothing for granted.

'I don't know why we're even here,' Boyd hissed. 'Dervla told us Jack Gallagher bought the car. We should be back at the station grilling him, not looking for this Kevin lad.'

'"This Kevin lad" is forty years old and he worked at Gallagher's house. Jack pushed him in the canal for some reason. And he told Dervla about seeing something being buried on the hill, which led her to find the bones of a child.' She stopped talking. Stayed stock still.

'What is it?' he whispered.

'What if Kevin has something to do with Lugmiran Enterprises? What if he lived in the Castlemain Drive house before hiding out here? What if he killed a child there and buried the body on the hill?'

'But why would he tell Dervla about it?'

'Jesus, Boyd, this is screwed.'

'You're telling me.'

'Keep watch. I'm taking a closer look.'

She felt his hand on her shoulder, tugging her down.

'No. We do this together.'

'I need you to warn me if anyone arrives,' she insisted.

'I'm staying with you.'

She sighed. 'If you want to help, head to the rear of the house. See if there's a back door. We don't want him escaping just when we've found him.'

'He could be armed and dangerous.'

'If he is the killer, he's only used knives. I'll be ready for him. Now go.'

She watched him making his way stealthily along the wall until he was out of sight. Straightening up, knees creaking, she pushed in past the useless gate, walked resolutely along the path and knocked on the door. Weather-beaten timber visible beneath peeling black paint, more like the entrance to a shed than a house.

Another knock. No answer.

At the tiny, dirty window she shielded her eyes with her hands and peered in. It was so dark inside she could only just make out the shape of a table and two chairs. Back at the door, she knocked for a third time.

'Mr Doran? Kevin? I'm Detective Inspector Parker. Come out, please.'

She heard the grass tremble in the breeze and the pad of footsteps from the side of the house. Raising her hands for a fight and holding her breath, she leaned against the door. It opened inwards and she stumbled inside.

'What the—'

'Are you okay? Did I scare you?' Boyd grabbed her flailing arm and hauled her to her feet.

'For feck's sake, Boyd, I told you to go round the back.'

'There's no back door. No chance of anyone escaping from the house unless they come out this way.'

'Ever heard of a window?'

'Yeah, but—'

'No buts.' She watched as he turned away. 'Where do you think you're going?'

'To guard a non-existent back door.'

'Don't be so petty.' She took a good look around the room, helped by the light flowing in through the doorway.

'His van is at the rear of the house,' Boyd said, flicking on a torch. 'If he's not here, he left on foot.'

'Or someone collected him.'

'Or took him.'

'You're a ray of sunshine today, Boyd.' She lifted up a wicker basket full of dirty clothes. 'Agh!' she yelled.

'What?'

'A bastard mouse. Fuck. Shit. Bollocks. Bastard nearly ran up inside my sleeve.' She flapped her arms. 'And it's not bloody funny either.'

'Listen. Stop. Shh.' Boyd held up a hand, the torch casting shadows along the walls.

She followed close on his heels as he moved to the only other room in the hovel, her eyes scanning all around her, fearful of more vermin. The place was rotten to the core.

'Lottie! He's here. Call an ambulance.'

She pushed past Boyd into the dark, dank room and stopped.

Their elusive Kevin Doran was lying on a pile of coats and filthy blankets, his skull caved in. She picked up Boyd's torch from the floor, where he'd dropped it, and saw the blood spatter on the walls. 'Shit, shit, shit.'

Boyd was leaning over the man. 'He's alive!'

'How the hell is he still alive? I can see his brains.'

'You can see feck all in here. Call an ambulance.'

The smell of the room caught in her throat. She gagged. Juggling her phone, she ran outside and made the call, giving directions as best she could. When she hung up, she noticed she had a missed call from Superintendent Farrell.

She called back.

'Parker, is that you?'

Of course it's me, Lottie thought. 'Yes.'

'Get your arse back here. We found Chris Dermody. At a checkpoint on the bypass, fifteen kilometres out. About half a million worth of cocaine in the boot of the car. What kind of a dope drives around with dope while the country is on high alert for the missing boy?'

'Did you ask him about Evan?'

'Parker, I'm not stupid. He says he didn't take him.'

'Where is Dermody now?'

'Locked up, and you better hurry if you want to interview him before the bureau guys arrive.'

'He must have said something about the boy.' Lottie knew she sounded hysterical.

'He was adamant he knew nothing about him. Get back here now. That's an order.'

Lottie rubbed a hand along her forehead, trying to ease the thumping headache taking root beneath her skull. 'I've found Kevin Doran. I don't think he'll be talking any time soon. He's alive, but only just. Send someone to secure and search his place.'

'You need to sort out this fiasco. It's gone from bad to worse. Time is running out for Evan.'

'Fuck's sake, I know that,' Lottie cried.

Farrell hung up.

Lottie took a deep breath of fresh air and returned to Boyd in the hovel. 'Ambulance is on its way,' she said.

'I don't know how long he can hold on.'

'Dermody is in custody. Says he knows nothing about Evan. Farrell is on the warpath. And the boy isn't here. Who the hell took him? Oh God, what a mess!' She felt she was about to crumble, but she had to stay strong.

She held a hand to her nose and mouth to keep out the stench and leaned in beside Boyd. 'Are his lips moving? Shit, Boyd, he's trying to say something.' She trained the torch on Kevin's face.

Boyd put his ear to the man's mouth. 'What is it, Kevin? Who did this to you? Come on, lad, help is on the way. Talk to me.'

Lottie watched, mesmerised, as Kevin's eyes flew open, two white lights in a face of rose blood. 'What's he saying?'

'Shut up for a minute and listen,' Boyd whispered.

A hand rose from the folds of rancid clothing and gripped Lottie's, tugging her close, and she inhaled the reek of blood and dirt. The place smelled like an abattoir, and whether Kevin Doran was a murderer or not, she was consumed with conflicting emotions, swamped by an avalanche of sorrow for the man and the way he lived.

'Talk to me, Kevin,' she said. 'Please. We want to help you.'

His eyes closed and darkness once again reigned on his face.

'Who was it, Kevin? Talk to me.'

'Tell … Sorry Isa … AJ … agh …'

She dared not breathe as she listened, but was unable to decipher what he was saying. As she leaned in closer, Kevin's body lurched upwards in a spasm. The walls trembled as if they were alive and the room filled with squeaks and tapping and skittering. The bloody place was crawling. She watched helplessly as the man fought for his life.

She tore at his clothing to begin massaging his heart, and then made another discovery. A series of lacerations criss-crossed his torso.

'He's been stabbed, Boyd. The wounds are the same as those on Joyce and Isabel's bodies. Kevin was attacked by the same fucker.'

'Jesus, Lottie, stop. His brains will fall out.'

She twirled round, frantically searching for something to wrap around the caved in, bleeding head. Nothing clean that she could see.

'Fucking hell.' She tore off her jacket and sweater and then her white T-shirt, which she handed to Boyd. 'Make a bandage.' He did his best, but the material was soaked red in seconds. She handed him her sweater, then tugged her jacket back on.

The wail of sirens broke through the air.

She ran out as an ambulance screamed down the narrow lane, bringing branches with it. Brakes squealed. Then doors opened and slammed.

As the paramedics entered the house, Boyd joined her outside.

'What do you think he was saying?' he asked.

A cold wind chewed her skin through her jacket and she shivered violently. Boyd drew her close, wrapping an arm around her. She welcomed the warmth, inhaled his scent, trying desperately to rid her nose and throat of the stench of decay from Kevin Doran's home.

'I think he said AJ,' she mumbled through chattering teeth. 'And the only AJ I know in relation to all this is AJ Lennon. The hardware tycoon. Who Jack Gallagher used to work for before Quality Electrical.'

'It makes no sense.'

'Nothing makes sense, Boyd.'

'Let's get back to the car before you freeze to death.' He squeezed her shoulder.

A trail of mice ran out of the door.

'I think I'm going to be sick.' And before Boyd could pull out of the way, Lottie threw up over his best shirt.

CHAPTER SEVENTY-ONE

Kirby thrust a bottle of water into Lottie's hand. She gulped it down before spitting out most of it in an effort to expel the foul taste lodged in her throat. She found a clean shirt in her locker. Dressing, she listened to Boyd giving out yards after discovering he hadn't a change of clothes at the station. He had to settle for the offer of a shirt from Kirby.

'It's rank,' he said, buttoning it up anyway.

'It's clean,' Kirby said.

'I doubt that, but thanks.'

'Any time.'

In the interview room, Lottie sat with Boyd and faced Chris Dermody.

The man stared at her, his arrogance seeping from his pores. He was short and stout, his chest barrelling against the table. His hair left a greasy stain on the collar of his puffer jacket.

'I want my solicitor.'

'Mr Dermody, you know all about the Drugs and Organised Crime Bureau, I'm sure.' She kept a close eye for a reaction, but he stared at a point on the wall. Fuck him.

'Well, those boys are on their way and they won't give a shit about you or your solicitor. We found nearly half a million euros' worth of cocaine concealed in the boot of your car. Stupid of you really, trying to move it with checkpoints all over the country searching for a missing child. But the drugs are not my concern, because right now my priority is the safety of a four-year-old boy.'

He moved his head, curling up his lip. 'I told your boss, I know nothing about him.'

'How come Nathan Monaghan tells me you threatened him on Monday evening by using Evan's name.'

'The prick said that? Look, lady, I was just throwing it out there. Monaghan was getting cold feet. A few weeks ago he was mouthing off that his missus was coming into a big payday. But I didn't give a fuck about that. I wanted him to remember he was working for me on my terms. Getting well paid for it too.'

'So how did you know his son's name?'

'Funny thing is, the kid isn't his son after all.'

'Answer the question.'

'I want my solicitor.'

Lottie slammed the table and Boyd's water cup hit the floor. 'Fuck you and your solicitor. I want to know where you're holding the boy. He is only four years old.'

'I never went near the kid. Monaghan told me the brat's name himself when I met him in the pub to recruit him. Never even laid eyes on him until his photo started popping up all over the place. I've enough to be doing without snatching kids.'

Leaning back in the chair, Lottie stared at the ball of arrogance in front of her. She believed him.

'Who do you work for?'

'I'm a self-made man.'

'Quit the shit, Dermody. I want a name.'

'Nope. I want a deal with the bureau for that information.'

She glared at Boyd, who was mopping up the spilled water with a tissue. He was no help.

Standing quickly, she said, 'If the boy dies, you will rot in hell.'

Dermody sat up straight and glanced at the recording equipment.
'Hey, wait a minute. I never took him. I swear. It was an idle threat to
keep that prick on board. I'm saying nothing here, right? But if I was
you, I'd take a long, hard luck at Monaghan's employer.'

Lottie turned at the door. 'AJ Lennon?'

'I'm saying nothing.' But he smirked and nodded emphatically.

'Bring in AJ Lennon,' Lottie ordered when she was back in the office.
'Where's Dervla Byrne being held?' She sat on the edge of McKeown's
desk as a wave of dizziness floored her.

'She's waiting to be interviewed. Kept screaming to speak to you.
Something about a phone in a fridge. Whatever all that is about.'
McKeown threw his hands in the air.

'I'll talk to her.'

'Wait a minute,' he said. 'When I heard that Dervla and Kevin had
been in foster care, I thought it would be an idea to check who else
had been fostered by Frank Maher.'

'And?'

'There's no way for me to look at files without good reason and a
warrant, so I contacted Dylan Foley, Sinéad's husband.'

'McKeown! He's a person of interest. Christ almighty, you'll land
us all in the shit-house.'

'Yeah, but he's also a social worker with access to files.'

Lottie was apt at bending the rules herself, so she hadn't a leg to
stand on. 'Go on, tell me.'

'I informed him that he could be charged as a conspirator because
it was likely his key had been used in the abduction.'

'That's bullshit and you know it.'

'He doesn't, though. Anyway, he came up with the goods. I told him to go back at least thirty years on Frank Maher's fostering records. He accessed the old files for me.'

'He could lose his job.'

'I told him his name wouldn't be used in connection with the information if we found anything relevant. Will I go on?'

'Do.'

'We know Dervla Byrne and Kevin Doran were fostered by Frank Maher and his wife, but did you know that the Mahers also fostered Joyce Breslin? At one stage, all three were there at the same time.'

'Wow!' This was news. 'I'll need to talk with Maher again. Any link to Isabel or Jack Gallagher in these records?'

His ears grew red. 'No. Not yet.'

'Keep looking. Talking of Dylan Foley, anything turn up regarding his key?'

His ears positively pulsed. 'I asked him for a list of clients he met on Monday and the names of those who attended the late meeting he had before he left for the gym. I have him scared shitless, so he's emailing the list to me.'

A gust of hot air blew into the office as Kirby shoved in the door and slapped a file on the desk.

'Forensic report on Jack Gallagher's van. No evidence that Gallagher held or transported Joyce in the vehicle. It's packed to the gills with electrical materials, and his boots don't match the footprint found at his house or those discovered at the pond where Joyce's body was found.'

'Any way of checking if the boot print belongs to AJ Lennon?' McKeown asked.

Lottie said, 'Lennon is a small man, probably a size nine or ten. Doubt it's him. But check it out.' She paced the room, tearing at her arms. She thought about the mice, and shivered again. 'What's the motive for killing Isabel and Joyce? Something to do with the smuggling? Or the crime that happened at Castlemain Drive?'

Boyd had come in behind Kirby, and the sound of his voice broke Lottie's concentration.

He held up a hand for silence. 'Thanks, Gráinne.'

'What did she have to say?' Lottie dared to hope the SOCO had been able to get DNA results.

'The teddy bear from the house at Castlemain Drive. You were right. She fast-tracked the DNA sample and it's a match for Evan Breslin. And the blood on the razor blades I found in the scarf is a match for Joyce.'

'That's proof that Joyce and Evan were in that house on Castlemain Drive at some stage.'

'Yeah,' Boyd said. 'They must have lived there before she moved in with Nathan.'

'Well, we can't ask either of them what happened, but it could be a motive for the current crimes,' McKeown said.

'It's clear that a child died there,' Boyd said. 'Forensics are still checking for more evidence.'

Lottie nodded. 'Okay. The boy's real father must have lived there too. But he is still an unknown. We need to look at what we know. Jack Gallagher bought a car from Frank Maher via Dervla Byrne. Then Joyce Breslin was in possession of said car. That car was registered to Lugmiran Enterprises, as was the Castlemain house. Anything from CAB or DOCB on finding the names behind Lugmiran?'

McKeown said, 'Not yet, but I have the revenue office digging into it too. Could be linked to the drug smuggling. By the way, Revenue have been following Jack Gallagher for back taxes for his freelance work.'

Lottie continued to pace, unaware that she was bumping into desks. 'If a crime occurred in that house while Joyce lived there, she may have told Isabel and that knowledge got them both killed. And Evan is caught in the crossfire. Can his DNA tell us who his father is?'

'No match to anyone on our system.'

'So it's not Jack Gallagher or Nathan Monaghan. What about Kevin Doran or Frank Maher? Did we take their DNA?'

'Jesus, Lottie,' Boyd said. 'Frank is eighty-three.'

'Get his DNA and fingerprints. Age is no barrier to crime.'

'Right.' Boyd made the call. 'I'll tell the lab to run Kevin's DNA too.'

She came to a stop in front of the boards. 'Anita is Isabel's mother. It's unlikely Isabel was ever in foster care, so … Wait a minute. Remember when Kevin was mumbling. He said something that sounded like AJ, but he also said sorry and something else. It could have been Isabel.'

'I didn't catch what he said,' Boyd said.

'Any update from the hospital? When can we interview him?'

'He's in surgery. Head wound and one of the stab wounds are their biggest concern. The rest of the cuts are superficial.'

'We know Kevin worked at Gallagher's house. Isabel was murdered the same day Joyce went missing,' Lottie said. 'Then Evan was abducted. Come on, lads, talk to me. What does it all mean?'

'I think you were right when you said they knew something they had to die for,' McKeown said. 'But it doesn't explain why Evan was taken.'

'We need to find Evan's father. He either knows what went on in the Castlemain house or he's responsible for all of this.'

'Doesn't bode well for finding the little boy alive when we don't know who we're looking for,' Kirby said.

'The ray of sun shines again,' McKeown said.

'I'll interview AJ Lennon when he's brought in,' Lottie said. 'Find out what's keeping them. I'm going down to have a word with Jack Gallagher, and then I'll talk to Frank Maher again.'

She turned on her heel and shut the door softly, leaned against it, closed her eyes and exhaled. She had to find Evan. Alive.

*

Lottie nodded at the guard and pressed the switch to release the cell door. It was cold down in the bowels of the station. She missed her sweater.

'Am I being released?' Jack asked half-heartedly, without standing. 'My daughter. I want to see Holly. My solicitor is working on a complaint against you.'

'Jack, shut up for a minute. Tell me about the car you bought from Frank Maher.' She leaned against the wall, the light hurting her eyes.

'What car?'

She sat beside him on the plastic mattress. 'You have a daughter. I believe you love her, and that you loved Isabel in some twisted way. I'd like to know what changed between you.'

'First you ask about a car I know nothing about, and now you want to know about my marriage. Make your mind up.' He folded his arms but didn't turn away.

'I'm racing against the clock to find a four-year-old boy alive. I don't have the full picture, though I believe whoever killed Isabel and Joyce has taken him. You've been our number one suspect, but now I honestly don't think you did it.'

'What's changed your tune?'

She rested her head against the granite wall, feet on the cot, and hugged her knees. She kept her eyes wide open, staring at the side of his head. Now that she suspected Evan's real father had taken him, it couldn't be Jack. His DNA was not a match. But was he innocent of everything? What about the car?

'Tell me what happened to the black Ford Focus you bought via Best Deals from Frank Maher five years ago.'

His muscles twitched, his hands tightening on each other between his knees, and he turned to look at her. 'Then can I see my daughter?'

'I'll see.'

He nodded slowly. 'There's nothing to tell really. I hadn't been working at Quality Electrical very long at the time, and one of the lads, Ciaran Grimes, asked me to answer an advert on Best Deals. So I did.'

'Bloody hell,' Lottie said. She'd talked to Ciaran Grimes at the site where Joyce's body had been found.

'I met a young woman at a house down by the harbour, handed over the five thousand cash Ciaran had given me and drove it back to him. That's it. That's the truth. Can't say I ever laid eyes on it after that.'

'Ciaran Grimes asked you to buy the car?' she asked incredulously.

'Yep.'

'Why couldn't he just go and buy it himself?'

'I didn't think about it, just did as I was told.'

'He might have been muddying the purchase trail.' She was thinking out loud now. 'Could Grimes have masterminded all this mayhem? He works for Michael Costello.' Jumping up from the cot, almost falling over her feet, she headed for the door. 'Holy shit!

'What does it mean?' Gallagher unwound his body and stood.

'I don't know.' She was totally confused. 'You ever hear of Lugmiran Enterprises?'

'Never.'

She paused by the door. 'Isabel worked for Costello for a time too.'

'Yeah.'

'Was there ever anything between them?'

'You mean an affair? No way. She never really liked him. He treated her like dirt.'

'Was Isabel ever in care? Fostered?'

He shook his head. 'I doubt it. You could check with Anita.'

Her mind was tumbling with scenarios. 'Did you ever see Grimes or Costello with Joyce Breslin?'

He shook his head. 'I don't think so, but I was on the road all day and only docked into the yard in the morning and evening. I know you think I had something to do with her murder, but I swear I was with Tanya at that time.'

'I believe you.'

'At last.'

'Don't go anywhere. I'll be back.' She pressed the buzzer to be released.

Outside the cell door, her phone rang.

'Hi, Jane.'

'I've had a quick look at the bones that were brought in from the hill.'

'Anything to identify who the child was?' Lottie held her breath, hoping the pathologist might be able to solve that mystery.

Jane continued, her voice low and soft, 'No but two of the tiny rib bones have marks consistent with knife wounds. Lottie, this child was stabbed.'

CHAPTER SEVENTY-TWO

AJ Lennon was a puddle of sweat when Lottie entered the interview room. He cut a sorry lump behind the table. She felt nothing for him as her body twitched with nervous energy. She sensed she was getting close to unravelling everything, and maybe, just maybe, she could find Evan before it was too late.

'AJ, I want you to be honest with me. There's a four-year-old's life on the line.'

'I know nothing about him or his abduction.'

She chanced a different tack. 'People are being murdered, AJ. Did you hear Kevin Doran was attacked this morning? He's very badly injured?'

'Kevin?' Lennon looked like he was about to puke all over the desk. She edged against the wall, just in case.

She forced a nonchalant cadence, though she was buzzing like an electric current had struck her. 'He mentioned you, you know, before he lost consciousness. Someone caved his head in and stabbed him.'

Lennon's pallor turned green. 'You're lying. I don't understand. Why would someone attack him? He's … h-harmless.' His words were caught in his throat.

'You know him, then?'

Lennon pursed his lips. Silence.

'Come on, AJ. A little boy could die. I need to know what you know. How is Kevin involved in all this?'

'He's not involved in anything.'

'Not even your smuggling ring?'

His eyes flashed like steel. 'I'm not smuggling anything.'

'Chris Dermody says different.'

'I don't know who that is.'

'Your lorries were smuggling cocaine into the country. You have to know that, because your employee Nathan Monaghan drove them. Across Europe and back to your warehouse.'

Lennon seemed to shrink into the collar of his shirt, jowls wobbling over the cotton. 'I'm not involved in the day-to-day running of the warehouse. How is Kevin?'

'It's your lorries that are involved in the smuggling operation.'

He tugged at the worry hole in his sweater, leaning towards her. 'I'm so sorry, but none of this is my fault.'

She shook her head and remained silent, watching him squirm. In reality she wanted to leap across the table and wring the truth out of him. Evan's life depended on speed.

'Okay, you win,' he said. 'Tell me how Kevin is and then I'll tell you what I know.'

'You're in no position to make a deal.'

'You need to find that little boy, don't you?' A dark streak skittered across his eyes, the steel glint morphing into black onyx.

Bastard, she thought. 'Kevin's in surgery. When I know more, I'll tell you.'

He nodded a couple of times, as if he had no choice but to believe her. He hadn't.

'Michael Costello was using my lorries for smuggling drugs. I had to turn a blind eye. I had no control; I was at his mercy.'

'What?'

'You heard me. He is one mean bastard in every sense.'

'You are a successful business man reported to be worth millions. Why would you let Costello use you like that?' She watched the small man shrink smaller, and she knew. 'What does he have on you, AJ? Why was he blackmailing you? Sexual harassment of your workers? Fraud in your business?'

'I'm not like that, I swear to God. I pride myself on my morality.'

'For heaven's sake, AJ, just tell me.'

'It was Kevin.'

'Kevin was smuggling?'

'No. Kevin … Kevin is my son.'

She hadn't seen that one coming. The cogs in her brain turned furiously, trying to catch up.

'Why was Kevin in foster care if he's your son?'

'I abandoned him like I abandoned his mother. He was put up for adoption and it didn't work out. I kept tabs on him as much as I could. Then one day he came to me and told me he'd found out about me, but he wanted nothing from me. Broke my heart.'

'I don't understand any of this.'

'Talk to Anita, though I only told her this week who Kevin is.'

'Isabel's mother? Anita Boland?' She couldn't believe what she was hearing.

'Anita is Kevin's mother too. We were teenagers, kids really. We had no other choice.'

'Sweet Jesus.' It dawned on her then. Kevin and Isabel were half-siblings. 'Did Kevin kill Isabel?'

'God, no. I think in some part of his brain he believed he was keeping watch over her.'

'But he lived like a hermit.' A filthy one at that. 'How could you allow your own son to live like that?'

'Kevin had his troubles.' AJ tapped the side of his head. 'It's hard to explain, but …'

'Go on, please.'

'I think it's all down to Michael Costello. He thrives on being in control of everyone. I believe he could have killed Isabel. She worked for him for a time, and he tried to control her until Jack stepped in. I don't think he ever forgave Jack for that.'

Lottie noticed how AJ was shifting blame, but his words held a hint of truth. 'How could Costello force you to allow your lorries to be used for drug smuggling?'

'He found out Kevin was my son. I don't know how, but he did. Threatened to sell the story to the papers. How I let my son live like a pauper while I wallowed in supposed millions. It wasn't like that at all. Kevin lived his life the way he did because he wanted to. He was damaged. Poor boy. I let him down terribly.'

You should be ashamed of yourself, she thought, but then who was she to judge?

'AJ, do you think Costello could be involved in Isabel and Joyce's murders, and Evan's abduction?'

'I wouldn't put anything past that bastard.'

Rushing out of the room, Lottie made her way up the stairs two at a time, adrenaline fuelling her steps.

She yelled at Kirby.

'Bring in Michael Costello and Ciaran Grimes for questioning. Boyd, we have a quick trip to make. Forget about your blasted coat. We won't be long.'

CHAPTER SEVENTY-THREE

Frank Maher was curled up beside his dog on the floor by the stove. No matter what Lottie or Boyd said, the man refused to move.

'Leave me alone. Go away.'

The one link they had appeared to stem from Frank Maher's fostering. She had to ask the question.

'Was Michael Costello one of the children you fostered?'

Frank looked up at her, eyes narrowing as if surprised by the question. 'Michael was the first child we ever took in. Like a son, he was. But he was hard work, poor Michael.'

She'd give him poor Michael if it turned out he was a devious murderer and kidnapper.

'Was it a formal fostering?' Michael's name hadn't been on Dylan Foley's list.

'No. You see, he was my wife's sister's kid. She fecked off to England once he was born and left him with us. Died of a drug overdose in Luton five years after that.'

'And you never registered with the relevant authorities the fact that you were raising someone else's child?'

'Why would we? He was family by blood.'

'Joyce Breslin was one of your foster kids, wasn't she?'

'She was.' The man looked too defeated to argue or lie. 'Poor little thing was like a lost bird. Michael was intrigued by her. He tried to fix her. They were all lost, and I couldn't help them find themselves. Michael tried, God love him.'

'Tell me more.' She ground her teeth in irritation.

'Michael was the brightest and smartest child I'd ever met. He grew up to be an intelligent and successful man. Made something of himself and I'm proud of that.'

'How did he get on with the other children you took in?'

Frank cried out as if in pain and the dog whined. 'Shush now, Bosco. It's okay, boy. No one is going to take you away from me.'

'Mr Maher?' Boyd said. 'Please talk to us, sir.'

'I like respect. Thank you. You see, Michael was very taken with Joyce when she arrived. She was the youngest and the last we took in. He had a place of his own by then and was on his way to building up his business, but he called in to see me regularly. Stayed the odd few nights too.'

'In what way was he taken with Joyce?'

'I'd go so far as to say he was in love with her, but I know Michael couldn't love anyone. Despite all his virtues, he has a hard heart. It pains me to tell you that. But that's what made his business a success.'

Plus funds from smuggling drugs, Lottie thought.

Frank was almost whispering by now. 'I think, even though she was young, she was stronger than the others, and he saw her as a challenge … he wanted to break her.'

'What do you mean?' A minute ago, Frank had said Costello wanted to fix Joyce.

'He loved a challenge. He always wanted to make the impossible possible.'

'Kevin and Dervla were here too. Kevin must be around Michael's age. Tell me about their relationship.'

'It was fiery from the start. We took in Dervla when she was only about five, and a few weeks later Kevin arrived. He was aged about ten when he came to us. He'd been adopted but it hadn't worked out, and I think he was in one of those awful industrial schools for a while. Broke the lad in a terrible way. We had to work hard with him, giving him lots of attention. That meant we had less time for Michael. He became sullen and mean. But after a while he seemed to take Kevin under his wing and it was like they were best buddies. It was a small miracle.'

'Why the change in Michael's behaviour?' Boyd asked.

'I didn't know at the time, but I think I do now. I believe he used Kevin for physical abuse. Time and again I found Kevin with cuts to his arms and legs. It had started with Dervla too.'

'What did you do about this abuse?' Lottie asked.

'Nothing, I'm sorry to say. Whatever was going on, it calmed Michael down and that made life easier for us. I'm ashamed. I turned a blind eye to what was going on.'

'It's criminal,' Lottie said.

'I just wanted to keep a calm house. When they got a bit older, he took them on trips up to Misneach. He always talked about the soul healing itself through pain.'

'He forced children to cut themselves?'

'I suspect so. Dervla might tell you about it.'

Lottie had seen the telltale signs on Dervla's arms when she'd brought the little bone into the station. 'Frank, we found the bones of a child up on Misneach. Do you know anything about that?'

'God, no.'

'The car you sold, did you ever see Michael driving it?'

Frank looked away, caressed his dog. 'My car wasn't in his league. Michael always drives something flashy.'

'You previously told my colleague you'd never heard of Lugmiran Enterprises. Are you sure?'

'Is it connected in some way to all that's happened?'

'The car was registered to this company. Also a house where we believe Joyce lived for a time.'

'What does it all mean?'

'Please, Frank, it's important. Anything you know about this Lugmiran is important.'

'Let me think. Ah, unless it has something to do with the sacred hill.'

'How?'

'It might be too far-fetched.'

'I'll take far-fetched at this stage,' Lottie said.

'There was an ancient god called Lugh, and Ail na Mireann means stone of division. It's rumoured to be on Misneach. Does that help?'

Another link to the hill where the bones had been discovered. 'Michael knew all this?'

'It was him who told me about it. He was fascinated by all that.'

'Was there a relationship between Michael and Joyce?'

Frank rubbed the dog's furry neck and kissed its head. 'I'd say there was something there all right. When Joyce left, Michael told me not to worry, he'd look after her. She never came back to see me and I never saw them together.'

'Did Michael ever have children?'

'God, I hope not.'

'Why do you say that?'

'Because if he did, I'd fear for their safety.' Tears sprang up in the old man's eyes. 'Michael doesn't know how to love anyone. How could he love a child?' Sobs broke from his throat and the dog whined in sympathy.

Lottie was building a mental picture of Michael Costello and shivered to think that he had been in her home and talked to her family. 'Frank, do you know of Kevin's true parentage?'

'Aye, I do. I got a copy of his adoptive birth cert when the social workers brought him here that first day, all those years ago. It was a bulky file for a ten-year-old, but it held the background of all his troubles. I think we were given the file so that we'd know who we were taking in.'

'But an adoption cert doesn't show the names of the birth parents.'

'No, but his original birth cert was attached to the file. Probably by accident.'

'Did you ever tell Kevin that you knew who his real parents were?'

'No, I did not.'

He kept his head down, allowing the dog to nuzzle his wrinkled chin. Lottie wasn't buying his innocence.

'You told Michael, didn't you?'

Frank squeezed the dog and the animal whimpered. 'I don't think he ever saw the cert, but I might have shouted it at him one time.'

'How did that happen?'

'Michael was in his late twenties or even thirties – I'm not good with ages. Kevin was still living here at the time. Michael was gloating, telling him how he was making a success of his business, that Kevin would always be a nobody. God forgive me, but I let fly at him.'

'What did you say?' But she knew.

'I told him Kevin's father was a millionaire businessman. Not that you'd think it to look at him.'

'Did you say the name?'

'I probably did, because Michael saw red. Stormed out and rarely called round after that.'

'What about Kevin?'

'Next day he upped and left. Never laid eyes on him again.'

'I'll need that birth cert.' Lottie tried to wrap her head around this information. She had one last question. 'Do you know of a Ciaran Grimes?'

Frank didn't hesitate. 'I don't.'

There was nothing else to do here. She had to put it all together and save Evan, if he was still alive. She felt hollow inside as she stood up, a crick in her neck from leaning downwards. At the door, she heard Frank's croaking voice.

'Inspector, I think I might have done something else stupid.'

'What is that?'

'I phoned Michael this morning, after you were here. I told him you were asking about Kevin, that you knew where he lived. God, I hope I didn't put Kevin in any danger.'

Boyd nudged her to say nothing. It would be the kind thing to do. But she knew that being kind rarely got her results.

'Kevin was attacked in his home this morning. He's fighting for his life. That, Frank, is your fault.'

CHAPTER SEVENTY-FOUR

He was still in control. Nothing was impossible for the smartest man on earth. He was cleverer than the lot of them put together.

No need to panic. He rarely panicked.

But after he'd received the phone calls earlier, Michael Costello knew he needed to accelerate his plans. First Dervla, the fucking bitch, trying to blackmail him over some phone she said had belonged to Isabel Gallagher. Then he'd got Frank's call.

Kevin.

That whiny little bastard knew nothing. Costello had racked his brains but couldn't take a chance on something unknown being revealed later.

He'd had no problem dispensing with him. Easy and timely. He'd actually passed the detectives' car on the road after the kill. It felt good to smash the stone into his skull. It surprised him how satisfying the rush was, and he'd relished scoring the skin with his knife before thrusting it into the bastard's flesh.

It had been the same with Isabel. Her flesh had felt soft and supple as he'd sliced her throat and knifed her back. He mourned the fact that he hadn't taken longer with her, but the baby wouldn't shut her mouth and it'd ruin his plan to frame interfering Jack if he killed the kid. Fathers didn't murder their kids, did they? Not unless their name was Michael Costello. He smirked at that.

Joyce had been a different story. The years he'd kept her holed up in that house. Clever of him to situate her in a housing estate, hiding in plain sight. He liked that. Ingenious. It had been good while it lasted, but the night he'd lost it, he really had lost it. Stupid kid had annoyed the fuck out of him. How many times had he told her not to call him Daddy? What if someone found out about his secret? He'd run down the stairs, grabbed the knife and used it on her in her cot. Threw the pillow over her face for good measure. She wouldn't call him Daddy ever again. The rush had been so high, he'd wanted to kill them all.

But Joyce had a way with her. She'd learned from the best, he supposed. He'd moulded her well during her time at Frank's. Brought her to Misneach many times, and the others too. Controlled them all by introducing them to the magic of the blades. Initiated them into discovering a pain they could not live without. He was a genius.

But now he knew that what he'd done the night he'd killed his daughter had been a mistake. Joyce had always had a rebellious streak and a backbone buried beneath the layers of cuts he'd inflicted to teach her a lesson.

That night, he'd come down from the high of the kill too quickly and allowed her to talk him into letting her and the boy live. She'd dictated the burial on their sacred hill. His one moment of weakness in a lifetime of control.

He'd given her the car and told her to get out of his life. And then she'd had the audacity to try to blackmail him! Her and that Isabel bitch. How had they even become friends? Ha, Isabel hadn't been too happy when he'd told her who she had for a brother. Her face! She'd been easy to coerce into cutting away her pain with a blade while she worked for him. That was until Jack came knocking on her door. Bastard.

The women thought they could blackmail him over the fortune he was making from the drugs. Idiots. And holding what happened that November night over him. Planning to tell the guards everything if he didn't pay up by Friday.

'Well, bitches, it's almost Friday, and you're both dead.'

He threw a bundle of food wrappers into the black bag. He'd been safe until Lottie Parker poked her nose in. Hadn't he done her job for her, leading her to Jack Gallagher? Why had she not charged that prick by now?

It was all down to the kid. Evan. Stupid name. 'Fucking hell!'

He marched around the house stuffing what he could into the bag. Anything that would leave evidence the kid had been here. He wasn't going to make another mistake.

When he was certain he had the house clear, he threw the refuse sack into the boot of his car and went back inside the house to make sure his plan was rock solid.

He'd killed Isabel and tried to frame Jack. Caught up with Joyce at the lake with the tracker he'd placed on her phone. She wouldn't be able to collect the kid from day care, and he knew her partner wouldn't be home till late. He'd paid his employee Ciaran Grimes to steal the door key from Dylan Foley. That had been the easy bit. Then all Michael had to do was walk into Foley's house. Knock out the wife if she was in the way and take the kid. But no force had been necessary. The woman wasn't around and the kid seemed to recognise him, which was good. He hardly whimpered.

It was easy after that. Grimes's girlfriend, Carla, cared for the boy during the day, while he and Grimes carried on working, beyond suspicion.

And now he'd paid Grimes and Carla enough to get to the Costa del Sol and stay there, with the promise of further payments if they kept their mouths firmly shut. The two had scuttled off with the sports bag full of cash and Michael knew he was still in control. One last job and he could go back to being who he was meant to be. A successful, upstanding Ragmullin citizen.

He stared at the boy.

'Well, kiddo, it's you and me now.' But not for long.

'Are you my daddy? My real daddy?' Two blue eyes, round and wide as coat buttons, stared up at him.

He kept his hands clenched in case he lashed out. He didn't want another screaming match.

'Shut your mouth or I'll stick a knife in it.'

The child snivelled and sniffed, snot running from his nose. Gross.

'Mummy wouldn't let me get a dog. But if I'm really good, I'd love a dog.'

'Your mummy is dead as a dodo. We're going on a trip.'

'I get car sick without Teddy. I want Teddy.'

'Fuck you and your bloody teddy,' Michael muttered as he picked up the boy, feeling absolutely nothing for him. If he was a dog, he might feel a little regret at what he was about to do.

Outside, he threw Evan onto the back seat. 'Seat belt. I might have to drive fast.'

'What's a dodo?'

'Jesus Christ, give me patience.' He fired up the engine and drove off at speed.

CHAPTER SEVENTY-FIVE

Boyd hung up the phone. 'Squad car arrived at Costello's house. There's no one home.'

'He's not at his office either,' Kirby said.

'Does anyone there know where he is?' Lottie said.

'No one's seen him all day. He didn't turn up this morning.'

'Where do we look next?' Lottie paced circles, prodding her forehead with a finger.

'What about Sinéad and Dylan Foley?'

'They're in the clear.' McKeown spoke up. 'Michael Costello used the same gym as Dylan, even though I can't find him on any security footage close to the place that evening. But it means he'd know Dylan's routine. And get this. Ciaran Grimes was the last client Dylan Foley saw on Monday evening. I asked Dylan if Grimes could have taken the key, and he said it was possible because he was flustered trying to get notes ready for his meeting straight afterwards.'

'And we were scouring useless CCTV from all the premises close to the gym. Damn.' She didn't even want to know why Grimes was seeing Dylan. It was probably made-up anyhow.

'Didn't I send a car to Grimes's house?'

'No one there, and he didn't turn up for work today,' Kirby said.

'His girlfriend is a hairdresser,' McKeown said, 'and she hasn't been at work since last Saturday.'

'Oh my God, what have they done with Evan?' Lottie tugged at her sleeve, pulling out threads. 'Find out what they drive and issue an alert to airports and ports for their car and Costello's, though I don't think Costello will run. He thinks he's too clever to be caught.'

'What is his motive?' Boyd said.

'By process of elimination, he must be Evan's father. We have DNA for almost everyone else involved, and no match. Lugmiran could be something to do with Misneach Hill, and that was a favourite spot of Costello's, according to Frank. When we eventually succeed in unpicking the layers of that company, I'm sure we'll find it was set up by Michael Costello.'

'And that means he owns 14 Castlemain and the car Joyce was driving,' Boyd said.

Lottie continued. 'We can assume he installed Joyce in the house in Castlemain after her time at Frank's. A child was stabbed in that house and her body buried on Misneach. That crime is the root cause of what's happening now. His motivation is in there somewhere.'

'But where is he?' Boyd said.

'Michael was in foster care for years and Frank told us he liked to cause pain to his foster siblings. The only one I can think of right now who might know where he'd take Evan is Dervla Byrne.'

Dervla fidgeted like a child waiting for the dentist.

'Leave me alone. I told you everything.'

Lottie pulled the chair from the far side of the table and sat beside her. 'Michael Costello. Tell me about him.'

'He's a prick.'

'We think he may have abducted Evan Breslin. Evan is only four years old. I saw how you felt when you brought me that child's bone. You care, Dervla. So do I. I want to find Evan. It's possible that Michael murdered Joyce and Isabel, and that he almost killed Kevin. He probably killed the child whose bones you found. I need to find that little boy before Michael murders him. Where would he take him?'

'Michael is a bully. He liked to cut us and then make us cut ourselves.' Dervla rocked, holding her arms around her waist.

'I'm sorry you had to suffer like that, but I need to know more about him.'

'Did you get the phone? It was Isabel's. Kevin was minding it for her. I think Joyce was trying to warn her. But Isabel was already dead.' She paused to catch her breath, her eyes wild.

'Warn her about what?'

'About Michael. Joyce knew what he was like but Isabel was never in care. She had no idea what he was capable of.'

'Where would Michael go when cornered?'

Without hesitation, Dervla said, 'Misneach. That's where he took us when he wanted to show us he was in control. He destroyed Kevin's life just because he could.'

'He wouldn't risk going there after all the activity on the hill yesterday.'

'I think he would. He is arrogant enough to assume he can get away with anything. Where's Kevin now?'

'He's in hospital. I don't know any more at the moment.'

'Poor Kevin. Will he get better?'

'I hope so.' Lottie felt the young woman spoke with little true emotion. Had Michael succeeded in cutting most of her empathy away? The bastard was a destroyer of lives.

Dervla said, 'I found the little bones on Misneach. Kevin often went up there seeking healing, even though we both feared the place. That's weird, isn't it?'

'What do you know about those bones?'

'Nothing. Kevin told me he'd been there one night a few years ago. He stayed hidden for fear of being seen. But he was certain some kind of ritual was going on. Was that what it was? Offering up a child?'

'No, I think it was two people covering up a horrendous crime. Are you the only person Kevin told?'

Dervla tugged at a piece of skin on her finger, causing it to bleed. 'I don't know, but I think he tackled Michael about it recently.'

'Why do you think that?'

'Because Michael called to my house late one night. Terrified me. Told me to keep my mouth shut about Misneach. At first I thought he meant about the time when he used to bring us there, but then, when I thought about it, I realised that maybe Kevin had let slip about the night he'd hid out there, and that was what he meant.'

'You think that's where Michael would go? Misneach?'

Dervla stared up into Lottie's eyes, her face a mask of indifference but her eyes dark and ferocious. 'That's where he'd go if he wanted to hurt someone, or even bury a body.'

CHAPTER SEVENTY-SIX

After she'd left Dervla, Lottie bumped into Boyd in the corridor.

'Misneach Hill. Michael Costello might be headed there. He could already be there. Shit, Boyd, we might be too late.'

'Slow down. I've scrambled air support from Baldonnell. There was a reported sighting of Costello's car heading west from Ragmullin. A silver Tesla.'

'What are we waiting for. Come on!'

The silver car had to be miles ahead of them.

'Put your foot down, Boyd.'

'What do you think I'm doing?'

'How can he drive that fast?'

'It's a powerful vehicle. And this is a heap of shite.'

'This is the newest in the fleet,' she yelled, trying to hear herself above the siren. 'Make it move.'

The fields and trees whizzed past as Boyd floored the accelerator. Sirens blasted through her skull. The road narrowed the further they drove and it seemed to her as if every farmer in the country had picked that exact moment to take their tractor out for a leisurely drive.

'I can't see him,' she yelled. 'Where is he?'

'Shit, shit, shit.' Boyd slowed the car, thumping the steering wheel. 'He must have pulled in somewhere.'

'Wait. Up ahead. Go! Turn right. Now!'

Boyd swerved past the farmer in his John Deere hogging the centre line of the road.

'Where am I going?'

'Park. There. No! Fuck. Over there, Boyd. Are you blind?'

'God almighty, Lottie. Stop shouting in my ear and I might be able to see.' He pulled up in a ditch behind Costello's Tesla.

Lottie jumped out and raced to the car shaded under a canopy of trees. Unlocked. She tugged open all the doors.

'Empty.' She scanned her surroundings. 'He's gone up the hill. We have to follow.'

'We need to wait for backup.'

'You can stand there dithering if you want to. I'm not waiting.' She fastened on her Kevlar vest and holstered her SIG Sauer, then took off up the mossy incline. She wasn't hanging around for Boyd to make up his mind while a little boy was held in the arms of death.

*

Michael Costello picked his steps carefully but still moved quickly.

The kid was heavy, not helped by his thrashing legs beating into his hip bone. He should have tied up the little shit. Should have killed him before he left the house. But a dead weight was worse. He knew that.

The memory of that night, however many years ago, was the root cause of this necessary re-enactment. He should never have listened to Joyce back then. Bury their daughter and walk away, she'd said. And that was what he had done, to his eternal regret. Then she'd had the cheek to come up with her blackmail plan, thinking she had fucked him over. No, sweetheart, you can't fuck over the master controller. Ingenious to send her the envelope with the address inside to remind her she was also involved. And a blade to maybe slice an artery.

The higher he climbed, the darker the evening fell around him. A fog slithered around his feet and he found it difficult to pick his steps.

He moved on upwards. Sweating. Panting. The kid stopped fighting him and was silent, as if fear had numbed and dumbed him. Good.

The tree loomed up ahead. White blossoms dotted the branches, with something circling about five metres from the trunk. Crime-scene tape.

'What the hell,' he muttered, dropping to his knees.

He kept a firm grip on the boy, squeezing his fingers into his bony arms, and looked all around, searching. He'd been sure they'd already have left, their job completed, but were they waiting for him? Was this a trap? No. There'd been no garda vehicles present when he'd arrived. He stared back down the hill, retracing his path with his gaze.

Imagination was a weird thing, he thought as he saw Joyce rising up from the fog. The bitch had come to haunt him. Impossible. He'd slit her throat and watched the blood seep from her body. No, it couldn't be her. She was dead. The vision took form as the woman stood tall and trained a weapon on him.

'It's over, Michael. Let Evan go.'

The detective.

'He's mine, and this is his final resting place.'

'Bollocks to that. You're surrounded, Michael. Release him.'

That was when he heard the whirr of rotor blades above his head. A helicopter came into view, circling in the sombre sky.

'Back off, or I'll slice his throat.' He brandished the knife. 'He must rest where his sister had lain.'

'I know what you've done, what you did to your little girl. Let your son go.'

'Dream on, bitch. Come here and let me teach you the power of the blade.' He held the knife high, knowing that one glorious swipe would be enough to end the life of the kid, and then he'd feel an exultation beyond comprehension.

*

Perspiration bubbled on Lottie's forehead and trickled down into her eyes. Her shirt stuck to her back beneath the Kevlar vest. Her feet slipped on the damp grass and her hands holding the gun shook violently. She tried to steady herself, but there was no way she could get a shot off without hitting the child. The bastard was using his own son as a shield.

Boyd reached her, his leather shoes useless as he slid to a slippery stop.

'What's the plan?' he whispered, breathless. 'The helicopter is above us and the ARU are en route.'

Lottie didn't have time to wait for the Armed Response Unit. Costello had to be talked down now.

She glanced up at the hovering helicopter. Costello had one hand raised, holding the knife, the child gripped to his chest with the other. The wind on the hill dipped as the helicopter flew away to one side. An icy stillness, a veil of fog shrouding the face of evil.

'Listen to me, Michael. Your little girl is no longer buried on Misneach. We've taken her bones away. She'll get a proper burial.'

'You're a bitch!'

'Come on, Michael. It's over. Let Evan go.'

'It's not over until I say so!' he raged, his voice demonic, his smooth control lost forever.

Her aim was to keep him talking until either she or Boyd could take a clean shot. 'What did Isabel and Joyce do to you to cause all this?'

'Stupid women. I had Joyce under my control. Then she betrayed me. The pair of bitches tried to blackmail me. Joyce should have known

421

better. As if I'd pay any of my hard-earned cash to them! I'm superior to everyone.'

'Were they blackmailing you over killing your own child or your drug smuggling business? Or both?'

Costello's face blanched under the glare of the helicopter spotlight.

'Yes, Michael. We know all about your drug money. Surrender now. Let Evan come to me.'

'You think I'm going to spend my life in jail because of those women and that skinny bastard Kevin.' He screamed and raised the knife again.

'Stop! No, Michael. Please. Kevin is alive.'

His hand relaxed a little. 'This all started with him. Kevin and Isabel … they must have coerced Joyce. I had her under my control. *My* control, you hear. And now this one will be under my control for ever as he rots to bone like his sister. I hate you all!'

He opened his mouth wide and waved the knife at the sky as if beseeching a miracle from some god. The blade glinted under the cone of light from the helicopter, illuminating them like something from a Gothic horror movie.

A blast rang out.

The child screamed.

The noise reverberated in Lottie's ears, followed by a smack as the boy fell to the ground. She jumped. Surely Costello hadn't … had he?

'No!'

All was silent then, save for the roar of rotors above their heads. Michael Costello dropped the knife, his arm an explosion of blood and bone. Like a slow-motion reel, he fell to the ground.

Lottie raced forward.

Evan had rolled away under the crime-scene tape, coming to rest on the dug-up earth where his sister had been unceremoniously buried. Lottie took him in her arms and cradled him to her chest.

Boyd ran to secure Costello.

'Is he dead?' she shouted, noticing the man's hair swept back on his forehead by the force of the gunshot. Above his grey eyes, a thin scar ran along his hairline.

'No, but he won't be cutting anyone again.'

She held Evan's shivering body tight. 'You're okay now, pet. It's all over.'

'Arm hurts. I'm scared. Want my mummy. Want my teddy.'

'I can get you your teddy, sweetheart. Ten teddies.'

But how was she going to explain about his mummy? The trembling child in her arms had no one left in the world. He would end up in the care system, just as his mother had. For now, though, he was safe. That was the main thing. She had not failed him as others had.

She felt her tears fall then, a mix of exhaustion and exhilaration. They dropped one by one onto the little boy's head.

CHAPTER SEVENTY-SEVEN

Lynch sank into her chair. 'I'm done with babysitting adults. I can't wait to get home and relax in the mayhem of my own house.'

McKeown pounced across the office like a cheetah. 'If you ever rat me out again, so help me God, I'll kill you with my bare hands.'

'Screw you, McKeown, you cheating prick,' Lynch said, breathing fire.

'Fuck you.' He stormed towards the door, grabbing Garda Brennan by the hand, propelling her out into the corridor with him.

Kirby swivelled on his chair and whistled.

'Why are you so happy?' Lynch said. 'Thought you fancied Martina?'

'Careful there, or you'll combust.'

'I know who I'd like to see combust.' She slapped files around on her desk before swiping them all to the floor.

'Not I, hopefully,' Kirby said dramatically. He craved a cigar to take the edge off the swirl of his emotions.

Lynch ceased her tantrum and looked over at him. Really looked. 'It was you, Kirby! I didn't phone his wife, so it had to be you. You could've warned me.'

He patted his shirt pocket. 'I'm heading out for a smoke.'

The door pushed inwards as Lottie and Boyd arrived.

'Good job, well done.' Kirby stepped back, cigar forgotten.

Boyd fell onto the nearest chair, his hands still shaking.

'Where's the boy?' Lynch said warily, hoping she wouldn't have to babysit again.

'At the hospital.' Lottie felt her legs would collapse if she didn't sit soon. 'He's bruised and has a broken arm. After that, I don't know.'

'Poor kid.' Boyd rolled his jacket into a ball on his knee.

Lottie heard the crinkle of the letter in his pocket and caught his eye. He lowered his head with a quick shake. Now wasn't the time. But she had to know. Sooner, rather than later.

'We got Isabel's phone from Dervla Byrne's fridge,' Kirby said. 'Messages on it between her and Joyce since her time working at Foley's day care. The whole plot laid out. They were blackmailing Costello over his drug smuggling.'

'They must have become friends then,' Lottie said. 'From the old cuts on Isabel's body, it looks like Costello treated her like everyone else in his life. Jack really did save her from him when he convinced her to give up that job.'

'McKeown received Gallagher's financial records from Revenue,' Kirby said. 'Seems Jack made money from his freelance work, but he had a huge tax bill outstanding. That may have been his reason for being stingy at home.'

'Maybe,' Lottie said. 'I still think it was a form of domestic abuse, the way he kept money from Isabel. Little did he know his wife was scheming to make her own fortune.'

'Which ultimately led to her murder,' Kirby said.

Lottie felt her feet go numb and craved one of Rose's hot dinners. 'I think that's enough for today, lads. We can continue this post-mortem tomorrow with a full-scale debrief.'

'Pub, anyone?' Kirby said.

'If you're buying.' Lynch grinned.

'That'll be the day,' Boyd said.

'I'll buy,' Lottie offered, and wondered how she'd get through the evening watching them all get drunk. She remembered her fridge was full of Boyd's beer which she'd left untouched. That thought might keep her going. She'd no intention of ever drinking again. Maybe. Maybe not.

EPILOGUE

Kevin's eyes flashed open.

He blinked rapidly, everything out of focus. He had no idea where he was or what had happened. He had the worst pain in his head he'd ever experienced and he couldn't shake the dream.

The foster home was the place Kevin thought he might be happy. The couple were older than he imagined parents should be, but no one could be worse than the people he'd encountered during his spell at the industrial school. His skin bore the raised lumps of belt beatings, all in places no one could see, unless he was stripped. He had no intention of ever stripping in front of anyone again. Frank and his wife looked like nice people. Not a bit like people who would make him bathe in front of them. He hoped not, anyhow.

He was huddled in the bathroom while they talked to the social worker downstairs when he heard a hysterical laugh. He peered through the large old keyhole.

An eye, so dark it might even be black but was probably navy blue, stared back at him. He jumped backwards, cracking his spine against the washbasin. He shrieked at the surge of pain.

The handle twisted and he realised he hadn't locked the door. There was no key in the lock, that was why.

'Hello, new boy. Are you going to live with us?'

'Don't know yet.'

She looked much younger than him, but she was tall and gangly, her hair cut unevenly — one side swept over her shoulder and the other up over her ear.

'Oh, they'll take you,' she said knowingly. 'They want the money. But you'll get no cuddles or bedtime stories here.'

'I'm too old for all that.'

'No you're not!' She stuck her chest out. 'I'm five, and I don't want you here.'

'We could be friends,' he said.

'Don't want to be your friend.'

He raised a shoulder. For some unexplained reason, he wanted this weird girl to like him. 'I can learn to be a good friend. You can tell me your secrets and I'll tell you mine.'

'Will you kiss me?' she said, sounding a lot older than she looked.

'Ugh! Gross.' He'd never kissed anyone in his life, nor been kissed. Not even by a mother or father.

She turned up her nose. 'Don't want to kiss you any more, so I don't.'

'You're weird.'

'I'm not. Have you seen Michael, yet?'

'Who's he?'

'He's the blade boy. He likes to watch when he makes me cut myself. He wants me to cut into my bones. He is weird.'

'I don't think I want to stay here.'

'Cheer up. I bet you'll like Misneach.'

'What's that?'

'It's a hill outside the town. Michael says it has evil spirits. It's not that high up really.'

'Think I'll take my chances down on the ground.'

'You'll do what Michael says. What's your name?'

'I'm Kevin. What's yours?'

'Dervla. Nice to meet you, weird boy Kevin.'

Her laugh followed him from the dark of his dream to his awakening.

The pillow was soft against his head, but it didn't ease the pain thrumming behind his eyes. His memory flashed again, of how Michael had abused him with blades. This recollection caused the pain to explode through his head. He put his hands around his skull to stop it, and felt a row of staples. He didn't understand.

The door opened.

He half expected to see Dervla standing there, with her crooked hairstyle, like the first time he'd seen her through the keyhole. But it wasn't her.

'Hello, Kevin.'

'Hi.'

'You know who I am?'

'Isabel's mother.' He bit down on his tongue, trying not to add that he also knew she was *his* mother. Why was she here, after all this time?

'The doctors say it's a miracle you survived. You're a lucky man.' Her words got caught on her breath. 'I want to say sorry, Kevin. For everything.'

A chair scraped across the floor and she sat close, her scent enveloping him. It was strangely comforting.

'It's okay.' He wasn't sure he'd got the words out or that she'd even heard him.

'I think you found AJ years ago, and you're aware he's your father. I'm your mother, Kevin. Why didn't you talk to me? I could have helped you like you tried to help Isabel.' She struggled to keep her voice even, and he wanted to reach out and hold her, but his hand wouldn't move.

'Kevin, I only found out about you this week. Who you are. I wanted to meet you and talk to you, but AJ warned me off. I'm so sorry he was ashamed of you. I would never have rejected you when you were born if it hadn't been for him. He was greedy and selfish as a teenager. He still is.' Her tears fell like silent raindrops.

'I was forced to put you up for adoption. I was only seventeen. AJ didn't stand up to his father. I know it's no excuse, but I was weak and young, and it was a different time. I should have fought to keep you.' She sobbed, covering his calloused hand with her own.

'Don't cry.' His voice sounded like it came from above. Anita, his mother, swam in and out of focus. 'I believe you. Saw how you loved

Isabel. I tried to protect her from Michael. I watched her, but I was never strong enough to confront him.'

'Don't blame yourself, son.'

Son! At last he belonged to someone.

'D'you know Joyce?' His words were beginning to slur. 'Michael forced her into an awful life. I think it was them I saw on Misneach that night, burying something. Do you know … about it?'

'Michael killed his own child. His and Joyce's.'

He felt reality slipping away. His mother disappearing from him. No, he'd only just found her.

'DNA from the bones confirms that she was Joyce and Michael's. Their daughter. He killed my Isabel because she and Joyce were attempting to blackmail him. He also tried to frame Jack. What kind of monster is he?'

'The … worst.' His voice sounded far away in his own ears.

'When you're better, Kevin, you're coming to live with me. I've lost Isabel. I won't lose you again. I am so sorry for all the years we've missed out on, but I want to be your mother now.'

Her voice floated around him like an ocean wave. Up and down and around. The sound of his mother's voice. A comfort blanket. And then Isabel appeared, her eyes bright and inviting.

He tried to reach out a hand, to touch her fingers. She was suspended above him with invisible wings. He tried to see, but his eyes were closing.

No, he couldn't lose sight of her. But others were joining her. Joyce, with a little girl curled in her arms. All smiling. Calling him.

He reached up, took his sister's hand and closed his eyes for the last time.

At last he had found peace.

*

Farranstown House brooded like a hungry monster behind them. In front of them, beyond the rolling fields, the lake reflected serenity. A thin pinkish-white line split the sky on the horizon, dark grey clouds above with the shimmering lake beneath. They were sitting on a wooden fence, a metre of space between them, their legs wrapped around the horizontal beam. Tension fizzed from their bodies like static electricity.

'I have to leave,' Boyd said quietly.

'Stay. Rose is in there cooking for you. Spoiling you.' Lottie laughed, edging along the beam, trying to bridge the emotional gap that had sprung up between them. 'After all that's happened in the last week, I realise how lucky I am to have Rose in my life. And you, of course. I need a night of hugs … and much more.' She winked. 'I think we deserve it.'

'I agree there. I'm in need of serious hugging time.' He laughed softly. 'But I do have to leave.'

'What do you mean?' She glanced at his face, shrouded in shadows. 'You're scaring me now.'

'I'm sorry about this, but I'm heading to Spain.'

'Come on, Boyd, now's not the time for a holiday. We have to finalise our reports, not to mention the debriefing. Superintendent Farrell is floating in glory because we found Evan alive. But we need to be sure we have an airtight case against Michael Costello. Plus, you injured him – he'll lose his hand – so you have that fallout to contend with.' Her voice was quivering. 'And listen, I need your help with Katie. She's in a state.'

'Because of Michael Costello offering her a job?'

'She had a lucky escape there.' Lottie inched closer to him. 'You've been great with Sean. You're a natural with my kids. Would you try talking to Katie for me? I'm sure she will—'

'Stop, Lottie.' He jumped from the fence and came to stand in front of her. 'I have to meet my ex, Jackie. She needs my help with … something. It's only for a few days.'

She breathed in through her nose, then slowly exhaled. Grounding herself so she wouldn't explode.

'What was in her letter?' She was unable to stop jealous tones coating her words, nor quell the increasing sense of doom. 'I thought you were done with her.'

'It's not what you're thinking.'

'You have no idea what I'm thinking.' She went to fold her arms defiantly, but he put an arm either side of her, bracing her in place. She eased in against his body. 'What does she want now?'

Boyd's mouth tightened, as if he was afraid the wrong words would escape. Dusk was quickly turning to night, casting his face in a deeper shadow. She couldn't read his eyes.

'This is difficult for me, Lottie.'

'You're not making it easy for *me*.' Fear came tumbling. 'Whatever she's written, she could be lying. It's a ruse to get you—'

'I have to go there, see for myself.'

'I love you, Boyd. Move in with me. Tonight. No more of this lodger lark. I want you with me all the time.' She knew she sounded desperate. Didn't care. She reached out and drew him in, kissed his lips.

He took her hand and held it. 'Jackie told me …'

'What?'

'It's hard to believe it could be true; that's why I have to go.' There were tears in his eyes, caught by the sparkle of the moon rising. 'She kept it secret for years. Something I always wanted, yearned for, and she always denied me. She's a vindictive character, so I suppose it could be a lie, but I have to know.'

'What are you trying to say, Boyd?' She wrapped her arms around his neck, looked into his eyes, willed him to tell her.

A steely mist swept up from the lake, enveloping them. His voice was no more than a whisper, caught on the breeze.

'Lottie, I dare not believe it, but if it's true, I have a son.'

'What?' She jumped down from the fence, pushing him away. 'She's a liar, Boyd, don't be taken in by her lies.'

'What if it's true?'

'How could it be? She's been gone years.'

'She says she was pregnant when she left me'

Lottie couldn't believe what she was hearing. Would never believe anything Boyd's ex-wife said.

'What does she want from you? To show you a boy who may or may not be yours and then deny you access to him?'

He dug into the earth with his shoe, his head bowed, then looked up at her, tears flickering the hazel in his eyes.

'We've just rescued a little boy who never experienced the love of his biological father. Not to talk about what Kevin went through … I can't allow that for a child of mine. You have to understand, Lottie.'

'Believe me, I'm trying.'

'And that little girl who was buried up on Misneach – no one even knows her name. Costello won't tell us and there's no one else who knows. How heartbreaking is that?'

She nodded. Maybe Evan would remember his sister's name in time, but she doubted it. Then she had an idea.

'Before you make a huge mistake, get Jackie to send a sample of the boy's DNA and you can it check against yours.' If there even was a kid, Lottie thought.

'What reason has she to lie?'

'What reason has she to only tell you now?'

He took a pack of cigarettes from his pocket and lit one, the taper burning red, casting his face in a warm hue.

'I thought you'd given them up,' she said.

'I need them now.'

'Here, give me one.'

He lit another and handed it over.

She didn't bring it to her lips, just watched it burn away in the silent swirling mist.

'I'll go with you.'

He threw down his cigarette, crushed it into the ground. 'That means the world to me, Lottie, but I have to do this alone.' He placed a hand over his heart.

'You'll come back to me?' She couldn't lose him, not now.

He smiled, lopsided, his ears sticking out. 'We don't know what the future holds for any of us, but trust me, I will come back to you.'

He put his hands either side of her head, lowered it and feathered her hair with his lips. Then he turned, and walked away, his silhouette outlined by the moon before he disappeared from view.

She glanced up at the house, surrounded by trees, their branches like tentacles grasping for something they might never catch. A void opened up in her heart, but she knew Boyd was doing the right thing. He always did the right thing. Always did what people asked of him. And she knew he would end up being hurt.

She ran back to the house to hug and hold each one of her children. She'd even hug Rose. She wanted to tell them all that she loved them more than life itself. She wanted them to know she would be around for them every day of her life.

She believed Boyd would return to her, but for now she had to give him the space he needed. She had to let him go.

This was one trip he had to make alone.

A LETTER FROM PATRICIA

Hello, dear reader,

I wish to thank you for reading my tenth novel, *Little Bones*.

Thank you for sharing your time with Lottie, her family, Boyd and the team in this the latest book in the series. I hope you enjoyed *Little Bones* and I'd love if you could follow Lottie throughout the series of novels.

To those of you who have already read the other nine Lottie Parker books, *The Missing Ones*, *The Stolen Girls*, *The Lost Child*, *No Safe Place*, *Tell Nobody*, *Final Betrayal*, *Broken Souls*, *Buried Angels* and *Silent Voices*, I thank you for your support and reviews. If *Little Bones* is your first encounter with Lottie, you are in for a treat when you read the previous books in the series.

I'm always delighted when readers leave reviews, so I'd be thrilled if you could post a review on Amazon or on the site where you purchased the eBook, paperback or audiobook. It would mean the world to me. Thank you so much for the reviews received so far.

You can connect with me on my Facebook author page, Instagram and Twitter. I also have a website, which I try to keep up to date.

Thanks again for reading *Little Bones*.

I hope you will join me for Book 11 in the series.

Love,
Patricia

KEEP IN TOUCH WITH PATRICIA

f trisha460

X @trisha460

⊙ patricia_gibney_author

⊕ www.patriciagibney.com

ACKNOWLEDGEMENTS

Little Bones was written during the second and third Irish lockdowns in the midst of the ongoing COVID-19 pandemic. I found writing in lockdown-enforced isolation difficult, which is odd as writing is mainly a solitary occupation. I couldn't have got over the end line without the support and encouragement of many people. First of all, thank you for reading *Little Bones*. To each and every person who continues to follow Lottie's journey, thank you for reading my books.

In these uncertain times, when personal contact is limited, I am lucky to have my family close to me. With all my heart I say a special thanks to my children, Aisling, Orla and Cathal. You are all brilliant and amazing young adults. Your dad, Aidan, would be so proud of you, as I am. I am forever thankful to have you in my life.

I am surrounded by endless love and affection in the form of my grandchildren, Daisy and Caitlyn, and Shay and Lola. Your grandad Aidan is laughing along with you and keeping an eye on you all. He is guiding us through life and spreading his love through each one of us. I love you all.

My parents, Kathleen and Willie Ward, are a constant support. Thank you both. Thanks also to my mother-in-law, Lily Gibney, and her family. Special thanks to my sister-in-law, Kate Gibney, in New Jersey for spreading the word Stateside. This book is dedicated to Kate and Eamonn's eldest son, Liam. Liam has overcome so much from the day he was born aided by his supportive mom and dad, his brother Brody, his strong faith and resilience. You are an inspiration to us adults, Liam.

I am lucky to have my sister, Marie Brennan, as an integral part of my writing process, always on hand to help me with my edits and proofreading. Thank you, Marie.

As always, my agent, Ger Nicol of The Book Bureau, is behind me with encouragement and support. I am indebted to Ger for advice and friendship. Thanks to Marianne Gunn O'Connor. Thanks also to Hannah Whitaker, at The Rights People, for sourcing foreign translation publishers to publish my books.

My editor, Lydia Vassar Smith, has been with me since my debut book, *The Missing Ones*. I am so grateful for her professionalism and expertise in encouraging me to raise the bar with each book. Cannot believe this is Book 10!

Kim Nash, head of publicity at Bookouture, is a rock! Thank you, Kim, for reading my books and for your encouragement. I'm delighted to see your own success as an author. Thanks also to Sarah Hardy and Noelle Holten for the social media shout-outs and your promotional work on my books.

Special thanks to those who work directly on my books at Bookouture: Alex Holmes (production) and Hamzah Hussain (publishing), Alex Crow and Hannah Deuce (marketing). Thanks to Tom Feltham for proofreading. I'm forever grateful to Jane Selley, whom I rely on for her excellent copyediting skills.

Thank you to all at Sphere and Hachette Ireland, who publish my books in paperback, and thanks to all my foreign translation publishers for bringing my books to readers in their native languages.

Michele Moran is the amazing voice on the audio format of my books. Bringing Lottie to life in the ears of those who listen to audio books is a special gift. Thanks, Michele and the team at The Audiobook Producers.

I am grateful to every reader who has posted reviews, because you all make a difference. Thank you to the brilliant book bloggers and reviewers who take time to read my books and in turn help readers find them.

I have found the writing community to be a very supportive network. Special thanks to my fellow Bookouture authors and the many Irish authors who offer me advice and encouragement, with special mention to Liz Nugent. Thanks to the local bookshops and libraries who have had to endure these difficult times but have been able to adapt to continue bringing books to readers.

Special thanks to John Quinn and Rita Gilmartin for responding to my queries. I usually fictionalise police procedures to add pace to the story. Inaccuracies are all my own.

Thanks to Patricia Ryan for the use of her remote cottage in Sligo overlooking the ocean. Perfect location for clearing the mind and enhancing concentration.

My friends have been brilliant through these unpredictable times. Antoinette Leslie, Jo Kelly, Jackie Walsh, Gráinne Daly, Niamh Brennan and Louise Phillips. Thank you for lifting me when my spirit flagged.

I was born and live in Mullingar, which is situated in the heart of Ireland. The support I've received from everyone is invaluable. Thank you to all media outlets, with special thanks to the local newspaper reporters for flying my flag – Olga Aughey, Eilis Ryan and Claire Corrigan.

Ragmullin and its characters are fictional, as is Misneach which features in *Little Bones*. If you follow an ancient path not far from my home town, you just might find a similar site steeped in mythology. Just ask Marty Mulligan or Justin Moffatt.

On a final note, dear reader, *you* make it all worthwhile and I hope to continue entertaining you with my crime and mystery stories. I'm currently writing the next book in the series (Book 11), so you shouldn't have too long to wait to see what happens next!

Sincere thanks for travelling this journey with me.